P9-DGF-291

#1 *New York Times* bestselling author
Nora Roberts writing as

J. D. Robb

"Any 'In Death' book should be at the top of any reading list. Eve, Roarke, and the rest of the cast will enchant you, and the murder plots will enthrall you."

—*Grand Forks Herald*

Mary Blayney

"Nicely nuanced, wonderfully complicated characters . . . quietly witty prose . . . simply superb."   —*Booklist*

New York Times bestselling author

Ruth Ryan Langan

"A popular writer of heartwarming, emotionally involving romances."   —*Library Journal*

Mary Kay McComas

"A remarkable talent."   —*Romantic Times*

Bump in the Night

J. D. Robb

Mary Blayney

Ruth Ryan Langan

Mary Kay McComas

JOVE BOOKS, NEW YORK

THE BERKLEY PUBLISHING GROUP
Published by the Penguin Group
Penguin Group (USA) Inc.
375 Hudson Street, New York, New York 10014, USA
Penguin Group (Canada), 90 Eglinton Avenue East, Suite 700, Toronto, Ontario M4P 2Y3, Canada
(a division of Pearson Penguin Canada Inc.)
Penguin Books Ltd., 80 Strand, London WC2R 0RL, England
Penguin Group Ireland, 25 St. Stephen's Green, Dublin 2, Ireland (a division of Penguin Books Ltd.)
Penguin Group (Australia), 250 Camberwell Road, Camberwell, Victoria 3124, Australia
(a division of Pearson Australia Group Pty. Ltd.)
Penguin Books India Pvt. Ltd., 11 Community Centre, Panchsheel Park, New Delhi—110 017, India
Penguin Group (NZ), Cnr. Airborne and Rosedale Roads, Albany, Auckland 1310, New Zealand
(a division of Pearson New Zealand Ltd.)
Penguin Books (South Africa) (Pty.) Ltd., 24 Sturdee Avenue, Rosebank, Johannesburg 2196,
South Africa

Penguin Books Ltd., Registered Offices: 80 Strand, London WC2R 0RL, England

These are works of fiction. Names, characters, places, and incidents either are the product of the authors' imaginations or are used fictitiously, and any resemblance to actual persons, living or dead, business establishments, events, or locales is entirely coincidental. The publisher does not have any control over and does not assume any responsibility for author or third-party websites or their content.

BUMP IN THE NIGHT

A Jove Book / published by arrangement with the authors.

PRINTING HISTORY
Jove mass-market edition / April 2006

ISBN: 0-515-14117-8

JOVE®
Jove Books are published by The Berkley Publishing Group,
a division of Penguin Group (USA) Inc.,
375 Hudson Street, New York, New York 10014.
JOVE is a registered trademark of Penguin Group (USA) Inc.
The "J" design is a trademark belonging to Penguin Group (USA) Inc.

PRINTED IN THE UNITED STATES OF AMERICA

10 9 8 7 6 5 4 3 2 1

Haunted in Death

J. D. Robb

There nearly always is method in madness.
—*G. K. Chesterton*

There needs no ghost, my lord,
come from the grave to tell us this.
—*William Shakespeare*

One

Winter could be murderous. The slick streets and icy sidewalks broke bones and cracked skulls with gleeful regularity. Plummeting temperatures froze the blood and stopped the hearts of a select few every night in the frigid misery of Sidewalk City.

Even those lucky enough to have warm, cozy homes were trapped inside by the bitter winds and icy rains. In the first two weeks of January 2060—post-holiday—bitch winter was a contributing factor to the sharp rise in domestic disturbance calls to the New York City Police and Security Department.

Even reasonably happy couples got twitchy when they were bound together long enough by the cold ropes of winter.

For Lieutenant Eve Dallas, double d's weren't on her plate. Unless some stir-crazy couple killed each other out of sheer boredom.

She was Homicide.

On this miserable, bone-chilling morning, she stood

over the dead. It wasn't the cold or the ice that had killed Radcliff C. Hopkins III. She couldn't say, as yet, if the blue-tipped fingers of winter had been a contributing factor. But it was clear someone had put numerous nasty holes in Radcliff C.'s chest. And another, neatly centered on his wide forehead.

Beside her, Eve's partner Detective Delia Peabody crouched for a closer look. "I've never seen these kinds of wounds before, outside of training vids."

"I have. Once."

It had been winter then, too, Eve remembered, when she'd stood over the first victim in a series of rape/murders. The gun ban had all but eliminated death by firearm, so gunshot wounds were rare. Not that people didn't continue to kill each other habitually. But the remote violence and simplicity of a bullet into flesh and bone wasn't often the method of choice these days.

Radcliff C. might have been done in by an antiquated method, but it didn't make him any less dead.

"Lab boys will rub their hands together over this one," Eve murmured. "They don't get much call to play with ballistics."

She was a tall woman, with a lean build inside a long black leather coat. Her face was sharp with angles, her eyes long and brown and observant. As a rare concession to the cold, she'd yanked a black watch cap over her short, usually untidy brown hair. But she'd lost her gloves again.

She continued to stand, let her partner run the gauge for time of death.

"Six wounds visible," Eve said. "Four in the body, one in the right leg, one to the head. From the blood spatter, blood trail, it looks like he was hit first there." She gestured a few feet away. "Force knocks him back, down, so he tries to crawl. Big guy, fleshy, with a strong look to him. He maybe had enough in him to crawl some, maybe to try to get up again."

"Time of death, oh-two-twenty." Peabody, her dark hair

in a short, sassy flip at the base of her neck, looked up. Her square, sturdy face was cop solemn, but there was a gleam in her eye, dark as her hair. "ID confirmed. You know who he is, right?"

"Hopkins, Radcliff C. With the fussy Roman numerals after."

"Your lack of interest in culture trivia's showing again. His grandfather was Hop Hopkins, and made a couple of fortunes in the swinging Sixties. Nineteen-sixties. Sex, drugs and rock 'n' roll. Night clubs, music venues. L.A.-based, mostly, before the big one hit California, but he had a hot spot here in New York."

Peabody shifted her weight. "Ran hot for a couple of decades, then hit a serious patch of bad luck. The even more legendary Bobbie Bray—she was—"

"I know who Bobbie Bray was." Eve hooked her thumbs in her pockets, rocking back on her heels as she continued to study the body, the scene. "I'm not completely oblivious to popular culture. Rock star, junkie, and a cult figure now. Vanished without a trace."

"Yeah, well, she was his wife—third or fourth—when she poofed. Rumor and gossip figured maybe he offed her or had her done, but the cops couldn't find enough evidence to indict. He went spooky, did the hermit thing, lost big fat piles of dough, and ended up OD'ing on his drug of choice—can't remember what it was—right here in New York."

Peabody pushed to her feet. "From there it's urban legend time. Place where he OD'd was upstairs from the club, that's where he'd holed himself up. In the luxury apartment he'd put in on the top floor. Building passed from hand to hand, but nobody could ever make a go of it. Because . . ."

Peabody paused now, for effect. "It's haunted. And cursed. Anyone who's ever tried to live there, or put a business in, suffers personal and/or physical misfortunes."

"Number Twelve. Yeah, I've heard of it. Interesting."

Hands still in her pockets, Eve scanned the large, dilapidated room. "Haunted and cursed. Seems redundant. Guess maybe Radcliff C. figured on bucking that."

"What do you mean?" Then Peabody's jaw dropped. "This is the place? *This?* Oh boy. Jeez."

"Anonymous tip does the nine-one-one. Gonna want to review that transmission, because it's likely it was the killer. What I've got is the vic owned the building, was having it rehabbed, redesigned. Maybe looking for some of his grandfather's glory days. But what's our boy doing hanging around in a cursed, haunted building at two in the morning?"

"This is the place," Peabody repeated, reverently now. "Number Twelve."

"Since the addy's Twelve East Twelfth, I'm going to go out on a limb and say, yeah. Let's turn him."

"Oh, right."

When they rolled the body, Eve pursed her lips. "Somebody really wanted this guy dead. Three more entry wounds on the back. Lab will confirm, but I'm thinking . . ."

She crossed the room toward a set of old circular iron stairs. "Standing about here, facing the attacker. Pow, pow. Takes it in the chest." She slapped a hand on her own. "Stumbles back, goes down. The smeared blood trail tells me the vic tried crawling away, probably toward the doors."

"Doors were locked from the inside. First on scene said," Peabody added.

"Yeah. So he's crawling, and the killer moves in. Pow, pow, into the back." *The sound of the shots must have blasted the air in here,* Eve thought. *Must have set the ears ringing.* "But it's not enough. No, we're not finished yet. Body falls, has to be dead or dying, but it's not enough. Turns the body over, puts the barrel of the gun to the forehead. See the burn marks around the forehead wound? Contact. I did a lot of studying up on firearms during the

DeBlass case a couple years ago. Puts the barrel right against the head and pow. Coup de grace."

Eve saw it in her head. Heard it, smelled it. "You put a gun like this." She pressed her fingertip to her own brow. "You put it right against the skin and fire, it's personal. You put that many steel missiles in somebody, you're seriously pissed off."

"Vic's got his bright, shiny wristwatch—looks antique— his wallet—cash and credit inside—key codes, ppc, pocket 'link. Killer didn't bother making it look like robbery."

"We'll run the electronics. Let's have a look at the 'link."

Eve took the 'link in her sealed hands, called up the last transmission. There was a whispering, windy sound which Eve had to admit tingled her spine just a bit. The husky female voice wove through it.

Number Twelve. Two A.M. Bring it. Bring it, and we'll party.

"Maybe robbery plays in after all."

"Did you hear that voice?" Peabody sent a cautious look over her shoulder. "It sounded, you know, unearthly."

"Funny, sounded computer-generated to me. But maybe that's because I know ghosts don't make 'link transmissions, or shoot guns. Because—and this may be news to you, Peabody—ghosts don't exist."

Peabody only shook her head, sagely. "Oh yeah? Tell that to my great-aunt Josie who died eight years ago and came back half a dozen times to nag my great-uncle Phil about fixing the leaky toilet in the powder room. She left him alone after he called the plumber."

"And how much does your great-uncle Phil drink?"

"Oh, come on. People see ghosts all the time."

"That's because people, by and large, are whacked. Let's work the case, Peabody. It wasn't a ghostly finger that pulled the trigger here. Or lured the vic to an empty building in the middle of the night. Let's do a run. Spouse, family, beneficiaries, business partners, friends, enemies. And let's keep it to the corporeal."

Eve re-examined the body, wondering if he'd brought whatever *it* was. "They can bag and tag. Start checking doors and windows. Let's find out how the killer got out of the building. I'll have another talk with the first on scene."

"You want me to stay in here? To wander around in here. Alone?"

"Are you kidding?" One look at Peabody's face told Eve her partner was absolutely serious. "Well, for God's sake. You take the first on scene. I'll take the building."

"Better plan. You want crime scene in now, and the body transported?"

"Get it done."

Eve took a visual sweep on the main floor. Maybe it had been a hot spot in the last century, but now it was derelict. She could see where some of the work had begun. Portions of the grimy walls had been stripped away to their bones to reveal the old, and certainly out-of-code, electrical wiring. Portable lights and heating units were set up, as well as stacks of materials in what seemed to be tidy and organized piles.

But the drop clothes, the material, the lights all had a coat of dust. Maybe Hopkins had started his rehab, but it looked as if there'd been a long lag since the last nail gun popped.

The remains of an old bar hulked in the center of the room. As it was draped with more dusty protective cloth, she assumed Hopkins had intended to restore it to whatever its former glory might have been.

She checked the rear exit door, found it too secured from inside. Through another door she found what might have been a store room at one time, and was now a junk heap. The two windows were about big enough for a cat to squeeze through, and were riot barred.

The toilet facilities on the main level were currently pits, with no outside access.

"Okay, unless you're still here, waiting for me to cuff you and read you your rights, you found a way up and out."

She glanced at the ancient elevator; opted for the spindly iron stairs.

The sweepers were going to have a hell of a time finding usable prints or physical evidence, she thought. There were decades of dust, grime, considerable water damage, what seemed to be old scorching from a fire.

She recorded and marked some blurry footprints smudged on the dirty floor.

Cold, she thought. *Freaking cold in here.*

She moved along the second floor landing, imagined it packed with tables and people during its heyday. Music pumping out to shatter ear drums, the fashionable drugs of the time passed around like party favors. The chrome safety railings would have been polished to a gleam, flashing with the wild colors of the lights.

She stood as she was a moment, looking down as the ME drones bagged the body. Good view from there, she mused. See whatever you want to see. People ass to elbow below, sweating and grinding on the dance floor and hoping somebody was watching.

Did you come up here tonight, Hopkins? Did you have enough brains before they got blown out to come early, scope the place out? Or did you just walk in?

She found the exit at a second story window, unlocked and partially open, with the emergency stairs deployed.

"So much for that mystery. Suspect most likely exited the building," she stated for the record, "from this point. Sweepers will process the window, stairs and surrounding areas for prints and other evidence. And lookie, lookie." She crouched, shined her light on the edge of the window-sill. "Got a little blood, probably vic's. Suspect may have had some spatter, or transferred some blood to his clothing when he moved in for the head shot."

Frowning, she shined the light further down, onto the floor where something sparkled. "Looks like jewelry. Or . . . hmm. Some sort of hair decoration," she amended when she lifted it with tweezers. "Damn if it doesn't look like diamonds to me, on some kind of clip. About a half inch wide, maybe two inches long. No dust on it—stones are clean and bright in what I'd guess to be a platinum setting. Antique-looking."

She bagged it.

She started to head back down, then thought she heard the floor creak overhead. Old buildings, she reminded herself, but drew her weapon. She moved to the back wall, which was partially caved in, and the old metal stairs behind it.

The sound came again, just a stealthy little creak. For a moment she thought she heard a woman's voice, raw and throaty, singing about a bleeding heart.

At the top of the stairs the floors had been scrubbed clean. They were scarred and scorched, but no dust lay on them. There was old smoke and fire damage on some of the interior walls, but she could see the area had been set up into a large apartment, and what might have been an office.

She swept, light and weapon, but saw nothing but rubble. The only sound now was the steady inhale, exhale of her own breath, which came out in veritable plumes.

If heat was supposed to rise, why the hell was it so much colder up here? She moved through the doorless opening to the left to do a thorough search.

Floors are too clean, she thought. And there was no debris here as there was in the other smaller unit, no faded graffiti decorating the walls. Eve cocked her head at the large hole in the wall on the far right. It looked as though it had been measured and cut, neatly, as a doorway.

She crossed the room to shine her light into the dark.

The skeleton lay as if in repose. In the center of the skull's forehead was a small, almost tidy hole.

Cupped in the yellowed fingers was the glittery mate to the diamond clip. And near the other was the chrome gleam of a semi-automatic.

"Well son of a bitch," Eve murmured, and pulled out her communicator to hail Peabody.

Two

"It's her. It's got to be her."

"Her being the current vic's ancestor's dead wife." Eve drove through spitting ice from the crime scene to the victim's home.

"Or lover. I'm not sure they were actually married now that I think about it. Gonna check on that," Peabody added, making a note in her memo book. "But here's what must've gone down: Hopkins, the first one, kills Bobbie, then bricks the body up in the wall of the apartment he used over the club."

"And the cops at the time didn't notice there was a spanking new brick wall in the apartment?"

"Maybe they didn't look very hard. Hopkins had a lot of money, and a river of illegal substances. A lot of connections, and probably a lot of information certain high connections wouldn't want made public."

"He bought off the investigation." Whether it happened eighty-five years ago or yesterday, the smell of bad cops offended Eve's senses. But . . . "Not impossible," she had to admit. "If it is the missing wife/girlfriend, it could be she wasn't reported missing until he had everything fairly tidied up. Then you got your payoff, or classic blackmail regarding the investigators, and he walks clean."

"He did sort of go crazy. Jeez, Dallas, he basically locked himself up there in that place for over ten years, with a body behind the wall."

"Maybe. Let's get the bones dated and identified before we jump there. The crime scene guys were all but weeping with joy over those bones. While they're having their fun, we've got an active case, from this century."

"But you're curious, right? You gotta wonder if we just found Bobbie Bray. And the hair clips. Is that spooky or what?"

"Nothing spooky about a killer planting them. Wanted us to find the bones, that's a given. So connecting the dots, the skeleton and our vic are linked, at least in the killer's mind. What do we have on Hopkins so far?"

"Vic was sixty-two at TOD. Three marriages, three divorces. Only offspring—son from second marriage." Peabody scanned her memo book. "Bounced back and forth between New York and New L.A., with a couple of stints in Europe. Entertainment field, mostly fringe. Didn't seem to have his grandfather's flair. Parents died in a private plane crash twenty-five years back. No sibs."

Peabody glanced over. "The Hopkins line doesn't go toward longevity and propagation. Part of the curse."

"Part of birth control practices and lousy luck," Eve corrected. "What else—salient—do we have?"

"You gotta wonder," Peabody went on. "I mean Hopkins number two was married four times. Four. One surviving son—or surviving until now. He had a daughter from another marriage who drowned when she was a teenager, and another son—still another marriage—who hanged himself when he was twenty-three. That's the kind of consistent bad luck that says curse to me."

"It says pretty irrelevant background data to me. Give me something on our vic."

"Okay, okay. Rad Hopkins went through a lot of the money his father managed to recoup, and most of what he'd inherited from his mother, who was a socialite with some traces of blue blood. He had a few minor smudges for illegals, solicitation, gray-area business practices. No time served. Oh, no collector's license for firearms."

"Where are the ex-wives?"

"Number one's based in New L.A. B-movie actress. Well, B-minus, really. Number three's in Europe, married to some minor English aristocrat. But Number two's here in New York. Fanny Gill—dance instructor. The son's Cliff Gill Hopkins—though he dropped the Hopkins legally at age twenty-one. They run a dance studio."

"New York's an easy place to get to and get out of. We'll run them all. Business partners?"

"None currently. He's had a mess of them, off and on. But he was the sole owner and proprietor of Number Twelve Productions, which has the same address as his residence. He bought the building he died in at auction about six months ago."

"Not much work done in there in six months."

"I tagged the construction company from the name on the building permit. Owner tells me they got called off after three weeks. Their scuttlebutt is Hopkins ran out of money, and scrambled around for some backers. But he said he had a call from the vic a few days ago, wanting to schedule work to start up again."

"So maybe he got some money, or wheeled some sort of deal."

She found the miracle of a street-level spot a half block from Hopkins's building.

"Decent digs," Eve noted. "Fancy antique wrist unit, designer wallet, pricey shoes. Doesn't give the appearance of hurting financially."

She flashed her badge at the doorman. "Hopkins," she said. "Radcliff C."

"I'll ring up and let him know you'd like to speak with him."

"Don't bother. He's in the morgue. When's the last time you saw him?"

"Dead?" The doorman, a short, stocky mixed-race man of about forty, stared at Eve as his jaw dropped. "Mr. Hopkins is dead? An accident?"

"Yes, he's dead. No, it wasn't an accident. When did you last see him?"

"Yesterday. He went out about twelve-thirty in the afternoon, came back around two. I went off duty at four. My replacement would have gone off at midnight. No doorman from midnight to eight."

"Anybody come to see him?"

"No one that checked in with me. The building's secured. Passcodes are required for the elevators. Mr. Hopkins's apartment is on the sixth floor." The doorman shook his head, rubbed a gloved hand over the back of his neck. "Dead. I just can't believe it."

"He live alone?"

"He did, yes."

"Entertain much?"

"Occasionally."

"Overnight entertaining? Come on, Cleeve," Eve prompted, scanning his brass name tag. "Guy's dead."

"Occasionally," he repeated and puffed out his cheeks. "He, ah, liked variety, so I couldn't say there was any particular lady. He also liked them young."

"How young?"

"Mid-twenties, primarily, by my gauge. I haven't noticed anyone visiting the last couple of weeks. He's been in and out nearly every day. Meetings, I assume, for the club he's opening. Was opening."

"Okay, good enough. We're going up."

"I'll clear the code for you." Cleeve held the door for

them, then walked to the first of two elevators. He
skimmed his passcode through the slot, then keyed in his
code. "I'm sorry to hear about Mr. Hopkins," he said as the
doors opened. "He never gave me any trouble."

"Not a bad epitaph," Eve decided as the elevator headed
up to six.

The apartment was single-level, but spacious. Particularly since it was nearly empty of furnishings. There was a
sleep chair in the living room, facing a wall screen. There
were a multitude of high-end electronics and carton after
carton of entertainment discs. It was all open space with a
colored-glass wall separating the sleeping area.

"There was art on the walls," Eve noted. "You can see
the squares and rectangles of darker paint where they
must've hung. Probably sold them to get some capital for
his project."

A second bedroom was set up as an office, and from the
state of it, Eve didn't judge Hopkins had been a tidy or organized businessman. The desk was heaped with scribbled
notes, sketches, memo cubes, coffee cups and plates from
working meals.

A playback of the desk 'link was loaded with oily conversation with the recently deceased pitching his project to
potential backers or arranging meetings where she supposed he'd have been doing the same.

"Let's have EDD go through all the data and communication." The Electronic Detective Division could comb
through the transmissions and data faster and more efficiently than she. "Doesn't look like he's entertained here
recently, which jibes with our doorman's statement. Nothing personal in the last little while on his home 'link. It's
all about money."

She walked through the apartment. The guy wasn't living there so much as surviving. Selling off his stuff, scrambling for capital. "The motive's not all about money,
though. He couldn't have had enough for that. The motive's
emotional. It's personal. Kill him where the yellowing

bones of a previous victim are hidden. Purposeful. Building was auctioned off six months ago? Private or public?"

"I can check," Peabody began.

"I got a quicker source."

It seemed to her the guy she'd married was always in, on his way to or coming back from some meeting. Then again, he seemed to like them. It took all kinds.

And she had to admit when that face of his filled her screen, it put a little boost in her step to think: *mine.*

"Quick question," she began. "Number Twelve. Any details on its auction?"

His dark brows raised over those intense blue eyes. "Bought for a song, which will likely turn out to be a dirge. Or has it already?" Roarke asked her.

"You're quick, too. Yeah, current owner's in the morgue. He got it on the cheap?"

"Previous owners had it on the market for several years, and put it up for public auction a few months ago after the last fire."

"Fire?"

"There've been several. Unexplained," he added with that Irish lilt cruising through his voice. "Hopkins, wasn't it? Descendent of infamy. How was he killed?"

"Nine millimeter Smith and Wesson."

Surprise moved over that extraordinary face. "Well now. Isn't that interesting? You recovered the weapon, I take it."

"Yeah, I got it. Fill you in on that later. The auction, you knew about it, right?"

"I did. It was well-publicized for several weeks. A building with that history generates considerable media attention as well."

"Yeah, that's what I figured. If it was a bargain, why didn't you snap it up to add it to your mega-Monopoly board?"

"Haunted. Cursed."

"Yeah, right." She snorted out a laugh, but he only continued to look out from the screen. "Okay, thanks. See you later."

"You certainly will."

"Couldn't you just listen to him?" Peabody let out a sigh. "I mean couldn't you just close your eyes and listen?"

"Snap out of it, Peabody. Hopkins's killer had to know the building was up for sale. Maybe he bid on it, maybe he didn't. He doesn't move on the previous owners, but waits for Hopkins. Goes back to personal. Lures him, kills him, leaves the weapon and the hair clips with the skeleton behind the brick. Making a statement."

Peabody huffed out a breath. "This place doesn't make much of a statement, personal or otherwise."

"Let's toss it anyway. Then we're going dancing."

The Gill School of Dance was on the third floor of a stubby post-Urban War building on the West Side. It boasted a large, echoing room with a mirrored wall, a barre, a huddle of chairs and a decorative screen that sectioned off a minute desk.

The space smelled of sweat heavily covered with floral air freshener.

Fanny Gill herself was skinny as an eel, with a hard, suspicious face and a lot of bright blond hair tied up with a red scarf. Her pinched face went even tighter as she set her tiny ass on the desk.

"So somebody killed the rat bastard. When's the funeral? I got a red dress I've been saving for a special occasion."

"No love lost, Ms. Gill?"

"Oh, all of it lost, honey. My boy out there?" She jerked a chin toward the screen. On the other side, a man in a sleeveless skinsuit was calling out time and steps to a group of grubby-looking ballerinas. "He's the only decent thing I ever got from Rad the Bad. I was twenty-two years old, fresh and green as a head of iceberg."

She didn't sigh so much as snort, as if to signal those salad days were long over.

"I sure did fall for him. He had a line, that bastard, he had a way. Got married, got pregnant. Had a little money, about twenty thou? He took it, *invested* it." Her lips flattened into one thin, red line. "Blew it, every dollar. Always going to wheel the deal, strike the big time. Like hell. Cheated on me, too. But I stuck, nearly ten years, because I wanted my boy to have a father. Finally figured out no father's better than a lousy one. Divorced him—hired a fucking shark lawyer—excuse the language."

"No problem. Cops hear words like *lawyer* all the time."

Fanny barked out a laugh, then seemed to relax. "Wasn't much to get, but I got my share. Enough to start this place up. And you know, that son of a bitch tried to hit me up for a loan? Called it a business investment, of course. Just a couple months ago. Never changes."

"Was this business investment regarding Number Twelve?"

"Yeah, that's it. Like I'd have anything to do with that place—or Rad."

"Could you tell us where you were last night, Ms. Gill? From say midnight to three?"

"In bed, asleep. I teach my first class at seven in the morning." She sniffed. looking more amused than offended to be considered a suspect in a homicide. "Hey, if I'd wanted to kill Rad, I'd've done it twenty years ago. You're going to ask my boy, too, aren't you?"

"It's routine."

Fanny nodded. "I sleep alone, but he doesn't."

"Dead? Murdered?" Cliff lowered the towel he'd used to dry his damp face. "How? When?"

"Early this morning. The how is classified for the moment. Can you give us your whereabouts between midnight and three?"

"We got home about one. We'd been out with friends. Um . . . give me a second." He picked up a bottle of water, stared at it, then drank. He was a well-built thirty, with streaked blond hair curling in a tail worn halfway down his back. "Lars Gavin, my cohab. We met some friends at Achilles. A club uptown. We went to bed right after we got home, and I got up about seven, seven-thirty. Sorry, I think I want to sit down."

"We're going to need names and contact information on the people you were with, and a number where we can reach your cohab."

"Yeah, sure. Okay. How? How did it happen?" He lifted dazed eyes to Eve's. "Was he mugged?"

"No. I'm not able to give you many details at this time. When's the last time you had contact with your father?"

"A couple months ago. He came by to try to hit my mother up for some money. Like that would work." Cliff managed a half smile, but it wobbled. "Then he put the line on me. I gave him five hundred."

He glanced over to where Fanny was running another group through barre exercises. "Mom'll skin me if she finds out, but I gave him the five."

"That's not the first time you gave him money," Eve deduced.

"No. I'd give him a few hundred now and then. It kept him off my mother's back, and we do okay here. The school, I mean. We do okay. And Lars, he understands."

"But this time he went to your mother first."

"Got to her before I could steer him off. Upsets her, you know? He figured he could sweet talk her out of a good chunk for this investment. Get rich deal—always a deal." Now Cliff scrubbed his hands over his face.

"They fight about it?" Eve asked him.

"No. My mother's done fighting with him. Been done a long time ago. And my father, he doesn't argue. He . . . he cajoles. Basically, she told him to come by again when Hell froze over. So he settled for me, on the sly, and the five hundred. He said he'd be in touch when the ball got rolling, but that was just another line. Didn't matter. It was only five. I don't know how to feel. I don't know how I'm supposed to feel."

"I can't tell you, Mr. Gill. Why did you remove Hopkins from your legal name?"

"This place—Gill School of Dance. My mother." He lifted his shoulder, looked a little abashed. "And well, it's got a rep. Hopkins. It's just bad luck."

Three

Eve wasn't surprised MD Morris had snagged Hopkins. Multiple gunshot wounds had to be a happy song and dance for a medical examiner. An interesting change of pace from the stabbings, the bludgeonings, strangulations and overdoses.

Morris, resplendent in a bronze-toned suit under his clear protective cape, his long dark hair in a shining tail, stood over the body with a sunny smile for Eve.

"You send me the most interesting things."

"We do what we can," Eve said. "What can you tell me I don't already know?"

"Members of one family of the fruit fly are called peacocks because they strut on the fruit."

"Huh. I'll file that one. Let's be more specific. What can you tell me about our dead guy?"

"The first four wounds—chest—and the leg wound—fifth—could have been repaired with timely medical intervention. The next severed the spine, the seventh damaged the kidney. Number eight was a slight wound, meaty part of the shoulder. But he was dead by then. The final, close contact, entered the brain, which had already closed down shop."

He gestured to his wall screen, and called up a program. "The first bullets entered at a near level angle." Morris continued as the graphics played out on-screen. "You see, the computer suggested, and I concur, that the assailant fired four times, rapidly, hitting body mass. The victim fell after the fourth shot."

Eve studied the reenactment as Morris did, noting the graphic of the victim took the first two shots standing, the second two slightly hunched forward in the beginning of a fall.

"Big guy," Peabody commented. "Stumbles back a little, but keeps his feet for the first couple shots. I've only seen training and entertainment vids with gun death," she added. "I'd have thought the first shot would slap him down."

"His size, the shock of the impact," Morris said, "and the rapidity of fire would have contributed to the delay in his fall. Again, from the angles by which the bullets entered the body, it's likely he stumbled back, then lurched forward slightly, then went down—knee, heels of the hand taking the brunt of the fall."

He turned to Eve. "Your report indicated that the blood pattern showed the victim tried to crawl or pull himself away across the floor."

"That'd be right."

"As he did, the assailant followed, firing over and down, according to the angle of the wounds in the back, leg, shoulder."

Eyes narrowed now, Eve studied the computer-generated replay. "Stalking him, firing while he's down. Bleeding, crawling. You ever shoot a gun, Morris?"

"Actually, no."

"I have," she continued. "Feels interesting in your hand. Gives this little kick when it fires. Makes you part of it, that little jolt. Runs through you. I'm betting the killer was juiced on that. The jolt, the *bang*! Gotta be juiced to put more missiles into a guy who's crawling away, leaving his blood smeared on the floor."

"People always find creative and ugly ways to kill. I'd have said using a gun makes the kill less personal. But it doesn't feel that way in this case."

She nodded. "Yeah, this was personal, almost intimate. The ninth shot in particular."

"For the head shot, the victim—who as you say had considerable girth—had to be shoved or rolled over. At that time, the gun was pressed to the forehead. There's not only burning and residue, but a circular bruising pattern. When I'm able to compare it, I'm betting my share that it matches the dimensions of the gun barrel. The killer pressed the gun down into the forehead before he fired."

"See how you like *that*, you bastard," Eve murmured.

"Yes, indeed. Other than being riddled with bullets, your vic was in reasonably good health, despite being about twenty pounds overweight. He dyed his hair, had an eye and chin tuck within the last five years. He'd last eaten about two hours prior to death. Soy chips, sour pickles, processed cheese, washed down with domestic beer."

"The bullets?"

"On their way to the lab. I ran them through my system first. Nine millimeter." Morris switched programs so that images of the spent bullets he'd recovered came on screen.

"Man, it messes them up, doesn't it?"

"It doesn't do tidy work on flesh, bone and organ either. The vic had no gunpowder residue on his hands, no defensive wounds. Bruising on the left knee, which would have been inflicted when he fell. As well as some scraping on the heels of both hands, consistent with the fall on the floor surface."

"So he didn't fight back, or have the chance to. Didn't turn away." She angled her own body as if preparing for flight. "No indication he tried to run when and if he saw the gun."

"That's not what his body tells me."

Nor was it what it had told her on scene.

"A guy doesn't usually snack on chips and pickles if he's nervous or worried," Peabody put in. "Run of his entertainment unit showed he last viewed a soft porn vid about the time he'd have had the nibbles. This meet didn't have him sweating."

"Somebody he knew and figured he could handle," Eve agreed. She looked at the body again. "Guess he was dead wrong about that one."

"Number Twelve," Morris said as Eve turned to go.

"That's right."

"So the legend of Bobbie Bray comes to a close."

"That would be the missing woman, presumed dead."

"It would. Gorgeous creature, Bobbie, with the voice of a tormented angel."

"If you remember Bobbie Bray, you're looking damn good for your age, Morris."

He flashed that smile again. "There are thousands of Web sites devoted to her, and a substantial cult following. Beautiful woman with her star just starting to rise vanishes. Poof! Of course, sightings of her continued for decades after. And talk of her ghost haunting Number Twelve continues even today. Cold spots, apparitions, music coming from thin air. You get any of that?"

Eve thought of the snatch of song, the deep chill. "What I've got, potentially, are her bones. They're real enough."

"I'll be working on them with the forensic anthropologist at the lab." Morris's smile stayed sunny. "Can't wait to get my hands on her."

Back at Central, Eve sat in her office to reconstruct Hopkins's last day. She'd verified his lunch meeting with a couple of local movers and shakers who were both alibied

tight for the time in question. A deeper check of his financials showed a sporadic income over the past year from a
shop called Bygones, with the last deposit mid-December.

"Still skimming it close, Rad. How the hell were you
going to pay for the rehab? Expecting a windfall, maybe?
What were you supposed to bring to Number Twelve last
night?"

Gets the call on his pocket 'link, she mused. *Deliberately spooky. But he doesn't panic. Sits around, has a
snack, watches some light porn.*

She sat back at her desk, closed her eyes. The security
disc from Hopkins's building showed him leaving at 1:35.
Alone. Looked like he was whistling a tune, Eve recalled.
Not a care in the world. Not carrying anything. No briefcase, no package, no bag.

"Yo."

Eve opened her eyes and looked at Feeney. The EDD
captain was comfortably rumpled, his wiry ginger hair exploding around his hangdog face. "Whatcha got?"

"More what you've got," he said and stepped into the
office. "Number Twelve."

"Jeez, why does everybody keep saying that? Like it
was its own country."

"Practically is. Hop Hopkins, Bobbie Bray, Andy
Warhol, Mick Jagger." For a moment, Feeney looked like a
devotee at a sacred altar. "Christ, Dallas, what a place it
must've been when it was still rocking."

"It's a dump now."

"Cursed," he said, so casually she blinked.

"Get out. You serious?"

"As a steak dinner. Found bricked-up bones, didn't you?
And a body, antique gun, diamonds. Stuff legends are
made of. And it gets better."

"Oh yeah?"

He held up a disc. "Ran your vic's last incoming transmission and the nine-one-one, and for the hell of it, did a
voice-print on both. Same voice on both. Guess whose it is?"

"Bobbie Bray's."

"Hey." He actually pouted.

"Has to figure. The killer did the computer-generated deal, used Bray's voice, probably pieced together from old media interviews and such. Unless you're going to sit there and tell me you think it was a voice from, you know, beyond the grave."

He pokered up. "I'm keeping an open mind."

"You do that. Were you able to dig up any old transmissions?"

He held up a second disc. "Dug them out, last two weeks. You're going to find lots of grease. Guy was working it, trying to pump up some financing. Same on the home unit. Some calls out for food, a couple to a licensed companion service. Couple more back and forth to some place called Bygones."

"Yeah, I'm going to check that out. Looks like he was selling off his stuff."

"You know, he probably had some original art from his grandfather's era. Music posters, photographs, memorabilia."

Considering, Eve cocked her head. "Enough to buy Number Twelve, then finance the rehab?"

"You never know what people'll pay. Got your finger pointed at anyone?"

"Talked to one of his exes, and a son. They don't pop for me, but I'm keeping an open mind. Going through some business associates, potential backers, other exes. No current lady friend, or recently dumped, that I can find. Fact is, the guy comes off as a little sleazy, a little slippery, but mostly harmless. A fuck-up who talked big. Got no motive at this point, except a mysterious something he may or may not have taken with him to Number Twelve."

She eased back. "Big guy. He was a big guy. Easy for a woman to take him down if she's got access to a gun, reasonable knowledge of how it works. Second ex-wife is the

kind who holds a grudge, hence my open mind. I've got
Peabody trying to run the weapon."

"The thing is," Peabody told her, "it's really old. A hundred
years back, a handgun didn't have to be registered on purchase, not in every state, and depending on how it was
bought. This one's definitely from the Hop Hopkins/Bob-
bie Bray era. They discontinued this model in the
Nineteen-eighties. I've got the list of owners with collector's licenses in the state of New York who own that make
and model, but . . ."

"It's not going to be there. Not when it was deliberately
planted on the scene. The killer wanted it found, identified.
Lab comes through, we should know tomorrow if the same
gun was used to kill Hopkins and our surprise guest."

She considered for a moment, then pushed away from
her desk. "Okay, I'm going to go by the lab, give them a
little kick in the ass."

"Always entertaining."

"Yeah, I make my own fun. After, I'm going by this collectibles place, scope it out. It's uptown, so I'll work from
home after. I've got Feeney's list of transmissions. You
want to take that? Check out the calls, the callers?"

"I'm your girl."

Dick Berenski, the chief lab tech, was known as Dickhead
for good reason. But besides being one, he was also a genius in his field. Generally, Eve handled him with bribes,
insults or outright threats. But with her current case, none
were necessary.

"Dallas!" He all but sang her name.

"Don't grin at me like that." She gave a little shudder.
"It's scary."

"You've brought me not one but two beauties. I'm going

to be writing these up for the trade journals and be the fair-haired boy for the next ten freaking years."

"Just tell me what you've got."

He scooted on his stool, and tapped his long, skinny fingers over a comp screen. He continued to grin out of his strangely egg-shaped head.

"Got my bone guy working with Morris with me running the show. You got yourself a female, between the age of twenty and twenty-five. Bobbie Bray was twenty twenty-three when she poofed. Caucasian, five-foot-five, about a hundred and fifteen pounds, same height and weight on Bobbie's ID at the time of her disappearance. Broken tibia, about the age of twelve. Healed well. Gonna wanna see if we can access any medical records on Bobbie to match the bone break. Got my forensic sculptor working on the face. Bobbie Bray, son of a bitch."

"Another fan."

"Shit yeah. That skirt was *hot*. Got your cause of death, single gunshot wound to the forehead. Spent bullet retrieved from inside the skull matches the caliber used on your other vic. Ballistics confirms both were fired from the weapon recovered from the scene. Same gun used, about eighty-five years apart. It's beautiful."

"I bet the killer thinks so, too."

Sarcasm flew over Dickhead like a puffy white cloud in a sunny blue sky. "Weapon was cleaned and oiled. Really shined it up. But . . ."

He grinned again, tapped again. "What you're looking at here is dust. Brick dust, drywall dust. Samples the sweepers took from the secondary crime scene. And here? Traces of dust found inside the weapon. Perfect match."

"Indicating that the gun was bricked up with the body."

"Guess Bobbie got tired of haunting the place and decided to take a more active role."

And that, Eve determined, didn't warrant even sarcasm as a response. "Shoot the reports to my home and office units, copy to Peabody's. Your sculptor gets an image, I want to see it."

She headed out again, pulling out her 'link as it beeped. "Dallas."

"Arrest any ghosts lately?"

"No. And I'm not planning on it. Why aren't you in a meeting about world domination?"

"Just stepped out," Roarke told her. "My curiosity's been nipping at me all day. Any leads?"

"Leads might be a strong word. I have avenues. I'm heading to one now. The vic was selling off his stuff—antique popular culture stuff, I gather—to some place uptown. I'm going to check it out."

"What's the address?"

"Why?"

"I'll meet you. I'll be your expert consultant on antiques and popular culture. You can pay my fee with food and sex."

"It's going to be pizza, and I think I've got a long line to credit on the sex."

But she gave him the address.

After ending the transmission, she called the collectibles shop to tell the proprietor to stay open and available. On a hunch, she asked if they carried any Bobbie Bray memorabilia.

And was assured they had the most extensive collection in the city.

Interesting.

Four

He beat her there, and was being served coffee and fawning attention by a young, elegant redhead in a slick black suit.

Eve couldn't blame the woman. Roarke was ridiculously handsome, and could, if it served him, ooze charm like pheromones. It seemed to suit him now as he had the redhead flushed and fluttering as she offered cookies with the coffee.

Eve figured she'd benefit from Roarke's charisma herself. She hardly ever got cookies on the job.

"Ah, here's the lieutenant now. Lieutenant Dallas, this is Maeve Buchanan, our hostess, and the daughter of the proprietor."

"Is the proprietor here?"

"My wife. Straight to business. Coffee, darling?"

"Sure. This is some place."

"We're very happy with it," Maeve agreed.

It was pretty, bright—like their hostess—and charmingly organized. Nothing at all like the cluttered junk heap

Eve had expected. Art and posters lined the walls, but in a way she supposed someone might arrange them in their home if they were crazy enough to want things everywhere.

Still, tables, display cabinets, shining shelves held memorabilia in a way that escaped the jumbled, crowded stocking style many shops of its kind were victim to. Music was playing unobtrusively—something full of instruments and certainly not of the current era. It added an easy appeal.

"Please, have a seat," Maeve invited. "Or browse if you like. My father's just in the back office. He's on the 'link with London."

"Late for business over there," Eve commented.

"Yes. Private collector. Most of our business is from or to private collections." Maeve swept a wave of that pretty red hair back from her face. "Is there anything I can do for you in the meantime?"

"You've bought a number of pieces over the last several months from Radcliff C. Hopkins."

"Mr. Hopkins, of course. Nineteen-sixties through Eighties primarily. We acquired a number of pieces from him. Is there a problem?"

"For Hopkins there is. He was killed last night."

"Oh!" Her cheery, personal-service smile flashed into shock. "Killed? Oh my God."

"Media's run reports on it through the day."

"I . . . I hadn't heard." Maeve's hands were pressed to her cheeks, and her round blue eyes were wide. "We've been open since ten. We don't keep any current screen shows or radio on in the shop. Spoils the . . . the timeless ambiance. My father's going to be so upset."

"They were friends?"

"Friendly, certainly. I don't know what to say. He was in only a few weeks ago. How did he die?"

"The details are confidential." *For the moment*, Eve thought. There were always leaks and the media couldn't wait to soak them up, wring them dry. "I can tell you he was murdered."

Maeve had a redhead's complexion, and her already pale skin went bone white. "Murdered? This is horrible. It's—" She turned as a door in the back opened.

The man who came out was tall and thin, with the red hair he'd passed to his daughter dusted with a little silver. He had eyes of quiet green, and a smile of greeting ready. It faded when he saw his daughter's face.

"Maeve? What's the matter? Is there a problem?"

"Daddy. Mr. Hopkins, he's been murdered."

He gripped his daughter's arm, and those quiet eyes skimmed from Roarke to Eve and back again. "Rad Hopkins?"

"That's right." Eve held out her badge. "I'm Lieutenant Dallas. You and Mr. Hopkins had business?"

"Yes. Yes. My God, this is such a shock. Was it a burglary?"

"Why would you ask?"

"His collection. He had a very extensive collection of antique art."

"You bought a good chunk of that collection."

"Bits and pieces. Excellent bits and pieces." He rubbed his daughter's shoulder and drew her down to the arm of the chair as he sat. The gesture seemed to help both of them compose themselves.

"I was hoping to eventually do a complete appraisal and give him a bid on the whole of it. But he was . . ." He pushed at his hair and smiled. "He was canny. Held me off, and whet my appetite with those bits."

"What do you know about Number Twelve?"

"Number Twelve?" He looked blank for a moment, then shook his head. "Sorry, I'm feeling muddled by all this. Urban legend. Haunted. Some say by Hop Hopkins's ghost, others by Bobbie Bray's. Others still say both, or any number of celebrities from that era. Bad luck building, though I admit I'm always on the lookout for something from its heyday that can be authenticated. Rad managed to acquire the building a few months ago, bring it back into his family."

"Do you know how it got out of his family?"

"Ah, I think Rad told me it was sold off when he was a boy. His father inherited it when his grandfather died. Tragically, a drug overdose. And it was Rad's plan to bring it back to its former glory, such as it was."

"He talked about it all the time," Maeve added. "Whenever he came in. Now he'll never . . . It's so sad."

"To be frank," Buchanan continued, "I think he might have overreached a bit. A huge undertaking, which is why he found it necessary—in my opinion—to sell some of his artwork and memorabilia. And because I have a number of contacts in the business who might have been helpful when and if he was ready to outfit the club, it was a good, symbiotic relationship. I'm sorry this happened."

"When was the last time you had contact with him?"

"Just last week. I joined him for a drink, at his invitation. That would be . . ." He closed his eyes a moment, held up a finger. "Wednesday. Wednesday evening of last week. I knew he was going to try to persuade me, again, to invest in this club of his. It's just not the sort of thing I do, but he's a good client, and we were friendly."

When he sighed, Maeve covered his hand with hers. "So I met with him. He was so excited. He told me he was ready to begin the rehab again, seriously this time. He projected opening next summer."

"But you turned him down, investmentwise."

"I did, but he took it well. To be frank again, I did a bit of research when he first approached me months ago. Nothing thrives in that building. Owners and backers go bankrupt or worse. I couldn't see this being any different."

"True enough," Roarke confirmed. "The owners before Hopkins had plans for a small, exclusive spa with restaurant and retail. The buyer fell, broke both his legs while doing a run-through with the architect. His brother and

cobuyer were brutally mugged just outside the building.
Then his accountant ran off with his wife, taking the bulk
of his portfolio."

"Bad luck happens," Eve said flatly. "Could you tell me
where you were last night, between midnight and three?"

"Are we suspects?" Maeve's eyes rounded. "Oh my
God."

"It's just information. The more I have, the more I
have."

"I was out—a date—until about eleven."

"Eleven-fifteen," Buchanan said. "I heard you come in."

"Daddy . . ." Maeve rolled her eyes. "He waits up. I'm
twenty-four and he still waits up."

"I was reading in bed." But her father smiled, a little
sheepishly. "Maeve came in, and I . . . well . . ." He sent
another look toward his daughter. "I went down about midnight and checked security. I know, I know," he said before
Maeve could speak. "You always set it if you come in after
I'm in bed, but I feel better doing that last round. I went to
bed after that. Maeve was already in her room. We had
breakfast together about eight this morning, then we were
here at nine-thirty. We open at ten."

"Thanks. Is it all right if we take a look around?"

"Absolutely. Please. If you have any questions—if
there's anything we can do . . ." Buchanan lifted his hands.
"I've never dealt with anything like this, so I'm not sure
what we can or should do."

"Just stay available," Eve told him. "And contact me at
Central if anything comes to mind. For now, maybe you
can point me toward what you've got on Bobbie Bray."

"Oh, we have quite a collection. Actually, one of my fa-
vorites is a portrait we bought from Rad a few months ago.
This way." Buchanan turned to lead them through the main
showroom. "It was done from the photograph taken for her
first album cover. Hop—the first Hopkins—had it painted,
and it hung in the apartment he kept over Number Twelve.
Rumor is he held long conversations with it after she dis-

appeared. Of course, he ingested all manner of hallucinogens. Here she is. Stunning, isn't it?"

The portrait was perhaps eighteen by twenty inches, in a horizontal pose. Bobbie reclined over a bed spread with vivid pink and mounded with white pillows.

Eve saw a woman with wild yards of curling blond hair. There were two sparkling diamond clips glinting in the masses of it. Her eyes were the green of new spring leaves, and a single tear—bright as the diamonds, spilled down her cheek. It was the face of a doomed angel—lovely rather than beautiful, full of tragedy and pathos.

She wore thin, filmy white, and between the breasts was deep red stain in the blurred shape of a heart.

"The album was *Bleeding Heart*, for the title track. She won three Grammys for it."

"She was twenty-two," Maeve put in. "Two years younger than me. Less than two years later, she vanished without a trace."

There was a trace, Eve thought. There always was, even if it was nearly a century coming to light.

Outside, Eve dug her hands into her pockets. The sky had stopped spitting out nasty stuff, but the wind had picked up. She was pretty sure she'd left her watch cap in her office.

"Everybody's got an alibi, nobody's got a motive. Yet. I think I'm going to go back to the scene, take another look around."

"Then you can fill me in with what must be a multitude of missing details on the way. I had my car taken home," Roarke continued when she frowned at him. "So I could get a lift with my lovely wife."

"You were just hoping to get a look at Number Twelve."

"And hope springs. Want me to drive?"

When she slid behind the wheel, she tapped her fingers on it. "What's something like that painting going to go for on the open market?"

"To the right collector? Sky would be the limit. But I'd say a million wouldn't be out of the park."

"A million? For a painting of a dead woman. What's wrong with people? Top transaction in the vic's account from Bygones was a quarter of that. Why'd Hopkins sell so cheap?"

"Scrambling for capital. Bird in the hand's worth a great deal more than a painting on the wall."

"Yeah, there's that. Buchanan had to know he was getting bargain basement there."

"So why kill the golden goose?"

"Exactly. But it's weird to me neither of them had heard by this time that Hopkins bought it at Number Twelve. They eat breakfast at eight? No media reports while you're scoping out the pickings on the AutoChef or pulling on your pants?"

"Not everyone turns on the news."

"Maybe not. And nobody pops in today, mentions it? Nobody say, 'Hey! Did you hear about that Hopkins guy? Number Twelve got another one.' Just doesn't sit level for me." Then she shrugged, pulled away from the curb.

"Hit the lab before this. The same gun that killed Hopkins killed the as yet unidentified female whose remains were found behind the wall at Number Twelve."

"Fascinating."

"Weapon was bricked up with her. Killer must have found her, and it. Cleaned the weapon. You see those, the hair jewelry, she had on in the picture? Recovered at the scene, also clean and shiny. One by the window which the killer likely used to escape, one left with the bones."

"Someone wants to make sure the remains are identified. Do you doubt it's her?"

"No, I don't doubt it's her. I don't doubt Hop Hopkins put a bullet in her brain, then got handy with brick and mortar. I don't know why. I don't know why someone used that same gun on Hop's grandson eighty-five years later."

"But you think there's a connection. A personal one."

"Had to reload to put the bullet in the brain. That's extremely cold. Guy's dead, or next to it. But you reload, roll the body over, press the barrel down hard enough to scorch the skin and leave an imprint of the barrel, and give him one last hit. Fucking cold."

Five

Eve gave him details on the drive. She could, with Roarke, run them through like a checklist, and it always lined them up in her mind. In addition, he always seemed to know something or someone that might fill in a few of the gaps.

"So, did you ever do business with Hopkins?"

"No. He had a reputation for being generous with the bullshit, and often short on results."

"Big plans, small action," Eve concluded.

"That would be it. Harmless, by all accounts. Not the sort to con the widow and orphans out of the rent money, but not above talking them out of a portion of it with a view to getting rich quick."

"He cheated on his wives, and recently squeezed five hundred out of the son he abandoned."

"Harmless doesn't always mean moral or admirable. I made a few calls—curiosity," he explained. "To people who like to buy and sell real estate."

"Which includes yourself."

"Most definitely. From what I'm told the bottom

dropped out of Twelve for Hopkins only a couple of weeks after he'd signed the papers on it. He was in fairly deep—purchase price, legal fees, architects and designers, construction crew, and so on. He'd done a lot of tap dancing to get as far as he did, and was running out of steam. He'd done some probing around—more legal fees—to see if he could wrangle having the property condemned, and get back some of his investment. Tried to wrangle some money from various federal agencies, historic societies. He played all the angles and had some success. A couple of small grants. Not nearly enough, not for his rather ambitious vision."

"What kind of money we talking, for the building and the vision?"

"Oh, easily a hundred and fifty million. He'd barely scratched the surface when he must have realized he couldn't make it without more capital. Then, word is, a few days ago, he pushed the green light again. Claimed Number Twelve was moving forward."

"I'm waiting on the lab to see if they can pinpoint when that wall was taken down. Could be talking days." Her fingers tapped out a rhythm on the wheel as she considered. "Hopkins finds the body. You get a wealth of publicity out of something like that. Maybe a vid deal, book deals. A guy with an entrepreneurial mindset, he could think of all kinds of ways to rake it in over those bones."

"He could," Roarke agreed. "But wouldn't the first question be how he knew where to look?"

"Or how his killer knew."

"Hop killed her," she began as she hunted for parking. "Argument, drug-induced, whatever. Bricks up the body, which takes some doing. Guy liked cocaine. That'll keep you revved for a few hours. Has to cover up the brick, put things back into reasonable shape. I'm trying to access the police reports from back then. It hasn't been easy so far. But anyway, no possible way the cops just missed a brand new section of wall, so he paid them off or blackmailed them."

"Corrupt cops? I'm stunned. I'm shocked."

"Shut up. Hop goes over the edge—guilt, drugs, fear of discovery. Goes hermit. Guy locks himself up with a body on the other side of the wall, he's going to go pretty buggy. Wouldn't surprise me if he wrote something down, told someone about it. If cops were involved, *they* knew or suspected something. The killer, or Hopkins does some homework, pokes around. Gets lucky, or unlucky as the case may be."

"It takes eight and a half decades to get lucky?"

"Place gets a rep," Eve said as they walked from the car toward Number Twelve. "Bray gets legend status. People report seeing her, talking to her. A lot of those people, and others, figure she just took off 'cause she couldn't handle the pressure of her own success. Hop has enough juice to keep people out of the apartment during his lifetime. By then, there're murmurs of curses and hauntings, and that just grows as time passes. A couple of people have some bad luck, and nobody much wants to play in Number Twelve anymore."

"More than a couple." Roarke frowned at the door as Eve uncoded the police seal. "The building just squats here, and everyone who's tried to disturb it, for whatever reason, ends up paying a price."

"It's brick and wood and glass."

"Brick and wood and glass form structure, not spirit."

She raised her brows at him. "Want to wait in the car, Sally?"

"Now you shut up." He nudged her aside to walk in first.

She turned on the lights, took out her flashlight for good measure. "Hopkins was between those iron stairs and the bar." She moved across the room, positioned herself by the stairs. "From the angles, the killer was here. I'm seeing he got here first, comes down when Hopkins walks in. Hopkins still had his coat on, his gloves, a muffler. Cold in here, sure, but a man's going to probably pull off his gloves, unwrap his scarf, maybe unbutton his coat when he's inside. You just do."

Understanding his wife, Roarke moved into what he thought had been Hopkins's standing position. "Unless you don't have the chance."

"Killer comes down. He'd told Hopkins to bring something, and Hopkins walks in empty-handed. Could have been small—pocket-sized—but why would the killer shoot him so quickly, and with such rage, if he'd cooperated?"

"The man liked to spin the wheels. If he came empty, he may have thought he could work a deal."

"So when he starts the whole Let's talk about this, the killer snaps. Shoots him. Chest, leg. Four shots from the front. Vic goes down, tries to crawl, killer keeps firing, moving toward the target. Leg, back, shoulder. Eight shots. Full clip for that model. Reloads, shoves the body over, leans down. Looks Hopkins right in the eyes. Eyes are dead, but he looks into them when he pulls the trigger the last time. He wants to see his face—as much as he needs to echo the head shot on Bray, he needs to see the face, the eyes, when he puts that last bullet in."

She crossed over, following what she thought was the killer's route as she'd spoken. "Could have gone out the front. But he chooses to go back upstairs."

Now she turned, started up. "Could have taken the weapon, thrown it in the river. We'd never have found it. Wants us to find it. Wants us to know. Cops didn't put Hop in the system. Why should we do anything about his grandson? Took care of that himself. Payment made. But he wants us to know, everyone to know, that Bobbie's been avenged at last."

She stopped in front of the open section of wall. " 'Look what he did to her. Put a bullet in that young, tragic face, silenced that voice. Ended her life when it was just getting started. Then he put a wall up, locked her away from the world. She's free now. I set her free.' "

"She'll be more famous, more infamous, than ever. Her fans will make a shrine out of this place. Heap flowers and tokens outside, stand in the cold with candles for vigils. And, to add a cynical note, there'll be Bobbie Bray merchandising through the roof. Fortunes will be made out of this."

Eve turned back to Roarke. "Damn right, they will. Hopkins would have known that. He'd have had visions of money falling on him from the sky. Number Twelve wouldn't just be a club, it would be a freaking cathedral. And he's got the main attraction. Fame and fortune off her bones. You bet your ass. Killer's not going to tolerate that. 'You think you can use her? You think I'd let you?'"

"Most who'd have known her personally, had a relationship with her, would be dead now. Or elderly."

"Don't have to be young to pull a trigger." But she frowned at the cut in the wall. "But you'd have to be pretty spry to handle the tools to do this. I just don't think this part was Hopkins's doing. Nothing in his financials to indicate he'd bought or rented the tools that could handle this. And he doesn't strike me as the type who'd be able to do this tidy a job with them. Not on his own. And the killer had the gun, the hair clips. The killer opened this grave."

The cold was sudden and intense, as if a door had been flung open to an ice floe, and through that frigid air drifted a raw and haunting voice.

In my dark there is no dawn, there is no light in my world since you've been gone. I thought my love would stand the test, but now my heart bleeds from my breast.

Even as Eve drew her weapon, the voice rose, with a hard, throbbing pump of bass and drums behind it. She rushed out to the level overlooking the main club.

The voice continued to rise, seemed to fill the building. Under it, over it, were voices, cheers and whistles. For an instant, she thought she could smell a heavy mix of perfume, sweat, smoke.

"Somebody's messing with us," she murmured.

Before she could swing toward the stairs to investigate,

there was a shout from the nearly gutted apartment above.
A woman's voice called out:

"No. Jesus, Hop. Don't!"

There was the explosion of a shot and a distinct thud.

Keeping her weapon out, she vaulted up the stairs again
with Roarke. At the doorway, his hand clamped over her
shoulder.

"Holy Mother of God. Do you see?"

She told herself it was a shadow—a trick of the poor
light, the dust. But for an instant there seemed to be a
woman, her mass of curling blond hair falling over her
shoulders, standing in front of the open section of wall.
And for an instant, it seemed her eyes looked straight into
Eve's.

Then there was nothing but a cold, empty room.

"You saw her," Roarke insisted as Eve crawled around
behind the wall.

"I saw shadows. Maybe an image. If I saw an image, it
was because someone put it there. Just like someone
flipped some switch to put on that music. Got some electronics set up somewhere. Triggered by remote, most
likely."

He crouched down. Eve's hair, face, hands were all
coated with dust and debris. "You felt that cold."

"So, he dropped the temp in here. He's putting on a
show, that's what he's doing. Circus time. So the cop goes
back and reports spooky happenings, apparitions. Bull-
shit!"

She swiped at her filthy face as she crawled out. "Hopkins left debts. His son is beneficiary of basically nada.
Building's no-man's-land until it goes up to public auction.
Keep the curse crap going, keep the price down. Snap it up
cheaper than dirt."

"With what's happened here, discovering the body here,
that could go exactly the opposite way. It could drive the
price up."

"That happens, you bet your ass someone's going to

have some document claiming they were partners with Hopkins. Maybe I was wrong about it being personal. Maybe it's been profit all along."

"You weren't wrong. You know you weren't. But you're sitting there, in a fairly disgusting state, I might add, trying to turn it around so you don't have to admit you've seen a ghost."

"I saw what some mope wants me to believe is a ghost and he apparently pulled one over on you, ace."

"I know electronic imagery when I see it." The faintest edge of irritation flickered into his eyes at her tone. "I know what I saw, what I heard, what I felt. Murder was done here, then adding to it, the insult, the callousness of what was done after."

He glanced back into the narrow opening, toward the former location of the long-imprisoned bones. And now there was a hint of pity in his eyes as well. "All while claiming to be so concerned, so upset, offering rewards for her safe return, or for substantiated proof she was alive and well. All that while she was moldering behind the wall he'd built to hide her.

"If her body never left here, why should her spirit?"

"Because—" With a shake of her head, Eve scattered dust. "Her body's not here now. So shouldn't she be haunting the morgue?"

"This place has been home to her for a long time, hasn't it?" *Pragmatism,* he thought, *thy name is Eve.* Then he took out a handkerchief, used it to rub the worst of the dust and grime from her face.

"Homemade crypts aren't what I'd call home, sweet home," she retorted. "And you know what? Ghosts don't clean guns or shoot them. I've got a DB in the morgue. And I'm ordering the sweepers, with a contingent from EDD in here tomorrow. They're going to take this place apart."

She brushed some of the dirt from her shirt and pants before picking up her coat. "I want a shower."

"I want you to have a shower, too."

As they went downstairs, she called in the order for two units to search Number Twelve for electronic devices. If she thought she heard a woman's husky laugh just before she closed and secured the door, Eve ignored it.

Six

When she'd showered and pulled on warm, comfortable sweats, Eve gave another thought to pizza. She figured she could down a slice or two at her desk while she worked.

She was headed toward the office she kept at home when she heard Bobbie Bray's voice, gritting out her signature song.

> Broken, battered, bleeding, and still I'm begging, pleading
>
> Come back. Come back and heal my heart
> Come back. Come back and heal my heart

With her own heart thudding, Eve covered the rest of the distance at a dash. Except for the fat cat, Galahad, snoring in her sleep chair, her office was empty.

Then she narrowed her eyes at the open door that joined her office to Roarke's. She found him at his desk, with the title track beginning its play again through the speakers of his entertainment unit.

"You trying to wig me out?"

"No." He smiled a little. "Did I?" When she gave him a stony stare, he shrugged. "I wanted to get better acquainted with our ghost. She was born in Louisville, Kentucky, and according to this biography, left home at sixteen to migrate to Haight-Ashbury, as many of her generation did. She sang in some clubs, primarily for food or a place to sleep, drifted around, joined a band called Luv—that's L-U-V—where she stood out like a rose among weeds, apparently. Did some backup singing for one or two important artists of the time, then met Hopkins in Los Angeles."

"Bad luck for her. Can you turn that off?"

"Music off," he ordered, and Bobbie's voice stopped. "She bothers you," Roarke realized. "Why is that?"

"She doesn't bother me." *The correct term*, Eve thought, *would be she creeps me*. But damned if she was going to fall into the accepted pattern on Number Twelve, or Bobbie Bray.

"She's part of my investigation—and a secondary vic, even though she was killed a half century before I was born. She's mine now, like Hopkins is mine. But she's always part of the motive."

"And as such, I'd think you'd want to know all you could about her."

"I do, and I will. But I don't have to hear her singing." It was too sad, Eve admitted to herself. And too spooky. "I'm going to order up some pizza. You want in on that?"

"All right." Roarke rose to follow her into the kitchen attached to her office. "She was twenty when Hop scooped her up. He was forty-three. Still, it was two years before her album came out—which he produced, allegedly hand-picking every song. She did perform during that period, exclusively in Hopkins's venues."

"So he ran her."

"All but owned her, from the sound of it. Young, naive girl—at least from a business standpoint, and from a generation and culture that prided itself on not being bound by property and possessions. Older, canny, experienced man, who discovered her, romanced her, and most certainly fed any appetite she might have had for illegal substances."

"She'd been on her own for five years." Eve debated for about five seconds on pepperoni and went for it. "Naive doesn't wash for me."

"But then you're not a sentimental fan or biographer. Still, I'd lean toward the naivete when it came to contracts, royalties, business and finance. And Hopkins was a pro. He stood as her agent, her manager, her producer."

"But she's the talent," Eve reasoned and snagged some napkins. "She's got the youth, the looks. Maybe her culture or whatever said pooh-pooh to big piles of money, but if she's bringing it in, getting the shine from it, she's going to start to want more."

"Agreed. She left him for a few months in 1972, just dropped off the radar. Which is one of the reasons, I'd assume, he got away with her murder three years later. She'd taken off once, why not again?"

He stepped out to choose a wine from the rack behind a wall panel. "When she came back, it was full-court press professionally, with a continual round of parties, clubs, drugs, sex. Her album hit, and big, with her touring internationally for six months. More sex, more drugs, and three Grammys. Her next album was in the works when she disappeared."

"Hop must've gotten a percentage of her earnings." Eve brought the pizza in, dumped it and plates on her desk.

"As her manager and producer, he'd have gotten a hefty one."

"Stupid to kill the goose."

"Passion plus drugs can equal extreme stupidity."

"Smart enough to cover it up, and keep it covered for eighty-five years. So his grandson ends up paying for it. Why? My vic wasn't even born when this went down. If it's revenge . . ."

"Served very cold," Roarke said as he poured wine.

"The killer has a connection with the older crime, the older players. Financial, emotional, physical. Maybe all three."

She lifted up a slice, tugged at the strings of cheese, expertly looping them up and over the triangle.

"If it's financial," she continued, "who stands to gain? The son inherits, but he's alibied and there isn't a hell of a lot to scoop once the debts are offset. So maybe something of value, something the killer wanted Hopkins to bring to Number Twelve. But if it's a straight give-me-what-I-want/deserve, why set the scene? Why put on that show for us tonight?"

When Roarke said nothing, Even chewed contemplatively on her slice. "You don't seriously believe that was some ghostly visitation? Grab a little corner of reality."

"Do you seriously believe your killer has been dogging that building, it's owners, for eight and a half decades? What makes that more logical than a restless, angry spirit?"

"Because dead people don't get angry. They're dead." She picked up her wine. "It's my job to get pissed for them."

Roarke studied her over his own glass, his gaze thoughtful, seeking. "Then there's nothing after? As close as you've been to the dead, you don't see something after?"

"I don't know what I see." This sort of conversation always made her uncomfortable, somehow sticky along the skin. "Because you don't see it—if it's there to see—until you're dead. But I don't believe the dead go all *whoooo*, or start singing. The original Hopkins paid an investigation off, this killer wants to weird one off. It's not going to work."

"Consider the possibility," he suggested. "Bobbie Bray's spirit wants her revenge as much as you want justice. It's a powerful desire, on both parts."

"That's not a possible possibility."

"Closed-minded."

"Rational," she corrected, with some heat now. "Jesus,

Roarke, she's bones. Why now then? Why here and now? How'd she manage to get someone—flesh and blood—to do the descendent of her killer? If Hop Hopkins *was* her killer—which hasn't yet been proven."

"Maybe she was waiting for you to prove it."

"Oh yeah, *that's* rational. She's been hanging around, waiting for the right murder cop to come along. Listen, I've got the reality of a dead body, an antique and banned weapon used in a previous crime. I've got no discernible motive and a media circus waiting to happen. I can't take the time to wonder and worry about the disposition of a woman who's been dead eighty-five years. You want to waste your time playing with ghosts, be my guest. But I've got serious work on my plate."

"Fine then, since it pisses you off, I'll just leave you to your serious work while I go waste my time."

She scowled at him when he got up and carried his glass of wine with him to his office. And she cursed under her breath when he closed the door behind him.

"Great, fine, fabulous. Now I've got a ghost causing marital discord. Just makes it all perfect."

She shoved away from her desk to set up the case board she used at home. Logic was what was needed here, she told herself. Logic, cop sense, facts and evidence.

Must be that Irish in Roarke's blood that tugged him into the fanciful. Who knew he'd head that way?

But her way was straight, narrow and rational.

Two murders, one weapon. Connection. Two murders, one location, second connection. Second vic, blood descendent of suspected killer in first murder. Connect those dots, too, she thought as she worked.

So, okay, she couldn't set the first murder aside. She'd use it.

Logic and evidence dictated that both victims knew their killer. The first appeared to be a crime of passion, likely enhanced by illegal substances. Maybe Bray cheated on Hop. Or wanted to break things off professionally and/or personally. She could have had something on him, threatened exposure.

Had to be an act of passion, heat of the moment. Hop had the money, the means. If he'd planned to kill Bray, why would he have done it in his own apartment?

But the second murder was a deliberate act. The killer lured the victim to the scene, had the weapon. Had, in all likelihood discovered the previous body. The killing had been an act of rage as well as deliberation.

"Always meant to kill him, didn't you?" she murmured as she studied the crime scene photos on her board. "Wanted whatever you wanted first—but whether or not you got it, he was a dead man. What did she mean to you?"

She studied the photos of Bobbie Bray.

Obsessed fan? Not out of the realm, she thought, but low on her list.

"Computer, run probability with evidence currently on active file. What is probability that the killers of Bray, Bobbie and Hopkins, Radcliff C. are linked?"

Working . . .

Absently, Eve picked up her wine, sipping as she worked various scenarios through her head.

Task complete. Probability is eighty-two-point-three . . .

Reasonably strong, Eve mused, and decided to take it one step further. "What is the probability that the killer of Hopkins, Radcliff C. is linked with the first victim, Bray, Bobbie?"

Working . . .

Family member, Eve thought. *Close friend, lover. Bray would be, what . . . Damn math*, she cursed as she calculated. *Bray would be around about one-oh-nine if she'd lived. People lived longer now than they did in the mid-twentieth. So a lover or tight friend isn't out of the realm either.*

But she couldn't see a centenarian, even a spry one, cutting through that brick.

Task complete. Probability is ninety-four-point-one that there is a connection between the first victim and the second killer . . .

"Yeah, that's what I think. And you know what else? Blood's the closest connection. So who did Bobbie leave behind? Computer, list all family members of first victim. Display on wall screen one."

Working . . . Display complete.

Parents and older brother deceased, Eve noted. A younger sister, age eighty-eight, living in Scottsdale Care Center, Arizona. Young for a care center, Eve mused, and made a note to find out what the sister's medical condition was.

Bobbie would have had a niece and nephew had she lived, and a couple of grandnieces and nephews.

Worth checking into, Eve decided, and began a standard run on all living relations.

While the computer worked, she set up a secondary task and took a closer look at Hopkins.

"Big starter," she said aloud. "Little finisher."

There were dozens of projects begun, abandoned. Failed. Now and then he'd hit, at least enough to keep the wolves from the door, set up the next project.

Failed marriages, ignored offspring. No criminal on any former spouse or offspring.

But you had to start somewhere, she figured.

She went back to the board. Diamond hair clips. Bray had worn them for her first album cover—possibly a gift from Hop. Most likely. The scene told Eve it was likely Bray had been wearing them when she'd been killed, or at least when she'd been bricked up.

But the killer hadn't taken them as a souvenir. Not a fan, just didn't play. The killer had shined them up and left them behind.

"She was a diamond," Eve murmured. "She shined. Is

that what you're telling me? Here's the gun he used to kill her, and here's where I found it. He never paid and payment needed to be made. Is that the message?"

She circled the boards, studied the runs when the computer displayed them. There were a couple of decent possibilities among Bobbie's descendents.

They'd all have to be interviewed, she decided.

One of them contacts Hopkins, she speculated. *Maybe even tries to buy the building but can't come up with the scratch. Has to get access though, to uncover the body. How was access gained?*

Money. Hopkins needed backers. Maybe charged his murderer a fee to tour Number Twelve. Get in once, you can get in again.

How'd you find the body? How did you know?

What did she have here? she asked herself. Younger sister in a care facility. Niece a data drone. Nephew deceased—Urban War fatality. Grandniece middle-management in sales, grandnephew an insurance salesman. Rank and file, no big successes, no big failures.

Ordinary.

Nothing flashy. Nobody managed to cash in on Bobbie's fame and fortune, or her untimely death.

Nobody, she mused, except Hopkins. That would be a pisser, wouldn't it? Your daughter, sister, aunt is a dead cult figure, but you've got to do the thirty-five hours a week to get by. And the grandson of the bastard who killed her is trying to rake it in. You're scraping by, getting old and . . .

"Wait a minute, wait a minute. Serenity Bray, age eighty-eight. Twenty-two years younger than Bobbie. Not a sister. A daughter."

She swung to the adjoining door, shoved it open. "Bobbie had a kid. Not a sister. The timing's right. She had a kid."

Roarke merely lifted an eyebrow. "Yes. Serenity Bray Massey, currently in Scottsdale in a full-care nursing facility. I've got that."

"Showoff. She had a kid, and the timing makes it most likely Hop's. There's no record of a child. No reports from that time of her pregnancy. But she separated from him for several months, which would coincide with the last few months of her pregnancy and the birth."

"After which, it would seem, she gave the child to her own mother. Who then moved her family to a ranch outside Scottsdale, and Bobbie went back to Hop, and her previous lifestyle. I've found some speculation that during her period of estrangement from Hop she went into rehab and seclusion. Interviews and articles from the time have her clean and sober when she returned to the scene, then backsliding, I suppose you could say, within weeks."

He angled his head. "I thought you were leaving Bobbie to me."

"The ghost part's yours. The dead part's mine."

Seven

They were into their second year of marriage, and being a trained observer, Eve knew when he was irritated with her. It seemed stupid, just *stupid* to have a fight or the undercurrent of one over something as ridiculous as ghosts.

Still, she brooded over it another moment, on the verge of stupidity. Then she huffed out a breath.

"Look," she began.

After a pause, he sat back. "I'm looking."

"What I'm getting at is . . . shit. Shit." She paced to his window, to the doorway, turned around again.

Rules of marriage—and hell, one of the benefits of it, she admitted—were that she could say to him what she might even find hard to say to herself.

"I have to live with so many of them." There was anger in her over it, and a kind of grief she could never fully explain. "They don't always go away when you close the case, never go away if you leave a crack in it. I got a freaking army of dead in my head."

"Whom you've defended," he reminded her. "Stood over, stood for."

"Yeah, well, that doesn't mean they're going to say 'Thanks, pal,' then shuffle off the mortal whatever."

"That would be coil—and they've already done the shuffle before you get there."

"Exactly. Dead. But they still have faces and voices and pain, at least in my head. I don't need to think about one wifting around sending me messages from beyond. It's too much, that's all. It's too much if I have to start wondering if there's some spirit hovering over my shoulder to make sure I do the job."

"All right."

"That's it?"

"Darling Eve," he said with the easy patience he could pull out and baffle her with at the oddest times. "Haven't we already proven that you and I don't have to stand on exactly the same spot on every issue? And wouldn't it be boring if we did?"

"Maybe." Tension oozed back out of her. "I guess. I just never expected you'd take something like this and run with it."

"Then perhaps I shouldn't tell you that if I die first, I'm planning to come back to see you naked as often as possible."

Her lips twitched, as he'd intended them to. "I'll be old, with my tits hanging to my waist."

"You don't have enough tit to hang that low."

She pursed her lips, looked down as if to check. "Gotta point. So are we good now?"

"We may be, if you come over here and kiss me. In payment for the insult."

She rolled her eyes. "Nothing's free around here." But she skirted the desk, leaned down to touch her lips to his.

The moment she did, he yanked her down into his lap. She'd seen it coming—she knew him too well not to—but was in the mood to indulge him.

"If you think I'm playing bimbo secretary and horny exec—"

"There were actually a few insults," he interrupted. "And you've reminded me that you're going to get old eventually. I should take advantage of your youth and vitality, and see you naked now."

"I'm not getting naked. Hey! Hey!"

"*Feel* you naked then," he amended, as his hands were already under her sweatshirt and on her breasts. "Good things, small packages."

"Oh yeah? Is that what I should say about your equipment?"

"Insult upon insult." Laughing, he slid his hand around to her back to hold her more firmly in place. "You have a lot of apologizing to do."

"Then I guess I'd better get started."

She put some punch into the kiss, swinging around to straddle him. It would take some agility as well as vitality to pull off a serious apology in his desk chair, but she thought she was up to the job.

He made her feel so many things, all of them vital and immediate. The hunger, the humor, the love, the lust. She could taste his heat for her, his greed for her as his mouth ravished hers. Her own body filled with that same heat and hunger as he tugged at her clothes.

Here was his life—in this complicated woman. Not just the long, alluring length of her, but the mind and spirit inside the form. She could excite and frustrate, charm and annoy—and all there was of her somehow managed to fit against him, and make him complete.

Now she surrounded him, shifting that body, using those quick hands, then taking him inside her with a long, low purr of satisfaction. They took each other, finished each other, and then the purr was a laughing groan.

"I think that squares us," she managed.

"You may even have some credit."

For a moment, she curled in, rested her head on his

shoulder. "Ghosts probably can't screw around in a desk chair."

"Unlikely."

"It's tough being dead."

At eight-fifteen in the morning, Eve was in her office at Central scowling at the latest sweeper and EDD reports.

"Nothing. They can't find anything. No sign of electronic surveillance, holographic paraphernalia, audio, video. Zilch."

"Could be it's telling you that you had a paranormal experience last night."

Eve spared one bland look for Peabody. "Paranormal my ass."

"Cases have been documented, Dallas."

"Fruitcakes have been documented, too. It's going to be a family member. That's where we push. That and whatever Hopkins may or may not have had in his possession that his killer wanted. Start with the family members. Let's eliminate any with solid alibis. We'll fan out from there."

She glanced at her desk as her 'link beeped—again— and, scanning the readout, sneered. "Another reporter. We're not feeding the hounds on this one until so ordered. Screen all your incomings. If you get cornered, straight no comment, investigation is active and ongoing. Period."

"Got that. Dallas, what was it like last night? Skin-crawly or wow?"

Eve started to snap, then blew out a breath. "Skin-crawly, then annoying that some jerk had played with me and made my skin crawl for a minute."

"But kind of frigid, too, right? Ghost of Bobbie Bray serenading you."

"If I believed it was the ghost of anyone, I'd say it was feeling more pissy than entertaining. What someone wants us to think is we're not welcome at Number Twelve. Trying to scare us off. I've got Feeney's notes on the report from EDD. He says a couple of his boys heard singing. Another swears he felt something pat his ass. Same sort of deal from the sweepers. Mass hysteria."

"Digging in, I found out two of the previous owners tried exorcisms. Hired priests, psychics, parapsychologists, that kind of deal. Nothing worked."

"Gee, mumbo didn't get rid of the jumbo? Why doesn't that surprise me? Get on the 'link, start checking alibis."

Eve took her share, eliminated two, and ended up tagging Serenity Massey's daughter in the woman's Scottsdale home.

"It's not even seven in the morning."

"I'm sorry, Ms. Sawyer."

"Not even seven," the woman said testily, "and I've already had three calls from reporters, and another from the head nurse at my mother's care center. Do you know a reporter tried to get to her? She has severe dementia—can barely remember me when I go see her—and some idiot reporter tries to get through to interview her over Bobbie Bray. My mother didn't even *know* her."

"Does your mother know she was Bobbie Bray's daughter?"

The woman's thin, tired face went blank. But it was there in her eyes, clear as glass. "What did you say?"

"She knows, then—certainly you do."

"I'm not going to have my mother harassed, not by reporters, not by the police."

"I don't intend to harass your mother. Why don't you tell me when and how she found out she was Bobbie's daughter, not her sister."

"I don't know." Ms. Sawyer rubbed her hands over her face. "She hasn't been well for a long time, a very long time. Even when I was a child . . ." She dropped her hands now and looked more than tired. She looked ill. "Lieutenant, is this necessary?"

"I've got two murders. Both of them relatives of yours.
You tell me."

"I don't think of the Hopkins family as relatives. Why
would I? I'm sorry that man was killed because it's
dredged all this up. I've been careful to separate myself
and my own family from the Bobbie phenomenon. Check,
why don't you? I've never given an interview, never agreed
to one or sought one out."

"Why? It's a rich pool, from what I can tell."

"Because I wanted *normal*. I'm entitled to it, and so are
my kids. My mother was always frail. Delicate, mind and
body. I'm not, and I've made damn sure to keep me and
mine out of that whirlpool. If it leaks out that I'm Bobbie's
granddaughter instead of a grandniece, they'll hound me."

"I can't promise to keep it quiet, I can only promise you
that I won't be giving interviews on that area of the investigation. I won't give out your name or the names of your
family members."

"Good for you," Sawyer said dully. "They're already
out."

"Then it won't hurt you to answer some questions. How
did your mother find out about her parentage?"

"She told me—my brother and me—that she found letters Bobbie had written. Bobbie's mother kept them. She
wrote asking how her baby was doing, called my mother
by name. Her Serenity she called her, as if she was a state
of mind instead of a child who needed her mother."

The bitterness in the words told Eve she wasn't talking
to one of Bobbie Bray's fans.

"Said she was sorry she'd messed up again. My mother
claimed Bobbie said she was going back into rehab, that
she was leaving Hop, the whole scene. She was going to
get clean and come back for her daughter. Of course, she
never came back. My mother was convinced Hop had
killed her, or had her killed."

"What do you think?"

"Sure, maybe." The words were the equivalent of a

shrug. "Or maybe she took off to Bimini to sell seashells by the seashore. Maybe she went back to San Francisco and jumped off the Golden Gate Bridge. I don't know, and frankly don't much care."

Sawyer let out a long sigh, pressed her fingers to her eyes. "She wasn't, and isn't, part of my world. But she all but became my mother's world. Mom swore Bobbie's ghost used to visit her, talk to her. I think it's part of the reason, this obsession, that she's been plagued by emotional and mental problems as long as I can remember. When my brother was killed in the Urbans, it just snapped her. He was her favorite."

"Do you have the letters?"

"No. That Hopkins man, he tracked my mother down. I was in college, my brother was overseas, so that was, God, about thirty years ago. He talked her out of nearly everything she had that was Bobbie's or pertained to her. Original recordings, letters, diaries, photographs. He said he was going to open some sort of museum in California. Nothing ever came of it. My brother came home and found out. He was furious. He and my mother had a horrible fight, one they never had a chance to reconcile. Now he's gone and she might as well be. I don't want to be Bobbie Bray's legacy. I just want to live my life."

Eve ended the transmission, tipped back in her chair. She was betting the letters were what the killer had been after.

With Peabody she went back to Hopkins's apartment for another thorough search.

"Letters Bobbie wrote that confirm a child she had with Hop. Letters or some sort of document or recording from Hop that eventually led his grandson to Serenity Massey. Something that explosive and therefore valuable," she said to her partner. "I bet he had a secure hidey-hole. Security box, vault. We'll start a search of bank boxes under his name or likely aliases."

"Maybe he took them with him and the killer already has them."

"I don't think so. The doorman said he walked out empty-handed. Something like that, figuring the value, he's going to want a briefcase, a portfolio. Guy liked accessories—good suit, shoes, antique watch—why miss a trick with something that earns one? But . . . he was hunting up money. Maybe he sold them, or at least dangled them."

"Bygones?"

"Worth a trip."

At the door, Eve paused, turned to study the apartment again. There'd be no ghosts here, she thought. Nothing here but stale air, stale dreams.

Legacies, she thought as she closed the door. Hopkins left one of unfulfilled ambitions, which to her mind carried on the one left by his father.

Bobbie Bray's granddaughter had worked hard to shut her own heritage out, to live simply. Didn't want to be Bobbie Bray's legacy, Eve recalled.

Who could blame her? Or anyone else for that matter.

"If you're handed crap and disappointment—*inherited* it," Eve amended, "what do you do?"

"Depends, I guess." Peabody frowned as they headed down. "You could wallow in it and curse your ancestors, or shovel yourself out of it."

"Yeah. You could try to shine it up into gold and live the high life—like Hopkins. Obsess over it like Bray's daughter. Or you could shut the door on it and walk away. Like Bray's granddaughter."

"Okay. And?"

"There's more than one way to shut a door. You drive," Eve said when they were outside.

"Drive? Me? It's not even my birthday!"

"Drive, Peabody." In the passenger seat, Eve took out her ppc and brought up John Massey's military ID data. She cocked her head as she studied the photo.

He'd been young, fresh-faced. A little soft around the mouth, she mused, a little guileless in the eyes. She didn't see either of his grandparents in him, but she saw something else.

Inherited traits, she thought. Legacies.

Using the dash 'link, she contacted police artist Detective Yancy.

"Got a quick one for you," she told him. "I'm going to shoot you an ID photo. I need you to age it for me."

Eight

Eve had Peabody stop at the bank Hopkins had used for his loan on Number Twelve. But there was no safety deposit box listed under his name, or Bray's, or any combination.

To Peabody's disappointment, Eve took the wheel when they left the bank.

She couldn't justify asking Roarke to do the search for a safety deposit box, though it passed through her mind. He could no doubt pinpoint one, if one was there to be pinpointed, faster than she could. Even faster than EDD. But she couldn't term it a matter of life and death.

Just a matter of irritation.

She put in a request to Feeney to assign the task to EDD ace, and Peabody's heartthrob, Ian McNab while she and Peabody headed back to Bygones.

"McNab will be so completely jazzed about this." Smiling—as if even saying his name put a dopey look on her face—Peabody wiggled in the passenger seat. "Looking for a ghost and all that."

"He's looking for a bank box."

"Well yeah, but in a roundabout way, it's about Bobbie Bray and the ghost thereof. Number Twelve."

"Stop saying that." Eve wanted to grip her own hair and yank, but her hands were currently busy on the wheel. She used those hands to whip around a farting maxibus with a few layers of paint to spare. "I'm going to write an order forbidding anyone within ten feet of me from saying *Number Twelve* in that—what is it—awed whisper."

"But you just gotta. Did you know there are all these books, and there are vids, based on Number Twelve, and Bobbie and the whole deal from back then? I did some research. McNab and I downloaded one of the vids last night. It was kind of hokey, but still. And we're working the case. Maybe they'll make a vid of *that*—you know, like they're going to do one of the Icove case. Completely uptown. We'll be famous, and—"

Eve stopped at a light, turned her body slowly so she faced her partner. "You even breathe that thought, I'll choke you until your eyes pop right out of their sockets, then plop into your open gasping mouth where you'll swallow them whole. And choke to death on your own eyeballs."

"Well, jeez."

"Think about it, think carefully, before you breathe again."

Peabody hunched in her seat and kept her breathing to a minimum.

When they found the shop closed and locked, they detoured to the home address on record.

Maeve opened the door of the three-level brownstone. "Lieutenant, Detective."

"Closed down shop, Ms. Buchanan?"

"For a day or two." She pushed at her hair. Eve watched the movement, the play of light on the striking red. "We were overrun yesterday, only about an hour after you left. Oh, come in, please. I'm a little flustered this morning."

"Overrun?" Eve repeated as she stepped into a long,

narrow hallway brightened by stained glass windows that let in the winter sun.

"Customers, and most of them looking for bargains. Or wanting to gawk over the Bobbie Bray collection." Maeve, dressed in loose white pants, a soft white sweater and white half boots led the way through a wide doorway into a spacious parlor.

Tidy, Eve thought, but not fussy. Antiques—she knew how to recognize the real thing, as Roarke had a penchant for them. Deep cushions in rich colors, old rugs, what looked to be old black-and-white photographs in pewter frames adorning the walls.

No gel cushions, no mood screen, no entertainment unit in sight. Old-world stuff, Eve decided, very much like their place of business.

"Please, have a seat. I've got tea or coffee."

"Don't worry about it," Eve told her. "Your father's here?"

"Yes, up in the office. We're working from here, at least for today. We're buried in inquiries for our Bray collection, and we can handle those from home."

She moved around the room, turning on lamps with colored shades. "Normally, we'd love the walk-in traffic at the shop, but not when it's a circus parade. With only the two of us, we just couldn't handle it. We have a lot of easily lifted merchandise."

"How about letters?"

"Letters?"

"You carry that sort of thing? Letters, diaries, journals?"

"We absolutely do. On Bobbie again?" Maeve walked back to sit on the edge of a chair, crossed her legs. "We have what's been authenticated as a letter she wrote to a friend she'd made in San Francisco—ah . . . 1968. Two notebooks containing original lyrics for songs she'd written. There may be more, but those spring to mind."

"How about letters to family, from her New York years?"

"I don't think so, but I can check the inventory. Or just ask my father," she added with a quick smile. "He's got the entire inventory in his head, I swear. I don't know how he does it."

"Maybe you could ask him if he could spare us a few minutes."

"Absolutely."

When she hesitated, Eve primed her. "Is there something else, something you remember?"

"Actually, I've been sort of wrestling with this. I don't think it makes any difference. I didn't want to say anything in front of my father." She glanced toward the doorway, then tugged lightly—nervously, Eve thought—on one of the sparkling silver hoops she wore in her ears. "But . . . well, Mr. Hopkins—Rad—he sort of hit on me. Flirted, you know. Asked me out to dinner, or drinks. He said I could be a model, and he could set me up with a photographer who'd do my portfolio at a discount."

She flushed, the color rising pink into her cheeks, and cleared her throat. "That kind of thing."

"And did you? Have drinks, dinner, a photo session?"

"No." She flushed a little deeper. "I know when I'm getting a line. He was old enough to be my father, and well, not really my type. I won't say there wasn't something appealing about him. Really, he could be charming. And it wasn't nasty, if you know what I mean. I don't want you to think . . ."

She waved a hand in the air. "It was all sort of friendly and foolish. I might have even been tempted, just for the fun. But I've been seeing someone, and it's turning into a thing. I didn't want to mess that up. And frankly, my father wouldn't have liked it."

"Because?"

"The age difference for one, and the type of man Rad was. Opportunistic, multiple marriages. Plus, he was a client and that can get sticky. Anyway." Maeve let out a long, relieved breath. "It was bothering me that I didn't mention it to you, and that you might hear about it and think I was hiding something."

"Appreciate that."

"I'll go get my father," she said as she rose. "You're sure you won't have coffee? Tea? It's bitter out there today."

"I wouldn't mind either," Peabody put in. "Dealer's choice. The lieutenant's coffee—always black."

"Fine. I'll be back in a few. Make yourselves comfortable."

"She was a little embarrassed about the Hopkins thing. She wanted to serve us something," Peabody said when Maeve left the room. "Makes it easier for her."

"Whatever floats." Eve got to her feet, wandered the room. It had a settled, family feel about it, with a thin sheen of class. The photos were arty black-and-whites of cities— old-timey stuff. She was frowning over one when Buchanan came in. Like his daughter, he was wearing at-home clothes. And still managed to look dignified in a blue sweater and gray pants.

"Ladies. What can I do for you?"

"You have a beautiful home, Mr. Buchanan," Peabody began. "Some wonderful old pieces. Lieutenant, it makes me wonder if Roarke's ever bought anything from Mr. Buchanan."

"Roarke?" Buchanan gave Peabody a puzzled look. "He has acquired a few pieces from us. You're not saying he's a suspect in this."

"No. He's Lieutenant Dallas's husband."

"Of course, I forgot for a moment." He shifted his gaze to Eve with a smile. "My business keeps me so much in the past, current events sometimes pass me by."

"I bet. And speaking of the past," Eve continued, "we're interested in any letters, journals, diaries you might have that pertain to Bobbie Bray."

"That's a name I've heard countless times today. Maeve might have told you that's why we decided to work from home. And here she is now."

Maeve wheeled in a cart holding china pots and cups.

"Just what we need. I've put the 'links on auto," her father told her. "We can take a short break. Letters." He took a seat while Maeve poured coffee and tea. "We do have a few she wrote to friends in San Francisco in 1968 and 1969. And one of our prizes is a workbook containing drafts of some of her song lyrics. It could, in a way, be considered a kind of diary as well. She wrote down some of her thoughts in it, or notes to herself. Little reminders. I've fielded countless inquiries about just that this morning. Including one from a Cliff Gill."

"Hopkins's son?"

"So he said. He was very upset, nearly incoherent really." Buchanan patted Maeve's hand when she passed him a cup. "Understandable under the circumstances."

"And he was looking specifically for letters?" Eve asked.

"He said his father had mentioned letters, a bombshell as he put it. Mr. Gill understood his father and I had done business and hoped I might know what it was about. I think he hopes to clear his family name."

"You going to help him with that?"

"I don't see how." Buchanan spread his hands. "Nothing I have pertains."

"If there was something that pertained, or correspondence written near the time of her disappearance, would you know about it?"

He pursed his lips in thought. "I can certainly put out feelers. There are always rumors, of course. Several years ago someone tried to auction off what they claimed was a letter written by Bobbie two years after her disappearance. It was a forgery, and there was quite a scandal."

"There have been photos, too," Maeve added. "Purportedly taken of Bobbie after she went missing. None have ever been authenticated."

"Exactly." Buchanan nodded. "So substantiating the rumors and the claims, well, that's a different matter. Do you know of correspondence from that time, Lieutenant?"

"I've got a source claiming there was some."

"Really." His eyes brightened. "If they're authentic, ac-quiring them would be quite a coup."

"Were you name-dropping, Peabody?" Eve gave her part-ner a mild look as she slid behind the wheel.

"Roarke's done business there before, and you guys went there together. But he doesn't mention Roarke at all. And being in business, I figured Buchanan would keep track of his more well-heeled clients, you know, and should've made an immediate connection."

"Yeah, you'd think. Plausible reason he didn't."

"You'd wondered, too."

"I wonder all kinds of things. Let's wonder our way over to talk to Cliff Gill."

Like Bygones, the dance school was locked up tight. But as Fanny Gill lived in the apartment overhead, it was a short trip.

Cliff answered looking flushed and harassed. "Thank God! I was about to contact you."

"About?"

"We had to close the school." He took a quick look up and down the narrow hallway then gestured them inside. "I had to give my mother a soother."

"Because?"

"Oh, this is a horrible mess. I'm having a Bloody Mary."

Unlike the Buchanan brownstone, Fanny's apartment was full of bright, clashing colors, a lot of filmy fabrics and chrome. Artistic funk, Eve supposed. It was seriously lived in to the point of messy.

Cliff was looking pretty lived-in himself, Eve noted. He hadn't shaved, and it looked like he'd slept in the sweats he was wearing. Shadows dogged his eyes.

"I stayed the night here," he began as he stood in the ad-joining kitchen pouring vodka. "People came into the studio yesterday afternoon, some of them saying horrible things. Or they'd just call, leaving horrible, nasty transmissions. I've turned her 'links off. She just can't take any more."

He added enough tomato juice and Tabasco to turn the vodka muddy red, then took a quick gulp. "Apparently we're being painted with the same brush as my grandfather. Spawn of Satan." He took another long drink, then blushed. "I'm sorry. I'm sorry, what can I get you?"

"We're fine," Eve told him. "Mr. Gill, have you been threatened?"

"With everything from eternal damnation to public flogging. My mother doesn't deserve this, Lieutenant. She's done nothing but choose poorly in the husband department, which she rectified. At least I carry the same blood as Hopkins." His mouth went grim. "If you think along those lines."

"Do you?"

"I don't know what I think any more." He came back into the living area, dropped onto a candy-pink sofa heaped with fluffy pillows. "At least I know what to feel now. Rage, and a little terror."

"Did you report any of the threats?"

"She asked me not to." He closed his eyes, seemed to gather some tattered rags of composure. "She's embarrassed and angry. Or she started out that way. She didn't want to make a big deal about it. But it just kept up. She handles things, my mother, she doesn't fall apart. But this has just knocked her flat. She's afraid we'll lose the school, all the publicity, the scandal. She's worked so hard, and now this."

"I want you to make a copy of any of the transmissions regarding this. We'll take care of it."

"Okay. Okay." He scooped his fingers through his disordered hair. "That's the right thing to do, isn't it? I'm just not thinking straight. I can't see what I should do."

"You contacted the owner of a shop called Bygones. Care to tell me why?"

"Bygones? Oh, oh, right. Mr. Buchanan. My father sold him some memorabilia. I think maybe Buchanan was one of the backers on Number Twelve. My father mentioned him when I gave him the five hundred. Said something like Bygones may be Bygones, but he wouldn't be nickel-and-diming it any more. How he'd pay me back the five ten times over because he was about to hit the jackpot."

"Any specific jackpot?"

"He talked a lot, my father. Bragged, actually, and a lot of the bragging was just hot air. But he said he'd been holding onto an ace in the hole, waiting for the right time. It was coming up."

"What was his hole card?"

"Can't say he actually had one." Cliff heaved out a breath. "Honestly, I didn't really listen because it was the same old, same old to me. And I wanted to get him moving before my mother got wind of the loan. But he said something about letters Bobbie Bray had written. A bombshell, he said, that was going to give Number Twelve just the push he needed. I didn't pay much attention at the time because he was mostly full of crap."

He winced now, drank again. "Hell of a thing to say about your dead father, huh?"

"His being dead doesn't make him more of a father to you, Mr. Gill," Peabody said gently.

Cliff's eyes went damp for a moment. "Guess not. Well, when all this started happening. I remembered how he talked about these letters, and I thought maybe he'd sold them to Bygones. Maybe there was something in them that would clear my grandfather. Something, I don't know. Maybe she committed suicide and he panicked."

He lowered his head, rubbed the heel of his hand in the center of his brow as if to push away some pain. "I don't even care, or wouldn't, except for what's falling down from it on my mother. I don't know what I expected Mr. Buchanan to do. I was desperate."

"Did your father give you any indication of the contents of the letters?" Eve asked. "The timing of them?"

"Not really, no. At the time I thought it was just saving face because I was giving him money. Probably all it was. Buchanan said he hadn't bought any letters from my father, but I could come in and look at what he had. Waste of time, I guess. But he was nice about it—Buchanan, I mean. Sympathetic."

"Have you discussed this with your mother at all?" Peabody asked him.

"No, and I won't." Any grief seemed to burn away as anger covered his face. "It's a terrible thing to say, but by dying my father's given her more trouble than he has since she divorced him. I'm not going to add to it. Chasing a wild goose anyway." He frowned into his glass. "I have to make some arrangements for—for the body. Cremation, I guess. I know it's cold, but I'm not going to have any sort of service or memorial. I'm not going to drag this out. We just have to get through this."

"Mr Gill—"

"Cliff," he said to Eve with a weak smile. "You should call me Cliff since I'm dumping all my problems on you."

"Cliff. Do you know if your father kept a safety deposit box?"

"He wouldn't have told me. We didn't see each other much. I don't know what he'd have kept in one. I got a call from some lawyer this morning. Said my father'd made a will, and I'd inherit. I asked him to ballpark it, and the gist was when it all shakes out, I'll be lucky to have enough credits to buy a soy dog at a corner cart."

"I guess you were hoping for better," Peabody commented.

Cliff let out a short, humorless laugh. "Hoping for better with Rad Hopkins would be another waste of time."

Nine

"You have to feel for the guy." Peabody bundled her scarf around her neck as they walked back outside.

"We'll pass off the copy of his 'link calls to a couple of burly uniforms, have them knock on some doors and issue some stern warnings. About all we can do there for now. We're going back to Central. I want a quick consult with Mira, and you can update the Commander."

"*Me?*" Peabody's voice hit squeak. "Alone? Myself?"

"I expect Commander Whitney would be present as you're updating him."

"But you do the updates."

"Today you're doing it. He's going to want to set up a media conference," Eve added as she got into their vehicle. "Hold him off."

"Oh my God."

"Twenty-four hours. Make it stick," Eve added and pulled out into traffic as Peabody sat pale and speechless beside her.

Mira was the top profiler attached to the NYPSD for

good reason. Her status kept her in high demand and made Eve's request for a consult without appointment similar to trying to squeeze her head through the eye of a needle that was already threaded.

She had a headache when she'd finished battling Mira's admin, but she got her ten minutes.

"You ought to give her a whip and a chain," Eve commented when she stepped into Mira's office. "Not that she needs one."

"You always manage to get past her. Have a seat."

"No thanks, I'll make it fast."

Mira settled behind her desk. She was a sleek, lovely woman who favored pretty suits. Today's was power red and worn with pearls.

"This would be pertaining to Number Twelve," Mira began. "Two murders, nearly a hundred years apart. Your consults are rarely routine. Bobbie Bray."

"You, too? People say that name like she's a deity."

"Do they?" Mira eased back in her chair, her blue eyes amused. "Apparently my grandmother actually heard her perform at Number Twelve in the early Nineteen-seventies. She claimed she exchanged an intimate sexual favor with the bouncer for the price of admission. My grandmother was a wild woman."

"Huh."

"And my parents are huge fans, so I grew up hearing that voice, that music. It's confirmed then? They were her remains?"

"Lab's forensic sculptor's putting her money on it as of this morning. I've got the facial image she reconstructed from the skull, and it looks like Bray."

"May I see?"

"I've got it in the file." Eve gave Mira the computer codes, then shifted so she, too, could watch the image come on-screen.

The lovely, tragic face, the deep-set eyes, the full, pouty lips somehow radiated both youth and trouble.

"Yes," Mira murmured. "It certainly looks like her. Something so sad and worn about her, despite her age."

"Living on drugs, booze and sex tends to make you sad and worn."

"I suppose it does. You don't feel for her?"

Eve realized she should have expected the question from Mira. Feelings were the order of the day in that office. "I feel for anyone who gets a bullet in the brain—then has their body closed up in a wall. She deserves justice for that—deserves it for the cops who looked the other way. But she chose the life she led to that point. So looking sad and worn at twenty-couple? No, I can't say I feel for that."

"A different age," Mira said, studying Eve as she'd studied the image on screen. "My grandmother always said you had to be there. I doubt Bobbie would have understood you and the choices you've made any more than you do her and hers."

Mira flicked the screen off. "Is there more to substantiate identity?"

"The bones we recovered had a broken left tibia, which corresponds with a documented childhood injury on Bray. We extracted DNA, and I've got a sample of a relative's on its way to the lab. It's going to confirm."

"A tragic waste. All that talent snuffed out."

"She didn't live what you could call a careful life."

"The most interesting people rarely do." Mira angled her head. "You certainly don't."

"Mine's about the job. Hers was about getting stoned and screwing around, best I can tell."

Now Mira raised a brow. "Not only don't you feel for her, you don't think you'd have liked her."

"Can't imagine we'd have had much in common, but that's not the issue. She had a kid."

"What? I've never heard that."

"She kept it locked. Likelihood is it was Hop Hopkins's offspring, though it's possible she got knocked up on the side. Either way, she went off, had the kid, dumped it on her mother. Sent money so the family could relocate—up the scale some. Mother passed the kid off as her own."

"And you find that deplorable, on all counts."

Irritation shadowed Eve's face, very briefly. "That's not the issue either. Female child eventually discovered her heritage through letters Bray allegedly wrote home. The ones shortly before her death, again allegedly, claimed that she was planning to clean up her act—again—and come back for the kid. This is hearsay. The daughter relayed it to her two children. Purportedly the letters and other items were sold, years ago, to Radcliff C. Hopkins—the last."

"Connections within connections. And this, you believe goes to motive."

"You know how Hopkins was killed?"

"The walls are buzzing with it. Violent, specific, personal—and somehow tidy."

"Yeah." It was always satisfying to have your instincts confirmed. "The last shot. Here's what he did to her. There's control there, an agenda fulfilled, even through the rage."

"Let me see if I understand. You suspect that a descendent of Bobbie Bray killed a descendent of Hopkins to avenge her murder."

"That's a chunk of it, buttonholed. According to Bray's granddaughter, the murder, the abandonment, the obsession ruined her mother's health. Series of breakdowns."

"You suspect the granddaughter?"

"No, she's covered. She's got two offspring herself, but I can't place them in New York during the time in question."

"Who does that leave you?"

"There was a grandson, reported killed in action during the Urbans."

"He had children?"

"None on record. He was pretty young, only seventeen. Lied about his age when he joined up—a lot of people did back then. Oddly enough, he was reported killed here in New York."

Pursing her lips, Mira considered. "As you're one of the most pragmatic women I know, I find it hard to believe you're theorizing that a ghost killed your victim to avenge yet another ghost."

"Flesh and blood pulled the trigger. I've got Yancy aging the military ID. The Urban Wars were a chaotic time, and the last months of them here in New York were confusing from a military standpoint. Wouldn't be hard, would it, for a young man, one who'd already lied about his age to enlist in the Home Force, to put his official ID on a mangled body and vanish? War's never what you think it's going to be. It's not heroic and adventurous. He could've deserted."

"The history of mental illness in the family—on both sides—the horrors of war, the guilt of abandoning his duty. It would make quite a powder keg. Your killer is purposeful, specific to his goal, would have some knowledge of firearms. Rumor is the victim was shot nine times—the weapon itself is a symbol—and there were no stray bullets found on scene."

"He hit nine out of nine, so he had some knowledge of handguns, or some really good luck. In addition, he had to reload for the ninth shot."

"Ah. The others were the rage, that slippery hold on control. The last, a signature. He's accomplished what he meant to do. There may be more, of course, but he has his eye for an eye, and he has the object of his obsession back in the light."

"Yeah." Eve nodded. "I'm thinking that matters here."

"With Bobbie's remains found, identified, and her killer identified—at least in the media—he's fulfilled his obligation. If the killer is the grandson—or connected to the grandson, as even if he did die in the Urbans, it's certainly possible to have produced an offspring at seventeen—he or she knows how to blend."

"Likely to just keep blending," Eve added.

"Most likely. I don't believe your killer will seek the spotlight. He doesn't need acknowledgment. He'll slide back into his routine, and essentially vanish again."

"I think I know where to find him."

"Yancy does good work." Eve held the photos of John Massey—youth and maturity—side-by-side.

"He does," Roarke agreed. "As do you, Lieutenant. I doubt I'd have looked at the boy and seen the man."

"It's about legacies. Redheads ran in Bray's family. Her father, her daughter. Her grandson."

"And Yancy's work indicates he's alive and living in New York."

"Yeah. But even with this I've got nothing but instinct and theories. There's no evidence linking the suspect to the crime."

"You've closed a case on a murder that happened decades before you were born," Roarke reminded her. "Now you're greedy."

"My current suspect did most of the work there. Discovered the body, unearthed it, led me to it. The rest was basically lab and leg work. Since the perpetrator of that crime is long dead, there's nothing to do but mark the file and do the media announcement."

"Not very satisfying for you."

"Not when somebody kills a surrogate figuring that evens things up. And plays games with me. So it's our turn to play." Eve shifted in the limo. She felt ridiculous riding around in the big black boat.

But no one would expect Roarke to ride the subway, or even use a common Rapid Cab. Perception was part of the game.

"I can't send you in wired," she added. "Never get a warrant for eyes or ears with what I've got. You know what to say, right? How to play it?"

"Lieutenant, have a little faith."

"I got all there is. Okay," she added, ducking down a little to check out the window when the limo glided to the curb. "Showtime. I'll be cruising around in this thing, making sure the rest of this little play is on schedule."

"One question. Can you be sure your suspect will hit his cue in this play of yours?"

"Nothing's a given, but I'm going with the odds on this. Obsession's a powerful motivator. The killer is obsessed with Bray, with Number Twelve—and there's a sense of theatrics there. Another legacy, I'd say. We dangle the bait, he's going to bite."

"I'll do my best to dangle it provocatively."

"Good luck."

"Give us a kiss then."

"That's what you said last night, and look what happened." But she gave him a quick one. When he slipped out of the limo, she pulled out her 'link to check on the rest of the game.

Roarke walked into Bygones looking like a man with plenty of money and an eye to spend it as he liked. He gave Maeve an easy smile and a warm handshake. "Ms. Buchanan? I appreciate you opening for me this afternoon. Well, it's nearly evening, isn't it?"

"We're happy to oblige. My father will be right out. Would you like a glass of wine? I have a very nice cabernet breathing."

"I'd love one. I've met your father, though it's been three or four years, I suppose, since we've done business."

"I'd have been in college. He mentioned you'd bought a particularly fine Georgian sideboard and a set of china, among other things."

"He has an excellent memory."

"He never forgets a thing." She offered the wine she'd poured, then gestured to a silver tray of fruit and cheese. "Would you like to sit? If you'd rather browse, I can point you in a direction, or show you whatever you'd like. My father has the piece you inquired about. He wanted to make sure it was properly cleaned before he showed it to you."

"I'll just wait then, if you'll join me." As he sat, he glanced toward the portrait of Bobbie on the far wall. "It's actually Bobbie Bray who put me in mind to come here."

"Oh? There's always interest in her and her memorabilia, but in the last day it's piqued."

"I imagine." He shifted as he spoke so he could scan the black-and-white photographs Eve had told him about. And two, as she'd mentioned, were desert landscapes. "Just as I imagine it won't ebb any time soon," he continued. "Certainly not with the publicity that will be generated from the case finally being solved."

Maeve's hands went very still for a moment. "It's certain then?"

"I have an inside source, as you might suspect. Yes, it's certain. She's been found, after all these years. And the evidence proves it was Hopkins who hid her body."

"Horrible. I—Daddy." She got to her feet as Buchanan came into the shop. He carried a velvet case. "You remember Roarke."

"I certainly do. It's good to see you again." They shook hands, sat. "Difficult circumstances when you were here recently with your wife."

"Yes. Terrible. I was just telling your daughter that they've confirmed the identity of the remains found at Number Twelve, and found Hopkins's—the first's—fingerprints on the inside of the wall, on several of the bricks."

"There's no doubt any longer then."

"Hardly a wonder he went mad, locking himself up in that building, knowing what he'd done, and that she was behind that wall, where he'd put her. A bit of 'The Telltale Heart,' really."

Keeping it conversational, Roarke settled back with his drink. "Still, it's fascinating, isn't it? Time and distance tend to give that sort of brutality an allure. No one can speak of anything else. And here I am, just as bad. Is that the necklace?"

"Oh, yes. Yes." Buchanan unsnapped the case, folded back the velvet leaves. "Charming, isn't it? All those little beads are hand-strung. I can't substantiate that Bobbie made it herself, though that's the story. But it was worn by her to the Grammy Awards, then given by her to one of her entourage. I was able to acquire it just last year."

"Very pretty." Roarke held up the multistrand necklace. The beads were of various sizes, shapes, colors, but strung in a way that showed the craftsman had a clever eye. "I think Eve might like this. A memento of Bobbie, since she's the one who's finally bringing her some sense of justice."

"Can there be, really?" Eyes downcast, Maeve murmured it. "After all this time?"

"For my cop, justice walks hand-in-hand with truth. She won't let the truth stay buried, as Bobbie was." He held up the beads again. "I'm hoping to take her away for a quick tropical holiday, and this sort of thing would suit the tropics, wouldn't it?"

"After this New York weather?" Maeve said with a laugh as she lifted her gaze once more. "The tropics would suit anything."

"With our schedules it's difficult to get away. I'm hoping we can find that window. Though with what they've found today, it may take a bit longer."

"They found something else?" Buchanan asked.

"Mmm. Something about a bank box, letters, and so on. And apparently something the former Hopkins recorded during his hermitage. My wife said he spoke of a small vault in Number Twelve, also walled in. Hopkins must have been very busy. They're looking for it, but it's a good-sized building. It may take days."

"A vault." Maeve breathed the words. "I wonder what's in it."

"More truth?" But Buchanan's voice was strained now.

"Or the ramblings of a madman, one who'd already killed?"

"Perhaps both," Roarke suggested. "I know my wife's hoping for something that will lead her to Rad Hopkins's killer. The truth, and justice for him as well."

He laid the necklace on the velvet. "I'm very interested in this piece." Roarke sipped his wine. "Shall we negotiate?"

Ten

In Number Twelve, Eve stood in the area that had once held a stage. Where there had been sound and light and motion, there was silence, dark and stillness. She could smell dust and a faint whiff of the chemicals the sweepers used on-scene. And could feel nothing but the pervading chill that burned through the brick and mortar of an old building.

Still, the stage was set, she thought. If her hunch was off, she'd have wasted a lot of departmental time, manpower and money. Better that, she decided, than to play into the current media hype that the curse of Number Twelve was still vital, still lethal.

"You've got to admit, it's creepy." Beside Eve, Peabody scanned the club room. There was a lot of white showing in her eyes. "This place gives me the jeebies."

"Keep your jeebies to yourself. We're set. I'm going up to my post."

"You don't have to go up right this minute." Peabody's hand clamped like a bundle of live wires on Eve's wrist. "Seriously. We've got plenty of room on the timetable."

"If you're afraid of the dark, Detective, maybe you should've brought a nice little teddy bear to hold onto."

"Couldn't hurt," Peabody mumbled when Eve pulled free. "You'll stay in contact, right? I mean, communications open? It's practically like you're standing beside me."

Eve only shook her head as she crossed to the stairs. She'd gone through doors with Peabody when death or certainly pain was poised on the other side. She'd crawled through blood with her. And here her usually stalwart partner was squeaking over ghosts.

Her bootsteps echoed against the metal steps—and okay, maybe it was a little creepy. But it wasn't creaking doors and disembodied moans they had to worry about tonight. It was a stone killer who could come for letters from the dead.

There were no letters, of course. None that she knew of, no vault to hide them in. But she had no doubt the prospect of them would lure Rad Hopkins's killer into Number Twelve.

No doubt that killer was descended from Bray and Hopkins. If her hunch didn't pay off tonight, she was going to face a media storm tomorrow—face it either way, she admitted. But she'd rather deal with it with the case closed.

Funny how Bygones had old-timey photos of the desert. Maybe they were Arizona, maybe not, but she was laying her money that they were. There'd been old photos of San Francisco, too, before the quake had given it a good, hard shake. Others of New York during that time period, and of L.A. All of Bobbie's haunts.

Coincidence, maybe. But she agreed with one of the detectives in her squad on a case recently closed—a case that also included switched identities.

Coincidences were hooey.

She crossed the second tier, and started up to the old apartments.

Eve didn't doubt Roarke had played his part, and played it well. With the bait he'd dangled, she was gambling that

Radcliff C. Hopkins's killer, and Bobbie Bray's murderous descendent, would bite quickly. Would bite tonight.

She took her position where she could keep the windows in view, put her back to the wall. Eve flipped her communications channel to Peabody's unit, and said, "Boo."

"Oh yeah, that's funny. I'm rib-cracking down here."

"When you're finished with your hilarity, we'll do a check. Feeney, you copy?"

"Got your eyes, your ears and the body-heat sensors. No movement."

"You eating a doughnut?"

"What do you need electronic eyes and ears for, you can tell I'm eating a cruller from in there?" There was a slurping sound as Feeney washed down the cruller with coffee. "Roarke bought the team a little something to keep us alert."

"Yeah, he's always buying something." She wished she had a damn cruller. Better, the coffee.

"You should have worn the beads, Lieutenant." Roarke's voice cruised on. "I think they might have appealed to Bobbie."

"Yeah, that's what I need. Baubles and beads. I could use them to—"

"Picking up something," Feeney interrupted.

"I hear it." Eve went silent, and as she focused, the sound—a humming—took on the pattern of a tune, and a female flavor. She drew her weapon.

"Exits and egresses," she murmured to Feeney.

"Undisturbed," he said in her ear. "I've got no motion, no visual, no heat-sensor reading on anything but you and Peabody."

So it was on a timer, Eve decided. An electronic loop EDD had missed.

"Dallas?" Peabody's voice was a frantic hiss. "You read? I see—"

The earpiece went to a waspy buzz. And the air went to ice.

She couldn't stop the chill from streaking up her spine, but no one had to know about it. She might have cursed the glitch in communications and surveillance, but she was too busy watching the amorphous figure drift toward her.

Bobbie Bray wore jeans widely belled from the knees down, slung low at the hips and decorated with flowers that twined up the side of each leg. The filmy white top seemed to float in a breeze. Her hair was a riotous tangle of curls with the glitter of diamond clips. As she walked, as she hummed, she lifted a cigarette to her lips and drew deeply.

For an instant, the sharp scent of tobacco stung the air.

From the way the image moved, Eve decided tobacco wasn't the only thing she'd been smoking. As ghosts went, this one was stoned to the eyeballs.

. "You think I'm buying this?" Eve pushed off the wall. But when she started to move forward something struck out at her. Later, she would think it was like being punched with an ice floe.

She shoved herself forward, following the figure into what had been the bedroom area of the apartment.

The figure stopped, as if startled.

I didn't know you were up here. What's it about? I told you, I'm bookin'. So I packed. Don't give me any more shit, Hop.

The figure moved as it spoke, mimed pouring something into a glass, drinking. There was weariness in the voice, and the blurriness of drugs.

Because I'm tired and I'm sick. I'm so fucking messed up. This whole scene is fucked up, and I can't do it anymore. I don't give a shit about my career. That was all you. It's always been all you.

She turned, stood hipshot and blearily defiant.

Yeah? Well, maybe I have lapped it up, and now I'm just puking it out. For Christ's sake look at us, Hop. Look at yourself. We're either stoned or strung out. We got a kid. Don't tell me to shut up. I'm sick of myself and I'm sick of you. I will stay straight this time.

The image flung an arm out as if heaving a glass against the wall.

I'm not humping some other guy. I'm not signing with another label. I'm done. Don't you get it? I'm done with this, and I'm done with you. You're fucking crazy, Hop. You need help more than I do. Put that down.

The image threw up its hands now, stumbling back.

You gotta calm down. You gotta come down. We'll talk about it, okay? I don't have to leave. I'm not lying. I'm not. Oh God. Don't. No. Jesus, Hop. Don't!

There was a sharp crack as the figure jerked back, then fell. The hole in the center of the forehead leaked blood.

"Hell of a show," Eve said, and her voice sounded hoarse to her own ears. "Hell of a performance."

Eve heard the faint creak behind her, pivoted. Maeve stepped into the room, tears pouring down her cheeks. And a knife gleaming dully in her hand.

"He shot me dead. Dead was better than gone—that's what he said."

Not John Massey, Eve realized. The Bray/Hopkins legacy had gone down another generation.

"You look alive to me, Maeve."

"Bobbie," she corrected. "She's in me. She speaks through me. She is me."

Eve let out a sigh, kept her weapon down at her side. "Oh step back. Ghosts aren't ridiculous enough, now we have to go into possession?"

"And he killed me." Maeve crooned it. "Took my life. He said I was nothing without him, just a junky whore with a lucky set of pipes."

"Harsh," Eve agreed. "I grant you. But it all happened before you were born. And both players are long dead. Why kill Hopkins?"

"He walled me up." Her eyes gleamed, tears and rage and madness. "He paid off the cops, and they did *nothing*."

"No, he didn't. His grandfather did."

"There's no difference." She turned a slow circle as she

spoke, arms out. "He was, I was. He is, I am." Then spun, pointed at Eve with the tip of the knife. "And you, you're no different than the cops who let me rot in there. You're just another pig."

"Nobody pays me off. I finish what I start, and let me tell you something: this stops here."

"It never stops. I can't get out, don't you get it?" Maeve slapped a hand over her lips as if to hold back the gurgle of laughter that ended on a muffled sob. "Every day, every night, it's the same thing. I can't get away from it, and I go round and round and round, just like he wanted."

"Well, I'm going to help you get out of here. And you can spend every day, every night of the rest of your natural life in a cage. Might be a nice padded one in your case."

Maeve smiled now. "You can't stop it. You can't stop me, you can't stop it. 'You're never leaving me.' That's what he said when he was walling me up in there. He made me, that's what he said, and I wasn't going anywhere. Ever. Fucking bastard killed me, cursed me, trapped me. What the hell are you going to do about it?"

"End it. Maeve Buchanan, you're under arrest for the murder of Radcliff Hopkins. You have the right to remain silent—"

"You'll pay for leaving me in there!" Maeve hacked out with the knife she held and missed by a foot.

"Jesus, you fight like a girl." Eve circled with her, watching Maeve's eyes. "I'm not an overweight dumbass, and you don't have a gun this time. So pay attention. Stunner, knife. Stunner always wins. You want a jolt, Maeve?"

"You can't hurt me. Not in this place. I can't be harmed here."

"Wanna bet?" Eve said, and hit Maeve with a low stun when the redhead charged again.

The knife skittered out of Maeve's hand as she fell back, hit hard on her ass. There was another swipe of cold, this time like ice-tipped nails raking Eve's cheek. But she pushed by it, yanking out her restraints as she dragged Maeve's arms behind her back.

Maeve struggled, her body bucking as she gasped out curses. And the cold, whipped by a vicious wind, went straight down to the bone.

"This stops here," Eve repeated, breathless as what felt like frigid fists pounded at her back. "Radcliff C. Hopkins will be charged with murder one in the unlawful death of Bobbie Bray, posthumously. That's my word. Period. Now leave me the hell alone so I can do my job."

Eve hauled Maeve to her feet as the wind began to die. "We're going to toss in breaking and entering and assault on an officer just for fun."

"My name is Bobbie Bray, and you can't touch me. I'm Bobbie Bray, do you hear me? I'm Bobbie Bray."

"Yeah, I hear you." Just as she heard the sudden frantic squawking of voices in her ear and the thunder of footsteps on the stairs.

"I couldn't get to the stairs," Peabody told her. "All of a sudden the place is full of people and music. Talk about jeebies. My communication's down, and I'm trying to push through this wall of bodies. Live bodies—well, not live. I don't know. It's all jumbled."

"We went to the doors soon as communications went down," Feeney added. "Couldn't get through them. Not even your man there with his magic fingers. Then all of a sudden, poof, com's back, locks open, and we're in. Damned place." Feeney stared at Number twelve as they stood on the sidewalk. "Ought to be leveled, you ask me. Level the bastard and salt the ground."

"Maeve Buchanan rigged it, that's all. We'll figure out how." That was her story, Eve told herself, and she was sticking with it. "I'm heading in, taking her into interview. She's just whacked enough she may not lawyer up straight off."

"Can I get a lift?"

Eve turned to Roarke. "Yeah, I'll haul you in. Uniforms are transporting the suspect to Central. Peabody, you want to supervise that?"

"On it. Glad to get the hell away from this place."

When he settled in the car beside Eve, Roarke said simply, "Tell me."

"Maeve was probably already inside. We just missed her in the sweep. She had a jammer and a program hidden somewhere."

"Eve."

She huffed out a breath, cursed a little. "If you want to be fanciful or whatever, I had a conversation with a dead woman."

She told him, working hard to be matter-of-fact.

"So it wasn't Maeve who bruised and scratched your face."

"I don't know what it was, but I know this is going to be wrapped, and wrapped tight tonight. Buchanan's being picked up now. We'll see if he was in this, or if Maeve worked alone. But I'm damn sure she's the one who fired the gun. She's the one who lured Hopkins there. He had a weakness for young women. He'd never have felt threatened by her. Walked right in, alone, unarmed."

"If she sticks with this story about being Bobbie Bray, she could end up in a psychiatric facility instead of prison."

"A cage is a cage—the shape of it isn't my call."

At Central, Eve let Maeve stew a little while as she waited for Mira to be brought in and take a post in observation. So she took Buchanan first.

He was shaking when she went into interview room B, his face pale, his eyes glossy with distress.

"They said—they said you arrested my daughter. I don't understand. She'll need a lawyer. I want to get her a lawyer."

"She's an adult, Mr. Buchanan. She'll request her own representation if she wants it."

"She won't be thinking straight. She'll be upset."

"Hasn't been thinking straight for a while, has she?"

"She's . . . she's delicate."

"Here." Peabody set a cup of water on the table for him. "Have a drink. Then you can help us help your daughter."

"She needs help," Eve added. "Do you know she claims to be Bobbie Bray?"

"Oh God. Oh God." He put his face in his hands. "It's my fault. It's all my fault."

"You are John Massey, grandson of Bobbie Bray and Radcliff Hopkins?"

"I got away from all that. I had to get away from it. It destroyed my mother. There was nothing I could do."

"So during the Urbans, you saw your chance. Planted your ID after an explosion. Mostly body parts. All that confusion. You walked away."

"I couldn't take all the killing. I couldn't go back home. I wanted peace. I just wanted some peace. I built a good life. Got married, had a child. When my wife died, I devoted myself to Maeve. She was the sweetest thing."

"Then you told her where she'd come from, who she'd come from."

He shook his head. "No. She told me. I don't know how she came to suspect, but she tracked down Rad Hopkins. She said it was business, and I wanted to believe her. But I was afraid it was more. Then one day she told me she'd been to Number Twelve, and she understood. She was going to take care of everything, but I never thought she meant . . . Is this ruining her life now, too? Is this ruining her life?"

"You knew she went back out the night Hopkins was killed," Eve said. "You knew what she'd done. She'd have told you. You covered for her. That makes you an accessory."

"No." Desperation was bright in his eyes as they darted around the room. "She was home all night. This is all a terrible mistake. She's upset and she's confused. That's all."

They let him sit, stepped out into the hall. "Impressions, Peabody?"

"I don't think he had an active part in the murder. But he knew—maybe put his head in the sand about it, but he knew. We can get him on accessory after the fact. He'll break once she has."

"Agreed. So let's go break her."

Maeve sat quietly. Her hair was smoothed again, her face was placid. "Lieutenant, Detective."

"Record on." Eve read the data into the recorder, recited the revised Miranda. Do you understand your rights and obligations, Ms. Buchanan?"

"Of course."

"So Maeve." Eve sat at the table across from her. "How long did you know Hopkins?"

A smirky little smile curved her lips. "Which one?"

"The one you shot nine times in Number Twelve."

"Oh, that Hopkins. I met him right after he bought the building. I read about it, and thought it was time we resolved some matters."

"What matters?"

"Him killing me."

"You don't look dead."

"He shot me so I couldn't leave him, so I wouldn't be someone else's money train. Then he covered it up. He covered me up. I've waited a long time to make him pay for it."

"So you sent him the message so he'd come to Number Twelve. Then you killed him."

"Yes, but we'd had a number of liaisons there before. We had to uncover my remains from that life."

"Bobbie Bray's remains."

"Yes. She's in me. I am Bobbie." She spoke calmly, as if they were once again sitting in the classy parlor in her brownstone. "I came back for justice. No one gave me any before."

"How did you know where the remains were?"

"Who'd know better? Do you know what he wanted to do? He wanted to bring in the media, to make another fortune off me. He had it all worked out. He'd bring the media in, let them put my poor bones on-screen, give interviews—at a hefty fee, of course. Using me again, like he always did. Not this time."

"You believed Rad Hopkins was Hop Hopkins reincarnated?" Peabody asked.

"Of course. It's obvious. Only this time I played him. Told him my father would pay and pay and pay for the letters I'd written. I told him where we had to open the wall. He didn't believe that part, but he wanted under my skirt."

She wrinkled her nose to show her mild distaste. "I could make him do what I wanted. We worked for hours cutting that brick. Then he believed."

"You took the hair clips and the gun."

"Later. We left them while he worked on his plan. While, basically, he dug his own grave. I cleaned them up. I really loved those hair clips. Oh, there were ammunition clips, too. I took them. I was there."

Her face changed, hardened, and her voice went raw, went throaty. "In me, in the building. So sad, so cold, so lost. Singing, singing every night. Why should I sing for him? Murdering bastard. I gave him a child, and he didn't want it."

"Did you?" Eve asked her.

"I was messed up. He got me hooked—the drugs, the life, the buzz, you know? Prime shit, always the prime shit for Hop. But I was going to get straight, give it up, go back for my kid. I was gonna—had my stuff packed up. I wrote and told my old lady, and I was walking on Hop. But he didn't want that. Big ticket, that's what I was. He never wanted the kid. Only me, only what I could bring in. Singing and singing."

"You sent Rad a message, to get him to Number Twelve."

"Sure. Public 'link, easy and quick. I told him to come,

and when to come. He liked when I used Bobbie's voice—spliced from old recordings—in the messages I sent him. He thought it was sexy. Asshole. He stood there, grinning at me. I brought it, he said."

"What was it?"

"His watch. The watch he had on the night he shot me. The one I bought him when my album hit number one. He had it on his wrist and was grinning at me. I shot him, and I kept shooting him until the clip was empty. Then I pushed the murdering bastard over, and I put the gun right against his head, right against it, and I shot him again. Like he did to me."

She sat back a little, smiled a little. "Now he can wander around in that damn place night after night after night. Let's see how he likes it."

Epilogue

When Eve stepped out, rubbed her hands over her face, Mira slipped out of observation.

"Don't tell me," Eve began. "Crazy as a shithouse rat."

"That might not be my precise diagnosis, but I believe we'll find with testing that Maeve Buchanan is legally insane and in desperate need of treatment."

"As long as she gets it in a cage. Not a bit of remorse. Not a bit of fear. No hedging."

"She believes everything she did was justified, even necessary. My impression, at least from observing this initial interview, is she's telling you the truth exactly as she knows it. There's the history of mental illness on both sides of her family. This may very well be genetic. Then discovering who her great-grandmother was helped push her over some edge she may very well have been teetering on."

"How did she discover it?" Eve added. "There's a question. Father must have let something slip."

"Possibly. Haven't you ever simply *known* something?

Or felt it? Of course, you have. And from what I'm told happened tonight, you had an encounter."

Frowning, Eve ran her fingers over her sore cheek. "I'm not going to stand here and say I was clocked by a ghost. I'm sure as hell not putting that in my report."

"Regardless, you may at the end of this discover the only reasonable way Maeve learned of her heritage was from Bobbie Bray herself. That she also learned of the location of the remains from the same source."

"That tips out of the reasonable."

"But not the plausible. And that learning these things snapped something inside her. Her way of coping was to make herself Bobbie. To believe she's the reincarnation of a woman who was killed before her full potential was realized. And who, if she'd lived—if she'd come back to claim her child—would have changed everything."

"Putting a lot of faith in a junkie," Eve commented. "And using, if you ask me, a woman who was used, exploited and murdered, to make your life a little more important."

Now she rubbed her eyes. "I'm going to get some coffee, then hit the father again. Thanks for coming down."

"It's been fascinating. I'd like to do the testing on her personally. If you've no objection."

"When I'm done, she's all yours."

Because her own AutoChef had the only real coffee in all of cop central, Eve detoured there first.

There he was, sitting at her desk, fiddling with his ppc.

"You should go home," Eve told Roarke. "I'm going to have an all-nighter on this."

"I will, but I wanted to see you first." He rose, touched his hand to her cheek. "Put something on that, will you?" Until she did, he put his lips there. "Do you have a confession?"

"She's singing—ha-ha. Chapter and verse. Mira says she's nuts, but that won't keep her out of lockup."

"Sad, really, that an obsession with one woman could cause so much grief, and for so long."

"Some of it ends tonight."

This time he laid his lips on hers. "Come back to me when you can."

"You can count on that one."

Alone, she sat. And alone she wrote up a report, and the paperwork that charged Radcliff C. Hopkins I with murder in the first degree in the unlawful death of Bobbie Bray. She filed it, then after a moment's thought, put in another form.

She requested the release of Bobbie Bray's remains to herself—if they weren't claimed by next of kin—so that she could arrange for their burial. Quietly.

"Somebody should do it," she stated aloud.

She got her coffee, rolled her aching shoulders. Then headed back to work.

In Number Twelve, there was silence in the dark. No one sang, or wept or laughed. No one walked there.

For the first time in eighty-five years, Number Twelve sat empty.

Poppy's Coin

Mary Blayney

For Nora, Mary Kay and Ruth

Prologue

LONDON, ENGLAND
APRIL 2006

The bright blue door opened into another world. She could tell the minute she stepped into the entry hall that this small museum was exactly the sort of place she liked best. History was about people, not politics. How they lived was what mattered. Whoever had preserved this townhouse felt the same.

Inside it was a tribute to the Regency period. A time before trains changed village life forever, when fifty miles in a carriage was a good day's travel. There was no electricity, computers or air-conditioning.

Jim groaned when she insisted she wanted to take the tour.

"How is this different from every other old house we've seen? I bet it has a basement kitchen, no bathroom, and they call the first floor the ground floor."

"This is different because it's in Mayfair, the primo neighborhood way back in 1800 and still one of the best addresses. It's where the rich lived for the spring months, when they came to London to see and be seen."

"Lots of parties."

"Exactly."

Jim shrugged, and she knew she could talk him into it. "Come on. We have one week left of our year abroad. We've spent enough time studying economics. Let's learn a little history. Let's see how they lived."

"Yeah, without indoor plumbing."

They dutifully worked their way through the belowstairs exhibits, the wine cellar, and servants' hall; watched the cooking demonstration, accepting a sample of syllabub, a cream and sugar concoction that tasted faintly of lemon.

"Boring," Jim said.

"Interesting," she insisted.

The feeling that the tour was little more than a lecture ended when she stood in the bedroom, surrounded by the trappings of everyday life for the woman who had lived here two centuries ago.

There was a display of clothing from the inside out. No real underwear as she knew it, but a long slip that she would wear today as a dress, covered by a corset that did not look as uncomfortable as it sounded. Stockings in both silk and cotton, and charming flower-embroidered garters to hold them up.

The high-waisted gown would do nothing for her figure but she bet women with big hips and butts loved them. She smiled. Gowns like these would make life very interesting for a lover, like unwrapping a surprise package. There had been a military uniform in the man's dressing room. If all guys wore breeches that form-fitting, then their bodies were much less of a mystery.

She stopped in front of a vanity, the top outlined with a Plexiglas cover, filled with the familiar combs and brushes, though these were silver-backed and monogrammed. A pile of coins spilled from the tiniest of purses. A "reticule," the posted sign called it.

"Hey, Jim, look at this."

He was halfway out the door but came back to her side.

"The sign says coinage has changed since 1810, but surely that shiny gold one with the dent in it is way different from the usual even in those days."

"Who knows. The money here is still a mystery to me. I hand over a pound coin and the only thing I know is that it's way more than a dollar."

The girl leaned closer. "It's weird. It has writing on it, but it's definitely not in any language I know. Is there a docent on this floor?"

She looked up to find that Jim was gone. But she was not alone. A man sat in a chair tucked behind the door. Dressed in something like a naval uniform, he stood up and bowed to her, his face all smiles.

"You wish to know something of the coin, miss? The writing is Arabic. The East India Company minted the coins to be used in India. This particular one never made it that far. It's one of the few that was saved when the ship sank in the Bay of Biscay barely a week after leaving port." He stood up. "Would you like to hold it?"

"Yes, please." She turned back to the vanity, surprised to see that the Plexiglas was gone. How did they do that?

The man picked up the coin and handed it to her. Just as she bent to look at it, Jim leaned in the doorway. "Hey, let's go. I'm starved and I want to catch that soccer match."

"Come look at this, Jim."

He shook his head, impatient to be gone. "I'll meet you at Earl's Place."

She nodded and let him go. Walking over to the window, she inspected the coin, tested its weight and wondered what could have happened that dented it so. She turned back to the docent.

"I wish I could have known what life was like then."

"Ach, miss," the man scolded, "don't waste a wish on that. Have a seat. I can tell you all you want to know."

One

"Here, Papa, take this. I do not want you to be sad anymore." Poppy held out the bright gold coin as she came into his study.

David Lindsay looked up from the bills that littered his desk. The child was only nine years old and already trying to rule the world.

"Poppy," he said, trying for kindness rather than exasperation, "you know I am not your father. I thought we agreed that you would call me 'uncle.'"

"'Uncle' is what I called Mama's friends," Poppy said, coming closer to his desk. "I know you are not my true papa. You are Major David Lindsay of the 28th Regiment of Foot. You fought Napoleon and beat him. But the war is over and you are the one who takes care of me and Billy. That makes you my papa."

Her papa and not her uncle. Now he understood the difference. How many men had she called uncle? The answer to that question would tell even strangers all they needed to know about her mother. If only he could afford a decent nanny for her; but Billy needed a wet nurse far more than Poppy needed to learn what to say and what to keep to herself. He wanted any number of things for them, some a deal more urgent than a teacher for this sweetheart of a child.

He pushed his chair away from the desk and gave her the only thing he had to give. His smile drew a grin from her. She came closer and, with a nod of permission, climbed into his lap. She tried to put the coin in his hand.

"No, Poppy. I appreciate your generosity but you must keep it. For an emergency."

She made a small sound of acceptance, wrapped her fingers tightly around the coin and leaned against his chest. "Tell me a story, Papa."

"You tell me one, Poppy."

"All right," she said, biting her lip, the way she did when she was thinking hard. Storytelling came as naturally to her as smiling.

"Once upon a time there was a little girl who lived in"— she paused—"in a little village. Her mother had lots of parties and the little girl was always sent to bed before the guests came and told to pray before she went to sleep. It was hard to pray when there was a party, but she closed her eyes tight"—Poppy leaned away and demonstrated how that was done—"and prayed for a brother." Opening her eyes, she added, "Not for a papa. She never prayed for a papa."

Lindsay knew he was not her father. He had spent the year of her conception as part of the expedition to Copenhagen and the rest of 1807 in a convent recovering from a leg wound. Until last year he had not been in England for ten years. He was not Poppy's father, but it was possible that her brother, Billy, was his son.

"God sent a brother, but then he took her mother to heaven and she knew better than to pray for anything ever again."

The little girl paused and leaned against him with a deep

sigh that brought tears to his eyes. They were quiet a while, the only sound the drip of rainwater from the gutter.

Poppy had not prayed for him to care for her. It was her mother who had made that arrangement. It had not been that odd a friendship. Lindsay could see now that they had a lot in common, the war-weary soldier and the fading courtesan, both tired of the work they were growing too old for and not at all sure that there was another choice. They had consoled each other in the only way they could.

There had, after all, been a price to pay for the sex she gave him for free. He would never forget the last time he had seen her. It had been months since her bed had been used for anything but sleep. Death was close, the room cold with it. He could still hear her asking him, begging in a hoarse whisper, to be the guardian of her children.

Of course he had taken them in, praying that their lives would be better with him than they would be in an orphanage.

"Since prayer did not work the way the little girl wanted," Poppy continued, "she decided she would make a wish instead. For you see, Papa, she had a magic coin. A coin that one of her mother's friends had given her. He'd told her to make one wish and then to pass it on."

Poppy leaned back to look at him and handed him the coin. "I want to give you the magic coin, Papa." She held it out to him, again. Her stubborn gaze was a command.

"Was your wish granted?" Lindsay asked as he took the coin, not looking at it, but God help him, wondering if it was worth enough to pay for something other than the butcher's leftovers.

"But yes, of course my wish was granted. I wished for a papa. Now close your eyes and think your wish. You will know it is the right one when the coin turns warm."

So much trust, so easily given. The least he could do was play her game. Lindsay closed his eyes as ordered. *A way out of this hell.*

But wait; if *he* was the answer to her wish for family,

then he had best be careful with the phrasing. He thought a moment. *I wish for the profitable sale of my commission.*

"Keep trying, Papa. When it is the right wish, you will know."

"Very well." What kind of magic coin was this if you had to make the "right" wish? With his eyes closed tight, Lindsay wished again for the prompt sale of his commission and that it would provide enough money to invest and live on.

The coin still felt cold in his hand. This was no more than a game. He smiled a little and wished for work that was satisfying and that paid an impressive wage. Even as he had the thought, the coin warmed his palm. Lindsay opened his eyes with a jerk and then opened his hand.

Poppy straightened, and at that very moment the sun broke through the clouds. A beam of sunlight found its way through the front window, falling directly on the coin. It glowed as golden and warm as the Mediterranean sun. "Very good, Papa. It must have been a very fine wish."

"I was always good at following orders." Lindsay kissed the top of her head. "Now I give the coin away?"

"No, Papa," she said with the long-suffering tone of women everywhere. "You keep it until you are sure your wish is granted. You will know."

"How? Will the coin glow again?"

"No." She snuggled closer.

That was reassuring. He had handled death and war and now poverty, but Lindsay was sure that he would find magic more unsettling than all the rest combined.

"At first I was not at all certain that you were the answer to my wish. You see, I had wished for a papa *and* a mama. The night before we came here, I was in the kitchen eating a syllabub that Cook had made as a treat. I took the coin out, laid it on the table and asked quite out loud if you were the answer to my wish. At that very moment, Mama's friend who had given me the coin came through the door. He told me he was sorry that Mama was gone and yes, indeed, you were the answer to my wish. Then he bowed and left."

She turned her head so she could see him as she explained. "And Papa, the man was right. It was my mistake, you see, for I did not think to ask for a papa and a mama both at the same time."

She drew a deep breath and closed her eyes. In one minute she was fast asleep. Lindsay examined the coin.

Ah, from the East India Company. He used his thumb and fingers to turn the coin and found something in Arabic. There was the Roman numeral X at the bottom and the word "CASH." Ten of whatever. How convenient, but of no use to him at all. He would hold the coin to please her, even though he was sure it was no more magic than his shirt button.

Two

Lindsay made his way down the crowded street. "Sorry," he said to the flower seller he nudged with his arm. She merely shrugged at his clumsiness. "Beg pardon, ma'am." He bowed to the woman who bumped into him. She made her own apology with a gap-toothed smile. Did the sun send rays of good humor as well as light? Or was it that after a week of rain, the people of London felt nothing but gratitude for even half a day of dry, fine weather?

Stepping aside, Lindsay watched a bunch of street urchins race from an alley. No matter the age or station, half of London had the same idea he did. Walking cost not a shilling and after days of rain was pure pleasure.

Or would be if he could lose the feeling of impending financial disaster. He could barely support himself, much less his new family, and it would take time to sell his commission. He could borrow against the sale, but the cost of the loan would seriously reduce the money that came his way. And he needed every guinea far more than the moneylenders did. Lindsay walked on as though time and distance were the key to his problems.

He might wish for employment every minute of every day, but it would hardly fall into his arms. Not without some effort on his part. But where to start? Lindsay looked up as if he would find the answer wherever his random walking had brought him.

Bond street. Far from his Chelsea neighborhood, in more ways than one. For all that the exalted streets of Mayfair had been his milieu until ten years ago, he felt a trespasser.

It did not seem to matter whether it had been ten years or ten days. The same well-dressed men and women made their way in and out of shops, pausing to bow, stopping to chat. Maids and footmen moved with more purpose than their betters, laden down with parcels.

Lindsay noted that dresses were more elaborate, with ruffles at the hem, and that the spencers had more trim. The subdued color and cut of the men's clothing made the red of his uniform stand out all the more. His shako looked as out of place here as a mob cap would have at Waterloo. No matter—he was entitled to wear his uniform until he sold his commission. It was all that stood between him and clothes from a secondhand stall.

The smell of sugar and molasses made him think of Poppy, and he made his way to the door of the confectioner's. He had the door open before he recalled that he had no real money with him. He could not spend Poppy's coin, and not only because the shop owner would throw it in his face.

Instead of going in, Lindsay held the door for two women who were leaving, a lady and her maid. Judging from their laughter, the maid was as much friend as servant.

"But, my lady, he should he giving me sweets."

"Kitty, some rules are made to be broken."

Kitty had no answer for that. She flashed him a smile of

thanks for both her and her lady. Her mistress never even noticed that someone had held the door for them.

Lindsay noticed her. Her laughter embodied a joie de vivre he envied. Everything about her was as fresh as the spring day. Her perfume, the pink in her cheeks, the golden hair, the delicacy of the lace fichu that framed the curve of her neck. Her pelisse, the blue-green of her gown. Every single element of her perfection embedded itself in his mind in that one moment. He had yet to see her face, but was sure he would know her again, if only by the sound of her voice, for the smile that echoed in her words.

Lindsay's steps took him in the same direction as them, and he followed her progress as she made her way toward Hanover Square. She paused at least three times to exchange greetings with other shoppers, two gentlemen and another woman. Not friends, mere acquaintances. And how did he know that? The way she stood. The way she moved, with self-conscious grace. The camaraderie she shared with her maid was absent. A natural caution, or did she have no friends in London?

Lindsay watched as she and Kitty considered the merits of a shop specializing in leather goods. Something for her husband, perhaps? For surely she was married. No one this lovely would remain unattached.

They took so long in consideration that by the time they moved on, Lindsay was only a few steps behind them. If he had been less of a gentleman he could have overheard their conversation.

Her laughter drifted back to him, and Lindsay decided that when he sold his commission . . .

He was distracted from his fantasy by the sound of a horse, moving at unsafe speed, racing down the crowded street. A moment later a rider came into view, mud-spattered and determined on losing not a moment.

Lindsay moved forward quickly, the battlefield instinct for survival still with him even if now it meant no more than protecting a lady's gown from ruin. He took her by the shoulders, her back pressed against his chest, and placed himself between her and the mud that the idiot rider was casting up as he raced by.

He felt the delicacy of her bones beneath his fingers, the way her head would fit just below his chin, the orange spice scent of her perfume. And he felt her stiffen under his grip. Lindsay loosened his hold immediately. Even as she turned to him, people around them cried out in consternation. In that instant the woman realized that she had been rescued and not assaulted. While the rest of the street muttered, cursed and cried over mud-damaged clothes, his lady turned to him.

"Thank you for the gallant sacrifice, Colonel." Even as she spoke, the practiced artifice disappeared, banished by a laugh that lit her eyes and touched his heart.

He bowed to her. *Those eyes,* he thought; *I could lose myself in them forever.* "It is major, my lady. Major David Lindsay of the 28th Foot."

"Of the 28th Foot." She spoke the words as he did, and he nodded.

"My cousin is in the 28th. He joined for the uniform, I think."

He looked down at the red jacket with the bright yellow facings.

"I am afraid, Major Lindsay, that your uniform will never be the same. Do turn around."

Lindsay obeyed her order, and she made a small sound that confirmed her suspicion.

"Quite ruined, I'm afraid."

He turned back to her, shaking his head. "Not at all, my lady, merely injured in your service. It has seen action for ten years and not failed me yet."

"Oh yes," she said, her smile fading, "I am sure it has survived far worse. I am sorry. I did not mean to make light of it."

"Not at all." Lindsay could have kicked himself for erasing her smile. *She's flirting with you, you dolt. Think of something to say, so she will remember you when you meet again.* "I am sure my coat will fully recover."

"I wish I were convinced of that. If it cannot be made like new, then I will buy you a new one."

That gave him pause. Not that he wanted a new uniform, but that she would offer something so personal to a complete stranger chance met on Bond Street.

"Will you come and show me that it is still wearable?" she continued with a smile that hinted at conspiracy. "On Friday. I am hosting a small party to announce my arrival for the Season. I would be pleased if you would join us for some music and a light supper before we all make our way to the evening's entertainments."

"Thank you." *Her* arrival for the Season. Did that mean no husband?

"Eight o'clock, then? I am on Norfolk Street, just off Green. My house is the only one on the street with a bright blue door."

She turned from him before he could agree. He watched her out of sight. She was as fresh as the spring air, for all that she was not a young girl. More than lighthearted. Less than brazen. Unconventional, he decided.

A bright blue door? The only one on Norfolk Street? More like the only one in London. It was as odd as extending an invitation and neglecting to give him her name.

Three

"Her name is Lady Grace Anderson, Major." Nancy came into the study with Billy asleep on her shoulder.

How was a man to find out a lady's name and situation when the usual options were no longer his? His club memberships were long gone, his contacts among society nonexistent. Lindsay thought asking Nancy's help had been rather clever, like the old days on the Peninsula when he would have Jesseck check the status of grain for the horses. Jesseck spent most of his time in the kitchen these days, but Nancy was out daily with the children.

"She is a widow and this is her third Season since her husband died. The house was part of her settlement, but she rented it out all during her marriage."

"And she was married to . . . ?"

"Viscount Anderson, heir to the Earl Draycott. He was fifteen years older than she and died from a heart ailment."

"No children."

"No children, sir, but, this Season her aunt and the aunt's son are staying with her.

For propriety or company? Or was the cousin courting?

The conversation played back in his head as he approached the three front steps. The house was narrow, only about twenty-five feet wide, but it rose four stories, and that didn't count the basement. Comfortable but unremarkable, except for the blue door.

The butler greeted him with genuine warmth, took his shako and told him that the gathering was meant to be informal and to please join the guests unannounced. Lindsay found the large salon filled with over thirty people and no sign of Lady Anderson.

Several people smiled and nodded. A moment later an old gentleman approached, introduced himself, thanked him for his service and then began a monologue on his hopes for England at peace.

And so it went. His uniform was the only invitation people needed to make an introduction or start a conversation. And the Waterloo medal drew the curious. It named him hero and victor. No one ever asked how it felt to wear a medal that represented suffering as well as victory.

One or two of the guests asked meaningful questions: How long before the troops of occupation would be withdrawn from France? Would Napoleon stay put this time? He had no sure answers, but it made for a break from the misplaced hero worship.

For the most part he enjoyed it. He enjoyed it tremendously. It had been years since society had found favor with him.

Through the whole he never spoke to his hostess. He would look up and find her watching him with a pleased smile, the one that lit her eyes. Lindsay returned the attention with a slight bow, but every time he made to move toward her there was another man or woman anxious to speak with him. He might not have been able to speak to her, but he would occasionally hear her laughter, the very sound making this party memorable.

When the clock struck ten, the guests began to drift

away. Even as he made to join them and finally speak to his hostess, a footman came to him and asked if he would wait in the library.

The footman showed him to a room at the front of the house. As he heard the sounds of farewell, he took stock of his surroundings.

Lady Grace Anderson's house was all that was fashionable. And proper. With the occasional touch that kept it from being dull. He examined the fireplace, admiring the fairies that were carved into the molding that held the mantel, the same fairies that decorated the fire screen, though these were painted gold and green.

"Good evening, Major."

Lindsay turned to see a woman of a certain age, not his hostess.

"Good evening, madam. David Lindsay at your service."

"Yes, my son knows you. Captain George Cardovan. Do you remember him?"

Cardovan, yes. A fine officer, badly wounded in an accident when the ship landed at Ostend.

"Of course I do. A pleasure to meet you, Mrs. Cardovan. Is your son with you?"

"He is. I have finally convinced him to come to town, though he is embarrassed that he cannot dance."

And, Lindsay was sure, embarrassed that he had missed Waterloo. No matter that his quick thinking had saved lives in Ostend. To be wounded weeks before the final campaign was worse than death in Belgium. "I do understand. May I call on him?"

"He would welcome it, I am sure, Major. In fact, my niece would like to invite you to join us for dinner. George will be there too."

"Why, thank you, Mrs. Cardovan."

"Good. Grace is rather given to impulse. I am glad that you are not repelled by it."

"A soldier learns to handle the unexpected."

"A useful trait in this household, I assure you."

Lindsay thought of the bright blue door, the fairies around the mantel, and wondered if they would be having cakes and cream for the first course at dinner.

Mrs. Cardovan walked away from him and stood with her back to the fire screen. "Have you known my niece long?"

Was she assessing his threat to her son's courtship or being protective of her niece? "I've known her long enough to appreciate her laughter and effervescent charm, ma'am."

She reached out and rapped his wrist with her fan. "Then not very long at all."

What did she mean by that?

"Grace is a different woman since the viscount died and has earned every bit of pleasure life offers."

"You have earned some fun as well, Major. Anyone at Waterloo deserves as much."

It was not Mrs. Cardovan who spoke, and he turned to find Grace Anderson standing in the doorway. Before he could think of a way to answer she went on, "Good evening, Major. I am so sorry that I did not have a chance to speak with you during the party. I had hoped to have time to speak to everyone, but I fear my guest list was too ambitious. Will you stay for dinner?"

"Yes, thank you, my lady," he said, giving her a slight bow.

"Wonderful." She offered him her arm. "Petkin tells me the soup is ready to be served."

Mrs. Cardovan hurried to the door. "I will go tell George." Even as she spoke, the older woman nodded to him and left the room.

"Aunt Louise means well, but I wish she was not so inclined to believe in fairy tales. She has me cast as some butterfly just burst from a cocoon and still trying my wings." She did not wait for a response but continued, "Tell me, have you ever had a soup made from apricots?"

Four

Dinner was . . . well, an adventure. Not the least of which was the apricot soup. Captain Cardovan's welcome was embarrassingly enthusiastic and the two spent the first half of the meal talking of friends. By the time the more conventional fish course was served, Lindsay was feeling guilty for talking of nothing but the military.

From then on the four of them covered a dozen subjects, largely centered on the Season. Plays and balls were on everyone's list, as well as excitement at the opening of the Waterloo Bridge sometime in June. "It will make for a break from the usual, will it not?" Lady Anderson said.

If by "the usual" she meant the constant parade of young girls making their bows and the speculation over what matches would be made, then she was right. He might not be part of that world any longer, but he could remember it well.

By the end of the meal it was clear to him that George Cardovan was no suitor, but was loved like a brother. Mrs.

Cardovan excused herself and, after a pointed look from his mother, George joined her.

"I wish someone could convince my aunt that George must be allowed to live his own life." Lady Anderson looked at him and shook her head. "He can hardly be expected to enjoy the Season if she is constantly worrying over him."

He made some sort of neutral response, not at all inclined to take sides in a family squabble. She did not seem to expect an answer, but invited him back into the library, where a decanter of port awaited them.

She poured a small glass for each of them. This was another nod to the unconventional. No tea in the small salon for this hostess. No aunt to play chaperone.

She handed him a glass and then moved away, leaving the scent of her perfume as she moved about the room, like the newly hatched butterfly she had alluded to. One not quite ready to light in any one spot. She looked over her shoulder. "Did you enjoy the party?"

"Yes, thank you. It was an intriguing mix of people."

"Yes, I suppose it was, but all dear friends of mine."

"A pleasure to be included in so select a company." Exactly how did he fit in this group?

She took a sip of her port as she swept around him again. Her orange spice scent was as intoxicating as the port he held. Before Lindsay could turn to face her, she was in front of him. "I see that your uniform looks as well as it did before Fetters tried to win his absurd bet racing down Bond Street."

"Yes, my lady. Jesseck learned magic as my batman during the war years."

"In truth, Major, it hardly matters what your coat looks like. All eyes are drawn to your medal."

Lindsay looked away from her. "Too much has been made of it." This was not quite what he meant, but he was not even going to try to explain.

"I can imagine that all the fuss does embarrass you." She set her glass on the mantel. "When so many died. But you must wear it in honor of them, if acknowledgment of your own valor makes you uncomfortable."

He did that sometimes when he first put it on or took it off. Thought of Winslow, Packard or any of a hundred others and prayed for their immortal souls.

She walked over and touched it. Not him. She touched the medal and looked up at him. "Or wear it in honor of all the things men and women have done that deserve medals and are never recognized."

"Like childbirth," he said, nodding, thinking of Billy and the mother who died to give him life.

She dropped her hand and looked at him with a start, her smile gone, her cheeks flushed as though he had just struck her, not with his words but with his hand. She turned from him.

"I beg your pardon, ma'am. That was most indelicate of me."

She did not answer for a moment, then turned back to him, her smile in place, though this time it looked less natural. Her caution increased his unease. Rather like the way he felt in the field when all the birds grew silent and the animals stilled.

She moved around the room again, more slowly, not looking at him as she began.

"George, in his boredom, has told me all about you. Your family is from Kent. You've had an estate there since the time of Henry VIII. You were the second son. Your father bought you a commission. Your family, all of them and most of the servants, died of smallpox while you were in Spain."

She stopped moving about and faced him. "I am so sorry for your loss, Major. To face death every day to save our way of life and to have your own family taken from you is the cruelest irony."

"Yes, my lady."

She came back to her original spot by the fire screen, took her glass but did not drink. She stared into the liquid as she continued.

"Then the land steward you hired to manage the estate brought it to ruin. You had to sell it to pay off the debt and were left with nothing but your commission, which you wish to sell so you can begin a new life."

She paused, put her glass down carefully and looked him in the eye. "But selling a major's commission in peacetime is slow work."

She waited for him to speak, but Lindsay kept silent and held her gaze, caught between a slowly simmering anger and curiosity. Was this sort of gossip Cardovan's idea of friendship?

"I should imagine that, um, positions are scarce for men whose truest skill are enduring the Spanish winter and staying alive in France."

"Yes, my lady." He tamped down anger he could ill afford. If she knew of employment he must listen.

"Really, Major." She spoke with a burst of irritation. "You do know how to converse, I saw that at dinner. This will not work if you cannot manage more than one-word sentences when we are alone."

"My apologies. I am doing my best to remain civil when I would prefer to walk out of the room. To use your cousin as a spy is offensive to both him and me. My years in the army taught me how to hold my tongue and my temper, but this is too much." He had expected her to be above such behavior. Like some callow boy, he had been mesmerized by her smile, her aura of sweetness.

Looking shocked and more than a little taken aback, she spoke in hurried apology. "I am sorry, Major. It is only that George thinks so highly of you and loves to talk of all things military. It was more than vulgar curiosity, I assure you. I truly did have a reason for asking."

He gave her a curt nod, already regretting his outburst. Did she know about Poppy and Billy? If her source was

Cardovan then she would probably know nothing of his present state of affairs. He could only imagine what society would make of his newfound family. He could at least be grateful he had been spared that.

She took a very small sip of the port. "I meant no offense, Major." She angled her head slightly, and her eyes held more curiosity than regret. "Did you not use your own resources, or 'spies' as you say, to find out what you could about me?"

He had to concede that he had, but turned away from her rather than say it aloud. "If the invitation to your party and to dinner was a test of Cardovan's understanding of me, then you are taking the long road to your 'reason for asking,' madam."

"Yes. Yes I am." She grimaced. "But it is a little unusual. I wonder how someone as, um, staid as you will receive it."

"You think I am staid? After that burst of temper?"

"It was a justified outburst, Major."

She bowed her head and spoke with such humility that he came close to forgiving her. "But you are right, sir, staid is the wrong word. Calm? No, perhaps not calm, either. Sober? Settled?" She tried each word and shook her head. "Not frivolous. Definitely not."

"And you are nervous," he said with some surprise. The realization erased the last of his anger, for it put him in charge.

"Nervous? Why, yes, I am a little."

"I find 'tis better to act than to merely think about acting."

"I suppose what you really mean is that fighting a battle is easier than thinking about one."

"Precisely, but I find the same applies in peacetime."

"Yes." She could agree with him on this. "In fact, I think the Season is merely a different kind of battle. Not that I mean to belittle your experience in any way."

"It has been years, my lady, but the nervousness before my first ball is unforgettable."

"I made my bow fifteen years ago, and worried that no one would notice that the embroidery on my gown matched the color of my eyes."

She looked up then, and he could see that there was more pain than pleasure in the memory. He took a step closer, then stopped himself.

"But that was a long time ago, Major. This time I am going into the battle certain of the outcome."

Five

"Major, are you interested in employment? I would like to offer you a position." She took a step closer. "A position for which I am willing to pay twenty-five pounds a week through the entire Season."

"Twenty-five pounds? A week?"

She watched him. It was hard to tell what he was thinking. Was that the army training?

"What sort of position is it, my lady?"

"To continue the military analogy, Major: I want to hire you to be my ally. Would you consider work as my escort?"

"Your escort?"

She nodded, doing her best not to duck her head, to look him straight in the eye, to be businesslike. How did men do this? She should have asked someone. But who?

"What kind of escort?"

"More than an escort, actually. Could you be my companion? I would like to hire you to come with me to dinner parties, to take me to plays and the opera."

Lindsay winced at the word "opera."

"You do not like the opera?" She spoke as though she had already known that too. "You see, that is one of the reasons I am willing to pay you. So that there will be some reward for doing what is less than your favorite."

"But surely you would have no trouble finding an escort."

"Thank you, for I assume that is a compliment. But you see, I am not looking for a husband. In fact, I want to do all I can to discourage suitors. I do not want to marry again. Not ever. You are on my arm to make that perfectly clear."

"If we are seen together all the time people will assume . . ."

He did not finish the sentence, and Grace was charmed that he was so straitlaced. "People will assume that we are lovers?"

"Yes, my lady."

"But that would be no one's business but ours."

Lindsay stiffened, hesitated and then asked, "Are you hiring me to sleep with you?"

"No indeed, Major. We hardly know each other. And I am woman enough to prefer some degree of acquaintance before moving to the bedroom."

"Then it is not a condition of the employment, but a possibility?" He did not wait for her to answer. "No, madam. This carries your eccentric inclinations too far. I am not so desperate that I must sell my body like some whore on the corner."

Did he find her so unattractive then? It was so impossible to consider her as a lover? Was this attraction she felt one-sided? Drat and blast. "Hardly a prostitute, Major, more like a well-paid courtesan."

He closed his eyes, and Grace could see him struggling to keep his temper in the face of the insult. This was entirely wrong. She should not even have made the offer tonight, but given him time to recover from the perceived insult of her learning all she could about him.

Now she'd deliberately baited him. Why? Because she wanted him to be at least as embarrassed as she was?

"I am sorry, Major. I did not mean to offend." Grace walked closer, her words earnest and intense. "I wished only to offer a solution to both of our problems. I have no intention of doing any more than dancing with you. Could this not be purely a business arrangement? I know you were not married when you left Belgium, and if you will assure me that you have no wife or fiancée, then that is all I wish to know about your personal life."

"I am not married and have no woman in my life."

The fact that he answered her question convinced her that he might actually be considering her offer, despite the insult. The fact that he'd hesitated a moment in answering made her wonder what he was not telling her.

"Then that is all I need to know. I am offering you the position purely in the nature of a business proposal."

"Business it may be, my lady, but not any that I wish to be a part of."

"Please, there is no need to answer me now." She wanted to touch him, but knew that even a hand on his arm was more contact than he would tolerate. "Lady Harriston told me that she plans to invite you to her ball. I hope to see you there. Can I count on your presence being your answer? And please, sir, do forgive the insult."

He gave a curt nod, bowed and without another word left her alone.

Grace grabbed the port and took a healthy sip, and before she'd finished coughing her aunt was in the room.

"It did not go well?" Louise sat as Grace shook her head.

"It was close to disaster. I sounded like a crude hussy, lacking in all sensibility."

"Grace! What in the world did you say to him?" Her aunt put a hand to her heart as though palpitations were starting.

"First he accused me of using George as a spy, when all I wanted to know was if he was available."

"Yes. Exactly."

"I am not going to endure the experience again by telling you any more of it. Trust me when I say that I have given him a disgust of me. I apologized and asked him to reconsider." Grace shook her head. "When I asked him if he had formed any attachments since returning from Europe he said no, but I was sure there was something he was not telling me."

"It would be easy enough to find out."

"Absolutely not, Aunt Louise. He was so angry. If there is any chance he will reconsider I am not going to jeopardize it by making any more inquiries. He is entitled to some privacy, as are all my employees." She drew a breath that was all disappointment. "I think it is hopeless."

"What a shame." Aunt Louise patted her hand. "It has worked so well for the last two years."

"Because Belney had no interest in women and all Wharton wanted was money to emigrate to Canada."

"I was sure the major was an ideal candidate, Grace."

"I think he did forgive me the first offense, the spying. But then I let his lack of interest provoke me into a deliberate insult." Why had she even mentioned that? Louise was all attention now. Grace waved her hand. "After that I cannot imagine the major will set aside his pride, even for twenty-five pounds a week."

"One good thing has come from this, Grace. This is the first time I have seen you interested enough in a man to make a mull of it. Very good, my dear. I will be grateful for small steps. I should so like you to learn that sex is about more than a responsibility."

Grace looked at the port, and the very thought of drinking more made her cough. "It is just as well, Aunt. I like my life as it is."

"Then why do you look disappointed?"

"Relieved. I am relieved," Grace insisted. "He is too used to command and would have been very difficult to manage."

She turned away from her aunt. She was relieved *and*

disappointed. She could still recall his hands on her shoulders, her back pressed against his chest, feeling overwhelmed and thrilled at the same time.

She shuddered. There were times when the body and the mind were not at all as one. She knew what sex was. Never mind Aunt Louise's intimations—she had had more than enough of it to last a lifetime.

Grace turned back to her aunt. "Thank God he was offended. Clearly he is more a gentleman than I am a lady."

Six

"Billy is sick?" Lindsay had returned home to find his household in chaos.

"Very sick, Papa. He is not breathing properly. Nancy has sent for the surgeon." Poppy's words came out in gasps that were filled with tears.

How would he pay for the surgeon? Panic slid through him. Lindsay took Poppy's hand and hurried up the two flights of stairs to the nursery. He would find the money. There had been enough death in his world. If the surgeon could cure the boy then he would do whatever he had to do to pay for it.

Lindsay went through the day nursery and into the room where both Poppy and Billy slept. No sooner was he through the door than fear nudged the panic aside. God, what if this was contagious? What if Billy infected Poppy and she died too?

"Jesseck is in the hall waiting for the surgeon. I want you to go downstairs and make sure he stays awake."

Poppy obeyed without question. It was a miserable few

hours, and close to dawn before the surgeon discovered that the labored breathing had been caused by nothing more than a pea the child had pushed up his nose.

Poppy and Nancy both began to cry, but this time they were tears of relief. Lindsay comforted them and in no time the house was settled into the rhythms of sleep. The surgeon promised to send a salve that would ease the boy's discomfort and Lindsay sent Jesseck to bed, insisting that he would stay up until it arrived. He decided to wait outside, so that a knock would not echo through the house and disturb the children.

The milkmaids were making their way through the neighborhood, the fruit and vegetable carts lumbering by. As he watched the morning parade, he pulled Poppy's coin from his pocket. The surgeon had looked skeptical when Lindsay promised prompt payment. How many others were on the list to be paid? How long before debtors' prison claimed him?

Lindsay stared at the coin, not golden now but dark and unresponsive. "Is Lady Anderson's offer the answer to my wish?"

Even as he spoke, a man approached him. "What was that, Captain?"

It's Major, Lindsay thought. The man was wearing some kind of naval uniform. He ought to know rank, but Lindsay was too tired to correct him.

"You want to know if your wish has been granted," the man said, answering his own question and stepping closer. "The thing is, sir, you can never tell with wishes."

"It is none of your business." Lindsay gave him a cold stare, but the man stood his ground.

"I beg your pardon, sir, but you asked about your wish and I am come to answer."

"You are an expert on wishes?" It was a comment bordering on the absurd, but the man answered anyway.

"Indeed I am." He took off his hat and bowed as if that

would be introduction enough. "You wished for employment that was pleasurable and profitable, did you not?"

Lindsay took a step back, aghast at the thought that this proposal had already found its way to the gossip mill.

The man held up his hand, his hat still in it. "Never fear, sir. I am no threat to the discretion so essential to this offer."

Lindsay pushed the coin back into his pocket and prayed the man was telling the truth.

"You see, sir, the coin interprets the wish in its own way." The man ran his hat through his fingers. "Sometimes an explanation is needed." He bowed again.

Lindsay shrugged, humoring the man while trying to think of some reasonable explanation for his appearance.

"Now, sir, you asked for employment both pleasurable and profitable. That is what has been offered, is it not? The position with Lady Anderson? It is what you need, sir, and not only for the money. You need to step back into your rightful place in the world."

He would throw the ridiculous coin in the river the very next chance he had.

"Surely it is not the amount, Major. Twenty-five pounds a week seems a princely sum to me."

"It is." Lindsay hesitated and then decided that anything that happened this early in the morning was no more than a dream. "The work I am offered is hardly honorable."

"Aha, but you see you did not include 'honorable' in your list." The man nodded, as if he were agreeing with himself. "And, sir, I ask you, what is *dis*honorable about the position? Any work that you take on to provide for your family would suit my definition of honorable." He spoke with a firm nod, as though that was the final word.

"Then we define honorable differently."

"No, we do not. It is only that your definition is clouded by pride. Honor and pride. They are not the same."

"And preserving my pride was something else I failed to include in my list."

"Very good, Colonel. Yes, indeed, your wish is granted. It is up to you to make the best of it without compromising what is most important to you."

And with a nod, the man put his cap back on and continued down the street.

Seven

"Major David Lindsay." The steward's voice was well suited to his current task announcing guests. His baritone carried across the ballroom and caught the attention of Grace Anderson.

Elation swept through her. He was here. There was still a chance he would agree to her offer. He was not particularly late—the Harristons were still receiving guests—but she had given up hope when he had not been among the first to arrive.

At the announcement of his name, the woman she was speaking with stopped talking and turned to take a look at him. Grace watched him study the crowd. When he found her, he nodded. More than one head turned to follow his gaze and see who merited such attention.

It was not hard to tell. Her answering smile was out of all proportion to his brief nod. She could not help it.

"Oooh, my dear," the lady next to her said, "aren't you the lucky one. I was rather hoping I was the one he had taken such particular notice of. Major Lindsay is quite a handsome man, and I daresay it is not just the uniform that gives him such distinction."

Grace reminded herself that a single exchange of glances was enough to start gossip. Rumors of a liaison might be her goal, but the last thing she wanted was for gossip to start before she knew if he was willing. She did her best to control her satisfaction. If he said no after the smile she gave his discreet nod, everyone would know that it was he who had snubbed her. Did it matter? Just enough to make her smile disappear.

She gave her full attention to the woman who had expressed such envy, a woman whose name she could not quite recall. Something like "rooster," but that may have come to mind because she was dressed as though her goal had been to look like one. Grace wondered if anyone else thought the rather lovely bronze-red taffeta dress and the huge pair of feathers rising from her crown gave the woman the look of a bantam. A ruby choker only added to the overall effect. Perhaps she was trying to compete with her husband, a colonel whose uniform was as impressive as Lindsay's, even without the Waterloo medal.

"I met the major the other day, when he saved my clothes from ruin." Grace pressed her lips together to erase the smile and tried for something more decorous.

"Did Fetters race down Bond Street again?"

"Yes." She resisted the urge to turn back to look for Lindsay. He had seen her. He would find her when the time was right.

"We will have more to talk of this Season than which girl has caught the eye of which gentleman if Fetters continues these absurdities." The woman shook her shoulders, looking more like a rooster with each gesture.

"Hopefully, he will not be here tonight," Grace said, only half attending. "This is one gown I would like to wear again."

"The major is coming this way," the woman whispered.

Grace could not resist a glance over her shoulder. His

uniform made him easy to find, the red standing out even among the glitter of society. It was both elegant and sober, as was the man wearing it.

"He's coming straight to you," the woman hissed, stating the obvious, and Grace turned to greet him.

"Lady Anderson." He bowed.

"Major Lindsay." She curtsied.

Her smile faded as he stared at her, silent. Then he shook his head in the same slight way he had nodded to her. He turned to her companion as though the two words of her name was all the attention she would have from him.

This, then, was not the good news she had hoped for. Now she was truly embarrassed at the enthusiasm of her earlier welcome.

She stood her ground, though she was sorely tempted to flee. She was embarrassed only. Not humiliated. It was his choice and could have been made for a dozen reasons, reasons that had nothing to do with the way she dressed or drank soup.

With a determination to end their brief acquaintance with civility and, by the by, give the woman in red no further fuel for gossip, Grace watched as the major bowed over the other woman's hand.

"Good evening to you, Mrs. Rooster."

Rooster? *Good heavens,* Grace thought, *did he really call her that?* Even as she had the thought he blushed.

"It's Schuster, Major. I believe we met at General Broadbent's. The name is Schuster."

He bowed low over her hand. "I do beg your pardon, Mrs. Schuster. How hen-witted of me."

The choice of words was deliberate, Grace was sure. With real effort, she kept from looking at him. As it was she could barely contain her laughter.

"You must excuse me, Major, Lady Anderson." Mrs. Schuster nodded to each of them. "Lady Harriston wants my opinion on some new bonnets for her chicks. They are lovely girls. But having all three make their bow in the same Season would be a burden for any mother. If you will excuse me? And I'm sure you will." The arch tone hinted that Mrs. Schuster was going to share more than her opinion on hats.

They both watched her leave, and as soon as she was out of earshot Lindsay turned to her.

"Is there any hope for me or have I ruined myself completely?" Despite the question, he did not look particularly worried. "Tell me, how important is Mrs. Schuster? You must know the pecking order here."

She could not hold back her laughter. It came out with a most unladylike gasp, thank heaven, not quite a snort. His own grin became a laugh as well.

"I think you will survive, for she has no idea what the joke is. 'Chicks,' Major. She called the Harriston girls 'chicks.'"

This sent them into gales of laughter, which were soon uncontrollable and attracting more than a little attention. So much so that he tugged her after him and through the doors onto a terrace and the back garden.

The dancing would not end for another hour and the garden was empty. Grace laughed until her sides hurt, as much a release of tension as amusement. Lindsay led her to a bench, dusted the seat with his handkerchief and gestured for her to sit.

They sat side by side, barely touching, the laughter gone as quickly as it had come. Finally, Grace cleared her throat. "I dared hope that your presence tonight meant that you had decided to accept the position."

"I thought I had." He sighed, the sound of indecision at odds with the uniform and the air of authority that seemed so naturally a part of him. After a long moment he said, "I have no choice but to accept, my lady." He sounded more resigned than interested.

"One always has a choice, sir." He'd made it sound as though he were choosing the guillotine over the hangman's noose.

"I need the money. Enough for that to be the deciding factor." He was staring through the window at the dancers as they made their way through a waltz. Anything to avoid looking at her, she thought.

He needed money that badly? George had said that he did not gamble, or at least no more than most officers with too much time on their hands. Or maybe he needed the money for an investment. She would not ask. She had learned already that he valued his privacy, and she would respect that.

She was silent so long that he finally did turn to look at her.

"Is that too blunt for you?"

"No. Actually I appreciate your honesty." Now it was her turn to look away. "I could wish for more enthusiasm, but will do my best not to be offended by the lack of it." This awkwardness was not a particularly good way to start out.

"And I will do my best not to be disgusted at the thought of being paid by a woman to do work that is an insult to both of us."

Oh dear. This could easily lead to an argument, one they had already had. As they sat in strained silence, Mrs. Schuster strutted past the doorway. Grace glanced at Lindsay, who was watching the woman as well.

"Do you think she did it deliberately?"

"I cannot imagine"—he shook his head—"but she is drawing attention."

Yes, Mrs. Schuster was leaving disbelief in her wake. "Perhaps her goal in life is to be immortalized by Rowlandson."

"Perhaps, my lady. Picturing her in one of his cartoons takes very little imagination."

As she passed from view, Grace looked at him directly for the first time since they had come out on the terrace. "We can make of our arrangement what we will: an insult or an adventure. For now I will be grateful that you agreed and, ahem, did not chicken out on me."

He showed as much disgust as amusement—at the pun, she hoped. She attempted a bland smile, and finally he laughed. So did she. She could not recall a time that she had laughed with a man. Belney had no sense of humor at all. Wharton's humor was too crude to be amusing. And her husband—around him she had been very careful to control all her sensibilities.

If they could keep each other laughing, this might work after all.

Eight

"Are you having fun, Papa?"

Lindsay glanced over at Poppy, who was sitting on his bed, concentrating on pulling on his too-large gloves.

"Yes, I am." More fun than he had expected.

"What's the best part?"

He ran the brush through his hair one last time and turned to face the child.

"Tell me, Papa, what's the best part about going out? The people you meet? The food you eat? The clothes they wear? Staying up until it's almost morning?"

He sat on the bed and gently pulled his gloves off her small hands. "You know how when you go to the park with your governess? And how it's so much more fun on those days when your friends are there?"

She nodded.

"Society is the same. The best part is finding people who enjoy the same things you do and seeing them as often as possible."

"Are you going to the play with friends tonight?"

"Yes."

"A particular friend?"

Where had she learned that phrase? From her governess? "And why are you so curious tonight?"

"Because I asked Miss Truslow why you never stay home and she said that you had a particular friend."

Now he was the one who was exasperated. "Poppy, I see you and Billy every day."

She nodded, and he took his gloves and walked over to collect his shako.

"Mama used to go out at night, too."

He felt her words like a punch to a healing wound. *Yes, my child, and I go out at night for the same reason your mama did. To keep food on the table and a roof over our heads.*

"Mama used to go out at night and she died."

Lindsay came back to the bed, where she was kneeling now, her eyes level with his cravat.

"Poppy, dearest, I am not going to die. Not for a very long time. And certainly not because I go out at night."

"Do you promise?"

"Yes." One thing he was sure of: If he had survived ten years in the army, he was not meant to die young.

Poppy nodded, very near tears. He put his arms around her and gave her a hug, which she tolerated for all of two seconds.

With a change of mood that always confused him, she pulled out of his arms, then jumped twice on the mattress and onto the floor. "Have fun tonight, Papa. And bring me a treat!"

He watched her bounce from the room and followed her, coming back a moment later to pick up the freshly laundered handkerchief he meant to return to Lady Anderson. He held it to his nose and smelled only the lavender water the laundress had used. It was no match for the orange spice scent that was as much a part of Grace Anderson as her hair and the small round beauty mark behind her ear. And her laughter.

The scent must have been specially blended for her. By her husband? By a lover? By someone who understood her. Someone who knew that for all her orange blossom sweetness there was a spark of passion banked oh so carefully. A passion that peeked out when she laughed, when she lost herself in music, sipped champagne or tasted an especially well-made pudding. A passion that fired an inquiring mind. At least that was one passion he could indulge in with her. One that did not compromise his precariously balanced sense of honor. He tucked the handkerchief in his pocket. How long would the passion of an active mind be enough to share? Was it complete in itself or fuel for greater passion? It was a subject that he knew would intrigue Grace, but one he was not going to introduce.

"Are you having fun, Grace?"

"Hmmm." Grace pretended that all her attention was on her choice of the garnets or the amethysts.

"Is that a yes or a no, dear?" Her aunt was comfortably ensconced in the slipper chair and showed no sign of leaving.

"If we start on that now, Aunt Louise, I'll be late."

"Nonsense. No one ever arrives at the theater on time."

Grace chose the garnets and began fastening the necklace. "Yes, I am having fun." She picked up the earrings and fastened them, then sat on the padded bench of her dressing table, facing her aunt, her back to the mirror.

"Yes, I am having fun," she repeated as she reached behind her and picked up the bracelet that made a matched set with the earrings and necklace. "Major Lindsay is a perfect gentleman. Attentive. Courteous." She made the two words sound inconsequential. She waved her hand. "You know what I mean."

"I know what you mean, Grace, but not why it annoys you."

"He is a very entertaining companion. We laugh at the same things and we both are happiest when we find someone willing to talk about something other than Fetters' latest bet.

"But you see, even with that, there is a reserve about him. He never talks about his life, never at all."

"And exactly what should he tell you? He is your employee, Grace. What do you know of Petkin's private life?"

She shrugged. "I spend more time with him than I do with the butler." After a careful inspection of the catch on her bracelet, she added, "He is doing exactly what I hired him for, but the truth is I wish there were something more, something closer to friendship."

"And are you friends with all your employees?"

"My maid and I are friends." Even she could hear how defensive that sounded. "But I take your point."

"Kitty is a rare exception. You grew up together. She will always be as much friend as servant. Grace, you know as well as I do that it is not wise to be friends with an employee."

"You are the one who encouraged me to become more intimate with him."

"Yes, and I still think that having a lover would be a very enlightening experience for you. But I have my doubts as to whether this is the best way to go about it."

"Men do it all the time."

"Yes, that's true, my dear, but friendship is not a prerequisite for them."

"Oh. I always thought that was what would make the difference between enjoying sex and merely tolerating it." She pressed her lips together. Why had she said that aloud?

"When it comes to sex, men do not think first with their heart"—Louise paused—"or even their brain. For a woman like you, some sort of connection is essential."

"And what do you mean by 'a woman like me'?" Grace

stood up. "Someone who is happier as a widow than I was as a married woman? Someone who has never had a lover?"

"Both of those, Grace, but mostly a woman who, despite an inclination to flout convention in private, is in public a lady and not given to the casual in any way." She stood up and took Grace's hands. "Perhaps that is the solution. Stop thinking so much, Grace. Let him know you are interested in more than . . . what was it you said?"

"He is very attentive and courteous."

"Yes, let him know that you are interested in more than attention and courtesy and see what he does."

"I wish this were easier." Grace looked down at her lap. "It is too much like walking an untested bridge over a deep ravine. It was so much simpler before."

"You know in your heart that you would rather be facing that bridge than a brick walk that does no more than circle the garden."

"Yes, yes." Grace closed her eyes. "That describes my marriage exactly. But that is the past. I have changed, have I not?"

"No one who knew you then could doubt that."

"I wish there were something between the safe path and the treacherous bridge. Why do I have to go from one extreme to the other?"

"Grace," her aunt said with an incredulous laugh, "it has taken you two years to risk the bridge. That is hardly going from one extreme to the other."

"Oh, Aunt Louise." Grace pulled her aunt into a hug. "I am so glad to have you with me this Season. Talking with you is so much more satisfying than letters. I will try it. I will, even though I have no idea how he will react."

"Neither do I, my dear. But I must admit that I am hopeful."

Nine

"Garrick has been dead almost forty years and still his plays entertain. I do think *The Clandestine Marriage* is my favorite." Grace looked down as the people below moved out of the theater. She nodded and waved to acquaintances in another box who, like her, preferred to make their departure after the crowd had thinned.

Lindsay had come to realize that she preferred to discuss the play while it was fresh in her mind, and lingering the twenty odd minutes presented the ideal opportunity. "Yes, my lady, Garrick was a genius. The proof being that his characters are true for any age. You must be acquainted with any number like the grasping sister and the snobbish aunt."

"They ring so true." She shook her head in some amusement. "Do you think they recognize themselves?"

"Do you recognize yourself in Fanny?"

"The secretly married daughter?" Grace looked at him in some surprise. ""No, not at all. What makes you say that we are alike?"

Lindsay looked away for a moment and considered if what he was about to say would offend her. And wondered for a moment how often Poppy's mama had to make the effort to guard her tongue lest she offend her patron. He spoke anyway. "You and Garrick's Fanny are both well-meaning, loyal, sweet."

Grace blushed a little, and was about to speak when he held up his hand. "Sweet," he repeated, "but like her, you play a game with society. In the play Fanny felt the need to keep her marriage a secret."

"Ah, yes. I see." She was silent a moment. "Well, at least it is a comedy and not a tragedy. Though I suppose you could make the same case for Romeo and Juliet. That they felt the need to keep their relationship a secret."

"We are not young, plagued by warring families or in love."

"Remind me of that, will you, when this seems entirely too complicated a charade."

She laughed a little as though it was a joke and he smiled, but it was the first time in the weeks they had been together that she had ever implied she was less than comfortable with their arrangement.

"Would you like to leave now?" She held up her cloak.

He took it. The cloak was a light wool with a silk lining. The weave was fine, soft to the touch. He suspected it was as soft as her skin would be. As much as he might have liked to test the theory, he did no more than drop the cloak around her shoulders.

They found a crowd still on the stairs, and waited, Grace chatting with an acquaintance as he considered her comment about their "charade."

If she was not entirely satisfied with their arrangement, then it showed they shared something beyond an appreciation of Garrick's plays. He hated the constraints of his position, and attending the opera was the least of them.

For a man who had spent most of his life in charge, taking orders from a woman was a dramatic change. Yes, he had always had to obey orders as well, but he had never been so low in rank that there were not others to obey him. It made him realize that the chain of command was a salve to the self-worth of a man. Now he was in a position where he took orders from someone who was more comfortable holding a reticule than a sword.

Hardly onerous, yet still, at times, maddening. Especially the way she phrased things as though he had a choice. "Shall we leave?" Or "Would you like some supper?"

Lindsay had watched her with the others she employed, and, as she was with him, she was unfailingly courteous. But probably like her other servants, he had learned to take her questions as they were intended: All that mattered was what *she* wanted to do, and *when* she wanted to do it.

How did the others handle fatigue that came with a teething baby? How did they handle worry about responsibilities that had nothing to do with employment but were what made it so necessary?

In the army he was focused on one thing only. His loyalties were not split between a family that wanted to know every detail of his life away from them and a woman who never asked about his life in the hours they were not together.

When it became unbearably irritating, like tonight, he would remind himself that in time he would sell his commission and leave her employ. It was an option that the others did not have.

He watched as she laughed at something and could not help but smile. He looked around and saw several others turn toward the sound. Her laughter was one of the most charming things about her. Always genuine and inviting, so that anyone who heard it wanted to be part of her party.

Her laughter and inquisitive mind were not the only things that made his employment bearable and, when he was less tired and frustrated, fair compensation for her maddening version of leadership. Grace Anderson found good almost everywhere. And if she could not see the good in something, she would wish for it. How many times had she said "I wish . . ."?

There was a long list of changes she would make if she had Poppy's magic coin. The Prince Regent would be more attentive to his wife, the Luddites would end their unrest, her aunt would let her son live his own life.

He watched as she complimented Mrs. Schuster on her earrings, truly the only item she wore that suited her. Which only proved his point that Grace could find good almost anywhere.

Satisfied that he had talked himself out of his ill humor, Lindsay moved to rejoin Grace.

"Fine Season for you, Lindsay. Eh?"

Fetters might be talking to him, but he was watching Grace with interest, and Lindsay could hardly miss his meaning. He decided to ignore the man.

"We could make a wager. Just between the two of us. A hundred guineas that you two are leg-shackled before Christmas."

"Do you know how to say anything that does not begin or end with a wager?" Lindsay kept his tone civil, but he trusted that his irritation was clear. "You are an embarrassment to society. Move out of my way."

"Looking for a little fun, that's all. All the young chits are paired up and the Season is only half over. It will be damn dull if I can't stir things up a bit. No need to take offense. It's a sure thing for you. You're as close as two pistols in a gun case."

"Fetters, I am not wasting money betting with you, not on anything."

"It would be quite a coup for an army major to marry such a wealthy widow. No money problems ever again. If you don't want to spare the blunt you could always wager that." He flicked a finger at the Waterloo medal.

He grabbed Fetters' arm and squeezed so hard that the man gasped. "This medal represents something you will never understand, Fetters. Thousands of men died so that you can spend your life making ridiculous wagers. You can insult me all you want. But you will treat this medal and Lady Anderson with the respect they deserve."

Finally he let go of the man. Grace was still talking to a group of women and had not seen their exchange. Several others had. *Wonderful,* he thought, praying the conversation would not find its way to the gossip sheets.

As he and Grace reached the lobby, they could see that a heavy rain was what had slowed the departures. Rain was common enough in London. In this case it was the cap on an evening that had been anything but perfect.

Grace turned to him. "Would you like to come to Norfolk Street with me? Then I can have the coachman take you home. It will save your uniform from the wet."

He bent closer to her so that no one would overhear. "If they see us leave together then we will be the next bit of gossip."

"Do you care what they think?" she asked, then waited the barest of moments before turning to the door the porter was holding for them.

As usual she expected no answer from him, but it was all he could do not to give one anyway. *No, madam, I am being well paid to not care what society thinks, but for once I would like to be the one making the decisions.*

The ride to Norfolk Street was silent. The rain beating on the carriage roof made any but the most perfunctory conversation difficult, and Grace seemed lost in thought.

He watched her through half-closed eyes. There was some internal debate going on, and he did not have to ask to know that he was at the heart of it. As the carriage made the turn from North Audley to Green, she turned to him. "Would you like to come in for a brandy?"

This one was different from the usual question, tentative and uncertain.

"If that is what you would like, my lady." What exactly did she want? She had never offered such an invitation before. They had thoroughly dissected the play. What was there left to do this evening? He grimaced at his naïveté.

"Major?"

He came back to the moment and realized that he had not heard her reply.

"What I wish," she repeated with some brusqueness, "what I wish is that you do what you wish."

A choice? She was giving him a choice? He did not have to think. "Then no thank you, my lady. I am needed at home." It was a lie. He was saying no only because he could.

Completely mortified, Grace tried for a casual "Very well," and hoped that he could not feel her chagrin. She wanted nothing more than to be out of the carriage, away from him, but it was clear that Petkin had not heard their arrival. The coachman jumped down and hurried to the door to rouse the butler, or at least find an umbrella.

The silence grew, and Grace's embarrassment gave way to a fury out of all proportion to his refusal. He was a complete and utter idiot. His instant "No" seemed so instinctive that she could only assume he had taken a dislike of her. Now he was pretending she did not exist.

"Major."

He was staring out the window, but with a slowly drawn breath he abandoned his study of the rain-soaked street and gave her his full attention.

"Perhaps you are bored with our arrangement. Shall we say good-bye as well as good night?"

He gave no sign that he understood her but stared into her eyes, infuriating her all the more, something she had not thought possible. "Is that a yes or a no, Major Lindsay? Have you had enough of this game—is that what your refusal means? I hate it when you expect me to read my mind. I would rather you yell at me, abuse me with words, than suffer this contest of wills."

He nodded slowly, and when he spoke it was with a

calm that was worse than a shout. "I would only bid you good night, madam."

He looked away from her again, and she saw that those few words had been a terrible blow to his pride. He did, after all, need the work. Need the money she paid him. This was not about his sensibilities, but his livelihood. How could she have forgotten that?

"I will see you tomorrow, then. At eight."

He nodded, and she admitted to herself that her own pride had been bruised. "The Prince Regent is expected to make an appearance. I want you to look your best."

He nodded again, his face still without expression. She turned toward the carriage door and the umbrella Petkin held out, wishing that her order had sounded more authoritative and less petulant.

Ten

It could be a very awkward evening, Grace decided. Unleashing anger, and then not apologizing for it, was as forbidden as picking roses from her mother's garden. It was also rather exhilarating.

Lindsay had come without his medal.

"The ribbon was too frayed and must be replaced."

"Is it? Did you bring the medal with you? I can send Petkin for a new ribbon."

"I left it with my man. He's been tending my uniform for years."

He glanced away from her as he spoke, and she was sure he was lying. He'd left the medal home solely because she had told him, demanded, that he look his best. In the military that would be called something heinous, she was sure—denying a direct order? And punishable by something equally awful. Whatever it might be, it was not an option for her. She waited until he looked at her again.

"I am disappointed. Very." Why was it that she was the one who sounded defiant?

He did no more than bow to her.

Clearly she did not have what it took to be an effective officer, for she had no idea how to handle this. She opted for escape. "Shall we go?"

Lindsay turned with the barest of nods and opened the door before Petkin could be called. The coachman held the carriage door, and she did not speak again until they were both seated.

"Major, would you please check the latch on my necklace? It feels loose."

She watched his hands while he pulled off his gloves and then turned her back to him, loosened her cloak and bent her neck so he would have a clear view of the necklace. It was still light out, but inside the carriage it was dim, and only now did she realize Lindsay would have to feel the clasp with his hands.

Grace had intended the request as a set-down, but the feel of his fingertips brushing her skin made her forget the need to remind him of his place.

Had any man ever touched her there before? Surely she would recall. His fingers left an exquisite fire on the back of her neck, a fire that warmed her from head to toe. She wished he would press his lips to the same spot. She closed her eyes and imagined the pleasure. Then she would turn into his arms and press her mouth to his. Her whole body responded to the fantasy. Oh dear, oh my, *this* was what lust felt like.

"Your necklace seems quite secure, my lady."

He was either exerting great control or was totally unmoved. Was that possible? For one party to be on fire and the other uninterested? Of course it was.

She turned and straightened her skirts, making sure that no part of even her clothing touched him. She endured that for a full five minutes before she felt more herself again.

Herself. Whoever that was. A widow, largely happy, interested in all manner of things, and, at the moment, tired of being angry with the one person who seemed to enjoy the same things she did.

She turned to him. "I declare you the winner."

"I beg your pardon, my lady?"

She really was beginning to hate those two words. Why would he not call her Grace? "I said that you are the winner." She let out a puff of breath that was as much annoyance as frustration. "I am tired of being in your bad books. I have never actually lost my temper with anyone before. And this is the second time I have done so with you. It takes entirely too much energy and ruins my sleep. So, I am sorry that I was rude last night. Sorry that I asked what you wanted to do and then was offended when it was not what I wanted to do."

Lindsay regarded her with some confusion. True, she did not sound gracious in her apology—there was too much of an edge to her voice—but she *was* speaking English.

"I beg your pardon, but did you say that you have never lost your temper before? Is that what you said?"

"Yes. At least not since I was mature enough to learn self-control."

He shook his head, but said nothing.

"And now you are not even going to accept my apology, Major? Is that some sort of military training? Never concede?"

He did not answer immediately, but took both her hands and kissed each in turn. Though his expression still bordered on amazement, there was humor in his eyes. "Grace Anderson, it has been my ambiguous pleasure to introduce you to your first burst of temper. May there be many more."

"What does that mean?" Now she was the one who was confused. It was hard to be detached when the object of annoyance was holding your hands. It felt almost as good as his touch on her neck.

"It means that no one should go through thirty years of life with such careful control of her sensibilities."

"One of the differences between men and women, Lindsay. I suspect that most women who are dependent on men control their feelings. I've spent most of my life keeping peace, making sure that my father or my brother and then my husband was happy, comfortable and, heaven forbid, not angry with me. Or anyone else."

"Like a junior officer with never a chance of promotion."

"If you say so."

"But you see, my lady, the roles are reversed now. You are the one in charge and I am the one who lives to see that you are happy and comfortable and, heaven forbid, not angry at me."

"How odd," she said, considering his words, "but I see that you are right." She laughed a little. "Perhaps that was the real reason I gave into the anger last night. To lose some of that self-control with someone I felt"—she paused, searching for the right word—"someone I felt safe with."

The word hung between them for a moment. She felt safe with him? How could any woman be so completely wrong? Safe? When all he wanted to do was lay her on the carriage seat and ravish her. That was what the anger was a cover for—for both of them, he suspected. Surely she knew that as well as he did. He cleared his throat and tried a smile. "As I said, it was my pleasure."

"Surely you do not mean you *liked* my ill temper?"

"No." He could at least be honest about this. "But it did make a refreshing change from your inclination to phrase all your wishes as questions." When she would have spoken, he raised his hand. "I see now where that comes from: a lifetime of caution, trying to appear thoughtful, while still making your wishes known."

"That makes me sound like one of those managing women that are so unappealing."

"Not at all. More like someone who feels the need to be circumspect." He stopped, realizing how carefully she did protect herself, how guarded she was except around friends or in the security of her home. Did she even grasp that he was another line of defense between herself and society? Probably not, since he himself had only this moment realized it.

She was watching him, waiting for more. But he was not sure how she would react to his revelation and chose to keep it to himself.

"My lady, I can see that your urge to please is much too well developed. Feel free to irritate me as often as you wish."

She laughed at this absurdity.

He leaned closer and pressed his mouth to hers, because he could no longer resist the look in her eyes, the invitation in her laugh. No coyness from his lady—another convention ignored. She leaned closer, her hands pressed between them, then sliding up to circle his neck. She was feminine, soft, willing. He tasted her passion and felt it rising to match his own.

Some small, still rational part of his brain resisted the temptation to deepen the kiss, to take them to a place beyond friendship. They ended this sweetest of kisses three times, but finally, end it they did. Her response touched his heart. He prayed it would not complicate his life too much.

"Ah," she whispered, her mouth still close enough to touch his lips, "I've been wishing that you would do that."

He smiled, a smile he was sure she could feel even with her eyes closed. "Wish or not, I'm not sure that was wise."

He moved away, and she opened her eyes. "Major, I do not think the pleasure of kissing and wisdom can exist in the same world."

He raised her gloved hand and kissed it. "Then the pleasure is mine."

"Not all of it, Major," she said with a mischievous grin.

Eleven

Lindsay heard two female voices in the entry and went to open his study door. "I need to talk to Poppy, Miss Truslow."

"Certainly, Major. As soon as she changes from her play clothes."

"Now, if you please. I would prefer her being dirty to my being late for my next appointment."

"Are you going to see your particular friend, Papa?"

He did not answer her, since that phrase was precisely what he wanted to talk to her about.

She took his hand and sat next to him on the settee. She sat very still and tried for a ladylike appearance, the effort seriously compromised by the dirt on her face and her muddy hem. Had Grace Cardovan looked like this as a child, before her natural enthusiasms were curbed by marriage to Anderson? Yes, it was entirely possible that this was the child's version of her rediscovered joie de vivre.

"Poppy?"

She turned to him with an expression of disdainful interest. He almost laughed out loud.

"Where did you learn that expression? Certainly not from Miss Truslow." At least he hoped not.

"From my friend Verity's governess. I was trying to look like she does when she comes to the park and Miss Truslow talks to her."

Miss Truslow must be desperate for friends, Lindsay thought.

"I think I like Poppy's smile much better."

She grinned, and he nodded his approval.

"So, Poppy." He cleared his throat and considered the best approach to the somewhat delicate subject. "I understand that you have been telling your friends some amazing stories."

"I have?"

"Yes. That your papa is going to be married and soon you will have a mama."

Poppy sat back and began to bounce her feet against the edge of the settee. "It is not a made-up story, is it? You do have a particular friend, and why else would you spend so much time with a real lady if you did not wish to marry her?"

A real lady? He could speak on that subject for an hour. He had met a dozen of society's "real ladies" who were more whore than Poppy's mother had been. He would, however, leave that discussion to Miss Truslow.

"Because I am seeing someone does not mean that I will marry her. Listen to me carefully, my girl: You must stop expecting me to bring a mama home to you."

"I do not precisely expect it, Papa. It's more like a wish." She nodded as if that was the perfect explanation, and stopped thumping her feet. "Like a wish."

"I see. Then shall I give your coin back to you so you can make the wish?"

"No, Papa, I already made one. You must keep the coin and give it to someone else. Do you remember I wished for a mama and a papa? But I told you that only part of it came true, and now I see that the other part will too."

"No, Poppy. It will not. Miss Truslow is as close to a mama as you will come."

"You are going to marry Miss Truslow?" She was wide-eyed with surprise.

"No, I am not." He closed his eyes and prayed for the right words. "I am not going to marry anyone. Do you understand that?"

"Yes, Papa."

"And you must stop telling your friends that it will happen. That is one way that very nasty gossip begins. And no true lady spreads gossip. Miss Truslow will agree with me on that."

"But Papa, if you sell your commission and have some money, then can you marry someone?"

"Where did you hear that?" He was going to have to curtail trips to the park if marriage and money were all they discussed there.

"I asked Jesseck how rich we were and he said that as soon as you sell your commission we will be quite comfortable."

"Am I all that anybody in this house talks about?"

"No, Papa. Sometimes we talk about Billy's new teeth."

That was a relief. Dared he hope that when Billy began to crawl it would push his papa to second place? "Yes, Poppy, we will be quite comfortable when I sell my commission, but that has nothing to do with the possibility of marriage."

"Why would she not want to marry you? You are very handsome and have the Waterloo medal."

"Because we are only friends, Poppy." This was worse than being questioned by the General. "It is all that we want to be to each other."

"Oh, like Jesseck and Miss Truslow. They take tea together, but Jesseck would rather hold Nancy's hand."

"Is that so?" Jesseck and Nancy. There was his own lit-tle bit of gossip.

The new clock in the hall struck the hour and Lindsay realized that he was on the verge of being embarrassingly late for his ride in the park with Grace. "I have to leave now. Do we understand each other, daughter?'

"Yes, Papa. I will stop talking about a new mama until you sell your commission." She spoke the last as though her patience with the process was a challenge.

Lindsay nodded and sent her off to clean up for supper. It was not the complete capitulation he had hoped for, but since it might well take years to sell his commission he would leave it at that.

He made his way to Norfolk Street, relieved to find that Grace was late herself. He spent some time with Cardovan, talking over the war years yet again. Cardovan spoke of the Peninsula as if they had been there yesterday. For his part, Lindsay had done his best to forget the misery of the win-ters.

"Can hardly help but think of it these days, Major. The dedication of the Waterloo Bridge is upon us."

"On the second anniversary of the battle."

"I've decided that I will go. Have no medal to show, but think I need to be there." He thumped his cane against the side of the chair. "You know, for all the men who are not there."

"Yes, George, I do know." He tried to think of some-thing to lighten the atmosphere. "Do you think they would have had the ceremony on the anniversary of Waterloo if we had fought on the eighteenth of February instead of the eighteenth of June?"

His question had the desired effect, and he left Car-dovan laughing.

The park was crowded. He and Grace sat in the open carriage even though they could have walked faster than the equipage progressed.

That one burst of temper, or perhaps the kiss, had cleared the air for the last week. He had joined her for brandy twice since that first ill-fated invitation. But there had been no more kisses.

Once Cardovan had joined them, and had spent an hour giving them all the details of a visit by Colonel Wendle, the battalion commander of the 28th.

The other time they had been alone, if you did not count the butler coming in with brandy and then with some cakes and then with word that the rain had let up and would the major be wanting a carriage.

"We seem to be drawing some stares today. Do I have dirt on my face?" She turned toward him and they smiled at each other. He shook his head, and she shrugged.

He knew why people were watching, and it was not because Poppy had made him self-conscious. Each dance, each dinner, each time they were together they were more drawn to each other. He felt as though she were a flower opening to the sun and he were a bee who longed to sip nectar. And that bad bit of poetry was more than enough to convince him that he was in danger of compromising the single thing that kept his employment honorable.

They could have found privacy if they had wanted it, but the lingering power of their first kiss made him, at least, fear the consequences of the next one. If he gave in to the wanting, if he took her and all she was offering, he would lose all respect for himself. Being cautious enough for both of them was infinitely better than saying good-bye.

Twelve

"We must leave now. If we wait any longer the Waterloo Bridge will be opened without us, and I do so want to see the Prince Regent," Grace said, urging them from the table and the meal she hoped would hold them through the afternoon. "George, would you like the last bit of wine?"

"Grace, this will guarantee that I sleep through the entire event." He leaned as if to speak confidentially, but did not lower his voice. "And I snore."

They were a merry group. George seemed to be in better humor than he had been for months. His mother was so pleased by her son's good spirits that she did not need wine to feel light-headed. Grace had plans of her own. Plans she had shared with no one but Kitty, who was given the day and night off to celebrate as she wished.

"I tell you what, George, you sit near Lindsay and he will nudge you if you nod off." She glanced over at the major to see if he would agree, and shook her head.

Lindsay was slumped down in his chair pretending he was already asleep, then an indelicate snore made the other two laugh. Rousing from his supposed stupor, he looked around. "What did I miss?"

They all crowded into the carriage, still laughing, and settled for the ride to the river and the Waterloo Bridge, the newest and most graceful addition to the river scene.

It was a day filled with extremes. Tears and laughter, cheers and solemn attention. The bridge was named for the battle so "that posterity would remember the great and glorious achievement." The tolls were excused for this first day and the span was crowded as people made the trip from the end of the Strand to Lambeth and back. It was slow progress, whether on foot or by carriage, but no one complained.

Grace declared that they would join the parade. Aunt Louise insisted that George put his leg up, and it was a testament to the overall good humor, or perhaps the wine, that he allowed her to fuss over him.

George rested his leg on the opposite seat. It meant that Grace and the major had to sit very close together. Grace loved the feel of Lindsay beside her, the way his broad chest made her feel safe and cared for. He put his arm along the cushions behind them in an effort to give her an inch more space, and the feeling of safety changed to a thrill of awareness.

The open carriage made the two men in uniform available to the crowd, and everyone from their friends to the lowliest flower seller paid their respects to the two soldiers who, as one man said, had "made England safe for the next hundred years." He included George in the praise despite his lack of a Waterloo medal. Today, any man in uniform was a hero.

There was a fair set up to the southeast of the bridge, and Grace was delighted when her suggestion that they stop a while was well received.

She and Lindsay made their way through the fair, his medal drawing so much attention that finally he took it off and stuffed it in his pocket. The crowd was a mix of every class and calling; it was one of those rare days when all of London gathered, remembering the celebration of the war's end a year earlier and determined to reprise the good feelings of peace and a secure future.

There was the occasional scuffle. When fists were flying very near where they stood, Lindsay leaned down to her. "Do you want to leave? It is a bit close here."

"No." She laughed as a missed punch resulted in a very comic tumble. "It gives me an excuse to hold on tight to you."

There were jugglers, trained animals and an illusionist who held their attention for so long that he asked them if they were interested in an apprenticeship.

When they shook their heads, the illusionist asked if Grace would like to assist him. She really did want to go, but her aunt hissed in her ear, "That is unacceptable, Grace." And the major held fast to her arm when it appeared she might have stepped forward anyway.

As they watched the young girl who took her place, Grace turned to Lindsay. "Do you believe in magic?"

He watched the lowering sun as it lit her from behind, creating an aura of light around her. Gradually the crowed faded away, until it was just the two of them. He must have watched her for a long time, because finally she whispered, "Are you not sure or have you forgotten the question?"

"Do I believe in magic?" If she meant the absurd wish that had brought them together, he could not deny it. But she had never heard of Poppy, much less Poppy's coin. "Do I believe in magic? See, I did hear your question. And my answer is no. What we saw are tricks that fool the eye."

"No, not what he does, for you are right, that is only illusion. I mean the kind of magic that changes your life."

He could feel Poppy's coin heavy in his pocket. "Well, I do believe in miracles."

"You do?" With unspoken agreement, they moved away from the exhibition and toward the spot where the carriage awaited them.

"You cannot see the amazing ways people survive in war and not believe in miracles."

"But not magic?" She did not wait for him to answer. "Well, I believe in magic, Major." She said it as though she was ready for a great debate. She turned to him, "Could it be that that magic is a miracle without God's blessing?"

"That sounds slightly pagan, my dear."

She looked at him in some surprise. What had he said? Surely she realized he did not really believe her a pagan?

"You may be right, my lady. Without God's intervention I suppose magic could be used for both good and ill." For he and God knew that the magic of Poppy's coin had been both a blessing and a bane.

Mrs. Cardovan ran into some friends who invited her to join them for the fireworks. Initially, she refused, insisting that she needed to escort her son home, but she was easily convinced when Lindsay insisted that he could give George all the help he needed. Neither man was particularly interested in the display, having seen too many of the bombardments they imitated, enough to last a lifetime.

They were as silent on the ride home as they had been talkative earlier. George made to speak at least once but both men could see that Grace was lost in thought, her face so clearly determined that they knew it must involve something serious. Whatever George had to say, he thought better of it, leaving Lindsay to wonder exactly what Grace was thinking.

Thirteen

Grace was determined to take advantage of this opportunity. She would make her own magic and hope for a miracle.

When they reached the house, Cardovan brushed Lindsay's assistance aside and seemed quite able to make his way up the front steps. Once through the door they all handed cloaks and hats to Petkin and, to Grace's surprise, George abandoned his cane.

With Lindsay at his side, he made his way up the stairs, if not with speed then with surprising ease.

Grace followed them as they proceeded up to the second-floor bedrooms but went into her own room at the back of the house. It was a long while before she heard Lindsay's footsteps. Opening her door, she called to him, "Major, is he all right?"

Lindsay shook his head. "Why does he even use the cane?" he said as he came to her door.

"I told you before, Aunt Louise is a loving mother, but

much too protective of him. And he is a loving son who wishes to make his mother happy."

"No wonder he prefers the army."

"No mothers there?"

The major nodded with a smile. She loved that smile, the way it made her feel that her words were an echo of his thoughts. Grace took a deep breath. "My maid is off tonight. Would you help with my stays?"

His smile vanished. "You want me to come into your bedroom?" He spoke the words slowly, as though he did not quite understand the concept.

"Yes, please. I hardly want to unlace them in the hall." When he said nothing she stepped back into her room, leaving the door open. She was terrified, but reminded herself that all she had asked for was help with her stays. No more.

He came in behind her and stood by the door. "Are there not other maids?"

Grace did not answer him, only walked back to the door and closed it. "Shall I wake them?"

When he did not answer, she turned her back so that he could begin to undo the buttons of her dress. It took an interminable amount of time, the silence complete save only for the sound of their breathing. His was a little ragged, and she almost told him to leave and that she would wait for her aunt.

Then her dress was loosed and she let it slide down her arms so he could easily reach the corset laces. She could feel the tips of his fingers as they worked the silk strings, each touch making her want more. It took him a moment to realize that he must undo them completely for her to remove the garment.

The last of the laces slipped through the holes and Lindsay grasped her shoulders and turned her to him. "God, Grace, what kind of test is this?"

"Test?" she whispered even as his mouth silenced hers with a desperate kiss.

At first the embrace was arousing, she half undressed, he fully clothed. It was like the conqueror demanding his prize. His touch reached into her with such power that she almost let him have his way, let him take her as though there was nothing more between them than lust. But there was something here beyond the anticipated pleasure. She could feel it in the way his arms held her, the way his body pressed hers. This was as much about anger as it was about sex.

"Stop, David," she whispered in his ear, not afraid, not yet; she would only be afraid if he did not stop. "Please, stop, David," she whispered again, near heartbroken for him.

He pulled away from her with a frustrated groan that held the echo of his rage. He did not let her go. Instead he leaned his forehead on hers and they stood together, until his breathing steadied, his bruising hold the only sign that he was still angry. *"Angry" is too gentle a word,* she thought, infuriated, disgusted.

She leaned back, and his grip eased. "I am so sorry, David. Sorry for teasing you when I did not mean to. I truly did not intend that at all. Kitty did have the evening off. But I did not quite know how to tell you that we would be undisturbed."

He said nothing. That was his way, she realized, when he was trying not to say something that would hurt her. He was such a gentleman. Most of the time.

He stepped away from her. "Good night then, my lady."

She nodded, trying to decide whether to speak or not. Either way it would change them forever. If she held silent he would never be more than an employee. Or she could share more of herself than she ever had with any man. She had to decide in the time it took for him to walk to the door.

His hand was on the latch before she spoke.

"I understand, you know." She pulled the shell of her dress over her nakedness.

With the door opened a crack, he turned back to her. "I think not, my lady."

"Then you must think again." She paused, trying for a practical tone, failing completely. "I understand exactly how it feels to be wanted only for your body. How humiliating it is, how used you feel."

The space of the room was between them, but she had his attention. "It was that way for most of my marriage. Oh, at first I could pretend that Anderson felt some regard for me. But I should have known better when he never once considered my—" Grace stopped herself. That was entirely too personal.

"For him sex was all about creating an heir. And in that I proved to be a disappointment. He married me for a son, because his father insisted it was time for him to get an heir.

"He did not care a whit that I enjoyed the theater, disliked eating before noon and the very idea of boxing. He only cared that I was young enough to bear a dozen children. But in ten years of marriage I had only four pregnancies, and all of them ended in miscarriage."

"Stop, Grace." He closed the door and moved back into the room. "You do not have to relive that life."

She looked away from his sympathy. It was not what she wanted. "No, I will tell you. I suppose it is like reliving a battle you would as soon forget, but I owe you this much, so that you can understand."

"Understand what? That you have lived through your own hell?"

"No, why I hired you. Why I never want to marry again. Why, until I met you, even the thought of a lover was distasteful."

He came closer, and it made it more difficult to speak. She could feel his distress. His now mixed with hers.

"I knew what my duty was, and he was never cruel. But it was as though I was a broodmare and of no other value. There was not a person at Beauville that did not know and did not measure my worth by my failure. No matter that I visited the sick or learned the servants' names. Because there was no heir I lost their respect.

"Oh, David, I know how awful it can be, but now I see that there is a big difference between knowing and understanding. I am sorry, sorry from the deepest part of my heart." She wanted to turn away, to recoup some of her detachment, to, quite literally, put some distance between them, but she would not allow herself even that small comfort.

"He was a fool."

"He was a man." No sooner had she spoken than she realized the insult. She opened her mouth to take the words back and realized David was smiling. He lowered his head and raised his hand to hide his amusement and took a long moment to recover himself. When he looked up all humor was gone, his expression loving and filled with anguish.

"Do not apologize, Grace." He came closer and took her hands, kissing each one as he had once before. "I want to thank you. You have given me so much. Much more than money. You have shown me that there is a place for me in a world without war. That what so many died for was worth preserving, even for a silly fop like Fetters, but especially for women like you, your aunt and the dozens of others I have met these last four months."

"You make it sound as though I considered you some sort of charity. David, you are the best friend I have ever had. It was hardly a burden sharing the Season with you." Why did this sound like a farewell? Something in his expression, his tone, his words? All of them, she realized.

"There is one thing more we can share." He pulled her into his arms. He slipped her dress from her shoulder and pressed a kiss there. "And Grace, I have no desire for an heir. There is not money to leave one, after all, and my life is full enough without one."

"I did not hire you to be my lover," she said.

He gave her a look that challenged her claim, and she let him slip the dress down farther.

"Though, David, I must admit that I lost sight of that the first time you kissed me."

He kissed the spot that he had uncovered. "A dangerous admission, Grace."

She smiled and bobbed her head.

"Very dangerous when you are mostly disrobed." He took her in his arms and kissed her lightly.

It was an invitation, and she accepted it. In moments she was dressed only in her chemise and stockings. She stayed his hand and played his valet, helping him out of his coat and then going to work on the buttons of his shirt.

He took her hands from his shirtfront. "Now is not the time to be a lady, my darling. This is not about a dozen fine buttons." He made quick work of the shirt, as she did her stockings.

She was sure she blushed when he drew the chemise over her head, but then it was about touching, feeling his skin against hers, his heart thundering, hers answering. There was nothing familiar about this. And Grace knew that love and lust made this as different from what she had known before as the difference between homespun and silk.

They were both experienced in the mechanics, but both novices when it came to love. It was exquisite and basic, torture and pleasure and finally release and a sunburst of pleasure that bound them, eclipsing all other experience.

She must have fallen asleep, though not for so long that she woke up disoriented. She knew exactly where she was and who she was with. She turned her head to look at him. He was deeply asleep, as though the act had exhausted him, exhausted more than his body. Her own felt well used, not hurt at all but as though she had not done this in a long time. One husband and one lover in fourteen years was hardly excess.

Lying next to him was as lovely as the pleasure he had

shown her. Feeling safe, secure. And more than that. Feeling a oneness with him, as though the places where they touched now—along the leg, at the shoulder—made them one. Even with only his deep, exhausted breaths beside her, she felt the union.

David Lindsay was everything she could want in a lover. In a companion.

But perhaps not in a husband. Not that his poverty mattered. She was wealthy enough for two.

No, she would not marry him because once she did, he would be the one in charge. She would be the one who must make him happy, who must obey his wishes and subdue her own. She liked her life as it was. If there were a chance for children she might think differently, but she was realist enough to know that there was little hope of that. One husband was enough. A lifetime of lovers would be far more satisfying.

At this moment, though, she could not imagine that lifetime filled with anyone but him.

She smiled, and then her eyes filled with tears. Oh dear. She had not done this since childhood. Felt so much happiness that tears slid down her cheeks. This was different, completely different from heartbreak. This was the heart overflowing with joy.

When had those happy tears stopped? Sometime after her marriage. Never once had she felt this with her husband. But then they had never made love. Despite the fact David was being paid, this was a more personal, intimate act than she had ever shared with her husband. She edged closer to his side and touched her lips to his shoulder.

Fourteen

Lindsay opened his eyes, instantly alert.

"Is that something you learned in the army? To come awake so quickly?"

He did not answer her, but stared at her as if trying to absorb every detail of her beside him. The silence drew out and Grace's own smile faded when he did not return it.

"This is the end, Grace."

"What do you mean? Was it that awful? I thought you found as much fulfillment as I did." She knew she was blushing, and knew why. Being naked together had been perfect until he had spoken. Now it felt all wrong.

"It was . . ." He bit off whatever he was going to say, and the tenderness that went with it. "It was very satisfying."

"'Very satisfying'?" It might have moved her heaven and earth but his was still solidly in place. She made to turn away from him, angry and chagrined both.

He pulled her back to him and kissed her. "I lied. It was wonderful." He kissed her again, this time longer and with rising passion. "You are the answer to my dreams. You are everything a man could want. I could love you again now, tonight and for a hundred years and it would not be enough." He kissed her one more time, lightly, and even though it was a bare touch of the lips she felt it in the deepest part of her, which still echoed with pleasure. He pulled the coverlet over her and sat up on the edge of her bed. "But this is the end, my lady."

He looked at her even as he pulled his clothes from the floor and began to dress. "You must know that I can no longer accept money from you, work for you—not when it comes to this."

"To what?" She did not mean to sound confused, but had he not just said that he wanted her?

"Do you now see that I am no better than a well-paid whore? Or perhaps a courtesan, as you once said."

She was at a loss for words, her happy tears evaporating.

"It is more than my self-worth can tolerate. It would be different if I had sold my commission and could come to you with some money of my own. But that has not happened; God only knows if it ever will. It is one thing for society to think we are lovers—I have no control over what others think. But now it is the truth."

"But it happens. We could name many couples so engaged."

"But how many men are paid for their night's work, Grace?"

She shook her head, knowing any answer would be the wrong one.

"Put yourself in my place. Tell me, how would you feel?"

She had deliberately avoided the thought.

"It is degrading. And I will have no more of it. I needed employment and so I accepted what you offered. But no need is worth this compromise of my honor."

"Then we can go back to the way we were before. Friends."

"Yes, I can see from your expression that you know as well as I do that is impossible." He came to her and pulled her from the bed and kissed her ruthlessly. The kiss trapped them both. She could feel his arousal and her own hunger. He stopped the kiss and pushed her away, none too gently. "This will always be there between us."

He returned to his shirt buttons and then reached for his cravat.

"I will not let you go."

He whirled back to her with his jacket in hand. "You have no choice in this. I am no longer your employee. You may command, but I am no longer compelled to obey." He had his jacket on, was across the room and out the door before she could think of any argument that might sway him.

She lay back down on a bed that was too big and cold without him, to a world that was made too small without him to laugh with. She moved over to feel the linen that still held his warmth, and the tears that trickled out of her eyes were not from an excess of happiness.

He had not been thinking with his brain but with his body, and, oh yes, his heart. No matter why he had made love to her, he could not go back. If he did he would have to live with the gradual destruction of his honor. And it was the only thing he had left. For she had surely taken all of his heart, and part of his soul.

The sounds of her pleasure, the look of complete surprise, had touched his heart as surely as it had aroused his body. Grace Anderson had never known the pleasure of sex before. Married for ten years and like a virgin for all that. And the pleasure had not been one-sided. Her wonder had made him feel powerful. She might have been the one paying for services, but he had been the one in command. He had shown her how fine it could be, and had proved the same to himself.

God help him, his heart ached as though he had taken a

blow to the chest. His mind was a muddle of memories he wanted to relive and banish at the same time. If only he could sell his commission. It was the last bit of magic he would ever ask for.

Grace could not sleep. It was possible that she could never sleep in this bed again. She got up, found a robe and went to the window to draw the curtains, then began to pick up the clothes they had let fall. How she wished she could do this night over. This whole Season. How she wished she had never offered Lindsay employment.

She dropped her clothes on the chair in her dressing room and pulled out her oldest, most comfortable nightgown.

Would she have met him someplace else? Would he have asked her to dance? Could they have reached her bedroom some other way that would not have wounded him so?

She sank into the chair at her dressing table and pulled the last of the pins from her hair, combing it out as she had every night for at least fifteen years. The rhythmic strokes often allowed a contemplation where truth revealed itself. It did not fail her tonight.

She was in love with David Lindsay. Not the man who wore a uniform with pride and a medal as a tribute. Not the man who was always a gentleman. She was in love with the man who had shown her passion. Tonight had been the culmination, but there was more to the passion they shared than sex. He had made her laugh, encouraged her anger, made her feel in ways she'd thought long lost.

She turned from her seat to face the door, seeing him as he said her name that one last time, stone-faced and in control. She knew she would not see him again.

Something lying on the red carpet caught her eye. At the edge of the chair where David had carelessly tossed his uniform, she saw a coin. She bent to pick it up. Certainly it belonged to him, for it was not a coin she recognized. Something foreign, with English on one side.

It was hers now. One little bit of him to keep. She squeezed her eyes shut. Where had her pride gone? She was a mature woman, not greatly experienced, but one who knew the ways of the world.

Yes, she knew the ways of society, but she wanted so much more, had always wanted more. Oh how she wished that he could love her in return. She wished it as much as she wished for children.

Even as she thought how foolish it was to make wishes, when none had ever been granted, the coin warmed her hand. *How odd,* she thought. She studied it more carefully. It was bright and shiny, as though well cared for despite the slight dent, and she wondered if it was some kind of talisman for him.

Had it saved his life? Would David worry when he found it missing?

George would give it to him if she asked. Yes, that is what she would do. She could not trust herself to see him again and not beg for his attention. She owed his honor and her own better than that.

From her point of view love might make all things allowable, but for David Lindsay honor outweighed every other consideration. She would respect that. She would, even if it broke her heart.

Fifteen

He did not want to come back to the house on Norfolk Street, but it would have been insulting to ignore Cardovan's request. Coward that he was, Lindsay waited until he saw Grace and her aunt leave in the carriage, then trusted they would be gone long enough for him to complete his business with George and depart before they returned.

Petkin met him at the door with a smile. "Ah, Major, you have only just missed her ladyship. She and Mrs. Cardovan have gone to the milliner's."

"Thank you, Petkin, but I am come to see Captain Cardovan today."

Petkin took his hat and gloves with an apology for the mistake and went off to see if the captain was available.

Cardovan came back with Petkin. Walking without his cane, looking amazingly fit. There was an air about him, a resolve that gave him the authority he had lost after the misfortune at Ostend.

"Major, come in. I did not expect you so quickly."

Cardovan led him into the library, a room David would have as soon avoided. It reminded him too forcefully of Grace. If he was honest with himself, everything about the place reminded him of Grace, from the bright front door to the whimsical unicorn on the weather vane four floors above them. He should have suggested they meet elsewhere.

He was so lost in thought that he missed the first of Cardovan's words. But he could not help but be brought to the moment when Cardovan finished with ". . . that I might buy your commission."

He must have looked as shocked as he felt, for Cardovan's confidence faded. "It's the real reason I was so pleased by the colonel's visit. He came to see if I was ready to rejoin the regiment. He was actually the one who suggested I consider your commission. Can you believe that?"

Of course he could. But Cardovan gave him no time to comment.

"Even though I missed the whole of the Waterloo campaign, he still wants me with the 28th. He was afraid I was aiming for another regiment. He said that I am the captain he most wants to move up. He says he wants someone who is equal to the challenge of replacing you—not that I think I can." Cardovan reddened a little. "There are two captains senior to me; one is selling out and the other Wendle does not want as a major."

Cardovan paused, and Lindsay grabbed the chance to speak. "That is by all means wonderful, George."

"Then you are sure that you will not regret it?"

Cardovan looked as though it was the height of folly to give up a commission.

"Yes, I'm sure, George. I have responsibilities here now, and ten years in uniform is as much as I wish to test fate."

"I'm not finished. It's because I missed Waterloo." He stopped a moment and considered before he spoke. "Do you think Boney will give us another chance?"

"Pray God, not."

Cardovan nodded and shrugged away his disappointment. One thing they both knew is that there would always be wars.

"I hesitated because I know my mother wants me here with her. But, Lindsay, I cannot live my life because some woman wants me to be safe, even if it is my mother. I hate it here. I want the army life. That's all there is to it."

"I understand completely. But have you told her yet?"

"No." He was smart enough to look slightly worried at the prospect. "I wanted to be sure this was not some fantastic dream."

"The colonel wants you. You hardly need my blessing."

"But I want it, sir. You have been my model for as long as we have served together. Even as an ensign I knew you were the best the 28th had to name."

It appeared as if Cardovan was ready to list his virtues, and Lindsay raised his hand. "Enough, George. The commission is yours and I thank you for the consideration."

As Cardovan chattered on about the new uniform he was to order from Westin and who was the best boot maker, Lindsay realized that this was the George Cardovan he had known in the Peninsula. The man who had spent the last two years in London was a pale imitation. Surely even his mother could see that he was meant for the military life.

They had not been together twenty minutes when he heard voices in the hall.

"I will not be a minute, Aunt. Come into the library while I send Petkin for George."

Suddenly Mrs. Cardovan and Grace were in the room. Grace stopped short when she saw him, George's mother's expression was guarded, but she greeted him with her usual good humor.

Lindsay could see that the impetuous George Cardovan was fully restored. He took his mother's arm. "Come with me, Mama. I must speak with you immediately."

"That would be rude, George. You have a guest."

"Now, Mother."

Lindsay smiled, Cardovan already sounded as though he was in command, and if he could make his mother obey him then the men of the 28th would be child's play.

"Grace and the major are quite capable of finding something to talk about."

With a glance over her shoulder, Mrs. Cardovan allowed herself to be led from the room.

Grace remained near the door, staring at him, still as a statue. Lindsay walked toward her, and his movement seemed to awaken her. She did not approach him but went to the mantel.

"I believe you left this here."

She handed him Poppy's coin and he took it, their hands barely touching.

"Ah, thank you, Grace. I would be lost without Poppy's magic coin."

"It is magic, then? Did it save your life? When I saw the dent in it I wondered."

How could his whole world have changed in less than twelve hours? When he'd walked out of her bedroom he thought he would never see her again. Cardovan's news had changed that. But Grace still looked as miserable as he had been. No wonder Poppy had asked him if he was ill or if someone had died.

"Grace, the first day I saw you, I followed you down Bond Street. You were laughing with Kitty, and that laugh was like a siren's song. It always has been. It always will be. I wanted you from that moment. Just before Fetters performed his version of an introduction, I was thinking that once I sold my commission I would discover an entrée into society and find you."

Lindsay walked over to her and took her hands. They were cold, and he raised each to his lips and would not let them go.

"I've sold my commission, Grace. To your cousin, of all people."

"You've sold it? To George? Why did he wait so long? Did he not know how important it was to you? To us?"

He could have answered each of those questions. He kissed her instead, and felt all the tension melt from her.

"I thought I would never see you again, David."

"I'm so sorry, Grace."

She pressed a kiss to his mouth to silence him. "Your sense of honor is one of the most admirable things about you. Never think you must apologize for it." She leaned back in his arms. "I should be furious with you, with George, for torturing me this way, but I love you too much to be anything but grateful that you are here again." Her kiss proved it, the love pouring from her as it had last night, filling him, making him more completely a person than he had ever been before.

Grace pulled him down onto the settee and sat as close to him as possible without actually being in his lap, though she did seem to be considering that. She nodded at the coin on the table. "Is this really magic?"

"Yes, I think it must be." For his wish had been granted and had brought him to this moment. "Magic, verging on a miracle."

"I wished on it." She leaned toward him and whispered, "I wished that you could love me."

"Oh darling, you did not waste a wish on that, did you? For you have had my heart from the first, and my love not long after. That night you were so angry with me. That first time you did your best to command me to do your bidding? How could I not love someone who was trying so hard?"

"That was the moment you knew you loved me? When you were so angry?"

"And you do not think that love and anger can exist together?"

"Well, yes, they can, since I have felt the same. But will it not make for an unsettled life?"

"It may well, but who could wish for more?"

She shook her head at his optimism but did not argue. There was no need for words. Their kisses ended in laughter, and Grace brushed away what she called her happy tears.

"You know, David, if we had met at some ball or picnic, I would not have let you close to me. You are used to command, and I wanted to be the one in charge. It would have taken no more than one dance for me to see that and to send you on your way."

"You think that what happened between us was meant to be, was the only way for you to come to know me and me to know you?"

"Yes, and I worry even now that we do not know each other as we really are." She was resting her head on his shoulder as she spoke, and he was sure that her worry was not so deep as to be an obstacle, especially since he had thought this through and had an answer.

"I think we have each lived the other's life, Grace. What could be a better way to learn? It is bound to make both of us more understanding. It is not what I asked for, but it is the true gift of that wish."

She stood up then, moved away from him and made a circuit of the room. "Clear thinking is impossible when we are so close. Do you think that door has a lock? I have never had any reason to care before."

As he went to the door, Grace faced her one last fear. David said he would have no money to leave an heir. But leaving money to one's offspring was not the only reason men longed for children.

He would never have a child from her. Heaven had decreed otherwise. They would have to talk about it sometime. But neither one of them had spoken of marriage; perhaps they never would. She would not ruin the joy of the moment. She would be selfish for a little longer before she reminded him that he had to make a choice.

He turned the key with a satisfied "Aha" and pulled it

from the lock. Holding it as though it was a battle prize, he came to her and presented it with a bow.

She took it and set it on the table with the coin, the glitter distracting her just a little. She turned to him. "How did you come to have a magic coin, David?"

"My daughter Poppy gave it to me."

Amazement and a little thread of fear trickled through her.

He stopped kissing her neck. "What is it?"

"You have a daughter?" She moved out of his arms, looked at the coin and wondered.

"Yes. They are not precisely my children. There is Poppy, who is nine, and Billy, who is not quite a year. I am their guardian and will raise them as if they were my own."

He was not smiling, but watching her with an intensity she had not seen before. She realized that he was afraid. "Children were the rest of my wish last night. I wished you would love me as much as I wished for children." She raised his hand and kissed it. "Oh, David, I will love Poppy and Billy. As I would my own."

She flung her arms around him and kissed him fully, then leaned back in his arms. "Why did you never tell me about them?"

"Because you never asked. You were very careful never to ask of my personal life."

"Only because you were so offended at all the information George had given me. You called it spying. After that, I was ever trying to respect your privacy." When he did no more than shake his head, she had to nod in agreement. "No more secrets. Never again."

"Did I hear you say that you would love my children as you would your own? Does that mean you might marry me?" He paused, then added, "Two children are not the traditional wedding gift, but will you at least consider it? I cannot imagine life without you."

This kiss was happiness, pure joy given from one to another. It would anchor their world forever. Another thought occurred to him, and he gave her a devilish smile. "Or can I use the children as a bribe?"

She laughed. "Children? *Two* children? And one is a babe? David, I cannot imagine a better wedding present."

Epilogue

The girl sat in silence as the docent ended his story. "Why, that was wonderful." She leaned forward in her chair. "Is it true?"

When he would have answered, she shook her head. "No, don't tell me. I want to believe that Grace and David are as real as you and I and lived forever happy. Did they ever have any children of their own?" Again she answered her own question. "No, but Poppy and Billy were enough.

"I guess I'd better catch up with Jim," she added, but she didn't move from the seat. The docent waited patiently. The question burst from her. "What do you do when you are just days from leaving a country that calls to your soul? I can't imagine leaving. The thought of Topeka makes me shudder, and not because it's still winter in Kansas."

"Why can't you stay?" the docent asked.

"There's the whole visa thing. Jim says I can come back, but once I'm home there are my sisters and mother and grandmother and best friends from school. Not a one of them would understand. They think Topeka is perfect."

"For them it may be." The docent handed her the coin. "Take this with you as a memento. It will remind you that anything is possible."

"You can't give that away!"

"Of course I can." The docent shrugged. "I can get another one easily."

She let him talk her into it. It was only later, as she sank onto a bar stool at Earl's Place, that she actually considered whether the coin was magic. She put it on the bar in front of her, then picked it up and held it tight. "I wish there was a way for me to stay here." The coin felt warm, but then, the place was filled with people, the room overheated, the crowd cheering as they watched the last minutes of a soccer game.

She hadn't spotted Jim yet, but it hardly mattered. He wouldn't be interested in anything but the score. Instead she watched as the bartender worked his way to her spot at the end of the bar. Not the usual guy. An extra hired because of the crowd? With a practiced efficiency he took orders, got drinks and made change.

He was nice enough looking, and then he smiled. It changed his pleasant face to fabulous. It was a smile that made the world a brighter place and drew an answering one from her.

"What can I get you?"

His accent was different, not at all suited to a pub. This voice belonged at Eton or Oxford. Or somewhere with Prince William.

She pointed to the wine bottle he held, for some stupid reason not wanting to open her mouth and betray the fact she was an American. She'd forgotten about the magic coin and it fell from her hand, rolled along the bar toward him and onto the floor.

She gasped and stood on the stool, trying to see where it had gone.

"Under the cooler." He considered. "Is it important to you?"

"Oh, yes," she answered, "it's very special."

"Right then." He squatted, reaching under the cooler. He looked up at her with a grimace. "Time to do a little cleaning down here." He stretched a little farther and with a triumphant "Yes!" stood up and handed her the coin.

"Thanks," she said, "thanks a lot."

He nodded and held up the wine bottle, and when she said, "Please," he poured her a glass. She reached for her purse, but he waved off payment. "Give me a look at the coin. That's all the pay I want."

She was about to hand it back to him when the room erupted into shouts and cheers. The game was over and any number of thirsty sports fiends surged toward the bar.

"If you like, I can wait until the crowd's gone."

He leaned across the bar and smiled at her. "Great. That's exactly what I wished you would say."

The Passenger

Ruth Ryan Langan

For Jennifer and Betty, who know why.

For Nora, Mary, and Mary Kay—
friends and fellow believers.

And for Tom. Always.

One

"Just one more shot, Josh."

"Josh. Over here."

The crush of photographers stood elbow to elbow, vying for that one special shot of this amazing athlete who had caught the attention of the world's media.

A reporter's voice could be heard speaking into his microphone. "Josh Cramer isn't your typical athlete. A free spirit, he doesn't fit into any mold. Having already set a new world's record for sailing the Atlantic solo, and taking an around-the-world hot air balloon trip, he has now completed his latest adventure, extreme skiing in the Alps. This isn't for the faint of heart. As our viewing audience can see by the footage that has been released, Josh was launched from a helicopter, skiing through narrow passageways that looked for all the world like ice chambers. Josh Cramer's fearlessness, as well as his rugged good looks and charm, have brought him international acclaim."

One of the photographers shouted, "Flash me that winner's smile, Josh."

"No problem." Josh leaned a hip against the skis propped up against the Swiss chalet and tipped down his sunglasses.

Though this session had run hours longer than anticipated, he managed, through discipline, to keep his smile intact.

A photographer leaned in and adjusted his lens. "Show us the gloves, Josh. The ones you always wear for luck."

It was a familiar request, and one Josh had fielded a hundred times or more. Still, each time someone mentioned the gloves, he felt the familiar jolt to his heart.

He reached into his back pocket and held them up.

"Is it true that they belonged to your father?"

"Yeah." His eyes narrowed as he slipped them on. "That's right."

"Now that's the look I wanted. Dark. Dangerous. A little bit introspective." The photographer grinned as he snapped off several quick shots before lowering his camera. "Thanks, Josh."

A short time later, while the photographers hurried away to file their reports and meet their deadlines, Josh made his way inside the lodge and up the lift to his suite, where yet another crowd had assembled.

His agent, Martin Phillips, was holding court before a cluster of reporters and publicity people who were peppering him with questions.

"What's next for Fearless Josh Cramer?"

Josh looked over the crowd, recognized the speaker as a reporter from World Sports, and promptly closed himself in his bedroom. Once there he ripped off his ski gear and pulled on comfortable jeans and a T-shirt before sinking onto the edge of the bed.

His head came up sharply when the door was opened. Martin Phillips paused on the threshold. "Good news. World Sports is calling the article 'Man on the Run.' They assured me that you'll be their lead story and have the cover of their October issue."

"That's great." Josh lowered his voice. "Can we talk, Marty?"

"Yeah. In a minute. There're some people out here you need to meet." His agent caught him by the arm and hauled him to the parlor while calling out to a reporter, "The timing of this photo spread couldn't be better. You'll want to end the article by mentioning Josh's next adventure, which he doesn't even know about yet."

At his words, Josh arched a brow.

"How could he possibly top what he's already done? Don't tell me he's about to leap tall buildings and catch bullets in his teeth before spitting them out."

The reporter's remarks had the entire room full of people laughing.

Martin Phillips joined in the laughter. "You've just described Josh perfectly. He's always up for something different and challenging. Tomorrow he's leaving for the ultimate wilderness trek. No electronics gear. No space-age gadgets. He'll carry a mini-cam and a few basic necessities, but he'll have to survive on what he can catch or kill along the way, until he joins a camera crew at the end of his journey."

Suddenly all business, the reporter's smile faded. "Sounds like something out of a reality television show, without the lifeline of a safety net."

"Exactly." Martin nodded. "I've just finalized the last of the details with SNN, the all-sports news network. If the public likes it, they're hoping to make it a regular series, with Josh in a different dangerous location every month."

One of the photographers turned to Josh. "You don't give yourself much time to relax, do you?"

Josh remained mute while his agent answered for him. "Got to make hay while the sun shines. You didn't call Josh the Man on the Run for nothing. Besides, they made an offer he couldn't refuse. Now gentlemen, if you don't mind, it's been a long day, requiring some superhuman activity. I think it's time we give Josh some space."

As the others set down their empty glasses and began

filing from the room, one of them paused to ask, "Want to meet us in the bar, Marty? Maybe you could fill in a few more details about this latest adventure."

"Sure thing. Publicity is my middle name." While the others chuckled, he glanced at his watch. "I'll see you in an hour."

When the room had emptied, Martin picked up a chilled bottle of water and twisted the cap, draining it in one long swallow before turning to his client.

Josh was sitting on the sofa, staring broodingly into the flames of the fire.

"Okay." Martin sat on the opposite end of the sofa. "Tell me what's wrong."

"A trek through the wilderness?"

Martin grinned. "Look, I know it's not as glamorous as skiing the Alps, but the offer was too good to pass up." He studied Josh's face. "I don't think that's what's bothering you. What is it?"

"I told you not to book anything more. I said I needed some time."

"Time for what?"

"Time for me. Just for me."

"You see? That's the whole idea. That's why I fought so hard to get this for you. After you land in the wilderness tomorrow, you'll have all the time in the world to yourself."

"Yeah. With a camera recording my every move. You know what I mean, Marty. I've been at this for years now, without a break. I'm losing my edge. I need to recharge my batteries."

"Recharge your batteries? Josh, these people are throwing millions of dollars at you for doing what you love."

"I know but . . ."

His agent held up a hand. "If you'd like, stay in your room for the rest of the day. I'll handle the press. Here we are in one of the most luxurious ski resorts in the world. Pamper yourself with room service in front of the fire while you watch the skiers coming down those glorious slopes. Will that give you enough time to get back your edge?"

"You're talking hours." Josh ran a hand through his hair in frustration. "Get serious, Marty. You know what I mean. I need some real time off. I'd like enough time to just be lazy. You know. Doing fun, relaxing things like real people."

"Real people." Martin stood and began to pace. "Listen to me, Josh. The reason you're such a hot property is because you don't live like real people. I don't know anybody else who could take on your adventures and make them look like a walk in the park." He paused, his voice lowering for emphasis. "Don't you get it? People love seeing you sailing solo across the Atlantic, or watching you drop from a helicopter to ski down the Alps, because it's something they couldn't possibly do on their best day. That's the basis of this planned television special. The director is hoping to turn it into a series that will make us both more money than we ever dreamed of. And do you know why? It's because you're what the average Joe will never be. Absolutely fearless."

Josh gave a dry laugh. "Yeah, that's me. Fearless Josh Cramer."

Martin's eyes narrowed. "Are you telling me you're not? That somehow, between yesterday and today you've lost your confidence?"

"Of course not." Josh gave a shake of his head. "It's not fear, Marty." In truth, he couldn't recall the last time he'd experienced real, gut-wrenching fear. He'd always lived for the adrenaline rush that came from placing himself in danger. "I'm just tired. I need a break. Think about it. When was the last time I went out on a date?"

"You want women?" Martin started toward the door. "I can go down to the bar right now and bring you half a dozen gorgeous models who'd like nothing better than to spend the night with Josh Cramer."

"Thanks." His frown was back. "That's not what I mean and you know it."

"Listen." Martin started back to the sofa, using his most persuasive tone. "You just get through this next adventure, and I promise you, I'll pencil in a nice long break."

"Pencil in?"

Martin grinned. "Okay. It'll be written in stone. For as long as you want. How's that?"

"What if they want me to do a series?"

"Then we'll negotiate a contract that allows you some time off between adventures."

"Don't say that unless you mean it."

"I mean it."

For the first time Josh managed a smile. "I intend to hold you to that, buddy boy."

Martin relaxed. "Get some rest, buddy boy." It was their favorite nickname for one another and was a signal to him that Josh's temper was evaporating. "We'll be meeting with the director of the television crew first thing in the morning. You'll need to acquaint yourself with the seaplane you'll be piloting. This is raw wilderness. The only way in or out is by landing on Spirit Lake."

"Is that a problem?"

His agent hesitated for a fraction. "A lot of strange things have happened on that lake through the years."

"What sort of strange things?"

"Boats and planes disappearing, without a trace. Drownings, but no bodies."

Josh sighed. "I'm suddenly starting to like this."

"If you believe in this sort of rubbish, the Native Americans believed the lake to be inhabited by spirits." Marty grinned. "Or it could be just a strong undertow. Either way, I'll admit that when I first heard it, it creeped me out. It still does, if you want to know the truth. But this isn't about me. It's about you. Sounds like you're okay with it."

"Instead of being afraid." Josh chuckled. "I kind of like the added challenge."

"Great. I think seeing Fearless Josh Cramer tame the demons of Spirit Lake will be a good career move."

"Gee, thanks."

At Josh's wry tone, Marty grinned. "Just doing what you pay me for. Can you master the seaplane by morning?"

"Piece of cake."

"That's what I like to hear." Martin walked out, humming a little tune. He'd been managing Josh ever since his meteoric rise to fame ten years ago. When they'd met, Josh had been a cocky college kid who couldn't resist taking on a challenge that most sane athletes wouldn't even consider. Marty had been a brash young lawyer who was already handling some of the biggest names in sports. In the years since, he'd had plenty of time to learn just how to play Josh's many moods.

Time off. He chuckled as he stepped into the lift that would take him to the main floor and his cronies. He had no doubt that one day the public would lose interest and move on to the next media celebrity, though he fervently hoped it wouldn't be for many years. He'd acquired a fondness for the things money could buy. But when that day came, Josh Cramer would find himself with all the time in the world. Until then, Martin would do the job he was being paid to do, and see that he kept Josh too busy to think about the things that he might be missing in his high-profile, celebrity lifestyle. Besides, though Josh would never admit it, he thrived on activity. He'd go stark raving mad if he had to stay in one place with nothing to challenge him. Marty was just doing what his client wanted done. And making a pile of money in the process.

Marty was beaming with pleasure. "Josh, this is Wayne Thompson, who'll be directing the television special."

The director, wearing baggy fatigues and a baseball cap, stepped away from the cluster of sound technicians and camera crew loading their equipment aboard the larger of the two planes parked on the runway, and offered his handshake.

"And this is Brady Stewart." Marty dropped his arm around the shoulders of a tall, white-haired man with a military bearing. "Brady will be piloting the second plane which will trail yours. That way they'll be able to snap some shots of you from the air, and get some aerial shots of the rugged terrain."

Josh arched a brow. "Don't trust me with a camera?"

The director shrugged and glanced at Josh's agent. "I'm aware of your athletic prowess, but I'm not so sure about your photography skills. I want to be certain we have good, clean shots of everything. Later we can splice your photos and theirs together, to make a continuous narrative of your adventure. We'll land with you at your base camp and get as much of the local color as we can while you set off on foot, then we'll fly on to the final destination where you'll meet up with us at the end of your trek."

Marty chuckled. "Since there's room for me, I've decided to go along on the first leg of the trip, too. After that, I'll head to New York."

"Sounds good to me." Josh looked up when one of the assistants approached carrying a clipboard. "Looks like it's time to get aboard and do a final flight check."

He shook hands all around before walking away.

Within the hour he was airborne, with the second plane trailing.

He pressed a hand to the knot of tension at the back of his neck. Though a night at the ski lodge hadn't been nearly enough time to recharge his batteries, it would have to do until this latest assignment was completed. Then he intended to hold Marty's feet to the fire and take some quality time alone.

"Below me is Spirit Lake." Josh flipped the switch that triggered the camera mounted below the belly of the plane and watched the view on a monitor mounted just above his instruments. He'd spent the previous night on the Internet, learning as much as he could about his destination. "Native Americans named it, believing that great spirits dwelled in those depths. It's said to be one of the coldest and deepest glacial lakes in the country. Even the most sophisticated sonar equipment hasn't been able to locate a bottom. What makes this area so exciting is the fact that there are a thousand miles of wilderness without any of the amenities of modern civilization. You see below me no power lines. Although there are a few cabins along the shoreline, most are occupied by rugged individuals strictly in the summertime, since the only way in or out is by boat or seaplane. Winter in this isolation would be pretty brutal."

While circling the lake he switched off the outside camera and turned on the one mounted on the instrument panel. "I'll be taking my seaplane down in just a few minutes, and you, my viewing audience, will be going with me for the ride. I'm looking forward to taking you along on my journey through this forest. I'm told it's so primitive, I might be able to make the entire trek without seeing another human being."

Out of the corner of his eye he caught a flash of shimmering light and turned his head, assuming it was sunlight bouncing off the water far below. Instead he was stunned to see a woman dressed all in white, just settling into the copilot seat beside him.

He had a quick impression of fiery hair and intense blue eyes as he let loose with a string of curses. A stowaway? Some stalker hoping to make a name for herself? Hadn't security checked out this plane before he boarded?

His tone was pure ice. "All right. Who are you and what's your game?"

Her voice, soft, breathy, was little more than a whisper. "Don't worry, Josh, I won't let anything bad happen to you."

"You won't let . . . ?" He swore as turned to the camera. "Brady, as you can see on your monitor, there's a stowaway here in my plane. A lunatic female. When you follow me down, I'll leave it up to you to deal with this nutcase."

Josh's head snapped toward the woman. "Lady, when my companions get through with you, you'll wish you'd never been . . ."

There was a series of beeps before a siren started blaring throughout the cabin. The instruments went crazy, as did the plane, which began spinning wildly out of control.

"Mayday. Mayday." Josh automatically called out the words while he struggled to maintain control of his craft.

The seaplane continued spinning, and as Josh fought to remain focused, he realized that they were too far from shore for a soft landing. Instead, they were about to crash into the forest.

He turned to the woman beside him. "Brace yourself. Make sure your seat belt is secure, and keep your head down."

He saw no fear in her eyes. In fact, the word that came to mind was serene, but he was too busy fighting the controls to risk looking at her again.

Since Brady and his crew were right behind, Josh had no doubt they were witnessing his trouble. They could be down behind him within minutes, ready to help. All he had to do was survive the crash.

Adrenaline pumping, he braced himself for impact. Was this how his father had felt when his plane crashed?

His father.

He reached into his pocket and withdrew the tattered gloves, drawing them on. As always, the mere touch of them against his skin brought a sense of calm.

His passenger reached over and took hold of his gloved hand. Along with the sense of peace, he felt a wave of compassion for this stranger. However foolish she might have been to hide aboard his plane, she didn't deserve this fate.

Too late for recriminations, he realized. Whatever would happen now was meant to happen.

That was his last conscious thought as his plane slammed to the ground and burst into a ball of fire.

Two

Grace Marin stowed her gear on the scarred wooden table in a corner of the cabin before straightening to take a look around. Rustic was too kind a description. This cabin was downright primitive. Log walls, stone fireplace soaring to a loft above, which presumably would offer a place to bunk. The small galley kitchen didn't even have a sink, which meant no running water.

With a shrug she snatched up her camera and made her way outside. She'd stayed in worse places. Her work as a photojournalist for the *World*, an international pictorial magazine, had taken her to mud huts in Africa and tarpaper shacks in South America. She'd learned to survive on a few hours of sleep a night. As for food, her coworkers accused her of having a cast-iron stomach. She could probably eat worms if they were the only food available.

Moving to the end of a long, wooden dock, she sat with her back to one of the piers, staring at the endless stretch of water, and tried to stay focused on the photos she intended to shoot. It wasn't easy, especially since that scene with Richard was still on her mind.

He'd been so angry when he'd learned that she'd accepted this assignment, proving, he said, that her career meant more to her than he did.

He'd been right, of course. Grace had never denied it. But until the words had been spoken aloud, she'd been able to pretend otherwise. Now she needed to face some cold, hard facts about herself. She was a loner. Always had been, and probably always would be. It's what made her so successful in her career, and such a mess when it came to relationships.

With a sigh she returned her attention to the job at hand. She'd fully anticipated spectacular autumn scenery. Aboard the small supply plane that brought her to this isolated spot, she'd been expecting to see a ring of fiery trees reflected in the waters of a clear crystal lake. What she'd found was this dull, almost muddy landscape of colorless trees, a bleak, biting wind whipping the waves into foam, and a sense of foreboding that had her glancing heavenward to check for storm clouds. There were none. The sky was a gray, blank canvas.

This assignment had initially been offered to one of her fiercest competitors, who was beginning to make a name for himself with the readers of the *World*. That fact hadn't been lost on Grace, whose ambition had carried her to the top of her profession. When he'd discovered a conflict of dates, Grace had generously stepped up, even though she'd just returned from an exhausting assignment in the Middle East.

"You need some time off, Grace." Her editor, Mark Wellington, though grateful for her offer, sat flipping through his file of photographers, looking for a replacement.

"Time off for what?" Grace shoved aside a mountain of papers from the chair beside his desk and took a seat.

He glanced over. "Visiting family. Shopping. Going to

the spa. Isn't that what women usually do when they have some time?"

"I have no family. I'm more comfortable in torn denims and hiking boots than designer dresses and stiletto heels. And having my chipped nails filled with gel and my sun-baked skin oiled would bore me silly."

Mark spared her a quick glance. "And then there's Richard."

"Richard is old news." She never even paused before adding, "Now about this assignment . . ."

Her editor heard the finality in her tone. This wasn't the first time Grace had chosen career over romance.

He held out a two-page document. "Here it is. Pilots and fishermen swear they see a light dancing across the water of Spirit Lake. Dozens of them have responded, thinking it was a boater in trouble. The closer they get, the more the light begins to take on the shape of a woman. By the time they guide their plane or boat to the spot, the light, or whatever, is gone. Now I figure it's the play of moonlight or starlight on the water, but you know how these things turn into folklore."

Grace met his smile with one of her own.

"I see you agree with me. If you're up for it, you'll leave tomorrow. You'll go in by supply seaplane and be picked up in three days, weather permitting. In, out, and a four-page spread in the next issue, depending on what you find. Even without solving the mystery, you ought to get some fabulous autumn shots of a lake that has all the curiosity factor of the Bermuda Triangle. Maybe you can play up the dark spirits angle."

"Done." She took the information from his hand and sauntered to the door of his office. "I'm betting this mystery light–woman is the long-suffering wife of one of the fishermen, who just got tired of staying home while he was off having all the fun."

Her editor chuckled. "You get a picture of that, we'll have her on all the talk shows. See you the end of the week. And Grace, thanks for volunteering."

"No problem. This one's easy. No fuss, no bother, just me and my trusty camera."

Her words came back to haunt her as she sat, deep in thought. If the mystery light never appeared, what was she going to use to fill four pages of one of the most popular news magazines in the world?

She gave a soft laugh. What did it matter? She would have the next few days to spend all by herself.

All by herself.

Didn't that define her life? If she felt a little twinge at the realization that her future was looking as empty as her past, she shrugged it aside. She was very good at being alone. She'd had plenty of practice.

With her feet dangling inches above the water, she stared at the endless stretch of water. What would it feel like to slip beneath the waves? Was it possible to embrace death without a fight? Or would her subconscious take over and force her to swim? Not that she was actually contemplating doing such a thing. But the sight of all that dark water, the ancient trees surrounding it like a fiery fortress, was hypnotic. She couldn't ignore the nagging little thought inside her head that kept asking if anybody would miss her. Oh, there were a few friends and acquaintances, but for the most part, she'd lived her entire life isolated from the world, trying to please just one person—her stern, unyielding father. When she'd chosen a career that would take her far from him, they'd had a terrible row. And now, like everyone else in her life, he was gone, and there was no chance to make it up to him.

At first Grace was so deep in thought, she wasn't aware of the drone of the plane's engines overhead. When the sound finally penetrated her consciousness, she looked up absently, wondering if the supply plane had doubled back on its route.

The drone of the engines grew louder, and she lifted a hand to her forehead to shield the sun from her eyes. What she saw had her leaping to her feet. It wasn't the supply

plane that had brought her here. It was another plane,
smaller and flying much too low. If the pilot wasn't careful,
his craft was going to clip the tops of those trees. Even as
the thought formed, the plane began spinning end over end.
Just as it disappeared from view there was a tremendous
explosion, followed by a fireball of smoke and flame that
billowed up from the forest.

Heart pounding, Grace started running toward the site.
It would be impossible for anyone to survive such a crash.

The acrid smell of smoke assaulted Grace as she picked
her way through the woods. She could feel the waves of
heat even before she pushed through the brush and into the
very heart of the crash site. Small trees had been leveled,
deep grooves cut into the earth where the plane had skidded before coming to rest against a solid wall of forest. All
that was left of the airplane was twisted metal and charred
rubble. If there were any bodies inside, they were beyond
rescuing now.

With a sigh she backed away from the intense heat of
the fire. As she turned she saw a blur of color against the
drab landscape. Stepping closer she caught sight of a
man's body.

Was he dead?

Grace knelt and touched a hand to his throat, searching
for a pulse. There it was. Faint. Thready.

Alive. Relief poured through her. But there was blood.
So much of it. Grace reached into her pockets. Where was
a clean tissue when she needed one? Whipping off her
hooded sweatshirt, she unbuttoned her cotton shirt underneath and used it to mop at the blood that spilled from a cut
on his arm, and another on his leg that had soaked through
his pants.

She tore away his shirtsleeve and pants leg and examined the wounds. Despite the amount of blood, the cuts appeared to be fairly superficial. With a sigh of resignation,

she tore her shirt from top to bottom, tying the torn fabric firmly around each cut to stem any further flow.

The fact that the stranger remained unconscious led her to probe the back of his head, but she could find no evidence of swelling or trauma. While she examined him, she thought he stirred. But when she looked down, his eyes were closed.

She debated the wisdom of moving him. If there were internal injuries, any movement could make matters worse.

Coming to a decision she wrapped her hooded sweatshirt around him for warmth. "You may be in shock. If so, you'll need blankets and . . ." She knew she was babbling to someone who couldn't possibly hear her, but she felt the need to say something comforting. "Don't worry. You're not alone now. I'll be back soon with some supplies. Just . . . hang in there."

She patted his arm before turning away and racing back to the cabin.

Josh felt gentle hands probing, and the warmth of breath against his temple. Angels, he concluded. After what he'd gone through, there was no other logical explanation.

He'd always known, of course, that the risks he took in the lifestyle he'd chosen carried the strong possibility of an early death.

Like his father.

He took in a long, deep breath, expecting it to be his last. Now, finally, he would see the face of the man who, though he had died far too young, had left an indelible imprint on his son's life.

Ignoring the occasional twinges of pain, he gave himself up to whatever fate awaited him in the afterlife.

Grace struggled to wheel the heavy cart over roots and rocks and mounds of earth. The forest was not only dense, but unforgiving. A backpack would have been more efficient, but since she had no idea how long she might have to survive without shelter, she'd brought all she could pack into the cart, and had replaced her bloody shirt with a warm sweater, and over that a heavy parka.

At the crash site she worked as efficiently as possible unzipping a down sleeping bag and struggling to get the unconscious man into it.

Draping his arm around her shoulder she gently eased him into a sitting position. "Come on now, work with me."

Though she coaxed and cajoled, the unresponsive man was a dead weight. Finally, through sheer effort, she managed to roll him into the sleeping bag and zip it closed.

Then she set about collecting wood for a bonfire. Getting the fire started was simple, since the remains of the plane were still smoldering. Holding a stick to the rubble until it flamed, she crossed to the logs and waited for the kindling to catch fire.

Draping a blanket around her shoulders, Grace sat cross-legged beside the unconscious man and touched a hand to his forehead. There seemed to be no fever. He made not a sound, so she couldn't determine whether or not he was suffering.

As the sun slowly made its arc across the sky, she drew the blanket more closely around her and studied the man in the sleeping bag. His chest rose and fell in a steady, silent rhythm. He looked warm and peaceful. If she hadn't witnessed his plane crash, she could easily believe he was just asleep.

Praying that he was in no immediate danger, she stretched out beside him and, for the first time in weeks, slept soundly.

Three

Josh lay very still, eyes closed, and listened to the soothing sounds around him. Water lapping somewhere nearby. A breeze whispering through the branches of a tree. A chorus of birdsong.

He seemed imprisoned in a cocoon of warmth that rendered him unable to move. That fact, and the absence of pain, had him convinced that he was indeed dead. His last conscious memory had been the moment of impact, when his plane had hit the ground and skidded several hundred yards before slamming into an impenetrable wall of forest.

He'd watched the windshield of his plane shatter inward. Had heard the terrible screeching sounds of metal twisting. Had felt the plane shudder beneath him. And then a feeling of weightlessness, as though he'd been lifted in the arms of angels and carried ever-so-gently to earth.

Another memory returned. A woman, wearing nothing but a lacy bra and snug denims, holding him close. Tying something around his arm.

An angel? In bra and denims?

The thought had him grinning as he opened his eyes and saw her asleep beside him. He couldn't see her face, but her hair was a glorious tangle of red-gold curls.

His mysterious passenger.

She'd shed her blanket and parka, and what he could see of her slender figure in the faded jeans and sweater was model-perfect. Too bad she'd pulled on that sweater. Still, the sight of her snug backside had his smile deepening.

He looked up at rays of golden light filtering through the leaves of the forest. Like a benediction from heaven.

The woman stirred and brushed hair from her eyes before sitting up and turning. He realized in that instant that she wasn't his passenger. This stranger's hair was more red than gold, and her eyes were a startling shade of green, with little gold flecks. The kind a man could happily drown in.

When she realized that he was looking at her she scrambled to her feet.

"You're awake."

He'd heard that same voice before. Soft. Breathy. Calming. It had penetrated deep into his subconscious and had given him the most amazing sense of peace. He'd been given the assurance that he wasn't alone. That someone was nearby, looking out for him.

"Yeah. I'm awake. Or whatever they call it here."

"Here?"

"Heaven. That's where I am, right?"

She gave a quick laugh. "I've never heard the Spirit Lake Wilderness Refuge called heaven before. But I suppose to some hardy souls it might be."

"Spirit Lake?" He blinked. "I'm alive?"

"You are, though I don't know how. There's nothing left of your plane but ash and twisted metal." She pointed, and he could see wisps of smoke still rising from the rubble.

"If I'm alive, why can't I move?"

"Oh." She knelt and reached for the zipper on his sleeping bag. "Sorry. I was worried that you might go into shock from the accident, so I did my best to keep you warm through the night."

"I've been here all night?"

"And most of today." She pointed to the sun slanting low on the horizon. "It'll be evening soon."

"Are you telling me I slept all night and half the day?"

She nodded. "I checked on you a dozen times or more, and each time you were sound asleep. I tried waking you, but when I couldn't, there didn't seem to be much I could do except wait for you to wake on your own." She looked embarrassed. "I don't know if it was seeing you sleeping, or the fact that I couldn't go anywhere or do anything until I knew you were going to be all right, but whatever the reason, I slept, too. Not as many hours as you, but a lot more than I've slept in a very long time."

He was watching her closely. "Am I dreaming this, or are you real?"

"I'm real enough."

"Who are you, and how did you find me?"

"Finding you was easy enough. I just followed the smoke through the forest." She wiped her hand on her jeans before extending it. "My name is Grace. Grace Marin. And you are . . . ?"

"Josh. Josh Cramer." He stuck out his hand, then, spying his gloves, he grinned before slipping them off.

At her arched question he felt the need to explain. "My good luck charms."

"They seem to have worked."

"They do the job every time."

"Every time? Are you telling me you've been through something like this before?"

"Not a plane crash. But close."

"Are you feeling all right? No fever?" She tentatively touched a hand to his forehead.

He experienced a rush of heat so intense he could feel it in every part of his body. How could there be such heat from one soft, cool hand? He found himself hoping she would keep it there, just so, against his flesh. He felt a wave of disappointment when she lowered her hand and sat back on her heels.

He struggled to sit up. Instinctively she placed a restraining hand on his chest. "I don't think you should move. There may be some internal injuries."

"I don't feel any pain."

"None?" She seemed stunned by his admission.

"Except for a little twinge in my arm." He wiggled a foot. "And some in my leg." He sat up and looked around. "Where're my friends?"

"Friends?"

This wasn't the response he'd been expecting. "There was a second plane following me. I figured they'd put down on the lake as soon as they saw the crash."

Grace shook her head. "Sorry. I never saw a second plane."

"That doesn't make any sense." He frowned. "What about my passenger?"

Her eyes widened before she looked away quickly. "I'm sorry. You're the only survivor I was able to find. I just assumed you were alone, especially since I searched every inch of this area, and there was no trace of anyone else, or any remains."

As the enormity of these events began to sink in, his demeanor became brisk and businesslike. "I need a phone. Right away."

Grace shook her head. "There's no power out here. Even cell phones won't work, since there are no relay towers."

He'd known, of course. Still, there had to be some emergency measure. "How do you summon help if you're in trouble?"

"I was told to use the ham radio at the cabin. While you were asleep, I tried to power up the generator to report the accident, but I must have done something wrong. I couldn't get it to work." Seeing his look of disgust she added,

"When you're strong enough to walk to the cabin, you can give it a try. Do you know anything about generators?"

He shrugged. "I wouldn't call electronics my strong point, but I'm pretty good with my hands. I'll take a look at it. I'm sure I can figure it out."

When he started to stand Grace reached out to steady him. "Are you sure you're strong enough?"

"I've got to get up and start moving. I need to get a message out to my friends right away."

"Then let me help." She got to her feet and offered her arm.

He leaned on her and absorbed a quick jolt as he stared into her eyes. A trickle of sweat worked its way between his shoulders and down his back. Instinctively he pushed free and took a step away. What was the matter with him? Like any man, he enjoyed being close to a woman. Especially a beautiful woman. But he'd never had a reaction to a woman like this before. The thought of tasting those lips was almost overwhelming.

Having his emotions so close to the surface was probably a result of the crash.

"Thanks. I'm fine now."

And he was, he realized. After a few tentative steps, he was aware that, despite a crash that had left his plane mangled and burned, he seemed to have suffered no serious injuries at all. What were the odds of such a thing? For anyone else, he supposed, a million to one.

He glanced at his watch. The crystal had shattered, the time stopped at the moment of impact. Four P.M.

He shook off the dozens of questions whirling around in his mind. Hadn't he always accepted his extraordinary luck as his right? What he needed to concentrate on now was the fact that his mysterious passenger was missing and probably dead. As for the plane carrying Marty and the crew, they must have landed somewhere nearby, perhaps to pick up emergency provisions and medical personnel before coming to his rescue.

For now, he consoled himself, his string of luck was holding. He was alive and well. And in the care of the very beautiful and apparently very capable Grace Marin.

On the trek of the cottage, Grace paused beside a fallen log. "Would you like to rest?"

Josh shook his head. "I'm doing fine. It's hard to believe I went through a crash."

"No fatigue? No weakness?"

"None. I'm feeling better than I have in a long time. Probably all those hours of sleep," he added with a laugh. *Or maybe*, he thought, *it was the company of this intriguing woman.* He glanced over. "What are you doing in the middle of nowhere?"

"I'm a photographer with the *World*. My editor sent me out here to get some pictures of a ghost light."

"Ghost light?"

Grace chuckled. "That's what I'm calling it. Pilots and fishermen in the area reported seeing a light dancing across the water. Thinking it's a boater in trouble, they follow it. But when they get close, it looks like a woman."

"A woman? You mean a ghost that walks on water?"

Grace shrugged. "I know. It sounds crazy. The latest urban legend. Still, my editor thought it would make an interesting report."

"So? Have you seen her?"

"No. I just got here a short time before your plane went down."

"Sorry to mess up your plans."

"Yeah. You had a lot of nerve crashing your plane at such an inconvenient time."

They were both grinning as they stepped from the tangle of forest to the clearing around the cabin.

Josh looked around with avid interest. The structure was built of sturdy weathered logs, with a high-pitched roof to dispel snow. Behind the cottage was a small storage shed almost completely hidden by the vines and shrubs that had taken over. Beneath a gnarled oak sat a scarred wooden picnic table that seemed to be an extension of the tree itself. A short distance from the cabin, a long wooden dock jutted out like a bony finger into the rough waters of the lake.

"Whose place is this?"

Grace shrugged. "I never asked. I figure the *World* contacted the owner and rented it for the week. I just wish they'd sent someone out to check on it before sending me here. It's a bit . . . primitive."

He shot her a grin. "As long as it's shelter, I'm not about to complain. Besides, it looks solid enough."

"It does." She looked around, before nodding toward the vine-covered outbuilding. "The gas-powered generator is in there."

Josh followed her to the little shed. While she stowed the cart, he studied the rusted parts to the ancient equipment with a frown. "No wonder you weren't able to get it started. I wonder how long it's been since anyone used this."

"I can't even guess." She paused beside him. "Think you can make it work?"

"I'm going to do my best." He looked around. "I'll need time to take it apart and see if I can remove some of this corrosion."

Grace nodded. "I'd like to help." She lay a hand on his arm. "After all that rest, I'd welcome some hard, physical work."

He studied her hand on his arm before looking up into her face and her heart-stopping smile. "Thanks. I'll take all the help I can get. And if you're looking for physical, I'm your man."

Grace's heart took an odd little dip. To steady herself she bent to the pile of supplies she'd unloaded from the cart.

Josh held out his hands. "I'll get back to the generator later. First, I'll help you carry some of this to the cabin."

"All right." She filled his arms with the folded sleeping bag and blanket and held the door before leading the way to the cabin.

When Josh stepped inside the cottage, he was pleased to discover that it was as snug and comfortable inside as it had appeared from the outside. A staircase led to a loft tucked beneath the high-pitched ceiling of rough-hewn beams. The main cabin was one large room dominated by a floor-to-ceiling fireplace made of stone, with a wide mantel made of the same wood as the beams overhead. Flanking the fireplace were two weathered wooden rockers that appeared to be as old as the cabin. Facing the fireplace was a comfortable sofa draped with a faded hand-made afghan. In front of the sofa was a weathered coffee table fashioned from scarred wood. A second table and chairs formed a kitchen area, beneath several pine cupboards.

"I'll take those." Grace took the blankets from his hands and deposited them in a cedar storage box.

Josh turned toward the hearth. "Want me to get a fire started?"

"That'd be nice." She pointed. "I see some logs and kindling in that basket."

Crossing the room Josh tossed several logs on the grate before holding a match to the kindling. "How about some coffee?"

"I brought some with me, along with bottled water." Grace turned toward the cupboards. "I'll rummage around and see if there's anything I can use for making coffee."

Josh pointed to a blackened pot on a warming shelf over the fire. "You mean you didn't notice this little treasure?"

She gave a laugh. "What an antique. I've only seen one of these in pictures."

Josh found an empty bucket and headed toward the door. "I'll get some water from the lake, and while I'm there I'll wash this."

By the time he returned, Grace had retrieved a can of coffee from her supplies.

Soon the little cabin was perfumed with the rich fragrance of wood smoke and coffee.

Filling two mugs, Josh handed one to Grace before taking a long drink. "Now that we've taken care of what to drink, I hope you have some food hidden somewhere. I'm famished."

Grace shrugged. "I'm afraid food isn't much of a priority for me." She flushed when she caught Josh studying her more closely. "But I did bring some milk and eggs and bread and some peanut butter."

"Sorry. Man wasn't meant to live on bread and peanut butter alone." He paused a moment in thought. "I noticed some fishing poles in that shed out back. Come on." He started toward the door, with Grace following. "Let's just see what other treasures we'll find."

Half an hour later the two were seated at the end of the dock, fishing poles in hand, lines in the water, contentedly sipping their coffee.

Josh leaned his back against one of the wooden posts that had been sunk deep into the river bottom to support the dock. He watched with amusement as Grace kept yanking her line out of the water. "What're you doing?"

"Seeing if I've caught a fish yet."

"Don't worry. You'll know when you've hooked one. You'll feel a quick tug . . ."

Just then Grace let out a squeal of excitement and jumped to her feet, lifting her pole high in the air. Wriggling on the end of the line was a fish as long as her arm.

"Look! Look! I've caught one. Oh, my gosh, it's a whale."

Josh was laughing as he took hold of her arm and guided the fish into a net. "Not quite a whale, but a good-sized trout. He'll make a great dinner tonight."

"This is going to be so much better than P, B, and J sandwiches."

"You've got that right." He worked out the hook and dropped the trout into a bucket of water.

Minutes later he felt a tug on his own pole and lifted it in the air to reveal another catch. "The way these fish are biting, it looks like we won't have to worry about starving any time soon."

Within the hour they'd carried the bucket with their catch to the picnic table, where Josh showed Grace the proper way to bone and fillet the fish for cooking.

She watched with interest. "Is this what you do for a living?"

He chuckled. "I do this just for the pure pleasure of it." He arranged the fillets in a blackened skillet before heading toward the cabin. "Come on. Let's stoke the fire and see if we can't get this feast started. By the time you're finished, you're going to think you were dining in one of New York City's finest gourmet restaurants."

"Promise?"

He was still laughing as he held the door and followed her inside. "You aren't going to believe your taste buds."

Four

Grace set out plates and flatware on the rustic wooden coffee table positioned in front of the sofa.

She studied Josh, cooking the fish in a blackened skillet over the flames of the fireplace. He'd rolled the sleeves of his denim shirt to his elbows. Despite the plane crash, he was the picture of robust health, his body trim, his back and arms corded with muscles. Every once in a while he paused to sip his coffee before flipping the fish. He looked at ease, natural, as though he did this every day of his life.

"What do you do? That is, when you're not crashing a plane into the wilderness?"

He shot her a grin. "Extreme sports."

"Extreme?"

"Instead of just taking a hot air balloon up, I take it around the world and beat the old world record in the process. If I decide to surf, I choose to do it where I'll be the most physically and emotionally challenged."

Her hands paused in midair. "Why?"

He grinned. "It beats working for a living. And it gets the adrenaline pumping."

Grace gave a quick shake of her head. "I once told my father the same thing when he asked me why I had to go gallivanting around the world taking pictures. He couldn't understand why I wasn't content to just work at a local newspaper."

"Hmmm." He shot her a grin. "Does that mean we're kindred souls?"

"I don't know about that. I doubt I'd volunteer to circle the world in a hot air balloon."

"I only did it once."

That had her laughing. "How do you hope to top that?"

His smile grew and he made a formal bow. "For my next trick, ladies and gentlemen, I'm going to explore the wilderness."

Grace couldn't help grinning at his imitation of a carnival barker. "Were you planning on staying in one of the cottages here?"

"Not really. I'd planned on camping in the open. Along the trail." He wrapped a towel around the handle of the skillet and removed it from the fire. "I was about to film my journey for a television special."

"You're a TV producer, too?"

He gave a quick shake of his head. "Just a guy who loves nature."

"How many people are going with you?"

"Just me. The rest of the crew planned on filming me here at the beginning, and then waiting for me at the end of the journey to wrap things up."

She flushed. "I'm afraid I don't watch much television. I'm out of the country more often than I'm home. I'm not familiar with your show."

"It isn't a TV show yet. The producer was hoping this special might create enough interest to make it into a regular feature on the Sports News Network."

"Now that's something I'm familiar with. SNN is seen everywhere."

The fish were still sizzling as Josh turned them onto a plate. He removed a packet of leaves from the fire and opened them to reveal a mixture of steaming roots that he'd collected from the wild vegetation growing in the woods around the cabin.

When he carried the platter to the table, Grace eyed it with naked hunger.

Josh shot her a wicked grin. "Wouldn't you like to know what you're about to eat?"

"I don't need the scientific names, if that's what you mean. As long as you assure me that they're edible."

"A girl after my own heart." He settled down beside her and began to fill both their plates. "But just so you know the food is safe to eat, I'll tell you the name of everything here."

She chuckled. "A lot of good that'll do. How will I know whether you've given me their real name, or something you just made up?"

"You won't." He popped a steaming green leaf into his mouth and gave a sigh of pleasure before swallowing. "Now this is what I call fresh."

Following his lead, Grace tasted the fish and couldn't stop the little sigh that escaped her lips. "You're right. It's wonderful." She speared a green leaf. "All right. Just to play along, what's this called?"

"Lamb's-quarter. It'll taste a lot like spinach."

She bit into it and gave a quick nod. "It does." She lifted a steaming tuber. "And this?"

"Wild yam. The Native Americans who lived here probably considered it a delicacy. It'll stay fresh all winter if left in the ground."

"It's delicious." Grace tasted yet another green. "And this?"

"Wild asparagus."

"Tasty." She found herself wondering if he actually

knew all these plants, or was having fun with her. Testing him, she pointed with her fork. "This?"

"That's wild mint. And that one is thyme."

She started to laugh. "Honestly?"

"Would I lie to the woman who saved my life?" He speared a tuber. "This is orris root. And this is verbena. I'll use some later to make you tea."

"You're trying to impress me with all this knowledge, aren't you?"

"Guilty." He grinned. "Is it working?"

"Yeah." She shot him a sideways glance. "How do you learn all this?"

He shrugged. "The same way a city girl quickly learns which restaurant has the best carryout. I've spent so much time in the wild, eating from the land has become second nature to me."

"Is this when you tell me your amazing tale of having been raised in the wilderness by wolves, and that you're actually an untamed mountain man?"

That had them both laughing.

It occurred to Josh that he was having a grand time, feeling more relaxed and carefree than he had in years. "I spent a lot of time with my grandmother. She used to tell me stories about my dad, and I wanted to be just like him. I was keen for any adventure. I was on skis as soon as I could walk. Climbing mountains when other kids were riding their bikes." His tone lowered. Softened. "Gram told me that there wasn't anything my father wouldn't attempt. When I was a kid, I thought he could walk on water."

Grace heard the affection in his tone and felt a sudden ache around her heart at the thought of all she'd missed with her own father. "No wonder you need to get the generator up and running. He'll be worried sick until he hears that you're safe."

"My father died when I was ten. Until then, I was a military brat, moving all around the world. Though my mother hated it, I was having the time of my life." He crossed to the fire, retrieving the coffeepot. "I think, if my father had lived, my parents would have gone their separate ways." When he'd topped off both their cups, he set the coffeepot aside before returning to the sofa and stretching out his legs toward the heat. "Within a year of my dad's death my mother remarried, and I was allowed to move in with my grandmother. It was a good move for all of us. My grandmother was an amazing woman."

Intrigued, Grace turned to him. "In what way?"

He shrugged. "She'd buried a husband, a son. Since I was the only family member she had left, it would have been natural for her to lock the doors and cling to me as tightly as possible."

He saw Grace's sudden frown and wondered where she'd just gone in her mind. "Instead of holding on too tightly, she seemed perfectly content to allow me to follow my heart, no matter where it took me. When I was fourteen I told her I wanted to hike the Appalachian Trail the way my dad had. She offered to come along, but I told her I wanted to do it alone. And I did."

"But you were only a kid."

"I grew up fast. I found out a lot about myself that summer. After that, I spent every summer doing the things my father had done. Hiking in Wyoming. Snowboarding in Colorado. Fishing in Montana."

"So young. Weren't you afraid and awfully lonely?"

He smiled, remembering. "There were times when I thought I'd taken on a challenge that was bigger than my talent. But I can't say I was ever afraid. As for feeling lonely . . ." He stared into the fire. "I've always felt the presence of my dad in my life."

Again that quick tug at her heart before Grace nodded toward the gloves in his breast pocket. "Your good luck charms."

"Yeah." His grin was quick and easy as he removed them and set them on the table. "These were the only things left. They arrived in a box with a typewritten note

saying my father had been wearing them when his plane
went down."

"A plane crash?" She was so startled, she sat up
straighter.

"Didn't I mention it? He was a soldier in Special
Forces."

Grace went very still, wondering how he could speak of
such a thing without emotion.

"You're quiet." He reached over and caught her hand in
his. "I'm sorry if I upset you. But if you're thinking I was
trying to emulate him by crashing my plane, you're
wrong."

She absorbed a jolt, but when she tried to pull away, she
found herself held firmly. She stared at their joined hands,
then up into his face. "I wonder how your grandmother
found the courage to allow you such freedom after dealing
with something so violent and unexpected?"

He moved his thumb along her wrist and felt the way
her pulse jumped. Was she feeling it, too? The heat? The
adrenaline from this simple touch? "Gram told me that
whenever we give in to our fears, the bad guys win. It's become my mantra. Never let fear rule."

"I like that. Though I never heard it put into words, it's
pretty much my motto, too."

"Really?" He looked at her with new interest. "Most
people I know prefer to avoid risks and live their lives quietly."

"It's what my father wanted for me." Grace's tone grew
pensive. "I was always sorry that I couldn't be what he
wanted."

"We can't always be what other people want us to be."
Josh continued holding her hand. It felt good, he realized,
to be connected with someone, if only for the moment.

Was that part of the reason for his wanderlust? Was it
because he'd never felt as connected to the living as he was
to the dead?

Uncomfortable with the silence, Grace withdrew her

hand and got to her feet. "I'd better tackle the dishes." As she gathered the plates she smiled. "You were right."

"About what?"

"That was every bit as good as any big city restaurant. Maybe even better. Especially the weeds."

"Thanks." With a grin, Josh drained his cup and leaned his head back, enjoying the warmth of the fire and puzzling over the fact that he wasn't feeling any stress over this abrupt change in plans.

Seeing his sudden stillness, Grace called, "I'm sorry about your friend."

He lifted a brow and turned to her.

"Your passenger."

"Oh. She wasn't a friend."

She. For some strange reason, that simple word had Grace's full attention.

Before she could ask more his tone became brisk. "In fact, I didn't even know her name."

Grace struggled to mentally shift gears. One moment she was thinking that his traveling companion had been someone important in his life, and the next he was telling her his passenger was a stranger. "That doesn't make any sense."

"It didn't make sense to me, either. I was busy flying the plane, and the next thing I knew, she was there beside me."

"A stowaway?"

He nodded. "Apparently. I certainly didn't invite her along for the flight. Still, I can't help but feel responsible. How could she vanish without a trace?"

"There was an explosion on impact. If she couldn't get out of the plane, she would have been incinerated. Maybe when the ashes cool, you'll find some clue."

"Maybe."

She saw the puzzled frown and decided to pursue another topic. "You say your friends were right behind you?"

"Yeah." Josh ran a hand through his hair. "We were in communication until just before I went down. But even after my systems failed, they had to be close enough to see everything."

"Maybe there were clouds shielding your plane from view."

He shrugged. "Maybe." But he could remember nothing except a clear, cloudless blue sky before all hell broke loose.

"If they saw the crash, they may have decided to fly back to civilization and bring help."

"That's what I'm thinking, too." He fell silent, mentally willing his friends to be unharmed. He couldn't stand to think that if their plane went down, too, they may have suffered a very different fate from his.

Her voice interrupted his thoughts. "You have to be exhausted from your ordeal. Would you like to lie down?"

Josh shook his head. "It just occurred to me that for the first time in years I have nowhere to go and nothing to do but wait until my backup crew arrives."

It had to be the result of the crash. It was the only explanation for this strange euphoria. Ordinarily he'd be pacing like a caged tiger at the thought of all the unanswered questions. But for tonight, for whatever reason, he intended to put aside all the troubling questions and simply enjoy this unplanned freedom from his relentless schedule.

Without a word Josh tore himself from the comforting fire and got to his feet. "I'll give you a hand."

"You've done enough." Grace removed a kettle of water from the fireplace and poured it into a basin. "I think it's only fair, since you did the cooking, that I wash the dishes."

"Just to satisfy your sense of fairness . . ." He crossed to her. "We'll do them together." He picked up a towel and began to dry. "This way, we'll have them done in half the time."

"Don't you want to tackle the generator tonight?"

"I wish I could." He glanced out the window. "But it's already dark outside."

"I brought along a battery-operated lantern. Feel free to use it."

"I appreciate the offer." He dried the first plate and set it down before reaching for the next. "But I'd hate to use up all your batteries on something that can be tackled just as easily tomorrow."

"What about the people who are worried about you?"

"I'm sure they'll be here by morning." He was rewarded with a rare sense of peace. He couldn't work up any anger at these odd circumstances. He was alive, unharmed, and in the company of a beautiful woman. Life didn't get much better than this. And in the morning, when Marty and the others got here, he'd have a great tale to tell them.

He set aside the towel and lifted the plates. "Where did you find these?"

Grace gave a nod toward the cupboard above her. Josh reached up and opened the door before stowing them on a shelf. As he did, their bodies brushed. He glanced down at the same instant that Grace's head came up and he knew, by the look in her eyes, that she was feeling exactly the same quick sexual tug that he'd just experienced.

He lowered his hand to her hair and trailed his fingers through the tangles. "Soft." He didn't even realize he was speaking aloud. "I knew it would be as soft as an angel's wings."

"Josh . . ." She lifted soapy hands from the basin. Before she could resist he dipped his head and his mouth covered hers.

The jolt to his system was instantaneous. At the first touch of his lips to hers, he felt his mind empty of all thought but one. He'd wanted this more than anything. Just the chance to taste her. Touch her. Hold her.

Though he hadn't planned it, there was no way he could back off now. The feelings rocketing through him were more shattering than his plane crash.

He felt the slight trembling of her lips and swallowed her little gasp of surprise. As she started to back away his arms came around her, molding her to the length of him. The thought of devouring her was nearly overpowering.

The need to kiss her until she surrendered was so strong, so compelling, he wondered how he could resist. It took all his willpower to go slowly, nibbling her lips until they softened beneath his and opened. Then he was feasting on her mouth. There was such sweetness here. Such goodness.

Grace couldn't think. Couldn't move. Could hardly breathe. As he took the kiss deeper, she brought her wet hands to his chest. She could feel the strength in him, and she had a desperate need to cling, at least for a moment. Instead of pushing away as she'd intended, she found herself giving a shaky sigh before wrapping her arms around his waist. With his mouth on hers, there was no thought of holding back. For this one moment, she would give him everything, if he but asked.

Her simple act of surrender rocked Josh as nothing else could. He'd never known anything to compare to the feelings that spiraled through him as she offered her lips. He took them with a raw, deep hunger that startled them both. He could feel his blood heating, his heartbeat racing, as his mouth moved over hers, kissing her with a thoroughness that had them both trembling.

Grace had no defense against these strange new emotions. She could feel her body burning for his touch, her bones beginning to melt like wax. She'd never known a man's kiss to have such a devastating effect. The floor beneath her feet seemed to shift and tilt as his mouth moved over hers. When he drew her closer, she could feel his heartbeat thundering inside her chest, its wild rhythm matching her own.

In some small corner of Josh's mind a warning bell sounded. He knew he was very close to crossing a line. Who would have expected one simple kiss to take him to the very edge of reason? But this was far from simple. The woman in his arms had awakened a hunger, a craving that was threatening to take them both down a dark and dangerous path.

One of them had to be sensible.

Head spinning, chest heaving, he drew on every last ounce of willpower and managed to lift his head.

Unwilling to completely break contact, he kept his hands at her shoulders and looked down into her eyes while he waited for his heartbeat to settle. "I hope you're not expecting an apology. The truth is, I've been wanting to kiss you like that since I woke earlier and saw you lying beside me."

"I suppose I should at least thank you for your honesty." She gave a shaky laugh, wondering if her heart would ever return to its normal rhythm. Just standing this close, his hands touching her, had her pulse thundering out of control.

"All right. Time for true confessions." He was studying her through narrowed eyes. "I wanted to act on that impulse sooner, but I was afraid."

"You?" She tossed her head. "Fearless world athlete? I find that hard to believe."

"Maybe I was afraid you weren't real. That you were a figment of my overwrought imagination. Or that you'd run away before I had a chance to know you better."

With that glint of humor in his eyes, she couldn't tell if he was serious or having fun with her. Either way, his smile was contagious. He was far too tempting. And too close for comfort.

She took a step back and picked up the dish towel before drying her hands. "Sorry I got your shirt wet."

She tried to appear casual as she picked up the basin of hot water and crossed to the door before tossing the contents outside. When she returned it to the kitchen table she was aware of the way he was watching her. His gaze swept her, lingering on her lips. It was as tempting as any kiss. And had the same strange effect on her, leaving her feeling more aroused than she cared to admit.

He turned away abruptly. "I think I'd better take you up on that offer of a lantern and work on the generator."

"Why the sudden change of heart?"

His tone was gruff. "I don't think it's safe for us to be together just now."

She felt a quick flutter around her heart and realized that she'd been thinking the same thing. "No need to go on my account. Now that it's growing dark outside, it's time to earn my keep. I'm taking my camera to the end of the dock to watch for spirit lights."

"Better dress in layers. I have a feeling that once the sun goes down, it'll feel more like winter than autumn out there."

As Grace watched Josh pick up the lantern, she struggled to keep things light. "While you wrap your mind around rusted machinery, I'll wrap mine around my assignment."

He paused and shot her a wicked grin as he turned toward the shed. "I'd rather just have your arms wrapped around me the way they were a minute ago."

She managed a laugh. "It's a good thing we both have something important to do. Too much spare time on our hands is definitely dangerous."

As she made her way by moonlight to the end of the dock, she stared out across the darkened water and found herself desperately hoping to see a light. That was the one thing that would keep her mind off what had just happened.

But what about later tonight? How could she and Josh possibly get through the night in such close quarters?

This cabin was beginning to feel much too small for the two of them.

Five

Josh set the lantern on the floor beside the generator and switched it on. A wide beam of light illuminated the rusted machine. Spying an old army blanket folded on the end of a workbench, he shook it open, intending to spread it out on the floor. But the moment he touched it, he felt an amazing warmth flowing through his veins.

He studied the threadbare fabric. There were no markings on it. Nothing to distinguish it from any other army blanket. Still, he decided that it was too fine to be used in such a cavalier manner. Carefully folding it up, he retrieved an old drop cloth spattered with paint to use instead.

Using a wire brush, he began scrubbing years of rust and corrosion from the first metal part. When it was clean he set it on the cloth before reaching for another.

He'd always enjoyed the challenge of taking machinery apart and putting it back together. There was something so satisfying about finding that one tiny piece, that one overlooked part that would make the entire system hum. Even as a small boy he'd loved fitting pieces of a puzzle together. This chore was much the same, except that the pieces were bigger and more complex.

From his father he'd inherited a sense of curiosity; from his mother, patience. The two traits had held him in good stead through the years.

It was one thing to take things apart and see what made them tick. But as the minutes turned into hours, and the work showed no end in sight, though his persistence never wavered, his concentration shifted and he found his thoughts drifting to Grace Marin and that kiss.

He couldn't recall the last time he'd been so rocked by a simple kiss. Of course, there'd been nothing simple about it. The moment his mouth touched hers, he'd felt as if some unseen force had taken over his control.

He supposed, if he had to fall this hard, it may as well be with someone not only easy to look at, but easy to be with, as well.

She was a puzzle. A fascinating, complex woman. But there was a sadness he could see in her eyes in unguarded moments. Who was she? What had happened in her past to make her so sad? Looking back over their meal, he realized that, though she'd been a good listener, she'd revealed almost nothing about herself. He figured he would patiently work out the puzzle of Grace, just as he did everything else, given enough time.

Time. There'd been so little of it in recent years. Now he seemed to have more than he needed. Funny how life could change in the space of a minute.

Sitting back on his heels, he studied the generator. As far as he could determine, once it was properly cleaned and oiled, it ought to work. He unscrewed a protective plate and set it aside before tackling the rusted parts underneath. He was looking forward to communicating with the outside world by morning. Not that he expected to need this outdated piece of equipment for that. He had no doubt that the plane carrying the crew would arrive long before he could get this generator up and running. Still, he needed to be prepared in case they were delayed further.

What was keeping them? Had the same sudden atmospheric change that had caused his crash, forced them to land somewhere nearby? He refused to blame the crash on anything else. He knew it hadn't been pilot error. Though he'd been distracted by his unexpected passenger, he hadn't done anything to bring about the accident.

He thought about the debris that had once been his plane. If the crew following him had suffered a similar crash, would any of them have survived? He wouldn't allow himself to think about that. It was simply unimaginable.

And what about his mysterious passenger? Why had there been no sign of her after the crash? He shuddered at the thought that she had perished, her body incinerated beyond recognition. What a cruel injustice, when she'd probably stowed away as a lark. Or maybe, having learned about the proposed television special, had hoped to find a measure of fame.

And then there was Marty's unease about this place and its reputation. Were there really planes and boats that vanished forever, without a trace?

Unhappy with the direction of his thoughts, he returned his full attention to the generator.

Grace sat at the end of the dock, staring across the darkened water. In a tree by the water's edge an owl hooted, and nearby, its mate answered. Waves lapped gently against the shore in a steady drumbeat. Wind stirred the leaves of the trees, causing them to rustle softly.

She loved the nighttime best. She'd always considered it her special time. As a child, she'd used that time to forget, at least for a little while, the need to please her stern, unyielding father. For that brief period before sleep overtook her, she could stop pushing herself to be perfect. For a little while she could simply allow her mind to drift. To wonder where her mother had gone and why. To allow herself to hope that her mother might give a thought to the daughter she'd abandoned, and wonder what Grace had made of her life. It had been pleasant to imagine what her mother looked like. Throughout the years, her curiosity about the woman who had given her life had never dimmed. If anything, her unanswered questions nagged the edges of her mind at the strangest times. They were especially strong when daylight faded, and darkness covered the land.

Was that why, even now that she was an adult, the night remained her special time? Night was the time to rid herself of any unpleasant thoughts. Anything that might rob her of precious sleep.

Sleep. Grace yawned and stretched and realized that her muscles were stiff and cramped. She'd been sitting on the cold dock for hours without seeing a trace of light anywhere on the water. If the so-called spirit was going to stir, it would have done so by now.

The thought of a warm cabin and a soft bed were far too tempting.

Getting to her feet Grace gathered up her camera equipment, stowing them in her backpack, and made her way along the dock. The grass brushing her ankles was cold and damp with dew as she took the distance to the cabin at a run.

Inside, the rush of air caused a glowing ember on the hearth to pop, sending up a spray of neon red sparks. Grace crossed the room and added a log and kindling. In no time a fire blazed, and she eagerly held out her hands to the warmth.

Too tired to do more than kick off her boots, she draped the afghan around her shoulders, stretched out on the sofa, and was soon asleep.

Josh paused in his work and stared at the generator parts that he'd managed to clean so far, neatly arranged on the drop cloth, and ready for assembly. He decided to finish the rest in the morning. For now, hot, sweaty and covered with grime, he decided to take a quick dip in the lake to wash away the residue of this project. He wondered if Grace would still be watching for her spirit light, camera in hand. Without his watch to tell him the time, he calculated that it was well past midnight.

After carefully closing the door of the shed, Josh dashed through the darkness, following the trail of moon-light that illuminated the dock. Seeing that it was deserted, he paused only long enough to strip off his clothes and boots and set them atop the folded army blanket before diving into the gold-tipped waves. After the initial shock of cold water against heated flesh, he dove deep before rising to the surface and, like a great shaggy dog, shook droplets from his hair.

He swam in lazy circles around and around, grateful for the chance to work out the kinks in his muscles caused by the long hours in the shed.

Far out on the lake he spotted a sudden flash of light. His first thought was that it was a ribbon of moonlight trail-ing across the water. But the shape of it was all wrong. This was a single light that shimmered like a spotlight and ap-peared to be dancing atop the waves.

His heart gave a quick, hard bounce. This wasn't merely the reflection of the moon or stars on water. This was a steady, shimmering light that seemed to be moving toward him. There was no doubt that this was Grace's mysterious spirit light.

Knowing that Grace was missing the opportunity of a lifetime, he cupped his hands to his mouth and shouted her name. In the darkness he could hear the echo of his voice bouncing across the water and echoing in the nearby forest. Several more times he shouted, keeping watch on the door of the cabin, hoping to see Grace.

Pulling himself onto the dock he shouted again at the top of his lungs, but there was no sign of her.

The mysterious light was closer now, and moving directly toward him.

He slipped into his jeans and stood watching as the light continued drawing near. While he watched, the light began to glimmer brightly before it gradually took on the unmistakable shape of a woman.

She was too far away to see clearly. Her hair was covered by some sort of hooded cape that left her face in shadow. The cape, long and flowing, swirled about her ankles and shimmered with golden light as she appeared to glide effortlessly across the silvery waves.

Josh knew his jaw had dropped. Though he thought briefly of fleeing, he stood riveted to the spot.

While he stared in amazement, she paused and extended her arms, palms uplifted toward the sky. At her movement, a gust of bitter wind whipped the waves to foam and sent the trees along the shore dipping and swaying. The wind ruffled his hair and bit into his flesh, leaving him shivering.

Through it all he experienced no fear, only a sense of wonder at what he was witnessing. The light around her grew brighter until it was nearly blinding in its intensity.

While he watched, the image of the woman began to shimmer and fade until it was gone. In its place there was only darkness.

Josh shuddered and realized that the air had grown frigid. Chilled to the bone, he snatched up the blanket and shirt and boots and made a mad dash toward the warmth of the cabin.

"Ummm." Hearing the sound of the cabin door, Grace was abruptly yanked from the most pleasant dream. She'd been a little girl again, warm and snug in the embrace of her mother. Though she couldn't see the woman's face, she'd known instinctively who she was.

Struggling to hold onto the memory, she sat up, shoving tangles of hair from her eyes. "Guess I fell asleep."

She turned and, seeing the look on Josh's face, was suddenly wide awake. "You look like you've just seen a ghost."

"Yeah. That's exactly what I'd call her." Too agitated to think about sleep, Josh set the coffeepot over the coals before pulling on his shirt.

"Her?"

He turned and gave a solemn nod. "Your spirit. She was out there."

"You saw her?" Grace was on her feet and across the room in an instant, clutching his hands. "What did she look like? What did she do?"

At her touch, he experienced again the quick flare of heat and blamed it on the fact that he was still wired from what he'd just experienced. "I never really saw her face, but she looked the way I'd expect a ghost to look."

"How?"

He shrugged. "Shimmering light, a kind of ethereal form that suggested a woman."

He was already questioning what he'd seen. Had it really been a spirit? Or had that icy swim after so many hours of hot, sweaty work affected his mind?

Grace squeezed his hands. "Did she say anything?"

"Not a word. But I had the feeling that she'd been expecting someone else." Or had he imagined that, as well? "Anyway, she lifted her arms and there was this sudden rush of cold air, almost as if she'd summoned it." He shivered, remembering. "The trees along the shore were bent low from it, and the waves turned to angry foam. And then, as quickly as she'd come, she was gone."

"And I missed it." She released his hands and turned away on a moan of disgust.

"If it's any consolation, I did my best to wake you."

She glanced over her shoulder. "You did?"

He nodded. "I shouted your name at the top of my voice. Actually, I called you a couple of times, but got no response."

"That doesn't make any sense. I'm the lightest sleeper in the world. The sound of a pin dropping can have me awake and pacing for hours. I can't believe I missed the reason I'm here." Grace gave a long, deep sigh of annoyance.

"Hey, you're only human. You've been through a lot since yesterday. We both have." He moved up behind her and closed his hands around her upper arms, rubbing gently. "Who knows? Maybe she'll visit again tomorrow night."

"You don't really believe that, do you?"

"Maybe I'm just trying to convince myself as well as you." His voice, so close to her ear, sent shivers along her spine.

She turned and found his face inches from hers. "You still look pale." She touched a hand to his cheek. "You sure you're all right?"

"I'm fine." His voice sounded husky to his own ears. "But I wouldn't object if you wanted to hold me." He gave her a heart-stopping grin. "Just for a minute, of course."

She couldn't stop the smile that curved her lips. "Oh, sure. Of course. Hold you."

"Hey, it's not every day I encounter a ghost."

"Well, at least you saw her. That's more than I can claim." Still smiling she wrapped her arms around his neck.

"Mmmm. That's helping a lot. I feel better already." With a sigh he drew her close and pressed his mouth to the tangle of hair at her temple. "But if you feel like kissing me, just until my heart settles down, you understand, I won't object to that, either."

Now she was laughing. A soft, rumbling laugh that welled up and spilled over. "That's a good line, Josh. I bet you've had a lot of luck with it."

His smile went straight to her heart. "Actually, this is the first time I've tried it. Is it working?"

"I'd say so. I am holding you. And I'm halfway tempted to kiss you."

"You are?"

Her laughter grew. "Just to see if I can soothe your poor, overworked heart."

"I knew, the first time I saw you, that you were an angel of mercy." His mouth covered hers in the softest of kisses before he drew back.

The laughter died on her lips.

Seeing it, he dragged her close, keeping his gaze steady on hers. "But the thoughts I'm having about you right now are far from heavenly." This time his kiss was neither soft nor gentle. The arms that held her were almost bruising as he savaged her mouth.

For the space of a heartbeat she pulled back, caught by surprise. Then, as his lips claimed hers again, she sighed and leaned into him, giving herself up to the moment.

His lips moved over hers until she opened to him, urging him to take more. And he did, holding her so close, she could feel every beat of his heart inside her own chest. The taste of him, wild and just a bit dangerous, excited her. The press of that hard, muscled body to hers had her brain scrambling until she couldn't seem to hold a single, coherent thought.

What would it be like to lie with him? To have those strong arms around her all night? To give in to the pleasure he offered, until they were both sated?

"Josh. Wait." Struggling for breath, she pushed free of his arms. "I'm . . . no good at this."

He caught her chin, forcing her to meet his eyes. "I'd say you're very good."

"I don't mean kissing. It's this . . . man-woman thing. Relationships. I'm just no good at it."

He started to draw her close. "Then we'll forget about relationships and just go back to kissing."

She started to laugh, but it came out on a sigh. "Sorry. I

really enjoy kissing you. But sooner or later it would lead to more. And that just never works for me."

His eyes narrowed slightly. "Maybe you've just never tried it with the right one."

"Maybe." She shrugged and backed away.

Picking up her jacket she slung her backpack over her arm and headed for the door.

"Where are you going?"

"Outside."

"It's cold and dark out there."

"Yeah. That ought to help me cool off. And who knows? Maybe the spirit will make another appearance. If she does, this time I'll be there to record her visit."

On a sigh of frustration Josh stood in the middle of the room, staring at the closed door. Finally he poured himself a cup of coffee and dropped onto a chair, staring into the flames of the fire. Unfolding the army blanket, he wrapped it around himself and felt the warmth envelop him.

He'd experienced so many things in his adventures, but this was a first. There was the ghost, of course. But that didn't even come close to what he'd just experienced in Grace's arms.

In his entire life, he'd never been so affected by a woman. What he was experiencing had to be full-blown lust. It wasn't possible to fall head-over-heels in love with someone he didn't even know.

Love or lust, he'd give just about everything he had right now to satisfy this gut-wrenching need.

Six

Josh woke with a start and stared around.

A fire blazed on the grate. The wonderful fragrance of coffee permeated the little cabin. Grace was kneeling on the hearth, filling a mug.

Without a word he stood and made his way to her. Dropping to his knees he touched a hand to her cheek. "You all right?"

Her head came up with a snap. "I'm fine."

"Yes, you are." His eyes were grave. "About last night . . ."

"No." She scrambled to her feet a little too quickly. "Nothing happened last night. I'm sorry I made such a fuss over a simple kiss."

"Grace, we both know there was nothing simple about that kiss." Because she was determined to keep her distance, he tucked his hands into his pockets, to keep from reaching out to her.

"It doesn't matter. It won't happen again."

He was watching her closely. "Want to bet? It will if I have anything to say about it."

"Josh, I . . ." At the barking of a dog, she turned to stare out the window.

A big yellow dog was heading toward the cabin, dancing along beside an old man.

"Who in the world . . . ?" Grace crossed the room and tore open the door. "Hello."

The old man smiled and touched a hand to the dog's head. At once the dog sat, tail thumping the ground in a steady rhythm. "I saw the smoke and realized that someone was staying in the old lodge."

"Lodge?"

He stepped closer. He wore a heavy parka and a felt hat with an eagle feather tucked into the brim. His face was the texture of aged leather, with deep creases around his eyes and mouth. "Many years ago, when I was a boy, the lodge of my people stood on this very spot."

Grace held the door wide. "Would you and your dog like to come in? I've made coffee."

"Thank you." The old man stepped inside, and the dog followed.

Grace extended her hand. "My name is Grace Marin."

The old man took her hand in his. "Grace. The name suits you." His eyes, dark as midnight, stared into hers. "Do you know what it means?"

"I'm afraid not."

"It means 'one who is blessed with beauty and grace.' "

From the way he was studying her, Grace had the strangest feeling that he could see clear into her soul. Flushing under his scrutiny, she turned away. "This is Josh Cramer."

"Josh means 'warrior on whom the spirits smile.' " The stranger extended his hand, and Josh accepted his handshake. "Forgive an old man. I have always been fascinated with the meaning of names. I am Wyatt Eagle."

Despite the man's age, Josh could feel the power in his grasp. "And what does Wyatt mean?"

"'Guide.' And my dog is Barnaby."

Josh ruffled the dog's fur. "Does his name have meaning as well?"

Wyatt nodded. "His name means 'consolation.' He has brought me much comfort since we first met. He seems to have that effect on all who meet him."

Josh knelt down and studied the dog's sleek coat. "He looks healthy. Have you had him since he was a pup?"

"He belonged to a woman who spent her last days here at Spirit Lake. When she knew the end of her life was near, she asked me to keep him safe until I found him the perfect home."

"I'd say you already have. He's lucky to have you."

"We are both fortunate." When Grace handed him a mug of steaming coffee, Wyatt gave her a smile. "Thank you."

Grace indicated the sofa. "Why don't you sit here by the fire? We were just thinking about some breakfast. Would you join us?"

"Thank you. I will." He sank down gratefully and sipped his coffee.

"So." Josh poured himself coffee and stood with his back to the fire. "You stay here all year round?"

The old man nodded. "I am surprised to find anyone else here. What brings you to Spirit Lake so late in the season?"

Grace poured water into a bowl and set it on the floor, watching as Barnaby began to drink. "Josh is here to film a journey through the wilderness for a television producer." She began breaking eggs into a bowl before stirring them. "And I work for a newsmagazine that wants me to photograph the light that dances across the lake." She paused before asking, "Have you ever seen it?"

"Not many have had that privilege. But in my youth

some of the old ones in our village claimed to have seen her."

"Her? You know for certain it's a woman?" The egg mixture was forgotten. Too excited to think about food, Grace sat beside him. "What can you tell me about her?"

Without a word Josh moved to the small kitchen counter to take up the chore that Grace had abandoned.

The old man turned to Grace, who was twitching with excitement. "What would you like to know?"

"For openers, who she is and why she's here."

The old man sipped his coffee before setting it aside. "Her name has been lost through the ages. She was accused by her husband, elderly chief of an ancient people, of lying with another man. She did not deny it, but said that the man was a warrior, who had left to fight the intruders on the border. Among the ancient people warriors were considered more worthy of esteem than even the chief, for without brave warriors to see to their safety, their small nation would surely disappear as so many others had before them. The council decreed that if the warrior claimed the woman upon his return, it would be his right, and the old chief must step aside for the good of the people. The chief had no choice but to agree, but he stipulated that, whatever the outcome, their young daughter would remain with him. Though the young wife wept bitter tears over the loss of her daughter, she was shut out of the chief's lodge and sent away to await her warrior lover."

As he crossed the room to place the egg mixture in a skillet over the fire, Josh glanced at Grace's face. She was clearly as fascinated by this old man's tale as he was. While he slowly heated the eggs and set bread on the grate to brown, he listened carefully to the old man's voice.

"The woman had been married to the old chief when she was but ten and three years, and now she was confined to a cold, tiny shelter outside the circle of the others."

Grace broke into his narrative. "She was only thirteen when they were married?"

The old man nodded. "The ancient ones married young, and often died young. And because he was chief, when his old wife joined the spirit world, he chose a young, strong maiden to see him through his old age. As you can imagine, this handsome young warrior, so brave, so full of passion and love and laughter, had brought spring into the young woman's life. She could no more resist him than she could refuse to breathe. But the excitement she felt for him was overshadowed by the loss of the daughter she loved above all things."

Josh filled three plates and carried them to the scarred coffee table, before pulling up a chair for himself. Besides the scrambled eggs, Josh had added fresh, pan-fried trout from the bucket of fish.

Wyatt Eagle studied the meal. "This is a rare treat. I have not tasted such as this for a very long time."

"Then I'm glad we had some to share with you." Grace glanced over at Josh. "I'm so glad you finished what I started. This is really good."

He winked at her, causing her heart to do an odd little dance. "Happy to oblige, ma'am."

They both fell silent as they savored their meal, but it was obvious that Grace wanted to know more about the legend.

When at last Wyatt Eagle sat back, sipping strong black coffee, she could wait no longer. "Did the maiden's warrior return?"

Wyatt watched as both she and Josh shared their food with Barnaby. The dog ate his fill, before stretching out in front of the fire. Only then did the old man return to his tale.

"One day, as the bleak winter days turned into weeks, and the weeks into months, the woman heard voices raised in celebration. Racing from her shelter she hurried to the cluster of people, searching for the face of her warrior. One of the young braves stepped forward to tell her that her beloved had died in battle. Dropping to the ground, she buried her face in her hands and wept bitter tears. As the hours passed, she realized how desperate her situation had become. A lone female, without the protection of a warrior, couldn't possibly survive in this harsh land. Swallowing her pride, she made her way to the chief's shelter. When she entered, the voices of the others fell silent. The chief stood, pushing his little daughter behind him. From the corner of her father's robe, the child peered at the mother who was now a stranger. The woman bowed before the chief and admitted the shame she had brought to him, asking him to find it in his heart to forgive her. She promised from that day forward to lie with him and cook for him, so that together they could raise up their child to take her proper place among their people. The chief's face became as dark as a thundercloud, and his voice roared like that of the black bear as he told her that because she had shamed him, he would never take her back. If she wished to survive, she must uncover the warrior within herself. Then he turned her fate over to the council, who ordered her to be tossed into the frigid waters of the lake."

Grace put a hand to her mouth. "In the dead of winter? What a cruel death."

Wyatt nodded. "Not so cruel. The woman was prepared to pay the price of her infidelity. The people knew that the Great Spirits lived in their kingdom beneath the water. Even now, the woman's warrior lover was dwelling there with them. Now would she go to him. When the tribal elders tossed her into the icy water, moonlight glinted off the waves, like a beacon. At once her body went numb with cold. Within minutes she could no longer feel her hands or feet. Her body sank below the water and she gave herself up to the fate awaiting her. Suddenly, with a great rush of sound, the lake came alive. Waves rose up taller than the trees that ringed the shore. Fish that had been sleeping in the deep awoke and swam in wild profusion around her.

Water that had been laced with ice floes was now as warm as if it had been heated over a fire. A mighty wave lifted the woman on its crest, sweeping her above the waves. Her body began to take on a new form, and the form became that of a beautiful but fierce warrior woman in flowing robes, her hair golden, skin luminous as freshwater pearls. It is said that even now she waits out there in the lake, hoping for a glimpse of the daughter she loved more than her own life. Thus was born the legend of the warrior woman of the lake, for there is no warrior more ferocious than a mother denied the love of her child. Like a she-bear, she will wait and watch and do whatever is necessary to reclaim the love that was lost."

Grace's tone grew hushed. "Do you think she was able to make peace with her child?"

He fixed her with a dark, knowing stare. "What do you think, Grace?"

She was silent for a long time. When at last she spoke, her voice was troubled. "I can't imagine any daughter who would be so hard-hearted that she could ignore her own mother's anguish and refuse to forgive a solitary mistake."

"Even if that mistake caused great pain to the girl's father?"

"I wonder. Was it pain that drove the chief to punish her? Or his wounded pride?"

The old man shrugged. "Perhaps a little of both."

Josh asked the question that was uppermost in his mind. "You said few had seen her, except for some of the old ones. Why do you think the warrior woman has begun showing herself again after all these years?"

Wyatt Eagle turned to him. "That is indeed a mystery. Perhaps it is she. Or perhaps a kindred spirit who must find some resolution to the pain of this life, before entering the Great Beyond."

Grace mused aloud, "Why have I never read of this legend in any of my research?"

Wyatt smiled. "Much of my people's lore has never

been recorded, but rather passed from father to son. It is, after all, an ancient tale, and there are none of my people left." He set aside his empty mug. "I thank you for that fine meal. And for your pleasant company. But now I must leave you."

As he stood, Barnaby looked up from the fire. At a soft command, the dog trotted over to stand beside the old man and looked up into his eyes as though sharing his innermost thoughts.

Touching a hand to the dog's head, Wyatt glanced from Grace to Josh. "It would seem that my companion feels at home here." He turned to Grace. "You remind me of the woman who left Barnaby in my care. She entrusted me with something else and told me I would recognize the one for whom it was meant." He reached into the pocket of his parka and handed Grace a manila envelope.

She stared at it, then up at him. "I don't understand."

"So much of life is a mystery." He bent forward and brushed a kiss on her cheek. "Good-bye, Grace Marin. I am honored that we met." He turned to Josh. "Barnaby loves the land. He would make a boon companion to one who enjoys exploring the wilderness."

Josh chuckled. "I'm sure he would. But I travel alone."

The old man opened the door and stepped outside, with the dog at his heels.

Grace and Josh stood in the doorway watching as Wyatt and Barnaby started toward the woods. Suddenly the wind picked up, yanking the door from Josh's hands and slamming it shut.

"Getting colder," he muttered.

When he'd finally managed to shove open the door again, both man and dog were out of sight. Though Josh and Grace strained to see their figures moving in the woods, there was no sign of them.

"Odd. For an old man, he moves like lightning." Josh glanced at the envelope in Grace's hand. "Going to open it?"

"Of course." But instead of tearing it open, she simply stared at it.

"You're looking at it as though it's some kind of magic bottle, and you're afraid of the genie inside."

"Maybe I am."

He started out the door. "You can open that envelope, or just stare at it for the next hour. While you decide, I'm going to the shed and see if I can get that generator started."

He sauntered away, leaving Grace alone in the cabin, her pulse racing, her throat as dry as dust.

Seven

Josh breezed into the cabin on a rush of cold air. Bracing a hip against the door, he closed and latched it before starting across the room toward the warmth of the fireplace.

He passed Grace, seated on the sofa, surrounded by a stack of letters and photographs.

"Getting cold out there. I didn't realize just how cold until I stepped out of the shed and decided to wash up in the lake. I must be losing my touch. Even though I cleaned every single part, I couldn't get that generator to . . ." His words died in midsentence when he caught sight of Grace's tear-streaked face. "Hey, I'm really sorry." His voice lowered. "I see you decided to free the genie. Is it something you can talk about?"

Before she could say a word, the tears started fresh.

"Here." He was beside her in an instant, his arms outstretched. "Let me help."

Grace stiffened. It simply wasn't her style to give in to any weakness, especially one involving something so private and painful. But his offer was too tempting. Right now, this minute, she was feeling so alone and so wounded. Where was the harm in allowing someone else to be strong for her, just for a little while? The moment the thought formed in her mind, it seemed the most natural thing in the world to accept the comfort he was offering.

On trembling legs she stood and nearly fell into his arms. "Oh, Josh."

"Oh, baby, whatever it is, you'll get through it." He gathered her close. Against her hair he whispered, "Hold on, Grace."

The instant his strong arms closed around her, she felt a measure of peace and safety. Comfort. As though, simply by being held, she would, as he'd promised, get through this terrible pain that had shattered her poor heart.

The tears started again, and this time she allowed them to fall until there were none left.

At last she sniffed and lifted her head. "Sorry. I don't usually blubber like a baby. In fact, I can't remember the last time I had a good cry. Now I've got the front of your shirt all wet again. I seem to do that a lot."

"I don't mind." He lowered his head to smile down into her eyes. "It was wet anyway, after my dip in the lake. Feeling better?"

"Yeah. Thanks."

"My pleasure." Despite his smile, there was a huskiness to his tone that had her heart speeding up. He made no move to release her. "You feel good here."

She blinked the moisture from her lashes. "I was thinking the same thing."

"Great minds." His gaze burned over her face before settling on her mouth. "If you'd like, we could try that again, only closer."

Why wasn't she drawing away now that her tears had run their course? What power did this man have that he could hold her with nothing more than an inviting look, a charming smile?

Her voice was a whisper. "If you don't mind, I'd like that."

"Mind?" On a sigh he drew her close and tipped up her chin. She felt the heat of his kiss even before his lips found hers.

He kept the kiss as light as air. As soft as the brush of butterfly wings against her mouth.

When she didn't draw back, he took the kiss deeper.

With a little hum of pleasure she breathed him in. He tasted so good. So right. As cool as the night. As fresh as the evening breeze. With just a tang of the mysterious.

Grace sighed and gave herself up to the moment. If she could, she would stay here, just this way, being held in these strong arms, kissed by this wonderful, clever mouth, all through the night. In some dark corner of her mind she knew that she was playing with fire, in order to hold back the rush of emotions that had left her bruised and battered.

When Josh lifted his head, he touched a hand to her cheek. Just a touch, but she could feel the genuine warmth of him and was moved by it.

Now that her tears had begun to dry, he sensed her need to take her grief a step further and talk about whatever it was that had caused her so much pain.

Catching her hand he dropped down beside her on the sofa. "Want to share?"

She lifted a handful of letters. "These belonged to my mother."

"Your mother? She was the woman who gave them to Wyatt Eagle?"

She nodded. "All of them were written to me."

"Why go to all this trouble and mystery? Why didn't she just mail them?"

"She did." Grace pointed to the envelopes. "Apparently they were all returned to her unopened."

"You never got any of them?"

"I never even knew about them. Or about my mother's

attempts to contact me." Grace took a deep breath. "There are things about me . . . about my past . . ." She was silent for so long, Josh thought she might be having second thoughts about opening up to him. Suddenly the words just tumbled out. "My mother left when I was three. I don't even remember her. After she left, I was raised by my father."

"Any brothers or sisters?"

She shook her head. "Just me and my dad. We moved a lot. From small town to small town. To say my life was sheltered would be an exaggeration."

He chuckled. "There's nothing wrong with small towns or living a sheltered life."

"I wasn't just sheltered." She paused a moment, deep in thought, before going on. "Looking back, I realize that I lived in total isolation. I can't recall a single childhood friend."

"What about the kids at school?"

"I was homeschooled. My father was a poet. A very successful one. That made it possible for him to be home with me, seeing to my education without the benefit of tutors. By the time I was ready for college, he took a job teaching creative writing at the local university. At the time, I thought he did it to make the transition easier for me. Now I realize that he had other reasons, as well."

"What reasons?"

She shrugged and avoided looking at Josh. "Now that I know how desperate my mother was to find me, I suspect he wanted to see to it that she didn't succeed."

"And you never searched for her?"

"I had no reason to. My father raised me to believe that she wanted no part of our lives."

"Now that's some kind of anger. Did you make friends in college?"

"I guess it was too late to change. By then I'd become so comfortable being alone, I found it hard to reach out to the other students. So I continued to be pretty much alone,

except for my father. But when I couldn't stand being
smothered by his need to control me any longer, I chose a
career that would take me as far away from him as possible. We had a terrible fight."

"He'll get over it. You have a right to your own life."

"My father passed away while I was photographing the
people of a small village in the Sahara. We were still es-
tranged and never got a chance to make peace." She gave a
dry laugh. "I'm not only as obstinate as my father, but as
unforgiving."

Josh closed a hand over hers. "You can't stay locked in
guilt, Grace. What happened in the past doesn't have to af-
fect your future."

"But don't you see? Whether I like it or not, the past has
shaped me. Having read these letters, I realize that there
was another half of my life. A piece of me had been missing, and I didn't even know about it."

He could feel her pain in every word and wished with
all his heart that he knew how to ease it. "What do the letters say?"

Grace's fingers traced the edge of an envelope. "They're
all the same. An outpouring of love from a woman whose
heart is broken by the separation from her only child. In
every letter my mother asks how I'm doing, and what sort
of person I've become. And she begs me to forgive her for
not being a part of her life."

"Does she say why she chose to leave?"

Grace shook her head. "She gave little explanation, except to say that she'd met a man who had been her soul mate.
When my father learned of it he told her she would never see
her daughter again. In one letter she claims to have obtained
court-mandated visitation rights, but by then we'd left the
state, and for years her efforts to find us were thwarted."

When she looked over at him, Josh could read in her
eyes the shock that was beginning to set in. "It's going to
take some time for you to process all this information,
Grace. You shouldn't try to digest it all in one big gulp."

She looked down. "I feel as if I've been in some horrible train wreck that took the lives of both my parents. And somehow, I was the cause of it."

"That's not fair. You didn't cause this, Grace. You were just a kid. Your parents were two consenting adults. Whatever they did to one another, it was their choice, not yours."

"I know. But there's more. I didn't just spend my life missing my mother. I was all too happy to mirror my father's hatred of her. I nurtured it. Embraced it. And now that I've learned the truth, it's too late. In her last letter to me, my mother writes of her impending death. Now there's no way to make things right between us. All because of my father's bitterness, and my willingness, in fact my eagerness, to share it. That's what makes this all so crushing. Not just knowing that my mother spent a lifetime trying to reconnect with me, but the fact that I swallowed my father's story without question."

"Don't do this to yourself, Grace. Don't let this new information make you angry and bitter."

"I have a right to be bitter." Her tone was harsh, brittle. "Looking back, it seems I spent my entire childhood trying to be the kind of person I thought my mother incapable of being, in order to placate a father who reveled in his darkness. And he'd been playing with my emotions." Her voice was a cry of pain. "I've been regretting the choices I made that caused our separation, believing that he was the only one capable of loving me. And now I find I've been grieving the loss of an unforgiving man who did everything he could to make me into his own image. And for that unforgiving man, I contemplated taking my own life."

Josh was staring at her with a puzzled look. "What do you mean by that?"

For a moment she fell silent. The only sound in the cabin was the hiss and snap of the logs on the fireplace.

Now that the words had been spoken, there was no way of taking them back.

Grace took a deep breath. "Just before your plane crashed, I was sitting on the end of the dock wondering what it would feel like to just slip into the water and let the lake take me."

Her words sent shockwaves through him. He treasured life so deeply. Lived his life every day to the fullest. Though many would accuse him of taking foolish, dangerous risks, he harbored no death wish, but only the desire to live in the moment.

He latched on to the only thing he could. "You didn't follow through on your impulse."

"I didn't." For the longest time she sat quietly, staring at the clutter of letters and photos. "But who knows what I might have done if your plane hadn't crashed at that very moment?"

"Then I'm grateful for my accident."

She glanced over. "Do you believe it was an accident?"

He shrugged. "Do you have a better explanation?"

"I don't know. I'm thinking about the legend, and the fact that the warrior woman's story mirrors my mother's so closely. Is it all a coincidence? Or is there something more here? How did Wyatt know I was here? What was he to my mother?" She sighed and rubbed at her temples. "Oh, Josh. I'm so tired of thinking."

He reached a hand to her shoulder and could feel the knots of tension. "Here. Let me help."

Turning her slightly away, he brought both hands to the back of her neck and began kneading. With a sigh of contentment she leaned her head to one side, then the other, while he continued working the tightly-coiled muscles of her neck and shoulders.

She gave a deep sigh of pleasure. "Oh, that feels heavenly."

"I've been told I have very talented hands."

Beneath the warmth of humor in his tone was something darker, deeper. She experienced a quick rush of heat and decided to throw caution to the wind. She'd been alone too long. And what better way to forget, at least for a little while, the sudden, wrenching pain that had been thrust on her?

Her voice grew sultry. "Maybe you'd like to show me just how talented those hands are."

For the space of a heartbeat he stilled his movements. She could feel the warmth of his breath on the back of her neck. Could sense the way he was watching her while weighing her words.

When he finally spoke his words were clipped. "That's a very tempting invitation, and one that's hard to resist. But you're exhausted. And you've just suffered a shock to the mind and soul. What you really need is sleep."

She turned toward him. "I don't sleep well alone. Maybe if I had company . . ."

"Lie here and I'll cover you." He lifted the army blanket from the back of the sofa and unfolded it.

His rejection was more shocking than a slap. "You want me to sleep alone?"

He winked. "Doctor's orders."

With a sigh of annoyance she turned away, but not before he saw the look of pain in her eyes.

Very deliberately he drew the cover over her, allowing his hands to linger a fraction. Then he stood and crossed to the fireplace, where he set another log in place.

Wiping his hands on his pants, Josh stared into the fire and watched as flames began to lick along the bark until it erupted into a blaze.

He turned to glance at the figure on the sofa. Grace's eyes were already closed; her breathing slow and easy.

It hadn't been easy to refuse what she was offering. But it had been necessary. He'd recognized her need and would have been only too happy to pleasure her and himself. But he'd also sensed her vulnerability. Right now she was too devastated to think clearly. Quick, mindless sex might be enough to hold the pain at bay through the night, but in the morning, her heart would still be broken, her soul still shattered.

The heart and soul of Grace Marin didn't need a bandage. What they needed was a miracle. And though he was beginning to care deeply about this haunted, lonely woman, he was fresh out of miracles.

Eight

Josh stood at the end of the dock, staring at the sky. It seemed almost colorless, neither blue nor gray, a total absence of clouds, as though an artist had stopped painting before the picture could be completed. Though the sun wouldn't set for hours, the horizon was already beginning to pale and blur into the surrounding forest.

He studied the lake for any sign of a dancing light, but all he could see under the leaden sky was dark water.

What secrets did it hide?

In some small corner of his mind, the question nagged. What was happening here? Had he really seen a ghost, or had he allowed his imagination to make a fool of him? And what about Marty and the crew in the second plane? What could possibly take them this long to bring help? What of his mysterious passenger? Why had she chosen his plane? Why was there no sign of her remains? And now Wyatt Eagle and those letters from Grace's mother. There were too many events to be considered mere coincidence. There was something eerie going on here, and he couldn't seem to unravel the mystery. Still, he had to admit that he didn't feel threatened in any way. In fact, he'd never felt so peaceful. In this place, in this simple, almost primitive cabin, he had the strangest sense that he'd come home.

Hearing a sound behind him he turned to see the big yellow dog trotting along the dock. Josh looked beyond him, but there was no trace of Wyatt.

He knelt down and scratched behind the dog's ears. "Hello, Barnaby. Where's your master?"

The dog's tail thumped against the wooden dock.

"Don't tell me you ran away." Standing, Josh peered across the space separating the cabin from the forest, expecting at any moment to see the old man stepping into the clearing.

When Wyatt didn't appear, Josh turned toward the cabin. "Okay. I guess you just went for a stroll through the woods. Come on. Let's see what there is to eat. You hungry, boy?"

As if in understanding the dog bounded ahead and stood waiting until Josh opened the door. Once inside Barnaby trotted over to the sofa and began licking Grace's hand.

She awoke slowly. When she spied the dog, she wrapped her arms around his neck and buried her face in his neck. "Hello. You're back." She sat up, shoving hair from her eyes. "I'm so glad, because I have so many questions . . ."

When she realized that Wyatt wasn't there, her words trailed off.

She glanced at Josh. "I don't understand. Why is Barnaby here without Wyatt?"

"My guess is that his dog just wanted a little adventure. I'm sure, after so much time in this forest, Wyatt doesn't have any problem with Barnaby wandering off. He knows how to find his way home."

She nodded. "I'm sure you're right." She got to her feet. "I can't believe I slept so soundly. I haven't had this much sleep in a year." Seeing the way he was searching the cupboards she grinned. "Hungry? Again?"

"Yeah. But I thought I'd feed Barnaby first. I figure he must have worked up quite an appetite."

"Why not give him the last of the fish, and then we'll catch more for our supper."

"Great idea." He heaped a bowl with the remains of their breakfast and set it on the floor.

At once the dog pounced on the food and devoured it. When he'd had his fill, Josh started toward the door. "Guess it's time to drop our lines in the lake and see what we'll catch for our own supper."

"I'll help." Grace pulled on a jacket and followed him.

When they stepped outside, the first thing they noticed was the change in temperature.

Josh grinned. "A few minutes ago, it was freezing out here. Now it's positively balmy."

"Another good thing about this place. If you don't like the weather, stick around. It's bound to change." Grace tossed aside her jacket and kicked off her boots before picking up one of the poles. For some unexplained reason, she felt as happy-go-lucky as a kid when school was out. It had to be that nap. She couldn't recall the last time she'd felt this rested and relaxed. Whatever pain and humiliation she'd been feeling before was pushed aside. "Race you to the dock."

Laughing, Josh hopped on one foot, then the other, disposing of his boots before snatching up the second pole and chasing after her. Barnaby joined in the fun, barking and running around them in circles. When they reached the end of the dock and cast their lines, the dog trotted up holding a stick in his mouth. He dropped it beside Josh.

"Oh, you want to play, do you?" Josh picked up the stick and tossed it into the lake. At once Barnaby dove in and paddled furiously until he managed to retrieve the stick. Then he scrambled to shore, shook himself, and trotted the length of the dock to drop the stick beside Josh.

For nearly an hour they played the game. Each time, Josh would toss the stick as far as he could manage. Each time, Barnaby retrieved it and raced along the dock to play again. Finally, panting from his efforts, the dog lay beside Grace and began chewing on the stick.

Sweating, Josh tossed aside his shirt. "When I was a kid, I always wanted a dog like Barnaby. In my mind, I could see myself playing just that way."

Trying not to stare at the ripple of muscle that sculpted his arms and shoulders, Grace nodded toward the bucket of water, where several fish were swimming. "At least one of us managed to bring home the bacon, or at least the fish, while you two were having all that fun."

"Barnaby and I are in your debt. Now about all that work you've been doing . . ." Without warning Josh scooped her up and strode to the very end of the dock. "What do you think, Barnaby? Should we let our lady have a turn at all that fun?"

In reply the dog's tail thumped a steady tattoo on the dock.

Wriggling and kicking, Grace let out a shriek. "Don't you dare."

"Did I hear the word dare?" Josh gave an imitation of an evil laugh. "Woman, never dare Fearless Josh Cramer. It's the one thing I simply can't resist."

"Josh. These are the only clothes I have."

"Hmm. Another reason to toss you in the lake. I have an idea you'd look cute in nothing but your birthday suit."

"Josh, I'm warning you. Put me down."

"Yes, ma'am." With another laugh he did just that, and watched as Grace landed in the water with a grand and glorious splash.

She came up sputtering, wiping hair from her eyes. "I can't believe you did that."

Josh was laughing so hard he could barely speak. "Just following orders, ma'am. You did tell me to put you down."

While he was distracted laughing Grace reached out and snagged his ankle. Before he realized what she was planning, she gave a fierce tug and he landed in the water almost on top of her.

His hand snaked out to reach for her, but she managed to evade him and ducked under the water. He followed, and this time, when he surfaced, he had hold of her.

She felt the heat where his hands were touching her.

"You're very quick, Ms. Marin." He arched one brow like a villain. "But not quite quick enough. Now, how will I make you atone for that crime you just committed?"

She couldn't help laughing as she batted her eyelashes and gave him a demure smile. "It's my nature to share. I figured it wouldn't be fair of me to hog all this warm water for myself."

He was grinning. "Sorry, kid. You'll never make it on the stage."

"And I thought I was such a good actress." She sighed and wiggled her toes. "This water really is warm. I expected to come up shivering when you tossed me. But it's as warm as a bath."

"Now that you mention it . . ." He drew her fractionally closer. "And here I was hoping you'd need me to warm you."

She was laughing, her face turned up to his. "Sorry to thwart your plans."

"Not a problem. I'm very good at changing tactics in midstream." He pressed his lips to the corner of her mouth and nibbled a droplet of water.

She sucked in a quick breath. "Oh, yes. That was a very good change of tactic."

"Thanks. But it was clumsy. Give me a second chance. I can do better." He dipped his head and covered her mouth fully with his.

Grace gave herself up to the pure pleasure of the moment. It was the most delicious feeling to be held suspended in the water by those strong arms while that clever mouth moved over hers, weaving its magic. Slivers of fire and ice curled along her spine. With every touch of his lips, she could feel her body growing soft and pliant against his.

"Umm. That's much better." She wrapped her arms around his waist and held on as he took the kiss deeper.

They stayed locked together, mouths mating, breath mingling, until the world around them seemed to fade away. When at last they came up for air, their hearts were racing.

"Grace." The way Josh spoke her name on a fervent whisper had her going still. "We both know a kiss isn't enough this time."

"I know." Her throat felt too tight.

"You know what I want." He tipped up her chin to stare down into her eyes. "But I need to know if it's what you want, too."

While he waited for her answer, he felt his heart stop. She'd become a hunger. A need that could no longer be ignored.

"I want the same thing you want, Josh." She touched her mouth to his in the softest of butterfly kisses.

His movements stilled. With his hands framing her face, he studied her. His voice, when he finally spoke, was gruff. "You're sure?"

She was afraid to speak over the lump in her throat, so she merely nodded before leaning into him and offering her mouth.

She could feel him fighting to keep the kiss soft as his lips claimed hers, alternately draining her, then filling her, until all she could taste was him. She was so caught up in the kiss, she wasn't even aware that he'd begun moving toward shore. When they reached the shallows he lifted her easily in his arms and strode toward the cabin.

Her heart was pounding so loudly in her chest, she wondered that he couldn't hear it. But when she wrapped her arms around his neck and pressed her mouth to his throat, she heard his quick intake of breath and knew that he was as caught up in the moment as she was.

He paused to kick in the door, then strode across the room and set her on her feet. Water sheeted from their bodies, forming puddles on the floor. Neither of them took any notice.

His hands were greedy as he fumbled with the buttons of her wet shirt, nearly shredding it in his haste to remove it. Beneath it was nude lace, clinging to her like a second skin. He disposed of it just as quickly, revealing a body so perfect it had him sucking in a breath.

"You're beautiful, Grace."

Seeing the desire in his eyes, hearing the husky quality of his voice, had her experiencing the familiar trickle of fear. Fear of what they were about to share. Not because she feared the act itself, but because the feelings she had for this man were too strong, too intense. He was the one she'd been waiting a lifetime to find. For that reason, she knew she was leaving herself open to heartbreak. If he didn't share these feelings, she would have only herself to blame.

His hands stilled. "Having second thoughts?"

She lifted her chin like a prizefighter. "Of course not."

He merely grinned. "I told you, Grace, you're not a very good actress. And a really lousy liar."

"I'm not afraid." But her voice wavered as he lowered his mouth to her breast.

Heat poured between them and she wondered that her trembling legs could still hold her. To anchor herself she wrapped her arms around his waist as his clever mouth slowly drove her closer and closer to the edge of madness.

Desperate to touch him as he was touching her, she reached blindly for the fasteners at his waist and tugged at his wet denims until they joined hers at their feet. As her hands moved over him, she was rewarded by his low hum of pleasure.

He'd been content to move slowly, to taste and touch and explore. But now, with her hands on him, the need was so sharp, there was no way of slowing the passion that was raging. Though he fought to bank the flame of desire, he could feel it burning out of control.

He cupped her hips and dragged her roughly against him, all the while lingering over her mouth. With lips and teeth and tongue he took her on a wild ride. One minute she was holding on tightly, the next she felt herself stepping over the edge of a high, sheer cliff and falling, until the next touch had her soaring.

"Afraid now?" The word was whispered inside her mouth.

"Should I be?" She spoke the words on a shudder of pleasure.

"I'll never hurt you, Grace."

"I know." But she knew, in some small corner of her mind, that he was the only man who could. When she left this place, she would be leaving her heart with him.

While he explored the wonders of her mouth, she drank him in. Dark. Exciting. When he dipped his mouth lower, to the sensitive hollow of her throat, she arched her neck and actually purred with pleasure. Encouraged, he pressed soft, feathery kisses along her shoulder, over her collarbone. When he dipped his mouth lower, to take her breast, she felt her legs buckle.

At once his arms were there to catch her. He lowered her to the rug in front of the fireplace. His mouth covered hers in a kiss so hot, so fierce, it had her breath backing up in her throat. There was an urgency now that had their hearts racing, their lungs straining.

"Come with me, Grace. Let me show you places you've never seen."

He found her, hot and moist, and took her to the first glorious peak. Stunned, she could only clutch at him as he gave her no time to recover before taking her up and over again. Her trembling body hummed with needs she hadn't even known she'd possessed.

"Josh." She struggled to see him through the haze of passion that clouded her vision. All she could see were his eyes, so fierce, fixed on hers with an intensity that had her heart stuttering.

There was no hesitation now, only a wild exhilaration at this passion they were sharing.

She lifted a hand to his mouth and traced the shape of his lips. "Show me, Josh. Take me with you."

"We'll take each other."

They came together in a kiss that spoke of all the loneliness, all the hunger, all the need. Their lives beyond this cabin no longer mattered. The world had slipped away. Outside a night bird cried, and its mate answered. Neither of them heard. The steady sound of waves slapping the shore matched the beating of two hearts. Their breathing grew shallow, and the air between them grew heated, until their bodies were slick with sweat.

As he entered her, she wrapped herself around him, taking him deep.

They came together in a firestorm of passion and began to climb, to soar. They were beyond thought, beyond words, beyond anything of this world as they felt themselves reach the very summit. For an instant they hovered there, staring into one another's eyes. In the next moment they felt themselves slipping over the edge, and flying among the stars.

It was the most amazing journey of their lives.

"You okay?" Too dazed to move, Josh whispered the words against her temple.

"I'm . . ." She couldn't speak over the lump in her throat. Instead, she merely brushed a finger across his lips until they curved into a smile.

"That was . . ." He gave a shake of his head. Words couldn't describe what he was feeling. So alive. As though everything he'd achieved until now was a mere rehearsal for this moment. As though everything that would come after would seem dull by comparison. "That was incredible."

He leaned up on his elbows to stare into her eyes. "You're incredible, Grace."

She managed a smile. "You're not bad yourself."

He rolled to one side and drew her into the circle of his arms, nibbling her ear. "That was definitely worth waiting for."

"I was thinking the same thing." She shivered at the delicious curls of pleasure spiraling through her.

He brushed her mouth with his. "Want me to get up and cook the fish?"

"Not especially. Are you hungry?"

He gave an impish grin. "I was. But a very beautiful woman just fed my hunger."

"Happy to oblige, stranger."

"Now I know what it means to live on love. Who needs food?"

"I'll remind you about this in the morning, when there's nothing to eat but those fish swimming around in a bucket."

They were both laughing. But moments later their laughter died as they came together in a long, slow kiss.

Inside her mouth he whispered, "Want to go for seconds?"

"Umm." It was all the invitation she needed. She wrapped herself around him.

With soft sighs and languid kisses they took each other once more to that place that only lovers know.

Nine

Josh pressed kisses over Grace's eyelids. "Think Barnaby gave up on us and went back home?"

They'd lost track of the time, but earlier he'd carried her to the sofa, where they now lay in a tangle of arms and legs, with only the army blanket for cover.

Grace sighed, too content to move. "I hope so. It must be dark by now."

Josh lifted his head to gaze at the window. "Not quite. The sun is just sinking. Want to go watch the sunset?"

She nodded, and he helped her up before slipping into his denims, drying in front of the fire.

Grace ignored her own clothes and merely wrapped the blanket around her shoulders for cover.

Hand in hand they walked outside. At once Barnaby came trotting over, looking happy to see them.

"Oh, look at you. You've been swimming in the lake." Grace paused to scratch behind the dog's ears. She was rewarded with a few quick licks of his tongue.

"And look at this." Josh pointed toward the trees that ringed the lake. The countryside was alive with the most amazing palette. Deep red maples and bright yellow cottonwoods. Flaming orange oaks and gold willows, and purple sumac so rich they looked like velvet.

As they made their way along the dock, they lifted their heads to the sky, painted with waving ribbons of pink and mauve and purple. To the west, the sun was a fiery globe just beginning to sink below the waves. The placid water was no longer dark, but like a looking glass, alive with a reflection of all the magnificent autumn colors.

Grace turned to Josh with a puzzled expression. "Is it possible that this was here all along, and I never noticed?"

Josh's voice was hushed. "If it was, I was as blind to it as you. But then, ever since I had my first glimpse of you, I've been blind to everything else." He brushed a kiss to her cheek. "Maybe it takes the two of us, looking through the rosy glow of love, to see what's really here."

His words had her going very still. Was that it? Had love cast some sort of spell over everything around them?

They stood together on the end of the dock, watching the spectacular sunset. For the longest time after the sun disappeared, leaving a sky washed with unbelievable color, they remained there, arms around each other, savoring the beauty of the moment. Neither of them seemed willing to break the spell.

It was the dog's barking that finally roused them. Barnaby brushed past them and raced to the door of the cabin, where he stood waiting for them to catch up.

Josh gave a laugh. "I'd say that's a very broad hint that one of us is hungry."

They were still laughing as they opened the door. Barnaby was the first one inside. He moved about the room, sniffing, pausing, then standing patiently by the fire, watching as Josh tossed a log on the hot coals. Within minutes a cozy fire was burning.

"Make yourself at home." Josh knelt to run a hand along the dog's coat before walking across the room. He picked up a knife and began to fillet the fish.

"Let's see what I can find to go with that." Grace began rummaging through the cupboard.

Josh winked. "We could always eat a salad made of weeds, as you called them."

"Very tasty weeds, by the way. Or we could drink this." Grace held up a dusty bottle of pale amber wine.

"Good thing it's white wine." At her arched brow, Josh added dryly, "I figured a city girl like you would realize that red wine just doesn't go with fish."

"Well then, the one who left this here had very good taste." While Josh set the fish over the fire, Grace washed out two old, elegant stem glasses that had been hidden in the back of the cupboard. When they were sparkling, she filled them with wine and crossed the room to hand one to Josh.

He touched his glass to hers. "What will we drink to?"

Grace thought a moment before saying softly, "To strangers meeting in the most unlikely places."

"And to lucky plane crashes." Josh's gaze locked on hers as he sipped.

When the fish was perfectly browned, Josh divided it into three portions. While he and Grace settled themselves at the scarred old coffee table, Barnaby noisily polished off his food in several quick bites before flopping down in front of the fire.

Josh nodded toward the dog. "Looks like he's ready to stay the night."

Grace chuckled. "I was thinking the same thing. I hope Wyatt won't mind."

"We'll take him back first thing in the morning." He continued to study the dog before turning to Grace with a strange look.

She placed a hand over his. "What were you just thinking?"

"How right everything is. Us. This cabin. A cozy fire. Even a dog. This is the exact homecoming I've been picturing in my mind for years. It's been my secret wish."

His words had Grace's eyes widening. "Now that you mention it, that's true for me, too. Except that in my secret wish, along with love I'd find my mother."

"You have." He motioned toward the packet of letters. "In a manner of speaking."

She sighed. "I hadn't thought of it that way, but you're right. I guess I'll have to be satisfied with her letters to tell me what she was like, until I can ask Wyatt for more information. And at least now I know what she looked like."

Josh seemed startled. "You didn't know what your own mother looked like?"

Grace shook her head. "My father was so furious when she left, he tore every picture of her from his albums. There were no photos of my mother holding me or feeding me. My father destroyed all of them. He even tore their wedding picture in two. All I ever saw was my father in a tuxedo, gazing solemnly at an empty space beside him."

"Now that's what I call bitter." Josh rounded the table and drew her close to press kisses to her eyes, her cheeks, the tip of her nose. Against her mouth he whispered, "That's a lot of pain to carry around for a lifetime. I wish I could do something to erase it."

"You have, Josh. Just being here with you has brought me so much peace." She wrapped her arms around his neck.

He trailed nibbling kisses along her jaw until he heard her sigh. It pleased him to pleasure her. He loved the expressive look on her face, as the shadows in her eyes lifted and her little frown turned into the languid look of a lover. Her eyes were open, and focused on him. Only him. It was as erotic as anything he could have imagined. Far more exciting than the thrill of adventure. And so much more rewarding than hearing the cheers from his adoring fans. With Grace this adventure had become deeply personal and intimate. There was something about this quiet woman that touched his very soul.

Forcing aside the need to take her quickly, he ran soft, feathery kisses across her shoulder, down her throat, burying his lips in the sensitive little hollow. When he moved lower still, her sigh became a moan. Still, he kept his touch light, his kisses soft as butterfly wings, as he ever-so-slowly took her.

"What's this?" Grace sat up, shoving hair out of her eyes.

"Nourishment. After the amount of energy we've consumed, I thought we needed sustenance."

"Very thoughtful of you." She eyed the sandwich, cut into quarters. "Peanut butter and jelly?"

"And the last of the wine. Can't have P, B, and J without wine."

"Of course not." She laughed. "Makes perfect sense to me."

"I've been waiting a lifetime to hear a woman say that. Now I know we're compatible. Will you marry me?" He settled himself beside her on the sofa, completely unconcerned about his nakedness.

"Only if you promise to make me this for a midnight snack at least once a month for the rest of my life." She bit into the sandwich and made little humming sounds as she devoured it.

"That will depend on just how you plan to express your . . . gratitude for this extravagance."

"I intend to be . . . extremely grateful."

"I love it when you purr like that." He set down his glass of wine and leaned over for a quick kiss. "I wasn't joking when I asked if you'd marry me."

She pulled away and sucked in a breath. "Josh . . ."

"I know. You told me you're no good at relationships. Neither am I. But it's different with us, Grace. There's something special here that I don't want to lose."

"I feel it, too. But . . ." The question she was about to ask died abruptly on her lips when she saw the fierce look in his eyes. "Oh, hold me, Josh."

Suddenly the midnight snack was forgotten as they took each other with all the force of a hurricane.

Grace's head was pillowed on Josh's chest. She awoke to the strong, steady beat of his heart and thought it the most wonderful music in the world. When she opened her eyes, she found him watching her with a look of such intensity, it had her breath hitching in her throat.

"Good morning."

He brushed a hand over her cheek. "Morning, sleepy-head."

She actually felt herself blushing. "Have you been watching me sleep?"

"Yeah. Did you know that you wiggle your nose while you're sleeping?"

"I do not." She started to sit up but his arm was around her, holding her close.

"I know what I saw. Don't worry. You looked sweet while you were doing it. And I promise to tell no one. It'll be our little secret." He kissed the tip of her nose. "In fact, I consider it a real turn-on."

"After the night we've put in, you probably consider breathing a turn-on."

"Depends on who's doing the breathing." There was that grin again, sending her heart into a series of somersaults. "There's a fantastic sunrise outside our window. Want to walk to the dock and watch it?"

Even before she could respond, Barnaby walked to the door and stood waiting.

"Is he a mind reader?" Josh held out his hand and helped Grace to her feet.

Within minutes they'd dressed and were padding barefoot along the dock, with Barnaby racing ahead.

"Oh, look at that." Grace pointed to the bright orange ball of sun on the horizon that seemed to be rising directly out of the lake.

"I wonder what the ancient people thought of that?" Josh kept her hand tucked firmly in his.

"It would be easy to believe the sun slept in the lake after dark."

He nodded. "Along with the spirits."

Her head swiveled to study him closely. "Does this mean you've decided not to believe Wyatt Eagle's tale?"

He shrugged. "I'm sure he believes it. But now that I've had some time to think it through, I'm not so sure."

"What about the ghost you saw?"

He grinned. "Ghost? You mean that wisp of fog that blew in and spooked me?"

"Do you honestly believe it was fog?"

"I don't know what I believe anymore. Not that it matters."

"It matters to me. What about my photo shoot of the dancing light?"

"You came here hoping to find something mystical. I think what we've found together is mystical enough. No harm in getting some shots of starlight on the water though. Now that the countryside is alive with color, at least you'll have some breathtaking pictures."

While Grace mulled his words, they stood watching until the sun had completely risen above the water. Then, almost reluctantly they turned toward the cabin.

"Time to return Barnaby to his owner." Josh pointed toward their jackets. "We'd better bring those along, just in case there's another sudden change in the weather."

"Good idea." Grace picked up her jacket and followed him out the door.

Once outside, the big yellow dog trotted eagerly ahead of them, leading the way along a well-worn path through the forest.

They traveled for more than a mile before spotting a

rustic cabin up ahead, almost hidden under a canopy of lush forest.

"There it is." Grace pointed, and they hurried to catch up with the dog, bounding ahead of them.

Josh caught her hand and helped her over a fallen log. "Looks like Barnaby is aware that he's almost home."

As they stepped into a clearing, they stared in surprise. Instead of the snug retreat they'd been expecting to see, this cabin looked deserted. The door was hanging by one rusted hinge. As they climbed the steps, Josh held up a hand.

"Watch out, or you could fall through that hole in the wood."

Stepping gingerly around the crumbling step, Grace trailed him inside, only to stare around in dismay. The interior was even worse than what they'd already seen. Cobwebs hung from rotting beams. The sparse furnishings appeared to have been chewed by creatures from the wild; the stuffing tossed about, the cushions of an ancient mattress damp and moldy from the elements.

"This can't belong to Wyatt." Grace couldn't control a shudder.

When the dog trotted out the open back door, they followed, then stopped in midstride at the sight of a grave marker.

Josh knelt to read the inscription before looking up at Grace. "It has Wyatt's name. But the date is all wrong. According to this, he's been dead for years."

Grace dropped down beside him to trace the name and date that had been carved into the marker. The color drained from her face. "What's going on here, Josh?"

His eyes narrowed. "That's what I'd like to know. If someone's trying to play a trick on us, they've got a really warped sense of humor."

"The grave certainly looks old." Grace studied the earth, overgrown with vegetation. "I don't think anybody could fake the condition of that cabin."

Josh looked around, then got to his feet and helped her to stand. Drawing an arm protectively around her shoulders, he whistled to the dog.

She looked alarmed. "Where are we going?"

"Back to our cabin. Whatever's going on here, I'd feel a lot safer in familiar surroundings."

They started back along the path toward their own cabin, with Barnaby happily running ahead. Once there the dog flopped down in front of the fireplace and was soon dozing.

For the first time since his arrival, Josh made certain that the cabin door was secured before tossing a log on the fire. Seeing it, Grace was grateful that she wasn't alone.

She touched a hand to his. "The supply plane will be here in a couple of days."

He looked at their joined hands, then up into her eyes. "We're not waiting for the supply plane. First thing in the morning, we're leaving."

"How?"

"The way I'd planned to leave in the first place. We'll hike out. That is, if you're willing to trust me to lead us both to safety."

She lifted a hand to his cheek. "I trust you completely, Josh."

He drew her close and pressed a kiss to her temple. "Whatever's going on here, we'll get through it together."

"Together." She drew a little away and smiled. "I can't think of a nicer word than that."

"Neither can I." He gathered her close and covered her mouth with his. "Come to think of it, it's a word neither of us has ever been able to say before. Together." He spoke the word inside her mouth as he took the kiss deeper.

And then there was no time for words as they came together to offer comfort in the only way they could.

Ten

"Listen to this." Darkness had settled over the land, but inside the cabin, with a cozy fire burning, Josh and Grace sipped coffee while she shared with him some words from one of her mother's letters. "My darling Grace, one of my greatest fears is that, without a mother's love, you will spend a lifetime just passing through . . ."

She sucked in a breath. "It's what I've been doing, Josh. Don't you see? All this time, I've just been passing through." She lowered her head and continued reading: ". . . instead of living your life to the fullest. Remember this, my darling. Each moment should be savored, for each moment we're on this earth is a treasure. And the richest treasure of all is having someone to share the moments."

"A wise woman, your mother." Josh topped off Grace's cup and his own, before settling on the sofa beside her.

Grace reached into the manila envelope and withdrew a stack of photos. "It's such a thrill to finally be able to see what my mother looked like."

As she sorted through them, Josh had quick glimpses of

baby Grace in a young woman's arms, of a laughing baby in a bathing suit at the beach, of a happy baby clapping her hands and reaching out for the string of a balloon.

Finally Grace came to the one she'd been looking for. "This is my favorite. The one in my father's album had been torn in half. Always, I'd only been able to see him looking at an empty space. But now I can understand the intense look on his face. Isn't she beautiful?"

Josh stared at the photograph of the gorgeous golden-haired woman in a fairy-tale wedding gown, standing beside a stern-looking man in a morning coat and tails. But it wasn't the scene that captured his interest; it was the woman.

"This is your mother?"

At the sharp edge of his tone, Grace glanced over. "What's wrong?"

He tapped a finger on the photo. "That's my passenger."

She couldn't seem to absorb his meaning. "I don't understand."

"That's the woman who mysteriously showed up just before my plane went down."

"You mean she resembles the woman in this photo."

"I know what I saw, Grace." He snatched the photograph from her hand to study it more carefully. "It doesn't just look like her. It was this woman. This hair. Even this dress. She was all in white. Dazzling as the sun."

Grace was instantly on her feet, backing away from him. "Why are you saying this?"

"Do you think I'm making it up? I'd never do that. I'm telling you that my passenger was this woman."

Though Grace tried to reject it, her heart knew. She felt it give a sudden hard bounce as her eyes filled with tears. "Did she say anything?"

He struggled to recall the words. "She said don't worry, Josh. I won't let anything bad happen to you."

"You said you'd never seen her before. How did she know your name?"

He shook his head. "I figured she was a groupie, hoping to get her fifteen minutes of fame by stowing aboard a celebrity's plane." His voice lowered. "I never dreamed . . ." His voice took on a more practical tone as he began to wrap his mind around the reality of it all. "Now we know why her remains were never found."

"I don't under . . ."

"She was already dead, Grace. Like Wyatt. And for some reason, they both made themselves known to us."

Grace turned away and buried her face in her hands. "None of this makes any sense."

He went to her and gathered her close. "I know what you're thinking. I'm thinking it, too. But we're not crazy, Grace. And it's not some sort of contagious mass hysteria. We're sane, sensible people. But we both know what we saw and heard. Wyatt was here. We both saw him and listened to his tale."

"But why? What possible reason could he have for . . . coming back?"

"I don't know. Maybe to explain about the legend of the lake." Josh began to pace. He turned suddenly. "Didn't Wyatt say his name meant 'guide'? Was he guiding us toward something?"

Grace sighed. "I have to admit that hearing about the legend gave me insight into what my mother and father may have gone through. But what about Barnaby?" She glanced over at the dog, whose head came up at the very mention of his name. "How do you explain him?"

"I can't. Maybe he's been surviving alone in these woods and needed a home."

Grace mulled that. "Wyatt said that Barnaby loved the forest and that he'd make a fine companion."

"And he seemed pleased when we both took to the dog." Josh knelt and Barnaby hurried over to lick his hand. In a softer tone he added, "He's the very dog I wanted as a kid. Right down to his color. Maybe that has something to do with his being here."

"All right. So we found some things we've both been searching for. You've got your dog, and I've got my mother, but that still doesn't explain . . ."

He stood and framed her face with his hands. "You're forgetting about the most important thing we both found." He leaned close. "Love. I love you, Grace. You're exactly what I've wanted in my life. The part that's been missing all these years."

At his words, she blinked back the tears that threatened. "I love you, too, Josh. I don't know how it happened. I certainly never expected anything like this, but here it is."

"Here it is." He lowered his mouth to hers. "So what are we going to do about it?"

"We could hide out here for the rest of our lives."

He nibbled her lower lip. "It's tempting. We could shut out the world and create our own little paradise."

Barnaby suddenly raced to the door and began barking.

Grace and Josh stepped apart. With his finger to his lips he shoved her behind him and picked up the fish knife before opening the door.

Barnaby rushed out and began racing along the dock, barking furiously.

When Josh stepped outside, Grace hurried to catch up. "Whatever is out here, you're not facing it alone. We're together now, remember?"

"I don't want you hurt, Grace."

"I'm not going back inside without you." She took hold of his hand.

When they reached the end of the dock, they paused beside Barnaby. The dog had gone eerily silent and was staring at the lake.

And then they saw the light, dancing across the dark waters, heading directly toward them.

Grace's hand tightened on Josh's as the light began to shimmer and glow, before it assumed the figure of a woman. As she drew closer, they could see her gown, dazzling white, and her hair, a glorious cascade of red-gold curls.

"Oh, I have waited so long for you. So long." Her musical voice was as clear as a bell. "I could not take my rest until I fulfilled my heart's desire to see you happy."

"Mother?" Grace said the word haltingly and wondered why it sounded so right. So perfect. It was the first time she'd ever said it aloud. She took a deep breath and said it again. "Mother."

The woman smiled. "I have waited a lifetime to hear my daughter say that word. It is the sweetest sound ever created."

"How long have you been . . . gone?" Grace couldn't bring herself to speak of death.

"In the world it would be a year or more. It is a mere moment in this place, where time is of no consequence. My love for you burns brighter than the sun, Grace. Far too bright to be dimmed even by death."

Grace was so moved by those words, she couldn't find her voice. She stood, tears streaming down her cheeks, drinking in the vision that was her beloved mother.

Beside her, Josh draped an arm around Grace's shoulder to offer his strength. "How does Wyatt Eagle fit into this?"

"Wyatt is my guide to the Great Beyond. It was he who taught me that great love can wield great power."

"And so you went through all this elaborate scheme"— Grace's hand swung to include Josh and the dog at their feet—"just to make me happy?"

"Your happiness has been my greatest concern. It was necessary for you to know how deeply you are loved, Grace. Without that knowledge, you would be incapable of fully giving love."

"But why Josh? How did he happen to get caught up in this?"

The woman turned to Josh. "Your father was . . . dear to my heart."

Grace turned to Josh, and knew, by the stunned look on his face, that his thoughts mirrored her own. His father had been a warrior who had given his life in battle.

"He was here once, wasn't he? That's his army blanket I found in the shed."

The woman nodded. "He and I were here together once, in that long ago time. And then, all too soon, he was gone."

"Why can't I see him? Why isn't he here, too?" Josh's voice rose in anguish.

"As much as he wanted to show himself to you, he ceded his power to me. My need was greater, because my daughter never knew me. You know your father, Josh. So well, in fact, that you have striven to emulate him all the days of your life. And he remains with you forever."

Her smile grew radiant. "He and I hoped, by bringing the two of you together in an idyllic setting, you would open yourselves to the love that is possible. Now that you have found it, the rest is up to you. But remember this. Love so easily found in paradise can be lost or squandered when the realities of the world intrude. Only the two of you can decide the final outcome."

Before the last word was spoken, the woman's image began to shimmer and fade.

"Wait. There's so much more I need to know." Grace reached out a hand, but like wisps of fog, the image dissipated and began drifting back across the dark waves until it was nothing more than a distant light.

As they continued to watch, the light flickered, then faded as it disappeared beneath the waves.

Before they could say a word they heard the sound of a plane coming in hard and fast.

The sky lightened, and they were startled to see the sun hanging low on the horizon. It was no longer nighttime, but late afternoon.

Grace was the first to speak. "That isn't my supply plane."

Josh stared in astonishment. "It's one of ours. The one that's been missing for days."

The plane made a perfect landing on the water and rolled up to the dock. As soon as the door opened, Josh strode forward.

Marty was the first to step out, followed by the pilot, Brady Stewart, with the rest of the crew spilling out behind him.

"Where've you been?" Josh strode forward to meet them.

"Following you, buddy boy." Marty removed his sunglasses and pointed. "Didn't you hear us applauding you? That was a hell of a fine landing."

"Landing?" Josh stared beyond the plane to see his own, bobbing in the water, tethered neatly to a buoy just offshore.

For the space of a heartbeat he couldn't find his voice. When at last he spoke, his tone was incredulous. "Are you saying I just came down?"

Marty glanced at his watch. "Not five minutes ago."

Josh looked at his own wrist and realized that his watch was now working perfectly. It read four-ten.

Grace stifled a cry and turned away, running blindly, with Barnaby following.

Brady Stewart chuckled. "Your agent warned us you'd manage to find some gorgeous model even in the wilderness. How'd you smuggle her in here?"

"We'll talk later." While the rest of the crew milled about, setting up camera equipment, Josh made a dash toward the cabin. When he stepped inside he saw the dog lying by the fire.

Grace was pacing the room. She looked up as he entered, and he saw the tears before she flew into his arms. Her words were muffled against his chest. "I was afraid I'd only imagined you as well."

"Yeah. I had the same fear." He ran a hand over her hair, down her back, as though to reassure himself that she was indeed real.

"What happened to us, Josh? Was all of this a dream?"

He gave a quick shake of his head. "We'll need some time to figure it all out. But this much I know. It was no dream. Barnaby is real. So are those letters and pictures of your mother." He took her mouth in a hot, fierce kiss. "And so is this."

She returned his kiss with one of her own. On a sigh she stepped back. "But what do we do about it?"

He shrugged. "You heard your mother. Now we deal with our feelings in the real world."

"But how can our love possibly survive? Our careers take us all over the world."

He nodded. "That's right. I have a contract to fulfill. A journey to take through the wilderness. And you have a photo essay to file." He grinned. "I'll be curious to see how you describe the mysterious legend of the lake now."

She was silent a moment, imagining the possibilities. Her breath came out in a long, deep sigh. "With all these responsibilities, where does that leave us?"

He could hear the director shouting orders, and the voices of the crew drawing closer, and knew that there was precious little time left.

"If you're willing, why not meet back here when we both complete our assignments? We'll plan our future."

"Our future." At a sudden thought she glanced at the dog drowsing by the fire. "And Barnaby?"

"You heard Wyatt. He'll make a boon companion on my journey. And when you and I are married, he'll make a boon companion on our journey together."

"Our journey together." She sighed and wrapped her arms around his waist. "Oh, Josh. I never thought I'd welcome those words. But it's what I want."

Josh could hear Marty shouting for him. He gave her a quick, hard kiss. "You'll be here when Barnaby and I return? No matter what?"

"No matter what. Count on it."

"I love you, Grace Marin. I want to spend the rest of my life with you."

Against his mouth she whispered, "And I love you, too, Josh Cramer. Forever and always. Please take care of yourself. I'll worry about you until we're together again."

"Don't worry. We have angels watching out for us, remember?"

After one final kiss he whistled up the dog, and the two of them walked out the door.

Grace stood staring at the closed door, her head spinning. There was so much she didn't understand and probably never would. But this much she knew without question. Through a series of events far stranger than anything she'd ever imagined, whether by magic, or mysticism, or simply the power of love, she'd just been granted her fondest wish. Now it would be up to her to write her own happy ending.

It would be a challenge. The world would do its best to intrude on paradise. But Grace didn't have a doubt in the world that she and Josh would be up to the task. After all, they had some pretty amazing ancestors showing them the way. Best of all, they had love. As her mother had made perfectly clear, true love could overcome any obstacle, even death.

Feeling as strong as any warrior woman, she picked up her camera. Time to complete her assignment. No more would she be just passing through this world. She intended to get down to the business of living her life to the fullest. With Josh's love as the beacon, the journey ahead was bright with promise.

Mellow Lemon Yellow

Mary Kay McComas

One

She didn't see him enter the room or hear his steps as he walked up the aisle to the coffin. She simply glanced up and there he was, weeping silently as he gazed down at the pasty white face with the brightly rouged cheeks—her father in his final slumber.

She sat in the first row of padded folding chairs and tried to look away again, uncomfortable with public displays of raw emotion. But not staring at him proved to be impossible.

Charlotte had no flare for fashion of her own, and she didn't like to judge . . . but the man was wearing sparkling, ruby-red sequined shoes—large ones—with squat heels and red bows across the toes just like . . . well, just like Dorothy's in the *Wizard of Oz*. With white sport socks. They hugged his ankles and climbed halfway up his thick, well-shaped, hairy calves—which were bare from there to his knees. His muscled thighs looked laminated in a pair of silver-gray football pants that disappeared beneath a baggy black overcoat with white piping around the collar and the large kangaroo-like pouches that took the place of normal pockets.

How could she not stare?

But who was he? Surely, not a friend of her father's and certainly no one she knew. Though after a quick second peek at his face he did look, somehow, almost vaguely familiar to her . . . sort of.

Aside from the clothes, he was a nice-looking man, clean shaven, his dark hair clipped short. He stood in partial profile to her, his head bent low, the strong angles of his face draped in sadness. He had the kind of square chin she always thought denoted a strong character—a hero's chin, with a nice straight nose, and his full lips curved downward at the corners, making his sorrow seem as real to her as her own.

But who was he?

She hated situations like this. What if he spoke to her? She was better with numbers than names and there was never a right thing to say, on either end, when someone died. What *had* she been thinking?

The funeral director, Mr. Robins, was a client of her father's—now officially her client, since she planned to continue the family bookkeeping and accounting business. He'd been kind and helpful over the last couple of days . . . though he'd still managed to take her to the cleaners with the funeral arrangements. It was her fault really. She knew better. He'd cut her a great deal on a two-hour viewing, even after she'd explained that her father had outlived all of his family but her, and all but a handful of friends. Ten minutes after signing the agreement and walking out the door, she realized that she'd let her grief overcompensate on a ritual she didn't need and her father would never know about, that she should have stuck to her guns about the simple, respectful grave side service she had originally asked for.

But then, she wasn't good at sticking to her guns, either.

The man reached up to wipe a stream of tears from his

cheek with the loose sleeve of his jacket, and sniffled, loudly. She turned to look behind her, hoping to catch Mr. Robin's eye as she was beginning to suspect that Mr. Ruby Shoes may have wandered in off the streets by accident and didn't quite understand where he was or what he was doing.

Three older gentlemen sat together, all accountants like her father, who played poker with him every other Saturday night, except during tax season. Sidney Clark and Sue Butterfield were old friends of hers from high school. The CPA who specialized in tax preparation, Kendall Watson, who they sometimes used for overflow, sat alone several rows ahead of Mrs. Kludinski and Joe and Martha White, and their young daughter, Ruth—neighbors from their building, who had apparently come together.

The rest of the chairs in the large elegant room were empty. There was no sign of the funeral director, and oddly enough, no one else seemed to have even noticed the strangely dressed man at the front of the room.

Several of them nodded and sent her sympathetic smiles. But none of them looked concerned when the man turned and started toward her.

This is it then, she thought, drawing a deep breath and squirming in her chair. She was truly on her own now—in every sense—and would have to handle him herself.

Should she ask him to leave? Maybe he'd just say he was sorry for her loss and go. No harm done, no fuss necessary. But if she didn't look at him, maybe he'd just leave—even better.

His crimson shoes twinkled into her field of vision and stopped in front of her. She couldn't pretend to not see them. Her gaze lifted in stages from the athletic socks to the V of a rainbow-colored Grateful Dead T-shirt beneath the baggy jacket, to his face.

Her breath caught in her hyper-extended throat and she emitted a nervous nasal-choking noise when she tried to breathe again.

The room seemed to teeter as she gazed up into stunning blue eyes, bright and keen with knowledge and know-how. She wanted to call them Infinite Sky Blue or Majestic Royal Blue or even Sexy Sapphire, give them some romantic name or label, but they defied all classification.

Magic.

Then, even before that word solidified in her mind, his eyes turned Vivid Clover Green.

She gasped and her heart went wild. Her brain telegraphed her muscles to jump and run; her nerve endings sputtered in response. Deeply alarmed, she turned to those behind her for help. They sat placidly, their expressions emphatically kind and benevolent toward her—but not one of them seemed to notice the man with her, much less his kaleidoscope eyes.

The urge to scream swelled in her throat.

Wait! Wait! Eyes don't change colors. Dad's viewing . . . don't make a scene. Maybe his eye trick is a trick of the eye . . . the dim lighting in here sucks . . . I didn't sleep well last night . . . I could be mistaken . . . Oh, God, let me be mistaken.

Sure enough, when she could look at him again, his eyes were the same mesmerizing blue as before.

She nearly fainted with relief.

He gave her a small, understanding smile. No. More than that . . . His tender expression seemed to be telling her that he not only understood but also *knew* what she was feeling. He'd startled her, and he was sorry. But that wasn't all. He *felt* all of it. He, too, was enduring the same sadness, the loneliness, the sense of loss and being lost that she was suffering.

Impossible. Irrational. Yet, for some strange, amazing reason, she believed him.

Maybe she just wanted to believe him.

Either way, he touched something inside her. Touched and coddled it. She couldn't remember ever feeling so . . .

warmly connected to someone on so short an acquaintance.

Not even an acquaintance really, she realized, her mind scrambling for something to say to him.

"Hi." He spoke in a soft, deep whisper that tickled her in very odd places.

"Hi."

"It's good to be back."

Back from . . . Mars? Before she could think of a better way to ask him, he gave her an amused you-silly-rabbit look and sat next to her. The sleeve of his tacky black jacket brushed the sleeve of her black blazer and she imagined a comforting warmth penetrating the right side of her body. He smelled of fir trees, spicy cider and warm vanilla.

Christmas.

They looked at one another and exchanged shy smiles.

"You don't remember me, do you?"

"No. I'm sorry, I don't. All—although you do look somewhat familiar. Except for the . . . ah . . ." Perhaps the less attention she gave his attire the better, for both of them. "Did you know my father well?"

"I knew him as well as you did. Maybe a little better, since my memory is longer."

"Are you a relative, then?"

"Not exactly."

"A close friend?"

"Of yours, yes." He was a friend of *hers*? Her cheeks grew numb as blood drained from her face and her heart struggled to handle the extra load. From where? From when? How could she have forgotten him? No, no! She did not know this man. And she was just about to tell him so when he added, "Strange, isn't it?"

"What?"

"That it doesn't really matter if someone dies quickly like your mother did, in the accident, or slips away slowly over several years, you're never really ready when it happens, are you? And the hurt is just the same."

She gave a slight nod and looked away, feeling overexposed by his innocent observation. She'd been trying to tell herself that very thing, trying to rationalize the overwhelming sense of being selfish and weak and cruel every time she wished her father back alive, knowing all the pain he'd suffered the last two years. A good daughter would set him free, feel his relief and be grateful for it. Wouldn't she?

A good daughter would also miss *him*.

She did miss him. Desperately. Though she hadn't thought of it that way before—missing him. It wasn't the same as wishing him back. Missing him was just . . . missing him, feeling the aching void of him in her life. Nothing weak or mean about that. That was just human.

She caught the strange man nodding in her peripheral vision and slanted her eyes toward him. There was a closed-lip smile on his face and an air of satisfaction as he angled one scarlet-shoed foot across a silver-coated thigh and settled himself more comfortably.

"I'm sorry, but where do I know you from? How do I know you?"

"It'll come to you." He looked at her then with genuine fondness. She felt a dither near her diaphragm, recognized the tug of attraction and wanted to laugh. Hysterically. Married men, gay men and now lunatics—her dating pool was nearly complete. Of course, if he was also a stone-cold killer, he would top it off nicely. She shook her head slightly. How could she have forgotten someone like him? He leaned close and murmured, "We can talk about all that later. For now, let's just sit here together and remember him. He was a fine old gentleman."

She was certain he didn't belong. He was a stranger—very likely an unhinged stranger escaped from a local facility—but she was struck once again by how much she

loathed sitting in the front row all alone, the last of the Gib-
sons, the sole survivor, the only one left.

There was plenty of room and he wasn't hurting anyone
by being there. And truth be told, she found his presence
beside her as consoling as it was disconcerting.

Her gaze returned to the pattern on the rug three feet in
front of her. She sighed and began to feel calm and content
for the first time in . . . a really long time. When he reached
over to gently pat her thigh, she found it reassuring, not
forward or offensive at all. Soothing. Relaxing.

She judged him to be about her age. As bizarrely dressed
as he was, and as unconcerned as he seemed about exposing
his emotions, there was a part of her that admired his spirit
and bravery. Envied him, really. He was extreme, unques-
tionably. Deranged, perhaps. But at least he wasn't afraid to
express himself, to stand out, to do what he wanted to do.

She couldn't recall the last time she'd made a major life
decision on her own and stuck to it. From the day she was
born, late in her parents' lives, until this very moment,
everything had been lovingly planned and laid out for her.
It was assumed that she would set her feet into the trail of
prints they left for her, step after step, and she had. Now
here she was, almost thirty years old, living the life her parents had chosen for themselves, and not at all the woman
she once dreamed of becoming.

She wore her long mousey brown hair in a simple knot
or a ponytail at the back of her head for convenience. Her
clothes were neat and functional rather than trendy and attractive. Makeup was a bother she didn't bother with. She
had her father's short thin nose, her mother's full lips, and
moss-colored, almond-shaped eyes—a gene from her
grandmother Gibson, whom she'd never met. All fine donations, but in the end, all they added up to was plain.
Charlotte was plain. It wasn't what she set out to be but—

She jumped when she felt a heavy hand on her left
shoulder, and was surprised to see Mr. Robins standing be-

side her chair. He was a tall somber man who couldn't have looked more like a mortician if he tried.

He bent at the waist and murmured, "Charlotte. I didn't mean to startle you."

"Oh. No. I was just . . ." Had he come to ask her new friend to leave? It was undoubtedly for the best, but she couldn't help feeling disappointed. The man was such a kind, gentle soul. She hoped there wouldn't be a scene as she envisioned the funeral director dragging him, kicking and screaming, from the room in his absurd outfit—ruby shoes flailing, giant jacket hiked up over the football pants, legs straining therein. "He isn't disturbing anything, is he?"

Mr. Robins glanced at her father's coffin. "No, of course not. And there's still plenty of time if you're expecting more people."

"More people?" She hadn't expected this many people. "No. I think . . . I think this is about it. Has it been two hours already?"

"Almost. But if you'd like more time—"

"No. God, no." She cut him off and snatched up her purse. "I've had plenty of time. Thank you so much for everything you've done. You've been very kind."

"Not at all. Everything has been arranged for the grave-side service in the morning, just as we discussed."

"Nine o'clock, right?" She stood up.

"Our car will pick you up at 8:30 sharp."

"Great." She hesitated. "Should we call someone—" She turned and discovered that her peculiar companion had already left his seat. She glanced around looking for him. "Did you see which way he went? It might not be safe for him to be wandering around on his own."

"Who?"

"That guy who was sitting here."

"I'm sorry. I just came in. I didn't see anyone leave."

"No, he was there a minute ago . . . when you first came up."

He smiled tolerantly. "You were deep in thought. Perhaps you didn't notice when he left."

She stared at the empty chair. Maybe it was just as well that he'd slipped out undetected. She disliked the idea of him locked up somewhere. She thought of electroshock therapy and shuddered. But he was so sweet and friendly and the world could be a terrible place for people like that. She hoped he would be all right.

Mr. Robins was looking at her askance.

"You're probably right. It's been a strange few days."

Two

The days got stranger as the week wore on.

Learning that Mrs. Kludinski and Martha White were planning to attend the graveside ceremony as well, Charlotte invited them to ride in the family limousine with her. In fact, she was prepared to *beg* them to join her rather than take the sad, solemn ride to and from the cemetery alone— but it hadn't been necessary.

Like most Seattle days it was cloudy and overcast, the early spring wind was still winter chilly. The service was short and dignified . . . *like Dad*, she thought, in a moment of light nostalgia. She thought back to her seventeenth birthday and her father's tradition of marking her height on the bright yellow wall behind the kitchen door. It surprised him and delighted her to discover they were both 5 feet 7 inches tall, and in a rare display of vanity, he'd stretched and wiggled and hyper-extended his spine a quarter of an inch up the wall to top her—then asked her please to stop growing. An inch later she did, though the marks on the wall never changed.

They were leaving the cemetery when she saw the peculiar man again. Dressed as he was in the same outrageous outfit, how could she miss him? He stood beside an angelic head stone and waved as the limo passed by.

"Stop! Please stop," she called to the driver. "He's missed the service."

"Who?" Elderly Mrs. Kludinski and Martha craned their necks to look out every window in every direction. "Who missed the service? I don't see anyone."

"That man standing over there by the angel." She made a vague gesture with her head as she scrambled closer to the door, waiting for the long black Cadillac to come to a complete stop before getting out. "I'm pretty sure I don't know who he is, but if he walked here I want to make sure he can get back to . . . to wherever he came from. He was at the viewing yesterday, remember? He sat with me?"

She glanced over in time to see the exchange of confused frowns.

"Nice-looking man? About my age? Wearing that weird black jacket?" She was reluctant to use the kicker but she would if they didn't stop staring at her like that. "Big, sparkling red shoes?"

"Are you feeling nauseated, dear?" Mrs. Kludinski was all concern. "Dizzy? Let's roll down the windows and get some air in here, shall we?"

Frustrated, Charlotte twisted around in her seat to look through the rear window, straight back to the stone angel, its hands extended in welcome, wings poised for flight— but there was no tall, handsome man in big red shoes. A hard, painful knot of anxiety formed just below her sternum as she got out of the limo. He was nowhere in sight.

And yes, she did feel a little sick about it.

He crossed her mind again two nights later as she sat alone at a table for two eating an early dinner in her father's favorite Italian restaurant just down the street from their apartment.

No, it was *her* apartment now.

She hadn't taken more than two bites when she glanced up and saw the bizarre man in the window, looking in longingly at her favorite scaloppini.

Thrilled, but mostly astounded to see him there, she sucked in a sharp breath and choked on a small piece of shrimp—coughing and hacking and beating her own chest. When she could breathe again and focus beyond the tears in her eyes, he was gone again.

It didn't occur to her until late the next afternoon that he might be ... well ... stalking her. It wasn't something she normally worried about. She wasn't rich or beautiful—there were whole days, in fact, when she suspected she was invisible to the human eye. What could be safer?

But all that changed as she sat in the narrow, second-story office of Chancellor's Furniture Store, downloading the last of the month's sales invoices off a tediously slow computer. It had been raining off and on all day, and she glanced out the small pane-window to see which it was, on or off.

It was gloomy and bleak and the street lights glowed in soft pools along the sidewalks below. In the pool directly across from the store, the pale light ricocheted off a very large pair of ruby slippers.

He leaned against the lamp post, as if waiting for a bus, but came to attention when he saw her looking down at him. He waved wildly and flashed a wide white grin. He looked delighted to see her. She felt a little delighted herself.

Still, the coincidence of him showing up at her father's viewing and funeral, then their favorite restaurant, and now outside a client's business were adding up. And not looking good.

But, weren't stalkers more stealthy than this? Considerably less obvious? Shouldn't she *feel* him watching her, not *see* him everywhere? And where were his keepers? Surely he'd been missed by now at whatever facility he'd escaped from. Shouldn't there be people out looking for him?

How could anyone miss seeing him, she wondered, observing the absolute indifference to him in the other pedestrians. Seattle was not an indifferent town. Big and busy, yes, but the absurd and outrageous still turned heads. Her heart twisted at the thought that she might be the only one watching this poor, unfortunate man slipping through the cracks of society.

She did have the good sense to be afraid of his sudden attachment to her . . . or would have had it, if he exuded even the mildest wave of rancor or aggression. But the plain fact was, he didn't. Approachability, congeniality and kindness. She sensed these things about him—along with a faint underlying familiarity.

The real problem was that even if he weren't dressed like a clown, even if he seemed like the most normal guy in the world, she still wouldn't know what to do about him. More to the point, what she should do about his perplexing interest in her. She wasn't great with men. He clearly needed a friend and for some reason he'd chosen her, but . . . wouldn't the best and kindest thing for her to do for him be to call the authorities, get him the help he so obviously needed?

"Charlotte?" She turned from the window as Henry Chancellor entered his office with two styrofoam cups of coffee. "Am I too late? Are you finished? You take yours black, don't you?"

She nodded and took the cup he handed her. "I just finished. You need a new computer up here, Henry."

"I know. The newer ones downstairs are much faster but . . . I *know* this one."

Comfort in familiarity, she'd invented the concept. "I need the social security number for the new mover you hired. But I have everything else I need for this month. Looks like your Beat the Bunny Pre-Easter sale did very well."

"It's the season. By the end of March people have forgotten how expensive Christmas was, they've spent the whole gloomy wet winter indoors with their furniture, so they're ready to buy new in the first light of spring. And don't worry about the boy. He's my wife's nephew. I hired him for the month, for the sale. Friday is his last day. He needed to earn some extra money. I've been paying him out of petty cash." He held up a hand to keep her from speaking. "And, yes, I wrote it down for you."

He started to cross behind her to a stack of papers on the far side of the desk, but she stood quickly and put her back to the window, giving him his place at his desk—and blocking his view of the street below.

"He wants to take his girlfriend to the prom in a limousine. Ah, here it is." He ripped off the top sheet of a note pad and handed it to her over his shoulder, waiting for her to walk around him, so he could lean back. But if she did that, he could see out the window. He scooted his chair forward, adding more room to the already adequate space for her to move around him. She glanced over her shoulder to the street and the man waved at her to come down to him. "Can you get through back there?"

"Oh. Yes. I just . . ." She'd have to distract him. She leaned down and picked up her brief case. "I was just thinking that I didn't go to my prom. Did you?"

He swiveled his chair to the left, away from the window, and smiled nostalgically. "I took my wife, as a matter of fact. My father lent me his 1959 Chevy Belair, and she was the prettiest one there." She smiled at the warmth in his voice. "My wife, that is . . . although that Chevy was something to look at, too." She laughed, as he'd hoped she would, and then he narrowed his eyes at her. "Do you have a moment to talk, Charlotte?"

She glanced at the window, at the coffee in her hand, then back at him. "Sure."

He waited for her to sit in the empty chair beside his desk, keeping his back to the window. "I wanted to tell you how sorry I am about your father."

"Thank you."

"Will you be all right? Businesswise? I know he had a great many clients. Will you be adding them to yours, or won't you have time for them?"

"Oh." She was anxious to get away—hoping her strange friend wouldn't wander off before she could get to him, then hoping he would. "I'll keep some of them. There are several companies that he started with as small businesses, they grew, and he stayed with them. They took up a lot of his time. A lot of my time, too, recently. But they should have their own in-house accountants now. I'll weed those out and keep most of the smaller businesses. The next few months will be a little hectic but it should work out fine."

"Not too much for just one person?"

"No. Well, yes, but I'll be fine." It wasn't like she had a lot of other things to do with her time.

"You're sure?" She recognized the look in his eyes and sighed. It was the sympathetic, well-meaning look that invariably preceded a discussion of her nonexistent love life. "The reason I'm asking is, my wife's ex-sister-in-law's nephew is the . . . ah, um . . . you know, the main money man for this big chain of hotels, actually several chains with different names. They do fast food, too. And rental cars. He's the vice president of money or something but they call it something else . . . ah . . ."

"Controller? Auditor? CFO? Chief financial officer?"

"Yes, that's it. In Chicago. He travels a good deal, works long hours. A very nice, quiet, young fellow. He was out here last fall on a visit and fell in love with the water and the mountains and all the greenery—you know how people do. Says he wants to downsize his life a little, enjoy more of it while he's still young . . ."

What if a patrol car happens to drive by? Cops get paid to notice the strange and unusual. Would they check with missing persons before or after they confiscated his shoes and locked him up? she wondered.

". . . up and quit his job." Henry went on. "Luckily, he's single, did I mention that? A very nice, quiet, young guy.

Anyway, he's packing up and moving out here. Expect him any day now."

"Bold move."

"Gutsy, I thought, and smart, too. Figuring out early that money isn't everything. Life is short, you know?" He looked uncomfortable in light of her recent loss. "Anyway, I believe he has plenty of money set aside but he's not ready to retire just yet, so he's looking for work. Something smaller. Something challenging. And when my wife told me all this, she seemed very enthused with the idea of the two of you at least meeting. Since you have so much in common," he added, looking even more uncomfortable. "Perhaps you could work out some sort of business arrangement. Maybe . . . who knows? A nice, quiet, single young man . . . and you. Who knows what might happen?"

It started as a low grumble deep in her belly, then escalated to a high pitched screaming in her head. *No, no, no! Nice, quiet man is a synonym for miserable, boring loser! I don't want to have anything in common with that! I want more! I need more! I want bold, confident and determined! I want exciting! I want sexy! I want Alpha! I want passion and laughter and . . . and someone who will see me as more than a nice, quiet woman! I want a life! I want to live! I want to get out of here!*

"It was awfully nice of her to think of me." It was a strain to control her voice. "But to tell you the truth, Henry, I don't think I'm going to need a partner. Not right away. Not for several years, if then. I'm feeling pretty confident that I can handle the whole business on my own, once I weed through it."

"I have no doubt that you can." Henry looked let off the hook. He could at least tell his wife he'd tried. "But it's something to keep in mind, down the road a bit. Working alone can get lonely."

"I know. Thanks, Henry." She stood, slipped the strap of her purse over her shoulder and picked up her briefcase with the same hand, leaving the other free for the rest of her coffee. "If you think it might help, have him call me when he gets settled. I'll give him the names of the companies I'll be cutting loose. They'll be looking for good accountants very soon."

He beamed at her. "You're a sweet girl, Charlotte Gibson."

She smiled and felt heat in her cheeks. "I'll see you next month, Henry."

"I always look forward to it."

"Me, too. Thanks for the coffee."

"Good night, Charlotte. Hurry home. I think it's going to rain."

The moment she stepped out of the front door onto the sidewalk, he called to her. "Well, it's about time. I thought you forgot about me again."

Charlotte took a deep breath. She was nonconfrontational by nature, but everyone had their limit. She glanced at the traffic, then marched across the street to deal with him.

Three

"Who are you? And why are you following me?"

He gave her a charming smile and slipped his hands into the pouches on his jacket. But the man walking on the sidewalk behind him, stopped short and frowned at her.

"Who me?" the second man said, surprised and annoyed by her accusation. "I'm not following you."

"No. Sorry. Not you." She held up her cup and spread her last three fingers. "Sorry."

She watched the second man stomp away, then curled all but her index finger around her coffee cup and directed it at her target. "You!"

"It's a long story," he said, calm and mildly amused. He spoke in a smooth, deep baritone that seemed to vibrate in the nicest way at the base of her spine. "Let's walk or we'll get caught in the rain."

Turning to his right, he started to walk, confident that she'd follow. She only did so, however, because he was aimed in the direction of her apartment—she might need to know if he knew where she lived.

"This part is always so much harder when you're dealing with adults who don't believe in anything anymore. But you, I'm pleased to say, are a rare and wonderful exception, Charlotte. Deep down, you still believe."

"In what?"

"In all the good stuff." He inhaled deeply through his nose as if he could smell it. "Peace. The power of hope. Love. The Spirit of Christmas. Happily ever after. All of it. Most of the time you are a True Believer."

"That's very nice, but who are you?"

He thought a moment. "I know you like to add things together and come up with a sum total at the end. But in this case I think we should use a little algebra. You were always good at math. I'll give you the answer, if you promise to stay and listen to the solution for X. You won't have a clear answer to your question until you have all the components."

"Okay. Shoot." She was proud that she sounded braver than she felt. How did he know so much about her? It was creepy . . . and fascinating. Mentally she kept track of the shops ahead that were still open for business, and possibly sanctuary if she needed it.

"We've been friends a long time, you and I."

"No, I—"

"Better friends when you were four and five, and for a while when you were six, but that doesn't mean we've forgotten each other or that I didn't exist all this time. I've always been here; you just wouldn't let yourself see me."

"Well I see you now, but I still don't know who you are."

"I am a figment of your ingenuity, the aggregate of your resourcefulness, a compendium of your dreams and wishes. In layman terms, I was once your imaginary playmate, and now I'm your—" Her feet took root in the sidewalk. He stopped to look back at her. "Oh, see? You're not going to believe me, are you?"

She stared at him. He gave her a smug smile and lifted his brows. "I do look familiar though, don't I? And how else would I know you had a make-believe friend if I didn't exist?" He walked back to her, took the lax arm hanging from her left shoulder and looped it over his. "Come on. I'll explain everything. It's not as complicated as you might think."

She allowed him to pull her along, taking careful note of the very real-feeling arm under her hand and the strange scent he had that remind her of winter holidays. *Some sort of drug that oozes through his skin like garlic? Doesn't cyanide smell like almonds?*

There was a convenience store three blocks up—she could call the police from there. For now, she needed to keep him calm, keep him talking.

"I've changed some, I admit." His tone was so casual it sounded like truth. "But, like you, I couldn't remain a child forever. So, I grew up with you. I changed when you changed." He laughed—not manically, but in a humorous way. A wonderful way. She liked his laugh. "I remember once, when you were fifteen, I looked like Kirk Cameron and Patrick Swayze in the same week. It was terrifying." He glanced down at her and turned sober. "You don't need to be afraid, Charlotte. If you really don't want me here all you have to do is stop thinking about me. I'll disappear again. Naturally, the reverse is true, as well. The more you think about me, the more real I'll become . . . to you."

How was she to *not* think about him when he stood right in front of her?

"To me." She recalled the viewing and the way no one else seemed to notice him—and the second man on the sidewalk a few minutes ago. "I'm the only one who can see you."

"That's right. I'm all yours." He winked at her. Her knees wobbled and she tripped on a crack in the sidewalk, staggering against him—against his solid and very real body.

He used his other hand to catch her and she looked up into his handsome face while he held her close by her upper arms. Her mouth went dry. He didn't feel imaginary. His out-of-this-world-blue eyes gazed into her soul and became soft and content with what he found there. He had the nicest mouth . . . a full, soft-looking lower lip that she suddenly ached to taste.

He frowned, looked puzzled, then set her back at arms length. "Uh-ah. Careful. You can't wish for things like that. I'm not real, remember?"

"You look real. You feel real."

"Only because you want me to." Suddenly his head and face faded in and out with the head, face and muzzle of a gray and black donkey. She made a startled noise and stepped back, and his image settled into place again. He raised a brow in censure and spoke sternly. "I am not a jackass."

"You can read my mind?"

"No. Not exactly." He collected himself and turned sympathetic. "I know. It's confusing at first, but you'll get the hang of it. Just . . . be careful what you wish for."

"So then . . . you're what I wish for?"

"And what you dream of and admire. What you think you need. I've been a long time in the making, I can tell you." He turned and started walking again. "Physically, I am now an accumulation of many men. You started putting me together, in this form, when you were in college . . . once you got over that Kevin Costner thing . . . and the, ah . . . Oh! Watch this." He stopped to assume a more distinguished pose. The shape of his eyes altered minutely and the color grew darker as he said, "Miss Bennet, for many months now I have considered you to be one of the handsomest women of my acquaintance."

"Mr. Darcy," she murmured in awe, stunned and fascinated by Colin Firth's eyes and voice.

He made a disgusted noise, rolled his chocolate brown eyes back to blue and started walking again. "What is it with you and that guy?"

"Can you do Mark Darcy, too?" She hurried to catch up with him.

"Of course, but it's not *him* telling Bridget Jones—the actor telling the actress—that he likes her *just the way she is* that makes your heart constrict like that. It's the thought of someone saying it to *you* that you love. And that's right here." He put his fist to his heart. "You made that a part of me. It's what I want, too."

She couldn't help it; she glanced at his shoes and his hideous jacket. "You want someone to tell you that they like you just the way you are?"

He cast her a vapid look. "Do not go there. Would it kill you to take even the slightest interest in male fashion? You should have seen my hair before you happened to decide, one random afternoon, that you preferred shorter hair on men in general."

"Not that many men can pull off really good-looking long hair. It always seems to look stringy or dirty. I don't think men have the patience to mess with their hair like women do. They're better off keeping it shorter."

"I know. I just told you that. But what about the rest of me? Open your eyes, Charlotte. Look around. This . . ." He held his hands out to display his getup. "This is the entire extent of memorable male clothing inside your head. And I'd be wearing Dorothy's shoes barefoot if you hadn't thought *tube* was an interesting way to describe a sock. Captain Kangaroo's jacket, of course, was a big hit with you *but* . . ." He paused to point an accusing finger at her. "Do not for one second think I don't know why you are so hugely impressed with these football pants. Sure. Laugh."

She giggled at his indignation even as a telling heat rose up her neck and into her cheeks. A woman passing by turned her head to look at Charlotte—seemingly alone and giggling to herself—and her face grew hotter.

"Ha! Serves you right, you should feel embarrassed.

You'll never know how close I came to wearing Julia Roberts' red *Pretty Woman* dress to your father's wake, just to make my point."

"I love that dress." She tossed her empty coffee cup in a trash receptacle outside a private gym and caught herself feeling completely at ease with him again.

"And the black-and-white one she wore to the Academy Awards the year she won. I know. Women's clothes you notice. But I can't work with your negative images of male fashion, the clothes you think are boring or tacky on men. They disintegrate almost immediately."

"I see men who dress nice. All the time. How memorable do a shirt and a pair of pants have to be?"

He shook his head. "It's the texture of the shirt and how you *feel* when you look at it or touch it. The way it drapes across a man's shoulders; the way his muscles ripple underneath it and how *that* makes you feel. The way it fits across his abdomen and tucks into the waistband of his pants, the way the pants hug his ass and how *that*—"

"Okay, okay. Really memorable. I get it. I'll try to pay closer attention."

"I'll help you." He looked down and up the long, drab black wool coat she had on. "You have good taste, Charlotte. You just need to use it more."

She prickled instantly. "I thought you liked me just the way I am? I thought you were my friend?"

He smiled. "I do, actually. And I am. Friends tell the truth, don't they? Besides, I can't say anything you don't already think. So we both know you could dress better."

She snorted. "What would be the point of that? What difference would it make?"

"Ah. There's that defeatist attitude we all know and love so well." He slapped a hand to his chest dramatically and looked heavenward. Then he was instantly serious as they started to cross the street just beyond the convenience store. "The point, dear Charlotte, is that you're never going to get what you want if you don't make some sort of effort to go out and get it. I know you think that some man, who looks just like me by the way, is going to come galloping up on a white horse and give you everything you've ever longed for, but that sort of thinking is as unreal as I am.

"And the difference is, you're on your own now. You can do whatever you want. You don't have to worry about disappointing your parents anymore. You don't need their approval. You don't have to worry about who will take care of them, or feel responsible for them. You've been a good daughter. But now it's time to start living your own life. They would want that. They never meant for you to hide yourself away in their ambitions. It just happened. All they ever really wanted was for you to be happy."

She couldn't help but wonder, how crazy was *she* to be taking advice from someone who didn't really exist? And if she made him and he didn't exist, did that mean she didn't exist? No, too *Matrix*-ish for her. So, if she existed and she made him, then he existed . . . somewhere. Maybe not in this plane of reality, but . . .

"Do you have a name?" she asked abruptly, acutely aware of the *real* people around her, barely moving her lips, keeping her head movements casual.

He looked startled, then a little wondrous. "You really don't remember me, even from before, when we were young?"

She shrugged. "I remember my parents teasing me sometimes about imaginary friends but . . . no, I don't remember you."

A slow, scintillating smile curved his lips. "So you don't remember the name you gave me." He whooped and laughed and did a little jig in Dorothy's shoes. "There, you see? There's some good in everything, Charlotte. You don't remember me, but you don't remember my name either." He seemed to grow slightly taller with relief and pride before he told her, "Just call me Mel."

"Mel?"

"Yeah." His gaze wandered as he tested the name. "Mel. I like it."

"What is it really? Melvin?"

He gave her a sly look. "If you can't honestly remember, I am not obligated to tell you. And frankly, that name was a flight of fancy taken first by Mr. Leitch and then by you that I have always resented. And, of course, you confused lemons with bananas but you were very young and may not have known the significance of—"

"You mean, you can remember things that I can't?" The first line finally sank in.

"Sure." He shrugged. "That's where I come from."

"Where?"

He sighed like he'd already explained a thousand times. He held out his hands. "You live here. Now. You are aware of everything going on around you. *This* is your consciousness. I usually hang out on the other side, just beyond the barrier. That's where everything you've ever heard or seen or felt or thought about exists, and the barrier is like a fine film that keeps all that information from flooding your mind all at once. It allows you to reach in and pluck out what you want, when you want it. Like a big boiling pot, let's say. Everything goes in there, all of it, from the moment your first two cells divide until . . ." He used one finger to poke her arm. "Now. And . . . now. And . . . now. And . . ."

"Okay. I get that it's all there."

"Most of what you put in the pot settles on the bottom because you don't need it or care about it. Sometimes a memory or a thought will bubble up to the surface on its own; sometimes you need to stir the pot to get them to rise. There are some, many, that float all the time. Things that have made a big impression on you, say. Images of people you think of often, works in progress, lists of phone numbers, tunes you like—things you want easy access to but don't want to think about constantly. You pick out what you want, think about it, throw it back in the pot a million times a day or more. Me, you think about *a lot*. I spend a great deal of time out of the pot."

"Right. I . . . you . . ." She flushed again, profoundly disconcerted that he knew her so well. All of her, so well. He smiled at her kindly.

"I'm not your conscience, Charlotte. I don't judge your fantasies or evaluate the legitimacy of your dreams or wishes. To me, they simply are what they are. I wouldn't exist without them."

"So why aren't you more like a hologram or a ghost or something then? If you're just a bunch of my memories and thoughts and . . . and desires. Why do you seem so real to me?"

"Because I am real to you." When he could see she still didn't quite grasp it, he took another track. He stopped and turned toward her. "Close your eyes."

"No. What if someone sees me standing here *alone*, in the middle of the sidewalk, with my eyes closed? You might as well hang a Mug Me sign on my back."

"Okay. Over here then, behind this potted shrub. Lean back against this building and close your eyes like you're just catching your breath. This'll only take a second. Close them and don't peek."

She leaned her head back against the brick wall and did as he told her. Immediately, she smelled bacon and could hear it sizzling in a pan.

More magic.

"Mmm. We love bacon, don't we, Charlotte?" She nodded blindly. "You want a bite?" She nodded again—in for a penny. "Open your mouth, then open your eyes."

She did both, only to find his fingers empty. She snapped her lips shut.

"Disappointed." He identified her primary emotion as he smoothed the backs of his knuckles slowly down her left cheek. "But you get the idea. The smell and the sound, they weren't real either. But your memories of them are strong enough to make your mouth salivate. Your desire to believe made the bacon real enough for you to open your mouth for it. Just like your desire to believe that someone like me exists makes me real enough for you to feel my fingers on your cheek."

It was a heavy concept inside her head, like God and black holes and why glue doesn't stick to the inside of the bottle. Things she accepted on faith alone. Her temples were starting to throb. It was more than she could assimilate all at once.

She pushed away from the building and started for home again. She needed to think . . . alone.

"You know," he said, dropping casually into step with her—seeming as comfortable out of her head as he was, apparently, inside it. "Maybe we could stop and buy a *GQ* magazine on our way home. We could browse through, see if I'm a shirt-and-tie guy, or more like a Marlboro Man, huh? We could pick up a *Glamour* and *Cosmopolitan*, too. I'm very in touch with your feminine side but it doesn't hurt to stay current. Tomorrow we can do some shopping and maybe—"

"Hey," she said, cutting him off as she spotted Mrs. Kludinski getting out of a car in front of their building. Her neighbor turned and bent at the waist to speak to the driver, with one small shopping bag in hand. "Don't start making a lot of plans, okay? Especially the *we* kind. I'm not sure I like you. I'm not sure I want you around. I'm not even sure I'm really awake here, so back off. Go . . ." She flipped her fingers as if to shoo away a fly. "Go . . . wherever you go when you're not around. I need to think."

"About me?" he asked smugly. Then she recalled she had to *stop* thinking about him to get rid of him. "Don't worry, Charlotte, Mrs. Kludinski can't see me, remember?"

"I can see you," she said through her clenched teeth, barely ten feet from her neighbor.

He hastened his pace to the front of the car and groaned. "It's Lacey. Looks like her husband bought her another new car. Brace yourself, sweetheart."

"Charlotte." Mrs. Kludinski caught sight of her and straightened out of the car with a smile. The elderly lady had been a widow for as long as Charlotte could remember. Social and friendly, she'd always made her feel like a special friend.

"Hi, Mrs. Kludinski. If this is Tuesday, that must be Lacey. Did you have a nice afternoon? Is this a new car?" She stepped into the street and over to the open car door. "Hello, Lacey."

A year behind Lacey Kludinski in school, Charlotte always thought her dark good looks were exotic rather than uncommonly beautiful. She was a popular cheerleader in high school and married a young doctor the year after she graduated from college with a degree in interior design— which she used solely to decorate her own home on Bainbridge Island. She was and had everything Charlotte wasn't and didn't—and couldn't be happier about it. Or more vocal about it.

"Oh, hi, Charlotte. Don't you just love it? Come feel this, real leather on these seats. Soft as butter. Sad thing is, we'll just have to trade it in next year for another new car because the humidity out on the Island is so hard on cars, you know. I swear, if I hadn't married a doctor, I don't know how we'd keep up with everything. It's just one thing after another, I'm telling you. So, how are you? Seeing anyone special yet?"

Charlotte smiled at her. Something inside her always wanted to think the best of Lacey. Really. She'd always been so nice to her aunt—tins of cookies and brownies in high school, Tuesday afternoon lunches and shopping trips since then. Lacey had a good side. Somewhere.

"What. A. Boob." Mel placed two big, hot hand prints on the shiny hood of Lacey's new car.

"I'm fine and no I'm not," she said quickly, thinking she

should go inside before Mel did something embarrassing. "I mean, I've been sort of busy and . . ."

"Her father passed away last week," Mrs. Kludinski injected.

"That's right. You told me. I'm sorry, Charlotte."

"Thanks."

"I bet she's wishing her aunt would take the hint and follow him." Mel stuck his finger in his mouth, wetting it, then doodled on the hood with it. "Your father was right about her being a gold digger, you know. She wouldn't give this nice old lady a bucket of bad luck, if she couldn't pay for it."

"All the more reason to keep your eyes open for a good catch," Lacey said, diligently. "I still think you ought to let me look into hooking you up with someone from my husband's hospital. He knows several male nurses, and most of them aren't even gay. A couple of them don't even *act* gay. You don't want to end up old and alone, do you?"

"Like your aunt, you twit?" But even before Mel said it, Charlotte felt the slightest stiffening in Mrs. Kludinski's posture and felt bad for her. Felt bad for them both really.

"There are worse things than old and alone, Lacey, but . . . thanks. And I will keep my eyes open. You drive safe now." She turned, stepped back onto the sidewalk and walked over to the steps of her building while Mrs. Kludinski said good-bye. Mel joined her, a derisive scowl on his magnanimous face.

The three of them watched the big, silver-colored Cayenne drive away.

"Well, her brain is the size of a pea and her heart is even smaller," Mrs. Kludinski announced as she turned around. "But she's real careful with her big fancy cars so she's a good, safe driver and she's cheaper than a taxi. Besides, I just wouldn't feel right about leaving her all my money if I didn't think shc'd carncd at lcast part of it. Wouldn't be good for her character."

Charlotte chuckled silently. The old woman started up

the four shallow steps and Charlotte followed her . . . and Mel followed her, ignoring her scowl and the hand she kept waving him away with.

"Sounds to me like Lacey's getting a pretty good deal." She stepped around the elderly lady, used her key to open the main door for her. "The two of you always seem to have a good time together. There are harder ways to earn money."

Charlotte scooted in after her, pushing the door closed behind her, locking him out. She glanced through the frosted glass in the door, turning completely around when she couldn't see him, to check the sidewalk in both directions. He was gone.

Four

"Oh no," she murmured softly, feeling mean and sorry and afraid she'd never see him again. Which would be for the best, right?

"What is it? Are you all right, dear?"

"Yes." She sighed, miserable. "I'm fine. I think I may have just done something truly awful and I'm not sure how to . . . if I want to . . ." Mrs. Kludinski looked concerned. "Never mind. I'll figure it out."

"Long day?"

"Incredibly."

"Can I help?"

Impulsively, she passed her briefcase to her other hand, then looped her arm around her frail shoulders and gave the old lady a quick peck on the cheek. "Thanks. But I'm okay."

"Yes, you are." She patted Charlotte's cheek with arthritic fingers and headed for the door of her first-floor apartment. "But if you need anything, call me."

"I will." She waited for her to go inside then turned to take the stairs to the second floor.

"Don't say you didn't miss me."

Mel grinned at her from the middle of the staircase.

"How long have you been there?"

"Since you locked the door on me."

"So you can walk through walls? Like a ghost?"

"Not exactly." His expression grew guarded. So, naturally, she said, "Explain."

With a belabored expression he got to his feet and let her by. "You didn't want me with you, but you didn't stop thinking about me, either. I didn't leave; I just got out of your way."

"Then get out of it again because I'm exhausted and I need to think . . . and you're a distraction."

"I can help you think. Two heads are better than one, right?"

"If I have this straight so far, you and I share a mind, so trying to solve a problem from two different heads might be a little tricky."

"Not really. You do it all the time. All those little mental debates." He stopped on the first landing and cupped both hands to his right. "Shall I have chicken or fish for dinner?" He moved his hands to the left and spoke at them in a slightly higher voice. "I feel like eating fish but the chicken is already thawed." Back to the right and the lower voice. "The chicken will be fine in the frig until tomorrow and I can nuke the fish in the microwave." Left. "Tomorrow I pick up the monthly receipts for Tops Chinese and they always send moo shoo pork home with me." Right. "I don't think it would be wise to risk that chicken on Thursday." Left. "That's okay, I can feed it to Mel and—" He gasped. "Charlotte!"

He sent a comically wounded look up the stairs and made her laugh. Taking steps two at a time he came to her side. She looked at him thoughtfully as little tumblers rolled back and forth in her brain.

"So . . . you can't really read my mind. You don't know what I'm going to say or think until I say or think it. You're on like a . . . a six- or eight-second delay, aren't you?"

"I love smart women." He started up the steps again. "I really do. Most smart men love smart women, as a matter of fact. That just makes sense, doesn't it? I told you there was nothing wrong with being smart."

"So I'm right," she said, following, recalling a short phase in her life when she'd actually pretended to be less intelligent to boost male egos. "And I bet there's some way to turn you off and on, too, isn't there?"

"In what sense? I have to admit that this sudden aversion to thinking in my presence is a definite turnoff for me. It would be for any man. But as to turning me on . . ." He slipped her a sizzling glance and she tripped on the next step. It amused him. "We've already discussed that."

"I *meant* off and on like a light bulb. You come, you go. You're here, you're gone. That's me too, right?"

"I am all you, babe." She squinted at him. "You, babe? Get it? Sonny and Cher?"

"I get it. I don't like it. I don't like being called sweetheart, either. You called me that earlier." She took her keys out of her coat pocket again and stopped at her apartment door. "Names like that annoy me."

"I know. But that's only because you hear them most often from old people and jerky men you don't know. But now you know me, and I'm not a jerk, so I'm testing endearments. There has to be one you like."

"Why?"

"Because they're one of the many components of the affection you crave. Once we find one that doesn't trigger a full-scale feminist reaction inside you, we can begin a desensitization program."

She sighed and lean against the door. "I have one more question." He pressed his shoulder to the door next to her and waited for it. He was a large presence and standing so close to him made her feel . . . not smothered, not intimidated, just . . . really good in a way she couldn't explain. Safe, maybe. "Why now? Why are you here now?"

"Because you need me now."

"For what?"

He glanced around as if the answer might be written on one of the walls, then looked straight into her eyes. "I'm not sure. We'll figure that one out together."

She could have stood there and looked at him for the rest of her life. His features were neither pretty nor beautiful; their appeal lay in the expressions that changed as often and diversely as his thoughts. An honest face. A trustworthy face.

He smiled suddenly and startled her. She turned quickly to unlock the door, then stopped.

"I actually have two last questions." He didn't seem surprised. "The second one is . . . will the man I fall in love with be exactly like you? Is that how I'll recognize him?"

"I don't know." She frowned and he held out the arm he wasn't leaning on. "I only know what you know, Charlotte, but . . . someone *exactly* like me would be perfect," he said without ego. "Perfect can be hard to live with. There would be no give and take of opinions, no surprises, no compromising. No growth. No friction, no push and pull. I think we're looking for someone *almost* like me, with as many of my strengths and virtues and attributes as possible. You'll feel comfortable with him. You'll sense parts of me in him. I think that's how you'll recognize him." He paused. "You gonna open the door now?"

"As soon as you leave."

He shook his head slowly. "Can't leave. Not while you're thinking of me."

"Then get out of my way again."

He backed away from the door. "Where am I supposed to go?"

"How would I know? Use your own imagination."

"Very funny. You want me to stand here in the hall all night?"

"I just want to be alone for a while. To think. To sort this out." She opened the door, went inside, then turned and blocked his entry. "I'm sorry."

He didn't look pleased and she thought he might argue, but all he said was, "I'm here for you."

She nodded, gave him a small apologetic smile and closed the door. Then turned to face the empty apartment with a heavy sigh. *Alone* sucked immediately.

She knew loneliness. Even before her few good friends got married, with her father still healthy and around all the time, there had been an underlying loneliness for as long as she could remember. She was simple and quiet and plain and so was her life for the most part. But now, she was alone *and* lonely and the difference overwhelmed her. Crushed her.

There was a soft knock on the door behind her. She looked through the peephole at him.

He smiled and waved. "You can change your mind and let me in. I'm good company."

"You're also a distraction. I need to think."

"I won't make a sound."

"No. Now leave me alone."

She dropped her briefcase and purse on the table beside the door, hung up her coat and went to the kitchen to cook the chicken she didn't feel like eating . . . also alone.

She had to face the facts. She was in deep trouble if she was resurrecting imaginary companions from her childhood. And while she was reluctant to give him any credit for his thinking, he was right about one thing: It was time to make some changes in her life. Big ones. Huge ones. Drastic ones.

It wasn't like it was a new concept to her; she'd been thinking about it, dreaming about it for years. It wasn't that she didn't *want* to change. She did, more than anything. So, what held her back?

As she thought about it, there came another knock on the door. She went to the kitchen doorway and stared across the room at it—decided to ignore him. A few seconds later, he called through the door, "Courage and self-confidence. That's all you need. And a plan. I can help you with the plan. I have some really great ideas."

"Stop bothering me!"

He was gutsy and self-confident enough for both of them . . . and stubborn and annoying. Was he everything she wasn't? No . . . that didn't work. She made him, so . . . she was brave and bold, too . . . right?

She took a few salad fixings from the frig, closed the door with her foot and carried them to the sink.

So say she suddenly went nuts and changed her entire life around, did everything she wanted to do, when she wanted to do it. What would people say? They were used to her being the way she was. *She* was used to it. Would they treat her differently? Would she be a different person? Would it make her happy? Or make her feel foolish for even trying?

Who cares what other people think? You're not changing for them; you're changing for yourself. You don't have to change your whole self, only what makes you unhappy, only what you want to change to make yourself happy. And why would you feel foolish for making yourself happy? Treat yourself better and other people will treat you better. That's just logical . . .

She threw the paring knife and cucumber in the sink, marched out of the kitchen, through the open dining room and across the living room to shout at the closed front door.

"Are you talking in my head now?"

"Well, you won't let me in to talk to your face, and you really shouldn't be making any unilateral decisions in there on your own. We're a team, remember?"

"If you don't leave me alone I'm going to . . . Ha! I have the entire six-hour mini-series of *Pride and Prejudice* on DVD in here. You want that?"

There was a thud on the door and a brushing sound of

something sliding to the floor on the other side . . . and then silence.

Charlotte put her hand over her mouth and laughed silently into it, all the way back to the kitchen.

Five

She woke abruptly the next morning from a heavy, dream-less sleep. Which was odd actually, because she usually woke slowly, attempting over and over to reenter the dreams her alarm clock interrupted, or sorting through the shadows and images to determine them too bizarre to re-visit. This morning she came wide awake without rem-nants, several minutes before her alarm rang with only one clear image in her mind.

"Mel?" She finished tying her robe as she walked down the hall toward the living room. Was it possible? Could the whole previous day have been last night's dream? "Mel? Are you still here?"

A muffled "Good morning" came through the front door.

He was on the floor in the hall with his back against the wall. He'd taken off his red shoes and stuffed his tube socks down inside them; rolled up his pouchy jacket to rest his head on. If he'd slept, he did it sitting up.

"Have you been out here all night?" she asked after opening the door.

"Where else would I be?" He started to gather his things and get up. He seemed a little snippy. "I can hardly engage in an active night life without you, now can I?"

"I guess I thought you would . . . pop out . . . or inside the apartment maybe, after I went to sleep."

He stood looking down at her. There was a hurt and a vulnerability in his eyes that was genuine. She felt something go warm and soft, and liquefy inside her. "I am powerless without you, Charlotte. If you want me in your life you have to let me in."

"What would happen to you if I didn't?"

He gave a little shrug, but she could tell the thought pained him. "Same as last time. You sent me under the bed to look for snakes and spiders and forgot all about me. I stayed there until you stopped worrying about such things. After that, you filled your mind with other issues, bigger problems. I tried to help you then, too, but you wouldn't let yourself see me. I had to do the best I could from inside your head—in dreams, in deep thought, through your imagination, but you got pretty good at closing me out in there, as well."

"I didn't mean to hurt you." And she didn't want him to go away again.

His dark brow furrowed. "I know. It's a sad fact of life, I believe, that growing up involves doubt and confusion, and that maturing so often becomes synonymous with sacrificing dreams and desires for what is logical and practical." He motioned to the open door, aware, apparently, that she was now ready to accept him. It was his awareness of it, of her, that was still very . . . weird. Following her inside, he continued. "Don't get me wrong; logical and practical are necessary. But not to the exclusion of everything else."

"And you think that's what I've done. Given up all my dreams and wishes for what's logical and practical?"

"Worse. You let your doubts and confusion run rampant and gave up everything for what your parents thought was logical and practical."

That hurt. More than she could say. Probably because it was too close to the truth, and mostly because he'd said it out loud. Was he deliberately trying to hurt her?

"That's not a very nice thing to say."

His smile was small as he dropped his shoes and coat on the couch. "I couldn't say it if you didn't already think it, remember?"

"Damn, that's annoying. There should be some rule about you hurting my feelings with my own thoughts. Put your shoes on the floor and hang that up in the closet. I like things tidy."

She turned on her heel and headed for the kitchen. She couldn't take much more of him without some coffee. The pot was on a timer and she emerged moments later with a steaming mug full.

"Actually, there are rules," he said, sliding into a chair across from her at the dining room table. "I can't lie to you. I need to be as honest with you as you'll let me." He looked sheepish. "I am sorry I hurt you, though. I could have said the same thing with a lot more finesse."

"So you're mad because I left you outside all night."

"No. I'm just tired of being ignored." He sighed and slouched in the chair. "I want everything to change now, today . . . yesterday even. I want it all to be as it could be . . . as it should be. But I can tell you're still not ready."

"Ready for what?"

"To listen to what I have to say. To trust me. To act on my advice."

"I let you in."

"That's not the same thing."

No, it wasn't. "I just met you. I need more time."

He stared at her for a moment, then closed his eyes, pressed his thumb and fingers to the middle of his brow, spread them out and rubbed his temples as if he had a headache.

"Do you want some coffee?"

"Do you really want me more awake than you are? And for future reference, that stuff goes straight to my nervous system. A hyper-stimulated imagination can be very scary, you know."

She wanted to laugh but just smiled instead. "Are you always this grumpy in the morning?"

"No, I . . . my internal clock is screwed up. I'm usually more active at night while you sleep, and I rest during the day when your brain is busy. . . ." he waved his hand vaguely, "creating cash and accrual systems . . . and auditing for errors and posting to general ledgers."

That's why she didn't dream last night . . . he'd been sleeping, too.

"What happens if you don't rest?"

"We get psychotic."

Unfortunately, that made sense to her, too.

"If it makes you feel any better, I missed my dreams last night," she said, her expression hopeful and cajoling.

A smile slowly curved his lips, and his eyes lit with reluctant fondness. He wagged his head a little, to appear not to be giving in too easily. "Well, maybe we can work something out. By nature, I'm considerably more flexible than you are. I can sleep anytime, anywhere. I'll just use my time more wisely."

"Like now? Because I'm going into my office to work for a while . . . until about noon."

"What about shopping?" He sat up straight. "We should get an early start. We need to work on your makeover plan. At least run down to the drugstore for some magazines. We don't even have to get a *GQ*. Ralph Lauren will have ads in everything. All I need is some warmer pants . . . and those shoes are throwing my back out of alignment."

"Maybe this afternoon, okay?" She stood with her coffee cup in hand. "I really do have a lot to do. The next few

weeks are going to be crazy until I incorporate Dad's clients
with my own." She sighed as the heavy ache of missing her
father settled in her chest, once again. Her throat grew
thick, her voice thin. "I should have done it months ago. I
knew he wasn't going to get any better. I knew he was getting weaker and weaker. I just kept hoping . . ."

She broke off when she saw tears welling in his eyes. It
was her pain, her sorrow looking back at her, still fresh and
tender and paralyzing if she gave into it.

"Anyway, I don't have time right now to . . . start changing a lot of other things." She went into the kitchen for
more coffee, calling, "I have a system. And once I get the
clients that I'm keeping set up in my system, I'll have more
time for shopping and . . . and whatever. Plus, I'll have to
close out the companies I'm not keeping, which could take
a while if they can't find someone to take over right away.
Dad would just die if I . . . he would expect me to stay with
them until they found new accountants."

She returned to find him with his elbow on the table, his
fist in his cheek, looking utterly bored.

"And . . ." he prompted.

"And what? That's it. I'm too busy."

"Have you ever noticed how easily that flows from your
lips? I'mtoobusy. It's like one word for you. It's your favorite excuse."

"Maybe because it's true."

"Ah-ha." He put on a long-suffering face and pushed
himself to his feet. "Fine. Swell. No problem." He shuffled
slowly over to the couch. "It's been twenty-eight years,
seven months, three days, ten hours and sixteen minutes. I
guess we can put life off a little longer."

"Oh, stop it." She watched him lie down and put his
hands under his head, the large muscles in his arms straining the sleeves of the Grateful Dead T-shirt. A vision of
those arms wrapping around her flashed through her mind
and she quickly blacked it out. "I have a life."

"Yeah, I know," he said to the ceiling, his tone jaded and

dull. "It's been one thrill right after another so far. I can hardly bear it."

"You're really obnoxious, you know that?"

"So sue me. You have your work, I have mine. You crunch numbers; I crunch the truth."

"You want a blanket?" She'd had enough truth for one day. The sooner he went back to sleep the better.

"No. I find warmth in your resentment."

That tickled her memory. "Where have I heard that before?"

"You read it in a poem by Isbin Rudger, poet and philosopher, 1422 to 1458, while you were researching a paper for English 404. You used to like poetry."

She read autobiographies and spy thrillers now. They were something her parents had liked, as well. They passed them around, discussed them like a mini book club. It was something else the three of them had in common, besides accounting.

"I'll be in my office if you need anything."

"Okay." He didn't sound particularly interested.

Had she stopped reading poetry because *she'd* lost interest in it or because her parents had no interest in it at all? She couldn't remember. But then, it probably wasn't one of those things lost in a single, memorable moment; rather one that slipped away gradually and unnoticed from neglect.

"You can watch TV if you keep it low."

"Great. Thanks." His tone told her he disliked daytime television as much as she did.

"Are you going to be mad at me all day?"

"Neither one of us can tell the future, Charlotte." He hesitated, then rolled over on his side to look at her. "If it makes you feel any better, try to remember who I am and that I'm more likely to reflect your emotions back to you then to generate my own."

He rolled onto his back again and closed his eyes.

So, she was bored and annoyed with herself. There wasn't anything new about that.

And yet, why would it seem so much more upsetting coming from someone else than from within? Was she so used to pleasing other people that pleasing herself had become so insignificant? Had she pushed her dreams aside so often that they didn't matter any more? Had she given up on them?

She took one last look at the large male body stretched out on her couch, then left in search of her copy of Emily Dickinson.

As it happened, Emily still spoke to Charlotte's soul and she'd missed that kinship. The revelation weighed heavily in her heart; her thoughts tied themselves in knots, with no clear answers.

She felt stifled in the large back bedroom, where two desks were positioned face to face; computers on the right at opposing angles; the walls lined with filing cabinets and bookshelves full of tax codes and books on marketing, finance and accounting.

It was her parent's office for as far back as she could remember—*their* bookkeeping and accounting business. It specialized in small businesses, which constituted 85 percent of the twenty million businesses in America, and was incredibly lucrative. It was a good business, and now it was hers.

But when she graduated from college she had plans . . . plans to get an apartment and set up her own office. She wanted to travel and take up scuba diving. She had exciting and wonderful plans for her life.

Looking back, she could remember the devastating disappointment she felt a few weeks after her mother's sudden death as she lowered herself into the chair across the desks from her father. It was logical, practical—and besides, he needed her. He was elderly. He'd be lonely. Who else would take care of him?

She stopped making plans, pictured herself living with

her father until she was as gray as he was. She started dressing and acting like the old lady she felt herself becoming. Her perspective narrowed to one monotonous day at a time.

She couldn't regret staying with him, especially now, but she could see that giving up on the rest of her life had been a huge mistake, and not one that was in any way his fault. *She'd* quit. She'd settled for dry meatloaf when juicy prime rib was just as easy to order and eat.

Finishing her entries much later than anticipated, and vowing to recheck them all a third time for errors the next day, Charlotte tiptoed into the living room.

She couldn't believe her good luck to find Mel still sleeping, his big masculine body curled toward the back of the couch, the colorful T-shirt scrunched to show part of his strong back, the football pants looking just as they ought to . . .

She blew out a short, hard breath to curb the excitement curling low in her belly. He wasn't real. Her disappointment had her sagging against the hall wall as she watched him sleep. Why was it so hard to remember that? Because she could see him, hear him, touch him, smell him . . . taste him maybe, if he'd let her? Because every sense she used to distinguish what was real and what wasn't was . . . malfunctioning? All of them? All at once?

She wasn't stupid. She'd heard of hallucinations, audio and visual, and how one or both can be so convincing people can actually *feel* them. People like . . . schizophrenics and drug addicts. She wasn't taking anything, so was she losing her mind? Was she crazy?

She listened to Mel's deep rhythmic breathing and occasional soft snoring noises and thought about it. Seriously. Because if she was nuts, Mel was the most exciting thing in her life since . . . ever, and she found it really hard to care, one way or the other. If she'd gone around the bend, she wanted to keep on going . . . and there didn't seem to be any reason for her not to.

Her gaze gravitated along his strong muscled back to

the football pants before she caught herself again. If she allowed herself to remain mentally impaired, there had to be rules; she had to draw some lines somewhere, right? Or did she?

She laughed silently and shook her head. Whatever Mel was, she was having fun. She liked him, except when he was grouchy and being too truthful. She liked having him here. He knew her, knew what she was feeling. He was something to think about besides how lonely and alone she was. He was company. He was . . . well, he was her dream man.

She snuck out quietly, hurrying over to West McGraw Street, and the one company her father represented that still kept its offices within walking distance of the apartment. Custom Window Coverings. They now had a large factory in Renton and did a booming catalogue business as well, and should have moved their offices out there, too, long ago, which she told the owner, Mike Woodall.

She was acutely aware that Mike's wrinkled suit jacket concealed the drape of his blue cotton oxford shirt across his thick shoulders and that his middle-aged spread hid the way it tucked into his baggy pants, and despaired over her negative imaging—but at least she'd tried.

He was reminiscent and sympathetic about her father, and grateful that she'd stick with them until a new accountant could be found. It was a good meeting, over all.

On the way home she stopped briefly to pick up the monthly checks, deposits and sales invoices from Al's Auto Repair, Royal Bowling and finally Garden Palace Chinese Restaurant, where she was always treated more like a guest than an employee. She traded Mrs. Chin a nice, flat, empty file folder for one that bulged with business receipts.

"Every month I pick up your folder, Mrs. Chin, and every month it gets fatter."

"That is good. A fat folder means good business," she said in rapid, clear, perfect English. She was barely five feet tall and Charlotte always felt the need to stoop in her presence. "Soon we will open restaurant number two, down the hill, under the Space Needle. Then we will give you two fat folders every month. Do you like hot and spicy?" Before Charlotte could answer, the woman pushed a large brown paper bag at her, saying, "Please try my kung pao shrimp this time. You are not allergic, are you? You can tell me if you like it when you come back next month."

"You don't have to keep doing this, Mrs. Chin."

"You do not have to pick up the folder. I have cousins in Renton who have to deliver the receipts themselves. I want to feed you for the pick up."

"I like to walk, so it's no . . ."

"Walking will make you hungry. So let me feed you."

"Thank you."

"You are welcome." She frowned briefly. "You are not married. Do you have a steady gentleman friend?"

Oh no. Was *Set Me Up* tattooed on her forehead?

"Not exactly," she said, hoping to ward off the inevitable without actually lying.

"I have a son who is ready to marry. He has been to college for a business degree. He can cook and clean and he lives alone. I am looking for a good wife for him."

Lie! Lie! Lie!

"Well, I am sort of seeing someone. Someone new. Too new to tell really."

"Good. That is good. But if it does not work out, you come back and date my son."

"I will. Thank you."

Mrs. Chin nodded and looked pleased.

Charlotte made one more stop, going several blocks out of her way, to the largest drugstore in the area. They had every magazine under the sun, and she plucked out several indiscriminately, as she combed the many copies for a recent *GQ*.

Suits and sport jackets, tuxedos and khaki slacks, button down and polo shirts. Is this how Mel wanted to dress? She contemplated a thick, white cable knit sweater she thought Mel would fill better than the model did and lingered—quite a while—over an ad for a pair of button-up-the-front jeans that lifted her eyebrows half-way up her forehead with the way they fit the bare-chested model. And it wasn't so much the blue-and-gray striped oxford shirt as the way it was open down the front of a broad and muscled chest with a flat, ridged stomach and the thin line of dark hair running straight down the middle of it to his . . .

Did Mel's chest look like this? Would the dark hair be coarse or downy soft? Would his skin be hot and smooth with hard pads of muscle beneath?

Oh my. She snapped the magazine closed. *Big, deep breath*. She glanced around to see if anyone watched as her cheeks flushed with heat, like some pervert in the magazine section of an adult bookstore. She gathered her things quickly, deciding it might be best to let Mel pick out his own clothes.

A few minutes later, watching the clerk fit a seven-inch stack of magazines into a bag for her, Charlotte trembled inside and out. She was excited. She couldn't wait to get back to Mel. He'd be pleased and proud of her for taking this first step, minuscule as it was. On her own. Without him. He'd smile that smile that made her insides lurch and tell her she was being bold, that she was finally doing the right thing, getting her life back on track.

She rushed out of the store in time to see a tall, well-built man in jeans and a white cable knit sweater with a black sports jacket on over it, jogging gracefully across the street toward her in large, sparkling red shoes.

She started to laugh.

He slowed down when he saw her, his face full of smiles, stopped three feet away, held out his arms and turned in a circle for her to see.

"Look at me," he kept saying. "Just look at me. I couldn't wait to see you. I'm a hunk, right? Look at me.

Real clothes. They feel amazing and they're warm. I look fantastic, don't I?"

"Yes. You do. I'm . . . I'm sorry about the shoes. I didn't even think about—"

She fell silent when he suddenly took her by the shoulders. "Baby steps, Charlotte. One thing at a time. To me this says I'm sticking around, that you believe in me, that you're beginning to trust me and you're finally willing to at least hear what I have to say." He leaned in, set a tender kiss between her brows, then pulled back to meet her gaze squarely. "You were hoping I'd be pleased and proud of you, and I am. But more than that, I . . . well, I'm beginning to believe in you, too, sugar."

He laughed at her expression and stepped away. They fell into an easy pace uphill toward home.

"Okay. Not sugar. But I'm still pretty impressed with the guts it took for you jump the hurdle, Charlotte. Most people ignore the voice inside them all their life. They play it safe, too afraid to take a chance on their dreams, and they regret it until the day they die. But not you. Not my Charlotte Gibson. You give your voice a body, and designer clothes . . . and body hair . . ." He whipped an evil and highly amused glanced her way. She felt fire in her cheeks. "*And* you listen. I admit, I had my doubts about you. You are a True Believer but up to now you gave me no reason to believe you were any different than most people." He looked down as he slid his hand over the front of his sweater. "Up until now."

He was like watching a little boy on his birthday. His obvious happiness brought a deep joy that settled around her heart like the gathering of rain clouds in a drought. And with it came hope, solid and true, like an object she could hold in her hand. There was something new and exciting in her life, and her world was on the verge of change. She could feel it. She was excited and scared . . . and so ready.

"And you were right this morning," he said, being generous in return. "I was unreasonable—you ignore someone long enough they get that way, you know. But you were right. This isn't the best time to drop the business ball and run off willy-nilly to play Barbie Gets A Makeover."

"Barbie?"

"Your transformation isn't going to happen overnight anyway. It shouldn't. We want to feel comfortable with the changes we make, one at a time, grow into the new you. There'll be plenty of time for that *and* to get the business settled again. Together, there isn't anything we can't handle, given a little time and a good attitude. Right?"

"Right."

"Right. We've already seen what all work and no play has done to you. All play and no work would make Charlotte . . . poor . . . and anxious and desperate. Depressed and frightened. Did I mention poor?"

She smiled and a woman walking toward her on the sidewalk smiled back.

"Besides, this is all about balance, isn't it? Yin and yang. Good and evil. Right and wrong. Work and play. You and me. We're a team. You listen to me, I listen to you, and together we build a new, well-balanced, well-dressed, well-groomed, considerably more attractive and confident businesswoman with a social life. How hard can it be?"

Did he want an answer to that? She looked up at him and he winked at her. Her breath caught and she swallowed, hard. She felt a little lightheaded.

"Piece of cake," he said, seeming not to notice the effect he had on her. "A pumpkin-and-ground-oatmeal bundt cake with rum-plumped raisins and a spiced-sugar glaze made from scratch, maybe. But cake nonetheless. And there's so much to think about." He threw his arms wide. "Clothes. Hair. Makeup. We need to call that stylist in Bellevue right away, the one from the newspaper article. He probably has a waiting list. What about joining a gym? All this walking is fine but a little upper body workout wouldn't hurt. Oh! Let's take that trip to Victoria like we always wanted. And what about revamping the apartment, too, while we're at it? It's yours now, so you might as well claim it. And shoes . . . for both of us. We should make a list of the hot spots in town, see where people go to meet people. There'll be plenty of dating tips in those magazines. We'll ask around a little and . . ."

Charlotte listened as he mapped out a new life for her. She'd never known anyone like Mel before, no one whose sole purpose for existence was . . . her. Her life, her fulfillment, her dreams. She'd never been the epicenter of anyone's universe before, the full focus of their energies. It was heady. Pleasing in a completely selfish way that she could easily get used to.

Mel saw her potential. He knew, as she had often wished, that there was so much more to her than a mind that was good with numbers and an overdeveloped sense of responsibility and duty. Her body and soul were starving for attention, and Mel planned to put both on a weight-gaining diet.

She planned to let him.

Six

Days slipped by and while the April weather remained wet, naturally, it also grew warm enough to shed her long, black wool coat for her old, tan trench coat.

"Halloween is six months off, Charlotte." Mel's expression was bland, his tone dry, and when she frowned in confusion, he held his hands out toward her coat and added, "This is your best impersonation of Detective Columbo, isn't it?"

"This happens to be a perfectly respectable Worthington raincoat. These kinds of overcoats never go out of style."

"Says who? And even if they didn't, they still lose buttons and get worn until they look threadbare and ratty. Much like this one." The phone rang. "Give it to me. I'll throw it in the trash."

"No," she said, backing up toward the phone, clutching the front of her coat. "Not until I have something to replace it with, and then it's going to someone who could use a perfectly good six-year-old coat. Along with everything else I own. Don't you like anything I have? Hello?"

"Charlotte Gibson? This is Axel Burton. I hope I'm not disturbing you." The baritone voice in her ear caused a slight hitch in her breathing. The deep, dark, purely masculine tones shivered along her nerve endings, as if she'd been touched. "Hello?"

"Yes. I'm sorry. What?"

Mel's thoughts were still in her closet. "I like that old, really soft flannel nightgown with the little pink bunnies on it. The long one? It feels so good when we're sick."

She tapped her closed lips with her index finger, listening intently.

"Is this Charlotte Gibson?" The man put a heavy inflection on the *Char* part of her name; it made her heart flutter.

"Yes. I was . . . distracted. I'm sorry. What did you say your name was?"

"Axel Burton. I'm calling from Chicago but I'm planning to be in Seattle later next week. Henry Chancellor said you might be able to turn me on to a couple of jobs coming up in the area."

"Henry? Oh." Memory kicked in and her stomach sank to the floor. "Right. You're his wife's sister's cousin's nephew or something. I remember. Henry seemed very fond of you."

He gave a soft laugh that made her want to weep with regret. It just wasn't fair that the voice belonged to the very nice, quiet, single, young, unemployed, *miserable, boring loser* Henry told her about. Money isn't everything? To a CFO? Get real.

And come to think of it, *Axel?*

"Actually, my mother's sister divorced Henry's wife's brother. But before they did, Henry and I got to know each other pretty well. At the family reunions. On vacation. Things like that. Henry's a good man."

"Yes, he is. And because he thinks so highly of you, I'd

be happy to recommend you to the clients I'm dropping from my practice. I don't know if Henry explained the situation to you or not, but my—"

"Yes. He did." He spoke quickly to spare her the pain of explaining. "I'm sorry about your father."

"Thank you. So you know that these companies are in transition, or permanently fixed in the 13 percent of all businesses that have between twenty and one hundred employees and no longer qualify as a small business?" She winced. She was talking like . . . like an accountant.

"Yes, but I was hoping you might agree to meet with me next week to discuss all this. Friday evening maybe, for drinks or dinner. I could explain briefly what I'm looking for, you could give me a short run down on what you've got and then we could discuss where you think I might fit best . . . if at all."

Oh, sure. Like she couldn't smell a blind date buried under a business meeting from a mile away.

"I'm sorry. I have plans for next Friday. In fact, the next few weeks are going to be crazy busy for me, and I know you're going to want to find a job fairly soon, so why don't you give me an email address or a fax or even a street address and I'll send you an overview and declaration of each company. You can take a few days to look them over and let me know which ones you're interested in. Then I'll write you a letter of introduction. How does that sound?"

"Like a lot of extra work for you, I'm sorry to say."

"Not at all. It's all right there on my computer. It's no problem at all."

"All right." He agreed and gave her his email address. "Maybe once we both get settled we can have that drink together anyway. Henry says, and I quote, that you're 'a pearl the oyster divers have somehow overlooked.' "

She rolled her eyes, *Oh brother*, then made a soft snorting noise in lieu of a laugh and brushed him off. "He has to say that. I do his taxes."

Politely, he didn't push the point and said good-bye.

She set the phone in its cradle and looked up to find Mel staring at her.

"What?"

"You're not even going to give him a chance?"

"Oh, please. There's a stigma to blind dating for a reason, you know. And it's not just because they're set up so you go into them blind." She picked up her briefcase, walked to the door, opened it and then waited for him. "It's because once you get there, your date makes you wish you *were* blind. Or even worse, your poor date is blind, and you dressed up for nothing. Trust me," she said, following him through the door and down the stairs to the foyer. "I've been on enough blind dates to know they never work. No more blind dates for me. I want to meet someone on my own. I want our gazes to lock across a crowded room. I want our souls to mate before we even speak. I want . . . *magic*. Love at first sight." Watching him shrug into an expensive looking brown leather bomber jacket, she let loose a tiny, wistful sigh. "Why didn't I conjure up a fairy godmother with a wand or a genie with a bottle full of wishes instead of a playmate with a fashion fetish?"

"Perhaps because, in your infinite wisdom, you knew it would be more fun to make your own magic." She gave him a look as he passed through the open door to the street. "Wait and see, my pet. When you do fall in love, you'll be glad there isn't any other magic around but your own."

A few weeks after that, when Mel proposed burning both of her coats in celebration of sweater weather, they made their first massive trip to the Goodwill.

These were not idle weeks by any means. Most days were consumed with the shifting of her father's remaining clients into a reasonable, and profitable, work schedule along with her own. Closing the books to-date for those she had to part with, designing several new client organizers and updating their methods of accounting to systems that were more efficient for them . . . and her.

She got new business cards and stationary, changing the

company name from Gibson & Gibson Financial Associates, Inc. to Gibson Financial Services, Inc. in standout Money Green ink, not the standard Profit Black.

The only thing Mel insisted on, other than waiting for Shamus—the famed hairdresser in Bellevue—was that she join the gym a few blocks south near Garfield Street. "Not just for your body, but also for your *soul*," he said, holding the tips of his fingers together like an Italian fresh off the boat.

She couldn't say that her soul enjoyed the exercise any more than her body did, but she was surprised at how quickly it became a part of her daily routine. The more energy she exerted, the more she seemed to have.

Late afternoons and early evenings were set aside for the evacuation of most things old. Her parents' old clothes. Her old clothes. Old books she didn't want to keep. Old adding machines three hundred times bigger than last year's model. Old kitchen utensils and furniture. And more of her old clothes that she couldn't part with the first time.

Mel was doggedly determined to wipe out her wardrobe completely.

"Ooh. *Now* we're talkin'." His voice echoed the admiration in his expression as she stepped out of the dressing room to look at the new jeans he talked her into trying on. He sat in a chair beside the mirror, nodding. "Look at this. We've found curves. And those are not so low on your hips that you're embarrassed every time you sit down, but they don't cut you off at the armpits either. Perfect. You've got a sweet little waist there and it's time to show it off." He did hesitate a moment. "We'll wait on the naval piercing. One thing at a time, right?"

"Right." Admiring the flattering fit of the jeans in the mirror, she didn't bother to scowl at him. She was used to his pushing the line of change to extremes with ideas like tattoos, thong underwear and lightweight Scandinavian furniture. These things were all fine and interesting to think about, but they were so not her, and he knew it. Still, he said he felt compelled to bring them to mind, just in case.

"The T-shirt could be a little shorter. You've got the belly for it, hun. No, hun, huh? Okay. Well, at least that one's tight enough to hug your curves, not just hang there like your body was a tree trunk."

She wished he'd stop talking about her curves. Stop looking at them with the warm approval that made her feel uneasy in a truly wonderful way. It was moments like this that she consciously fought to cling to reality, like a climber on the sheer face of a mountain, by the tips of her fingers and a prayer. He wasn't real. No matter how much or how hard she wished he was, he wasn't real.

"Let's burn the old ones."

"Pyromaniac."

"Obsessive-compulsive-frumpy-clothes-hoarder."

She bit her lower lip to keep her smile small.

"At least wear these home," he suggested, reaching out to pull the sizing tape off the back of her thigh, then the price tag. She reached up and yanked one from under her arm, then looked in the mirror again.

There was a distinctive . . . *exposed* sensation in wearing clothes that exhibited the exact shape of her body, the true size of her breasts and the tone of her bottom. Like being naked, but not. Exciting and disturbing and . . . sexual in a way she never dreamed she could be. Seductive. Soft and feminine. Not like a tree trunk. Like a woman. And it was potent.

Those weeks with Mel were special. As they cleaned and sorted, they made piles for consignment shops, another for charity and one more for a planned weekend at the Stop'n Swap near Lake Union. And they talked. About everything. The funny things her parents used to do, the girl who bullied her in sixth grade, the strife in the Middle East, why there was no special name for the tops of their feet.

When first Sidney and then Sue called with their bian-
nual invitations to a casual dinner to meet someone new
from their husband's office or the latest addition to their
company baseball team, neither she nor Mel felt any com-
punction in declining.

Late in the evenings they would curl up, exhausted, on
opposite ends of the sofa and share a blanket between
them. Sometimes Mel rubbed her feet, sometimes she tickled his, and at all times she was content and happy in his
company.

"I like Tony Soprano," Mel mumbled late one Sunday
night.

"He's a cold-blooded gangster."

"He loves his children."

"He kills people. With his hands."

"He's always sorry afterward."

"He cheats on his wife."

"Lots of men do."

"Why?"

"I don't know. But I don't think it's always because of
the wife. I don't think it is most of the time. And I know for
a fact that it wasn't your fault when Eddie Boise cheated on
you."

"You do?"

"Of course. You jumped through hoops trying to make
that guy happy, but it was the challenge he loved. He
cheated on everyone once he got what he wanted from
them. It wasn't you, it was him playing games."

"How can you tell if someone's playing games?"

"You can't always. Eddie fooled me too, or I'd have
voiced my suspicions earlier, but . . . it doesn't really matter. That's not what's important. Having your heart broken
sucks, but it beats the alternative."

"Feeling nothing at all."

"Mmm," he agreed, his gaze glued to the television as
the mob boss talked to a topless waitress in his bar.

"It's better to have loved and lost then never to have loved at all, huh?"

He glanced at her, looked away and then met her eye to eye. "Don't you think so? I mean, when all is said and done, it's never the number of people who loved you that counts, is it? It's the love you fill your heart with for others that matters. So, if you don't love, your heart stays empty, and so does your life."

That's what made those busy weeks with Mel so special, she supposed. His healing outlook on life; his simple, sensible answers to the most profound complexities of her life. His complete honesty about the mistakes she'd made and his total support when the fault wasn't hers. He helped her make subtle changes to her self-image, patch some of the holes in her confidence, led her to windows into her personality she never knew existed.

Seven

The doorbell rang one afternoon and she climbed over stacked boxes and bulging garbage bags to answer it. Mrs. Kludinski stood in the hall holding a CD case in both hands.

"Try this one it's . . . Good heavens! Your hair!"

The old lady's eyes grew round with wonder and Charlotte reached with both hands to be sure what hair she had left was still there. Soft and airy and shorter than she'd ever worn it before, she combed her hair forward with her finger tips and stated the obvious. "I had it cut."

"It's fabulous."

"Really? You like it?"

"I do. It's perfect for you. It shows off your long graceful neck, and your eyes look enormous. You look so young and fresh."

She grinned and for several long seconds she allowed herself to bask in the admiration she saw in her neighbor's face. "Thank you. I needed a change."

"Changing your music, too?"

"What?"

She tried to look around Charlotte into the apartment, her curiosity large. "I heard blues last night and country this morning, but I didn't hear any classical. This is Debussy. Piano mostly. You might like it."

"Is this your very sweet way of telling me I'm playing my music too loud?"

"No. This is my very sweet way of telling you that it's nice to hear signs of life up here. I was beginning to worry."

"Oh. Well." *Mel is pretty light on his feet for someone his size.* "I used to enjoy all sorts of music but all my parents ever listened to was Rock from the fifties and sixties and . . . well, I've been cleaning and I found some old tapes, but if it's too loud for you, I can turn it down."

"It's fine for me. I love music, too. And it's not that loud. I only used it as an excuse to come up here and see for myself what's been going on," she said frankly, once again trying to peer inside the apartment. Charlotte glanced over her shoulder at the furniture in the middle of the room, the boxes and bare walls. "What *is* going on up here? You've got Joe and Martha worried, too. Marty said she came across the hall one day last week to see how you were doing and she thought she heard you talking to yourself in here." She stepped into the apartment as Charlotte stepped back to let her in.

"Maybe it was the television."

"That's what I said. But she said it was too early in the day, that you never turn it on until the news hour."

"Yeah. Well. Maybe I'm getting sick of being so predictable. Maybe I had it on just to mess with her head." She leaned out the door to glower at her neighbor's door across the large empty hallway. *Busybody.*

"She was worried." She put her hands on her hips and looked around. "It looks like you're redecorating."

"Well, the furniture's old and . . ."

"And it's not yours, is it? Thank the Lord." She threw

her hands in the air. "I was afraid you were thinking of moving. When you get to be my age and you have good neighbors, you like to keep them. So, you're changing *everything*. Fantastic! What color have you decided on for the walls in here?"

"I haven't yet. I was . . ."

"Yes, you have. Tell her," Mel said.

"Red."

"Red?"

"Not bright red. Ah . . . a deep, warm Chinese red with a rich cream-colored trim, I think. And I want to pull up the rugs and refinish the hardwood floors, then put down an area rug . . . maybe something oriental with lush greens and that yellowish gold color . . ." Her voice trailed off. Mrs. Kludinski didn't need all the details to call the scheme grotesque.

"And a lovely blue, too, and maybe more of the red in the rug to pull it together because it sounds just fabulous. Charlotte, I'm so proud of you. It's about time you cut loose and let that bright, colorful personality of yours shine."

"You see?" Mel folded his arms across his chest. "Bold is beautiful. And thinking outside the neutral box is creative, not crazy."

"And what is this you have going on over here?" She walked slowly toward the far wall, lifting the glasses that hung at her bosom up to her nose as she carefully examined the wide and varied assortment of pictures taped thereon.

"Oh, that's a . . . sort of a shopping spree waiting to happen. You shop all the time, but I find all the styles and colors and . . . everything in the stores overwhelming. Too many choices. Too many decisions. I . . . I thought if I knew pretty much what I was looking for and what I didn't want, ahead of time, it would be easier."

"So organized and logical." She wasn't making a judgment, just taking note as she scanned the scraps of magazines and catalogs on the wall. "And yet, you have two very different styles emerging here, dear. Both are very nice, and a vast improvement on what you've worn in the past. No offense, but improvement *is* what you're looking for, isn't it?"

"Just a change, really." She sighed, resigned to the truth.

"Yes. Improvement. Big time."

"Yes. Indeed." She stepped back to see the bigger picture. "And the men in black leather?"

Charlotte's whole body cringed with embarrassment and she squeaked as she quickly ripped several of Mel's donations off the wall. "Those are . . . you know . . . just . . . nothing."

Mrs. Kludinski's smirk relaxed as she continued to study the wall.

"Fascinating. One style so . . . conservative."

"She means *boring*," Mel said, *I told you so* written all over his face.

"And the other so . . . revealing."

"Slutty." She pinned Mel with a look.

"Gracious, no!" Mrs. Kludinski looked surprised, and not by the word. "Revealing as in expressive, interesting, intriguing. It's fine to cover yourself neck to toe in these lovely suits for business if you want, if dressing like a man helps you feel as powerful as a man. But the rest of the time . . . well, I would love to see you—all women really—be open and honest and proud of your female form, no matter what shape it is."

"I couldn't have said that better myself." Mel nodded and smiled fondly at the old lady.

"But all that skin . . . Professionally, I can't—"

"Dear Charlotte." A sage smile curved her thin lips, and her pale blue eyes were positively wicked. "There is more power in the curve of a woman's neck and the turn of her ankle than in ten male bodies put together. And with every additional inch of leg and cleavage shone, the strength increases tenfold."

"Oh my." Mel was impressed.

"It's how you use the power that defines your professionalism. Until you get to be my age, of course. Then it's wise to have an alternate power source. Like money." She laughed.

But Charlotte was only half-listening as she reconsidered the pictures on the wall. "What if we compromise and do a little of both? I don't want to be too intimidating." She grinned. "But maybe a conservative suit with a more *revealing* blouse . . . or from the other direction, a shortish skirt instead of slacks."

"There you go. Or this little strapless sheath with the shorter bolero jacket. Or even just a little thin shawl while they're still in style." They made several other possible combinations, lifting the pictures off the wall and retaping them closer together, laughing when they didn't quite work and gasping with pleasure when they did. "There. See? Show enough to be enticing, leave a little to mystery, and avoid being *so* mysterious you're like the grab bag at a charity auction."

Mel whistled. "I bet this old broad was hell on wheels when she was young."

Mrs. Kludinski turned as if she'd heard him, but only looked around the room again. "I also know of a nice young man who does a good job painting. He's reasonable and fast. Would you like his number?"

"Well, we were . . . I was . . ." She heard Mel moan laboriously behind her. She wasn't all that keen on doing the job herself either. She realized it was the *nice young man* that had her balking. "He isn't single is he?"

"I don't know. It didn't come up while he was painting my guest room last fall, and I didn't ask. Does it matter?"

"No. Not really." She felt foolish. She wasn't really the sad victim of an international blind-date conspiracy—it just felt as if she was sometimes.

* * *

Shortly after the varnish dried on the freshly sanded floors, the air in the apartment grew thick with the smell of latex paint.

Guy Westfield, the painter, was a prompt and efficient man in his early thirties, who liked to stand around and talk in the mornings if Charlotte didn't make herself scarce.

"He's a sociable guy, our Guy," Mel said, following her into her office, where she'd spent most of the previous two days hiding from the painter.

Mel didn't usually join her in the office. When she worked, when she needed time to herself, he was very good about sensing it and getting out of her way for a while. And then he would just be there later, as if he were simply returning from the kitchen with a glass of water or had been reading in another room. It was one of his many tricks that she appreciated, and didn't question—it was best not to question.

"A sociable guy I'm paying by the hour, thank you very much." She sat down at her desk and brought her computer screen to life. "Besides, I hate watching someone else doing a job I'm paying them to do simply because I hate doing it myself. I hate to vacuum and dust and I haven't hired a maid service for the exact same reason."

"Yeah, well, that's secondhand guilt from your parents who grew up in a frugal do-it-yourself era." He flopped into the chair at the opposite desk. "I'm the one who's been nagging you to get someone part-time and rationalizing it as good for the economy, spreading the wealth around and supporting the job market."

She stared at him. "That was you? I thought it was the devil, tempting me with sloth."

"I know. And don't think I wasn't insulted. Not to mention frustrated that, once again, you couldn't distinguish his voice from mine. This is something we need to discuss sometime before I leave, by the way."

Her heart flipped and constricted; tears pushed and stung in her eyelids. "You're leaving me?"

His smile was reassuring. "Not while you still need me."

Charlotte didn't want to think about him leaving, couldn't bare thinking about it. So quickly he'd become the best and truest friend she'd ever known.

Oh, he teased her and provoked her and was difficult to take to a crowded movie theater where empty-looking seats were hard to hold on to, but he was also wise and comforting and a companion who made even the most mundane everyday activities more pleasurable.

And she was happy. She couldn't remember the last time she'd been so happy. She couldn't help it. He made her feel all gooey and girly inside. He was feeding huge portions of faith and fervor to her femininity, and she found she was as dependent on him as she was the new diffuser on her blow dryer.

"And, little lady, please don't think that you have successfully changed the subject from Guy to God," he went on, leaning back in the padded chair that once belonged to her father. "Because we both noticed he wasn't wearing a wedding ring and he seems like a nice enough guy. Guy, not God—though, I suppose He's probably nice enough too, just a little out of your league."

"God, not Guy, right?"

"Right."

"Well, I'm not going to hit on the painter."

"Why not? He's already seen you in that shirt with the baggy jeans I distinctly recall putting in the Goodwill box myself, and he can still bring himself to look you in the eye. He is obviously a man with great depth perception who can see beyond your foolish attachment to all that is dumpy and ill-fitting to the real you ... who is still screaming to get out, I might add."

She simpered at him. "They're comfortable."

"So are the new ones. You admitted as much."

"But why wear out my new jeans just hanging around the house working?"

"Because dressing well and looking nice is going to become your second skin." He held up his hand when she started to object. "You can be comfortable in clothes that look nice on you as easily as you can in ... what you've been wearing and ..." His eyes narrowed suspiciously. "And stop trying to change the subject."

"I'm not attracted to him, okay?"

"How do you know until you try?"

"You don't *try* to be attracted to someone; you just are."

"Not always. Sometimes you meet someone, you become friends, and *then* you become attracted. They grow on you. We've read all the same articles, seen all the same movies, listened to all the same talk shows. This love-at-first-sight you're so hung up on is usually just an infatuation and those never last. You know that."

"I know that for two people to be friends even, they must first have something in common. What do I have in common with this man?"

"How should I know? But you can't tell just from looking at him that you have nothing in common. He might be a painter who loves poetry and sappy movies, who likes music and dancing and books about Edna St. Vincent Millay. You never know. He could be the man who opens up the new world of skydiving for you."

"Scuba," she said, her expression bored. "I want to try scuba diving."

"I know. Just checking. And ... Guy could be the guy to teach you."

"So, if I ask him if he scuba dives and he says no, we can drop this?" His stare was taxed. She sighed. "I'll think about it. But not until after the painting is done. If it gets ugly I don't want him running off and leaving me with a half-painted apartment."

"Oh, ye of little faith. What if it turns out great and he decides to forego his bill?"

"Then I'd know we were incompatible, for sure. I never heard of anything so stupid." She turned back to the computer and her own work. "What sort of incompetent businessman is he that he'd paint someone's apartment for free, just for a date?"

"Not for a date and not for free. For love." He said it like a prayer.

She shook her head. "That's bartering. You can't barter for love. I told you it wouldn't work out with him."

And besides, I have you. Out of the corner of her eye she saw him squirm in his chair a few seconds later and buried the thought in numbers.

Eight

They watched the Mariners play at Safeco Field and spit off the observation deck of the Space Needle. They drove to Port Angeles and rode the Black Ball Ferry to Victoria, British Columbia, quite possibly the prettiest city in the northern hemisphere, in Charlotte's opinion, and they stayed for all three days of the Tall Ships Challenge. Mel liked the Ballard Locks. More than once she found herself standing at the rail watching boats of all shapes and sizes move up and down, passing from the Puget Sound to the fresh water of Salmon Bay—or vice versa.

August was already September before she began to feel as if she were finally settling into her own skin. Her reflection in the store front was as young and alive as she felt. *Her* reflection, not some stranger with similar features; *her* all stylish and put-together, eyes sparkling, head high.

Mel turned his head and then turned his body completely to walk backwards as they strolled Bellevue Square pretending to window shop at the various high-end stores and boutiques. Pretending, as they'd already blown her new clothing budget on an Ann Taylor suit and a pair of croco-embossed T-strap pumps at Banana Republic.

"Did you see that?" he asked.

"What?" She turned from the window. "And it better not be another Fuzzi skirt. I never would have bought that skirt if it hadn't been for you."

"It's a beautiful skirt. But no, did you see that guy, the one in the yellow shirt, the sandy brown hair? He almost broke his neck trying to get a good look at you."

She smiled but didn't look back. It wasn't the first time she'd turned a head in the last few weeks, and it was almost as satisfying as not being recognized by people she'd known for years. That look of confusion on their faces, then the surprise, then the awe and admiration was better than . . . well . . . better than anything she'd ever known but . . .

"That's not why I did all this, you know. It's a nice side effect, having men notice me, but I'd be just as happy if they didn't. Or maybe not as much anyway. I mean, everyone wants to be noticed, of course, but they don't have to stop traffic and stare. That's not what all this is about."

"I know."

"This is about me doing everything I should have done years ago to become the woman I always thought I'd be."

"I know."

"This is about reclaiming my life."

"I know. Let's cross over here." He was barely paying attention to her. He snatched up her hand and started for the shops on the other side of the second level.

"Victoria's Secret? Again?"

"They might have something new."

"You're not even listening to me." She stopped short, and one of two teenage girls rammed her from behind. "Oh! I'm sorry. Excuse me. I . . . should invest in a set of tail lights, I guess." The girl wasn't amused. "Sorry."

"Whatever." Glaring, she walked around Charlotte like she was something not to step in.

Mel watched her. "Do you think that attitude is nature or nurtured?"

"Looked pretty natural to me," she muttered, then turned to him. "Do I have a withering look like that?"

She tried a scowl and a snarl on him before he looked up and around, took her hand and started them walking again. "No, you don't. You do anger and disbelief very well . . . and boredom . . . and frustration, too. Your face is very expressive, but there's nothing that would make anyone feel subhuman like that." He paused, then sighed and rolled his eyes. "Did I mention stubborn? It seems to be your most frequent expression lately." He glanced over at her and wasn't disappointed. "I *do* listen to you, Charlotte. All the time. Every second of every day. It's what I do. But I can't be expected to react to every thought in your head—most aren't even whole thoughts; they're wisps and snippets mostly. And when you're thinking out loud, as you were just then, it might help to remember that *I'm* getting it in stereo—what you're saying and what you're thinking." He released her hand to point at both ears, then tipped his head. "Or in this case, what you're saying and what you're trying not to think."

"Ho! So now you know what I'm not thinking. That's great—and incredibly presumptuous of you." She increased the length of her stride.

He chuckled. "Not what you're not thinking, what you're trying not to think—that you did all this to attract men."

"Which I didn't."

"Of course you did." Once again she dug in her heels. "Well, what's wrong with that? If you were going to sell your car wouldn't you wash it and vacuum out the trunk, make it look nice, show off its best features, hoping to make someone else want it?"

"I'm selling myself?"

Mel recognized the edge in her voice and took a bracing stance. "Yes, in a way. Everyone does it, every day. You sell yourself to your clients. You're polite and professional; you work hard and you finish their financials on time—and they pay you and keep you on for another year. Are you going to tell me you wouldn't put as much effort into finding someone to love? Why, making yourself appealing to the opposite sex is as natural as . . . well, it is nature, isn't it? Birds do it. Animals do it. Maybe not as deliberately or as consciously as humans do it, but even then there's a great deal of basic human instinct involved. So why not admit it? Yes, you're reclaiming your life, and yes, you should have done so years ago, but you're also hoping to make someone else want you. You hate being alone." He stooped to meet her at eye level. "And there's nothing wrong with that. You can say it out loud."

Charlotte sighed, wandered over to a convenient bench and sat down. "I do hate being alone. And I do want somebody to want me."

"Amen to that, honey." The woman on the bench behind her turned her head and smiled. "You and me both."

"Why does it have to be so complicated?"

The woman shrugged a shoulder and took a guess. "If it was easy it wouldn't be special. It wouldn't mean anything to us. We'd take love for granted, like clean air—and look what's happening to that."

They exchanged a thoughtful smile.

"And so," Mel said, using his arms to draw a large circle in the space in front of him, as the woman turned away with a nod. "There you have it. Now let's shop." There was nothing Mel liked better but . . . he watched as she scrunched her face at the Victoria's Secret window display one shop down and let loose a sigh that could have been Job's. "You can have all the nice new clothes in the world but if you don't feel pretty and sexy and desirable in them, what's the point? And there's nothing that will make you feel pretty and sexy and desirable faster than pretty, sexy, desirable underwear."

"And you know this how?"

"Laurel's Lingerie on the Home Shopping Network. They say it repeatedly. Are you coming or not?"

"We practically bought Vicki out of business the last time we were here." She watched him fill his head with the subtle, feminine scent before entering the shop. "How many frilly underpants and bras do I have to have?"

"The question is, can you have too many?"

Apparently not.

But it wasn't her ravaged budget that bothered her that afternoon. It was the conversation she had with Mel that kept poking at her like a mean kid with a stick. She went over and over it in her mind. It made perfect sense on the surface—she didn't want to be alone and she wanted someone to want her—but there was something missing, a nail or a screw or some glue that would hold the two statements together.

Mel was nowhere in sight when she emerged from her long steamy bath that evening, bundled in a new blue terry robe that was softer than her old one, which had been washed so many times most of the pile had rubbed off. She brewed a mug of hot tea, added honey and curled up on one end of her new couch to study the fall television lineup in the *TV Guide*—but it didn't hold her attention for long. She read the first page of the new Elinor Lipman novel six times before she realized she wasn't in a very good mood. She felt restless and testy and . . . where the hell was Mel?

She wondered where he went when he wasn't with her—to play nine holes of golf? To get his teeth cleaned? Maybe he floated on clouds above the ozone, napping. Maybe something simpler . . . maybe he was off taking a shower, too?

A warm steamy fog broke and shifted before her eyes like a dream, and the damp musky scent of man and soap filled the air. She could almost see him in the mist, drops of water like diamonds in his thick dark hair, one lock hanging over his forehead, not quite touching his brow; his eyelashes spiked around deep blue eyes, his lips moist. His bare chest glistened; the skin across his broad shoulders was smooth and sun-kissed, and a fascinating river of course dark hair traveled the shallow valley between the rippled muscles of his abdomen, lower and lower until it—

"Charlotte!" A cloud billowed into the hall from the bathroom and Mel emerged, wrapping a large white towel around his middle—he was clearly steamed. "Have you lost our mind?"

"Oh God," she said, watching Mel turn to face the-wetter-than-he-was vision of himself as the image slowly faded away. Once it was gone he looked back at her.

"You can't keep doing this. I think I've been extremely tolerant of your feelings toward me—I am after all you're perfect man—but now you've gone too far. I can ignore only so much. We both know where this fantasy would have landed us and you know we can't go there."

"I know. I know." She drew her legs up close to her chest and buried her face between her terry covered knees. She was mortified . . . and completely shaken. The neurons in her brain began to fizzle and spit, signaling a mental meltdown as the schism between her mind and her emotions became so wide she couldn't bridge them any longer. "In my head I know, but not in my heart. I can't help it. I'm in love. With you. And it's hopeless. I'm hopeless." She stood abruptly, her face wet with tears, and marched toward the kitchen for a tissue, arms waving. "How pathetic and desperate does a person have to be to dream up someone like you? I watch Discovery Channel. They've never done a documentary on imaginary adult companions. I've hit bottom, haven't I? I'm insane. Pretty soon Joe and Martha will sneak across the hall and figure out that I'm sitting in here talking to myself and have me committed. You and I, we can chase imaginary bugs up the walls together."

"Stop it."

"What's the matter with me? Why did I ever think that listening to you would change anything? Merry Mel, come to fix poor Charlotte. What was I thinking? It's never going to matter if I change the way I dress or the way I look or the color of my apartment or . . . or if I date or don't date or . . . or have sexy underwear." She blew her nose and sniffed loudly, realizing then what had been missing from their earlier conversation: She didn't want to be alone and she wanted someone to want her, *but* she was alone and she'd stay that way as long as she had Mel. "Underneath it all, I'll still be me. I'll be plain and weak and awkward and I won't fit in anywhere. I'll be the same old Charlotte who screws up every relationship she has with a man, who sits at home and watches her friends get married and make new lives and . . . and babies and are happy and . . . plant gerbera daisies in their strip gardens. If I'm ever going to be the woman I've always wanted to be, if I'm ever to be truly happy with myself, then *I'm* going to have to change things . . . inside. Alone. Without you."

She turned to him expectantly, certain he wouldn't be able to come up with one of his unfailingly optimistic responses to this particular truth.

His expression was oddly unreadable, not a reflection of her anger, not sympathetic, not cheerful. After a short moment he said mildly, "You're being dramatic."

"Am I?" She nodded and thought about it. "Maybe I am. I don't know why I let you in . . . or out . . . or however this ridiculous thing works, but I can see now it was a mistake. You made everything so easy for me, but you're really just another excuse for me to keep avoiding the rest of the world. The changes we made together are amazing, but none of them are the kind that count. None of them really changed *me*. I know who I am. And I know who you are." Suddenly, the wind died and her sails went flat. "And I know what you're not. I do love you, Mel, but you have to go."

He looked like a small child who'd just had someone walk up and prick his balloon with a pin, confused and hurt.

"And please don't think I'm not grateful for all you've done for me, but don't you see, Mel? I need to make a real life with real people."

His shoulders began to droop in defeat—in a defeat he seemed to be expecting. As he sighed, a thick, velvety green robe grew clearer and more solid over his body. He gathered the front together in a fist at his chest as if he were cold and weakly sat in the chair a few feet away. In another flash of reality she realized how careful he must have been to so rarely let her see his magic—perhaps because the strangeness of it might have startled her awake sooner to the fact that he was *all* magic.

"This is the way of it, I suppose. Good enough when you're unhappy and lonely, but always a poor substitute for real life. It was the same when you were a little girl. If there were other children to play with, you didn't give me a thought." He looked and sounded heartbroken and dejected.

"I'm sorry, Mel."

He shrugged. "You know, I didn't expect you to see me that day at the viewing. And I sure *never* expected to get a second chance with you. It happens so rarely. All children have imaginations strong enough to create a playmate but only a brave few will admit it to adults, and fewer still take it the one step further to anthropomorphize it. Most make-believe buddies are lost in youth, trapped in childhood memories. If they're quick, a few can relocate to siblings or neighbor kids . . . the family pet. But only a lucky few get the chance to grow up and come out again. Didn't I say you were a rare and wonderful exception? A True Believer."

Her smile was sad. "Yes, you did."

"Charlotte." When she looked at him, he rearranged himself in the chair and patted the cushion, inviting her to sit with him. The chair was new and big, not nearly wide enough to be a loveseat but wider than most, perfect for curling up . . . or sharing. She snuggled close and he put his arm around her. "I've had a great time."

"Me, too. I've never had a friend like you before."

"Yes, you have. When you were four and five and for a while when you were six." She gave a soft laugh and turned her ear to his chest. The steady rhythm of his heart was soothing; she felt safe and warm and completely attracted in the circle of his arms. She closed her eyes to concentrate on safe and warm. "The trick is to remember that the very best parts of me are actually you. And you were wrong before—some of the changes we made are the kinds that count, or you wouldn't have had the strength to send me away. I'm very proud of you, Charlotte. It takes a big heart to forgive yourself for past mistakes, real courage to stand up for yourself and a keen mind to know what you want from life. All you ever needed was a little confidence . . . and a friend you couldn't ignore."

Her limbs grew heavy; her respirations slower and deeper as his holiday scent filled her head. "I'm afraid," she murmured from that half-awake, half-asleep state that was like flood water from the basement, heading for the attic. "I don't want to be alone."

"Everyone's afraid. Remember that. And you'll only be alone if you want to be," she heard him say clearly, but the next words came like those in a dream. *"Forget me, Charlotte."*

Nine

"Forget me? That's it? That's the best you can do? I can't say something and hop three times on my left foot to make you disappear?" She stomped around in the kitchen getting her coffee, having not ten minutes ago come blissfully awake in his arms.

"As far as I know, that's how it works. If you're thinking about me, I'm here."

"I'm thinking about you because you're standing right in front of me. I thought you'd disappear last night while I was sleeping?"

"Without saying good-bye?"

She narrowed her eyes at him. "You're doing this on purpose. You changed your mind. You're not going to leave."

"It's not up to me," he said, looking entirely too pleased. "You know that."

"Can't you just, you know, go where you go when you're not here and stay there?"

"Not if you're thinking about me."

"Not if I'm. . . ."

She thought about the times when he wasn't with her, when she felt he was being discrete and giving her time alone to think and meditate . . . and to work and read and do crossword puzzles . . . until she got stuck on a word. Then all she had to do was call out and he would answer from another room or join her if her concentration was not just momentarily broken but shattered completely by the riddle.

He loved going out and went everywhere with her except . . . that first morning when she wasn't sure she wanted him around, when she'd snuck out of her office hoping he'd still be asleep, hoping she could leave the apartment without him.

No, it was more than hope. It was will; she willed him to stay asleep because she didn't want to have another losing conversation with him that morning, because she wanted to leave without him, to be alone to mull things over.

The day before that she'd thrown up a mental *and* physical wall between them by commanding him to stay out of the apartment . . . so he stayed in the hall.

"I am all you, babe."

Her gaze rose slowly from the floor and their eyes met, one pair doubtful, the other pleased.

"All I have to do is fill my head with other things. That's the trick, isn't it? That's how it works. This is my life and I control it."

"Some of it."

"Well, yes but . . . you, for sure. I can control you."

He puffed his cheeks and blew out a deep breath as he folded his arms across his chest and leaned back against the kitchen counter with great forbearing. "Ah-ha."

"I woke up a little shaky this morning, a little nervous about being on my own and that's why you're still here. I'm over it."

"Ah-ha."

There was nothing to do but show him. She turned on

her heel and headed for the shower, thinking how good the hot water would feel on her skin, deciding to use a soft-scented soap instead of her usual body wash, gloating over the great deal she found on her new towels. She thought about the little collagen particles soaking into her skin from her moisturizer, the softness of her sweater and the perfect length of her slacks—tried to remember all the words to Joyce Kilmer's poem *Trees*. Listening to the heels of her shoes ticking on her gorgeous new hardwood, she remembered exactly where she left her keys and let herself out of the apartment . . . and looking across at the Whites' door, she elected to knock on it.

Joe, of course, had gone off to work already, but Marty was happy to see her when she opened the door.

"It's so good to see you, Charlotte. I've been meaning to get over and see you but Ruth has been so busy this summer that, well, I don't know where the time goes."

"That's alright, that's one of the reasons I came over. I . . . I've been meaning to tell you that if you'd ever like an afternoon off or you'd like to go out to lunch or if anything happens to your regular sitter, I'd be glad to watch her . . . Ruth . . . for you, I mean. I didn't feel like I could offer before—my dad liked his peace and he wasn't used to children—but now . . . well, I'm available if you need me. I like children. I just don't know many."

"That's so sweet of you." The amazed look on her face made Charlotte self-conscious. What? She couldn't be sweet? "But I'd much rather get a sitter and take *you* to lunch, if you're interested, that is. I've always wanted to get to know you better. I'm not that much older than you, I don't think. But you looked so busy all the time with your business and your father . . . we barely had time for a 'howdy' and a 'how's things' here in the hallway. I'm glad to see you have more time for yourself now."

Being available was three-quarters of the cure for loneliness. Who knew it was so easy? The first time the front-desk attendant at the gym said, "Good morning, Charlotte," before she'd even had a chance to sign in, it was . . . a nice surprise. She was quick and enthusiastic when Sidney and Sue invited her shopping—she was a much better shopper now than the last time they'd ventured out together.

"When *was* the last time the three of us shopped like this?" Sidney asked, scooting—exhausted—into a high-backed booth in the restaurant where they'd stopped for a late lunch and a drink.

"So long ago I don't remember." Charlotte remembered perfectly.

"Well, I remember," said Sue, her brown shoulder-length bob swinging as she got in on the other side. "It was my wedding. We were looking for bridesmaids' shoes, and my cousin Loretta, who's always trying to fart higher than her ass, was with us and would not even try on a shoe that didn't have a four-inch heel and a three-figure price tag, and you said you couldn't walk in four-inch heels, three was your limit, and Charlotte kept wandering around muttering '$250 for a pair of purple shoes that can't be deducted.' "

"Wait." Sidney picked up a menu but didn't look at it. "Speaking of farting, wasn't that the same day you found out that weird aunt of your mother's, who you didn't want to invite to your wedding because of her toxic flatulence problem, was, according to your mother, supposedly too sick to come to the wedding, so she insisted that it was safe to send her an invitation but who was, however, feeling very well and would be attending with her son, who, by the way, could power a windmill with his own noxious gases?"

"Yesss! I forgot about that. I remember I sent you off on your own and told you to pick out whatever shoes you wanted, I'd had it. And not only did Charlotte come back in about fifteen minutes, but she'd bought a pair of *black loafers* and told me no one would see them under her dress. I thought my head would explode." They all laughed. "I vowed then and there that cars would fly before we shopped together again."

Charlotte felt her cheeks burning and covered them with

her hands. "I was such a dork. Why did you put up with me for so long?"

"You mean aside from the fact that you were the sweetest, most gentle and giving dork at McClure Middle School? I don't know. Do you, Sidney?"

Sidney shrugged and glanced down at her menu, then up with a droll expression to keep the moment light. "Maybe because friends don't give up on each other. You haven't given up on me actually putting money in that savings account you made me open, have you?"

"No, but that reminds me—"

"NO!" they said together. "No job talk today."

"And no kid talk. This is my afternoon off." Sue tried to sound firm but there was nothing she liked better than talking about her children.

"Okay, then how about some juicy information on Mrs. Doctor Lacey Booth that I got directly from her aunt?"

Their ears twitched.

It wasn't hard keeping busy, stuffing her head with the hundreds of things she wanted to do and see. There were moments, of course, when her mind wandered—she glanced up once and saw Mel sitting in a chair across the room, then again leaning against a fence up the street and again riding the down escalator as she rode up. He smiled and gave a little wave; she smiled back, felt the pang of desire and looked away . . . *I think that I shall never see . . .*

She finally went out with Henry Chancellor's wife's uncle's sister's nephew, or whatever, Axel Burton, who was quite possibly the nicest man to ever leave Chicago. They liked each other very much but . . . there was no spark, no mating of souls, no *magic*.

He was, however, interested in scuba diving, so they took lessons together, driving all the way over to Alki Beach in West Seattle three evenings a week.

"We were crazy doing this in November." Her teeth chattered as she pulled on her thick down jacket, apple green with pink and yellow piping. They were past the pool work and actually swimming off Alki Beach in wet suits, which kept them fairly warm, until they took them off. "Why didn't we wait until summer?"

"Umm." He shivered, his knit cap pulled down over his wet hair. "The fewer off-season students get more one-on-one with the instructor? More underwater time? We were too eager? We're nuts?"

"That's the one." She stuffed her damp hair inside her cap and gave him a calculating look. He was only a little taller than she, maybe six foot, a nice, plain-looking man in his early thirties, with true brown hair and kind green eyes behind frameless glasses.

"What?" He held the door open for her.

"Well, don't take this wrong, it doesn't *mean* anything except that I don't know that many single people, but . . ." As she passed through the door, she saw Mel leaning against a pickup truck on the other side of the parking lot. He held out both hands as if to say it wasn't his fault she was missing him. She turned to Axel. "Well, I was thinking of trying speed dating and I didn't want to go alone. I thought if we went together it might not be . . ."

"As humiliating?"

"No, not humiliating just . . . less awkward. Who knows who we'll meet? And if you do meet someone nice and want to go out afterward for coffee or, you know, whatever, I can take a taxi home. Or vice versa."

It could happen.

They tried it twice to be fair, and to be fair, they didn't want to try it again.

She spent Thanksgiving with Sue Butterfield and her young family, her parents and her grandfather, who fell asleep during dessert and tipped whipped cream and pumpkin pie into his lap.

Christmas Eve she and Mrs. Kludinski made reservations and ate dinner in the Space Needle, which she hadn't done since she was seven or eight years old. She gave more than she received and that was okay. She had the spirit.

The mid-winter months were bleak and lonely. It rained nearly every day, turned to ice at night. She had only to look out her window to see Mel looking entirely pimplike, but warm, in a full-length red-fox fur—faux, naturally. Generally he sat on the bus bench on the corner, reading a newspaper until he felt her looking at him. He'd look up askance; did she want him to come up?

I think that I shall never see . . .

One night, he knocked on her door.

"You can't come in, Mel; you know that," she said, watching him through the peephole, enjoying the sight of him, too much.

"Just for tonight. I'll leave in the morning."

"I'm going to Cancun." This was news to her, too.

"Mexico?"

"A winter vacation before tax season hits full bloom." She wasn't used to living spontaneously; her hands were shaking. "I can take in the beach or go to the Mayan ruins. Boating. Oh, scuba!" Her enthusiasm soared. "*Warm* water scuba."

She was gone for ten days.

She was sorry to see him waiting at the airport for her, but she walked right by him, and for the rest of February, all of March and the first fifteen days of April, she was too busy to look more than two feet in front of her.

And then it was spring again.

Ten

"Thank you for coming," the bride said, extending her white-gloved hand and smiling ear to ear. "And thank you so much for your help, Charlotte."

"It was my pleasure and I'm glad things worked out well for you. Everything is so beautiful." She couldn't remember being more sincere about anything.

Her simple suggestion to hold the small wedding in Parsons Garden was a minimal contribution to the charming, almost fairy-tale scene around them. The small garden that had once belonged to the Parsons family was in full bloom with large snow-white magnolia blossoms; bright yellow and pale pink flowers flourished on the Cornelian dogwood and the Japanese weeping cherry. Spring plantings and thick shrubs and the neatly trimmed walk surrounded the carpet of deep green grass where sixty-odd chairs were quietly being rearranged in small groups around tables for a light reception. The string trio that had been playing softly since she stepped through the small iron gate lent an air of magic that hung like a canopy over the garden.

"And I don't think I've ever seen a prettier bride."

"Me, either," the groom said, beaming at both women as Charlotte gave the bride a gentle embrace then moved on to give him one meant for a bear.

"I'm so happy for you, Axel."

"I'm just glad Uncle Henry isn't too disappointed. If Janet hadn't charmed his socks off, I'd be in big trouble right now."

"That's not true. All he ever wanted was for you to be happy. And you so obviously are, I'll bet he's delighted. In fact, I think I'll go over right now and make sure he is."

Henry was, of course, thrilled and felt the need to drag her from one cluster of guests to another introducing her as his brilliant accountant—a term that attested to her sharp mind but did little to invoke the image of a sparkling personality. The Chancellor family was a jolly bunch; Janet's family was welcoming and kind, and the afternoon wore on in weather that seemed special ordered, clear and bright.

In an unguarded moment of weakness she caught a whiff of fir and fresh snow and turned, expecting to face Mel, there in a crowd of people.

He was nowhere in sight. She missed him.

A small lattice-covered bench located on a shady curve of the path beckoned to her—well, beckoned her sore feet anyway. She wasn't the only one who'd worn heels to stand on the grass but . . . what had she been thinking?

She closed her eyes for just a moment, felt the sun on her face, listened to the birds in the bushes . . . heard the bushes rustling, twigs snapping and opened her eyes again.

From behind the rhododendron on her right a small boy of three or four crawled on his hands and knees—his mother was going to kill him—in his white shirt and khaki dress pants. He grinned when he saw her and didn't exactly stick his tongue out *at* her but opened his mouth and let his tongue hang out like a—

"Woof." He crawled closer. "Woof. Woof. Woof."

"Oh my, what a sweet little puppy you are," she said,

sticking her hand toward him to see if he'd come to her. "Can I pet you?"

"Woof. Woof." He came close to her leg and sat back on his legs, putting his front paws on her thigh. He let her smooth down his bowl-shaped cap of chestnut-colored hair, remove a leaf and pat him lightly on the back. "Woof."

"Do you have a name, little doggy?"

"Woof. Charlie."

"Charlie is a great name. How old are you, Charlie?"

"Woof. Woof." He held up four fingers on his right paw, looking around.

"How many is that?" She started to count.

"Woof. Four."

"Four. And where is your keeper, you nice little dog?"

"Woof," he said, turning his head. "Hi, Dad. I'm a dog. Woof. Woof."

"So I see." A tall man stepped out of the shadows as he spoke to the boy, but he didn't take his eyes off Charlotte's face as she turned to look up at him.

He had the same thick, rich chestnut-colored hair as his son in a much shorter, hipper version of the comb-it-forward style his son had. He, too, wore a white shirt and khakis but he'd added a tie and carried a brown tweed sport jacket in his left hand. He had a strong chin and his lower lip was fuller than his top; shaded glasses covered his eyes . . . but it didn't really matter. She knew him immediately.

"Hi." She felt as if she'd greeted him a million times before, yet her throat was tight and her voice sounded strange. She felt tense, her hands trembled in her lap.

"Hello." He seemed to suddenly remember his glasses and removed them. His eyes were so dark they looked like holes with no bottoms . . . she toppled straight into them. "I hope he's not bothering you. Actually, I know he is . . . I'm hoping you don't mind."

She reached down blindly to pet the boy. "I don't. I like dogs."

They continued to stare at one another for one full minute before he motioned for permission to sit beside her. She smiled and tried to move to give him more room but the boy leaned against her right leg and she didn't get far. The man's slacks brushed against her leg when he sat; she made a minute adjustment with her thigh and felt the warmth of his skin beneath two thin layers of fabric. Her heart kicked once then flew, lighter than air.

A second later it stopped dead when it finally occurred to her that where there was a small boy and a daddy there was generally a mommy as well.

"All . . . Although maybe I shouldn't encourage him. His mother may not appreciate him getting so dirty."

He wasn't fooled. He knew what she was asking.

"His mother died three years ago and I don't think even she could have kept him clean for more then six minutes at a time." His stare was intense but she didn't mind, she couldn't look away either. "Friend of the bride or the groom?"

"Groom. You?"

"The bride is my cousin." So that made him, what, her client Henry's wife's ex-sister-in-law's nephew's new wife's cousin . . . and his son? Small world.

"The groom's my scuba partner."

"You dive?"

She nodded. "Do you?"

"Since I was a teenager but I . . . haven't for a while. I've been a little busy."

"Woof." Charlie crawled several feet away, bent his head down to pick something invisible up in his mouth, crawled back and dropped it at Charlotte's feet. "Woof. Throw my ball."

"Please," his father said automatically.

"Please. Woof."

She picked the ball up, threw it and Charlie chased it . . . and his dad was still staring at her when she turned back. "I bet you've been busy. He's a cute little boy."

He nodded, his mind on something else. He frowned briefly, then decided to tell her.

"You know I feel like I ought to know your name but I don't."

"Charlotte."

"It suits you. I mean, I think it does. It feels like it should. I know this is going to sound strange—or like some pick-up line or something—but I feel like I know you. Have we met before? I'm Sam Rutherford."

"I don't think so." But she knew exactly how he felt as something deep inside snapped and let go, became tranquil and easy, spreading a sense of rightness through her soul. "What do you do?"

"I'm an associate professor of the Romantics and Victorian literature at U Dub." A University of Washington professor, of poetry and heartfelt literature—*Do not swoon! Don't do it!* "That's Keats and Shelley, Tennyson and Browning, those guys."

"I know." And she'd bet every class he taught was packed full of girls. "I'm an accountant." That sounded so dumb she almost slapped her forehead. Her mind was exploding with ideas, but it was so hard to *think*. "I own my own business."

In her peripheral vision she knew Charlie had returned with the make-believe ball and, seeing he'd lost her full attention, dropped it a few feet away. He lifted his head, looked over his shoulder as if watching another toss and went to fetch it once more.

"If we haven't met before, it's good to meet you now, Sam Rutherford."

There wasn't a doubt in her mind that what she saw in his face was her future. Happy, earnest, genuine, solid and real—he had an honest face, a trustworthy face. He glanced down, saw her hands and took one in his to examine it as if he'd never seen one before . . . or maybe to determine if it was strong enough to hold his heart. Finally, he wove his fingers between hers and held them with his other hand.

"How would you like to walk over to Kerry Park and see a spectacular view of the Sound? It's only a few blocks away, an easy walk even in those shoes."

"I know where it is." She stood and he came up with her. "Can we bring the dog along?"

"That was my plan. If we wear him out with a walk I can put him to bed early, get my niece to sit with him and then we can go out for a drink, or dinner . . . or anything."

She smiled her approval of his plan and he turned to Charlie, who was still on all fours, humming an oddly familiar tune. "Hey, Big Guy, wanna go for a walk?"

"Woof. Woof."

Big Guy. An endearment. She imagined him calling her honey or sweetie or dear and her stomach didn't hiss and spit. She'd answer to his sugar and darling . . . but not babe. There was just something about babe that rubbed her wrong.

She put out her free hand hoping Charlie would give her one of his. "Can I hold your leash, little doggie, so you don't get lost?"

"Woof." He shook his head. "My boy has my leash."

"Your boy?"

"My new friend." He turned his head and looked pointedly into thin air. "He's four like me."

She looked at Sam who shrugged to say you-know-kids and grinned at his son. Her skin prickled.

"What did you name your new friend?" Sam asked him, playing along.

Charlie looked confused. "I didn't name him nothing. He gots a name already."

"Then please introduce us." He started them down the path toward the gate. She felt him hesitate at her side and turned her head in time to catch him sniffing the air. "Do you smell that?"

She inhaled deeply, smelled nothing and took a wild guess. "Christmas?"

"Yes!" He was confused and amazed.

"That's Mel," said Charlie, proud of his pal. "He smells like cookies, doesn't he, Dad?"

Sam sniffed again, moved his head about to catch a second whiff but it was gone—his adult defenses were up. Charlotte had a sudden, brilliant thought and squatted down to the boy's level; her smile was casual and cunning.

"Charlie, you know how your long name is really Charles Rutherford?" He nodded. "What's Mel's long name? Do you know?"

Charlie giggled. "Sure. It's dumb. He sang me the song to it. He says it sticks in your head and you can't get rid of it."

"What is it?"

"Mellow Lemon Yellow."

"Mellow Yellow?"

"Donovan," said Sam, identifying the song immediately. He laughed. "Your pal's a hippie, Big Guy."

"What's a hippie?"

Epilogue

"Careful now, Big Guy."

"Keep your eyes closed tight, Mom."

"I will, Charlie. Just don't walk me into another wall. I'll break my nose."

She felt Sam's strong arm across her lower back and knew she had nothing more to worry about. Charlie was so excited his six-year-old fingers could barely hold still long enough to keep a good grip on hers as he led her up the stairs and down the hall toward his bedroom.

They were married, the three of them—that's what Charlie told everyone. Charlotte adopted him the same day she married his dad, so they were a real, true family now.

The ink had barely dried on those papers when they were signing again for a pretty three-story Victorian in the university district. All three of them fell in love with the old house and had spent every spare minute and extra dime restoring it. Sam, who'd put himself through college working construction every summer, was a wonderful carpenter.

In her opinion, there wasn't anything he couldn't do with a hammer and a piece of wood.

"We're almost there. No peekin.' "

"I promise. No peeking."

But when they were halfway down the hall and should have turned left into Charlie's room, they proceeded on to the next room, an unfinished room they had plenty of plans for but not enough time or money, just yet. She knew when they passed through the doorway as Sam stepped back and used his free hand at the small of her back to guide her safely to the center of the room.

The first thing she noticed was the soft scent of new paint and wallpaper paste—two smells she now knew as well as coffee and bacon. She felt a soft breeze on her left and heard the gentle rustle of fabric. The window was open and . . . there were curtains. But how—?

"Okay, Mom. Open your eyes!"

"Oh!" was all she could say with her heart stuck in her throat.

They'd finished the room. Sanded and refinished the floors, built in shelves as had been discussed, removed all the old painted trim and replaced it with finished maple to match the floors. The furniture she and Sam picked out and bought together, and had temporarily set up in their bedroom, stood exactly where she'd dreamed of putting it—well, the crib was six inches too close to the window, but everything else was right on. He'd even remembered the pale apple-green walls and the pink buttons-and-bows trim she'd picked out if the baby was a girl.

"Sam. Sam." Her eyes welled with tears that were only half-hormonal as she watched him shift their daughter, Lily, from the curve of his left arm into the crib. He fussed with the receiving blanket then put his big hand lightly over the baby's small torso, clearly checking her breathing and heartbeat, before he turned back to Charlotte. "Sam."

"Me, too, Mom, I helped."

"You must have or it wouldn't have gotten done so quickly, and it wouldn't be nearly so beautiful. Thank you, Charlie." Still a little fragile from the delivery, she bent at the waist, spread her arms wide and held him tight as he hugged her. He was so sturdy and strong compared to Lily. She kissed the top of his head and he ran off, too excited to stand still.

"When did you do all this?" Her face glowed as she turned to Sam. "You were with me all day Tuesday and most of yesterday. When did you have time?"

"I had a little help." He looked tired but as pleased with his efforts as she was—though when their eyes met she could see it made him even happier knowing she was pleased. "That all-day shopping trip with the girls. Marty's two-day yard sale. The afternoons you visited Mrs. Kludinski, she'd call when you were on your way home. It was pretty much a conspiracy." He grinned and it was like dawn again, like a fresh, bright, new day. He had the longest dark eyelashes she'd ever seen on a man, and he'd passed them on to Charlie. If Lily didn't get them, it would be a crime. "You like it then?"

"I do. I love it. It's perfect." She heard Charlie in his room next door. She glanced at the baby, pale and pink and sleeping peacefully. Mother of two, wife of one, was this really her life? She watched the late afternoon sun stir red in Sam's dark brown hair, fell in love all over again with the way his eyes lit up when he looked at her. Oh yeah, it was her life all right, and she wouldn't change a second of it. "The room is perfect. We're perfect. How can this be?"

A few happy tears spilled down her cheek, and he chuckled. The only times he'd seen her cry was when she was too happy to do anything else. Taking her hand, he led her across the room to an easy chair that both swiveled and rocked and pulled her down onto his lap.

"It's perfect because we both remember what it was like before we had this amazing, huge love in our lives, so we don't take it for granted." Palming her left cheek, he dabbed at her tears with his thumb then pulled her close for a sweet lingering kiss. His lips were soft and skilled . . . and sensuous, as if each kiss was a new adventure. She sank into the moment, her head filled with the scent of him and new baby and . . . home. "You are my life, Charlotte."

Charlotte. She'd asked him once why he didn't call her honey or dear and he'd said, "Because *Charlotte* is like poetry and as pretty as you are." It worked for her.

Charlotte smoothed her knuckles down his clean-shaven cheek. This was so much more than she ever dreamed love could be, so much better. Studying the strong features she'd come to know and love so well, she wondered, "What if one of us hadn't gone to the wedding that day?"

He shook his head; his gaze was like a caress. "It wouldn't have mattered. We would have found each other eventually. The moment I saw you I knew I wanted to grow old with you. I knew that I'd love every second of our life together. And there you were, treating my son like a dog."

He laughed when her mouth fell open and she gasped. She tugged his earlobe. "He was so cute. I was so glad to hear that the two of you came as a package. And now Lily." Her voice quivered.

She let her kiss tell him how deeply she loved him, how happy she was, how thankful she was for the life they were building together. He had no problem reading her and rose up to slant his mouth over hers, pulling her closer and closer until the right side of her body came to rest against him. Cheek to cheek they clung to one another, warm and tender, and they tried to capture that special moment forever in their hearts.

"Not more kissing again." Charlie's high-pitched voice was packed with boredom and repugnance. "I might have to hurl."

"Hurl?"

Charlie's grin was gapped now that he'd lost his front teeth. "Kevin says that's the same as barfing."

"What happened to 'throwing up'?"

"It's a guy thing," Sam whispered in her ear. "The worse it sounds, the better it is."

"Oh."

There was a lot she didn't understand about guys, a lot she took on faith as being right and true in both boys and men. She knew that the responsibilities of first grade and now the duties of an older brother had taken their toll on Charlie. He rarely spoke of Mel anymore—not that he was gone for good because from time to time she would still hear Charlie talking to him at night before he went to sleep. But he no longer requested a place for Mel at the dinner table or held the door open for him when they went out to play, and, well, growing up was a sad thing sometimes, she decided.

"I brung some of my old toys in here for that baby to have. All she's got is stuffed stuff and I'm too old for these now." A fire engine slipped out of his grasp and he picked it up, dropping a Marble Run Vortex as he did so. "I tried to get my jumping horse, too, but it got stuck in the door. Can you go get it, Dad?"

Charlotte noticed his beloved Super Stretch Mr. Fantastic and Thing in the heavy armload of miscellaneous toys. His generous heart made hers crack a little.

"Do you remember that baby's name?" his dad asked him. Sam gave her a little nudge and helped her to stand before getting up himself. "We need to use it so she'll know who she is."

"Lily." Charlie shuddered. "It's a good thing she's a girl."

"That's for sure. And the one thing we don't want is for her to wake up. So, why don't you put all your gifts here on the chair for now, and maybe Mom can go into our room and lie down to rest for a few minutes while you and I cook dinner. Does that sound like a plan?" Walking behind her, Sam put his long-fingered hands on her shoulders, gave a little squeeze and placed a loving kiss on the top of her head before heading for the door.

"Yes, it does." Dumping his possessions on the chair, Charlie leaned toward Charlotte and whispered, "It's KFC."

She laughed silently with him and zipped her lips together to keep their secret, before he trotted off to catch up with his father.

Charlotte stood over Lily for several long minutes, touching the fuzz of dark hair that capped her head, skimming a finger over the petal-soft skin of her tiny-fisted hand.

"You can be anything you want when you grow up, you know," she spoke softly to her daughter. "Even if you make a couple of mistakes along the way, it's never too late to change. Just keep an eye on your dreams and you'll make it. I know. I'm proof."

She walked softly across the room to the door, heard Sam and Charlie talking and laughing downstairs. Just as she was about to leave the room she caught a hint of spicy cider and fir trees in the air . . .

And smiled.